TAKE CARE, MR BAKER!

A selection from the advice
on the Government's Education
Reform Bill which the Secretary
of State for Education invited
but decided not to publish

Compiled and
edited by
Julian Haviland

FOURTH ESTATE · LONDON

First published in Great Britain by
Fourth Estate Ltd
113 Westbourne Grove
London W2 4UP

British Library Cataloguing in Publication Data

Take care Mr. Baker!: a selection from the advice on
  education which the government collected
  but decided not to publish.
  1. Great Britain. Education. Reform
  I. Haviland, Julian
  370'.941

  ISBN 0-947795-87-1

Typeset in Plantin by York House Typographic, London.
Printed and bound in Great Britain by
Richard Clay (The Chaucer Press) Ltd, Bungay, Suffolk.

Contents

Acknowledgements

The editor is grateful to innumerable people who gave generously of their time, energy and wisdom merely because they believed that a book on these lines was needed. He acknowledges special debts to the distinguished and busy men who contributed introductory essays for no reward and at almost no notice; to the resourceful staff of the House of Commons library; to the hard-pressed staff of the Inner London Education Authority; and to his co-workers who helped to read and to choose 100,000 words from several millions – Neil Grant, Celia Ellicott, Shervie Price, Caroline Haviland. He and the publishers wish also to thank all who helped by sending them copies of their own submissions to Mr Kenneth Baker; and to apologize to those whose golden words had after all to be omitted or – perhaps worse – truncated. For the inevitable mistakes and misjudgements in selections he alone is responsible.

Editor's Preface

Most of this book has been written by the public. They are specialist members of the public, in many cases, in that they have a particular interest in education, but the ordinary tax-paying Clapham-omnibus-travelling public all the same. Most have votes. Many are to be numbered among the present Government's supporters. What they almost all have in common is anxiety – that the Education Reform Bill is fundamentally wrong, or that parts of it are, or that its ideas are good but their working-out defective, or that Mr Kenneth Baker is moving too fast and is in danger of overlooking important details. I think it will be found that the book's title is an accurate guide to its contents.

The body of the book consists of selections from the public's invited responses to Mr Baker's consultation papers, in which he outlined most of the ideas which were later set out in his Bill. In making this material available, the only purpose of the editor and the publishers – self-righteous though it may sound – is to help to promote informed public debate on crucial legislation of which the final form is not yet determined.

Public opinion may yet have an important part to play. It will depend partly on whether those who broadly approve of the Government's declared aims decide to interest themselves in the detail of what is being done; and partly on their making their MPs aware of their interest. It is seldom safe to assume that Parliament knows what it is doing. Busy men and women, not all of them possessing special competence, spend their working weeks passing laws which they do not fully understand and have often not read. If their party is in office and the minister in charge of a Bill is well regarded, and if that Bill is more or less in line with something that was promised at the last election, many a backbench MP or peer will be happy to take it largely on trust. That can be risky. Even popular and energetic ministers may not know what they are about; and the fastest rising ministers are naturally the most transient.

The publication of this selection from what might be called the Baker papers is not intended to be hostile to either Mr Baker or his Bill. I say this because some have supposed it was. Only the simple-minded or those who have not looked at the Bill could say they were wholly for or wholly against a measure so complex. It seems to me, a non-expert, to have great potential both for good and for harm, with much still depending on how Parliament does its work.

Like the Bill, this book may show one or two signs of the great haste with which it had to be assembled. I would like to apologise to any readers who may feel let down, and I hope they will be few. The haste could not be avoided: the work of selecting and editing the material could not begin until January, and it had to be completed within a month for the book to be available before the public debate intensified in March with the Bill's return to the chamber of the Commons and the start of its critical passage through the Lords. Ideally, as the Royal Society of Arts says of the planning of a national curriculum (see Chapter 2), the design for a book also "should start by determining not the components but the whole." But that again requires time. We had no choice but to plan the framework before we could see the material that was to fill it. Happily, this difficulty proved a blessing: because we feared, wrongly, that some of the material might prove indigestible, we approached expert guides from different parts of the world of education (and in one case, that of Professor McAuslan, from outside it) each to open the debate contained in one of the chapters. Their brief was to prepare interested but inexpert readers for the possibly unfamiliar arguments they were about to encounter. They were also welcome to give their own views if they wished. In the event, the basic material proved absorbing; but the book has been greatly enriched by the essayists. (The original plan was that each essayist should be able to see the source material for his chapter. Shortage of time prevented even that, and only Mr Everest, who introduces Chapter 7, was able to read the evidence and to refer to specific submissions. But this apparent handicap caused no difficulties for the writers, each of whom had followed the debate closely.)

The material in the Commons library, to which I had privileged access, is almost all from institutions, big and small, writing corporately. It was deposited by Mr Baker at the urging of his Opposition "shadow", Mr Jack Straw (to whom, with his deputy Mr Derek Fatchett, I am indebted for practical help as well as for his contribution to Chapter 4.) Mr Baker took the view that he should not release letters sent him by private persons who might have written in confidence. So the solo voice is usually heard in the book only where a teacher, governor or education officer has replied on behalf of colleagues. (Some had no choice in this: the consultation process was at its height during the summer holiday weeks of 1987 when, for many, consultation was not possible. Almost every letter in the Commons library starts by reproaching Mr Baker for allowing too little time.)

Some private people sent me their own views, which I was happy to read and sometimes able to include. The London chapter has more solo voices because the Inner London Education Authority (sentenced to death by the Cabinet on the day this was written) collected them and kindly allowed me to read them.

It may seem that institutional voices predominate and that the combined voices of the educational "establishment" tend to drown the others. I hope not. There are institutions which are not of that establishment, and I have sought them out. The Audit Commission and CIPFA cannot be dismissed as beasts of the education jungle. Theirs is the voice of the shrewd man or woman who has understood that most of the proposed reforms are going to be expensive, some of them very expensive, and that someone must decide who is to pick up the bill.

The educational establishment is real enough, a leviathan which I could no more ignore than Mr Baker can. It would have been unwise to pretend that its members' evidence was unimportant. The Association of County Councils (ACC) is given a good run in Chapter 5 because every point they brought forward seemed to be substantial and to require a serious answer. Its sister body, the Association of Municipal Authorities (AMA), with its slightly brusquer tones, is just as trenchant. Their evidence, of course, is special pleading and there are those who say that for that reason much of it can safely be discounted. Not so: it is pleading of a high order, full of experience and knowledge, which only fools will fail to take into account. The teachers' unions have been accused in the past, by Labour as well as Conservative politicians, of being too narrowly interested in their own people. I found their testimony – particularly that of the National Union of Teachers – often political (as it has every right to be) and occasionally strident; but their submissions were full of vital points which others had not noticed, and showed at least as much concern for the schools and their pupils as for their teacher members.

Objectivity it is impossible in an exercise like this, and I did not attempt it. There could be no rules. I could only plunge in and pull out what seemed to matter most. I have a preference for lucid expression, but there was some vital evidence in more difficult language which had to be included too. I have not tried to describe the political colour of contributors, which is sometimes obscure and seldom relevant. Intelligent writing recommends itself. Most readers will know what they need to know about the more prominent respondents, for instance that the AMA is Labour-controlled but that at present no party controls the ACC. I tried to favour constructive advice. It was depressing occasionally to find experienced and articulate witnesses wasting their ink by telling Mr Baker at length that he had no right to legislate at all. But the preponderant mass of evidence is impressive in its practicality, its carefulness and its anxiety to help the minister and his department get their legislation right. There is a genuineness about most of the writing, whether its slant is fashionable or unfashionable, and even in the expression of the most arcane minority views. I included one short piece of pure invective, mainly for light relief but partly also to show that this ancient political art is not lost. But usually I found even among Mr Baker's most determined opponents a willingness to meet him in argument and to take at face value his request for advice. For anyone who believes that controversial legislation is best fashioned in debate, no matter how angry, this may be encouraging.

If the burden of this book seems overwhelmingly critical it is because it accurately reflects the weight of the advice offered. Naturally even the Government's supporters thought it their duty to point to what they considered mistaken. To counter this natural bias and to add interest, I ransacked the documents to find eloquent Conservative witnesses and have, for example, quoted at length the vigorous views of the Centre for Policy Studies in Chapter 4. Mrs Angela Rumbold, the Minister of State, told a supporter on January 19 that of 11,790 representations on the national curriculum examined in the DES only 1,536 were opposed in principle. Her answer was no doubt accurate, but it was also incomplete. I made no count, but I can confirm that the principle was overwhelmingly approved: I cannot recall one response, however, that endorsed without reservation the structure for the curriculum which the Government was proposing. On financial delegation to schools, very few voices were raised against the idea; but every respondent had particular and often grave objections to some part of the specific proposals. Here as elsewhere the prevalent tone of voice indicated a bewilderment, by no means confined to Mr Baker's opponents, that so much of the detail of what was proposed appeared to have been given so little serious thought.

It is important to remember that these were responses not to the Bill but to the outline proposals which preceded it. But the Bill when published showed only a few adjustments to take account of the critics' points. These I have tried to indicate. (Chapter 9 differs from Chapters 2–8 in containing several submissions made after the Bill was published. Many of the most forceful of these, from the universities' representatives in particular, were pressed upon Mr Baker with growing urgency as the Bill advanced through committee with ministers showing no wish to amend its offending clauses.) Clearly the Government will itself propose a number of changes in the legislation, perhaps while this book is in gestation, more likely when the Bill returns to the floor of the Commons at the report stage. But (except on the matter of London where the Government's thoughts have moved on) it does not seem likely that changes freely brought forward by the Government will be many or substantial.

I believe that readers will find the weight of the testimony gathered here very persuasive. It is hard to read what follows without believing that Parliament will still have much to do to make the Bill, with all the regulations and circulars that will flow from it, a respectable piece of work.

Julian Haviland
February 1988

To those at Westminster
who would surely wish to do their duty
by the Education Reform Bill,
if only they had time
to study its 147 clauses (so far)
and its 11 schedules,
this illuminating book is inscribed in sympathy
and in hope.

Abbreviations

AEG	Aggregate Exchequer Grant
AFE	Advanced further education
A level	Advanced level
APU	Assessment of Performance Unit
AS level	Advanced supplementary level
BTEC	Business and Technical Education Council
CDT	Craft, design and technology
CEO	Chief Education Officer
CNAA	Council for National Academic Awards
CPVE	Certificate of Pre-Vocational Education
CTC	City technology college
CVCP	Committee of Vice-Chancellors and Principals
DES	Department of Education and Science
ESL	English as a Second Language
EWO	Education Welfare Officer
FE	Further education
FHE	Further and higher education
FTE	Full-time equivalent
GCE	General Certificate of Education
GCSE	General Certificate of Secondary Education
GLC	Greater London Council
GM	Grant-maintained
GREA	Grant-related expenditure assessment
GRIST	Graduate in-service training
HE	Higher education
HMI	Her Majesty's Inspectorate of Schools
ILEA	Inner London Education Authority
INSET	In-service training
LEA	Local education authority
LFM	Local financial management
MSC	Manpower Services Commission
NAB	National Advisory Body for Public Sector Higher Education
NAFE	Non-advanced further education
NCC	National Curriculum Council (also National Consumer Council)
NCVQ	National Council for Vocational Qualifications
NDPB	Non-departmental public body
PCFC	Polytechnics and Colleges Funding Council
RE	Religious education
SCDC	School Curriculum Development Committee
SEAC	Schools Examination and Assessment Council
SED	Scottish Education Department
SEN	Special educational need
SERC	Science and Engineering Research Council
SSEN	Statement of special educational need
SSR	Student:staff ratio
TVEI	Technical and Vocational Education Initiative
UFC	Universities Funding Council
UGC	University Grants Committee
YTS	Youth Training Scheme

Introduction

Stuart Maclure
Editor, The Times Educational Supplement

Anyone who cares about education in Britain must be grateful for this book. Its central core is drawn from the 18,000 replies which Kenneth Baker, the Education Secretary, received in the wake of the spate of discussion documents which he issued while his Education Reform Bill was in preparation.

The consultation process which yielded this extraordinary response was a scrambled affair. The Bill was to be introduced at the end of November 1987. The general election had not been held till June, five months earlier. The discussion papers spilled out at the beginning of the holiday season, and respondents had eight inconvenient weeks in which to forward their considered observations.

Few people thought this reasonable or businesslike, but the fact is that, if the measure of success is the level of participation, it was undoubtedly successful. No other consultative exercise ever conducted by a Secretary of State for Education brought in such a flood of comment. It certainly took ministers and civil servants by surprise, and there must be some scepticism as to how closely they studied the tens of millions of words which descended on them while they were already heavily engaged in drafting the Bill.

It would, however, have been a dreadful waste if so much effort had simply ended there. What Julian Haviland and his researchers have done is to rescue some of this material, by sifting through the mountain of paper (now lodged in the House of Commons library) and making a selection available to a wider public.

This 'instant' book is an admirable attempt to extend the knowledge base on which public discussion can draw. For consultation is not just about drawing points to the notice of ministers. It is also about generating informed debate in both Houses of Parliament and in the country at large.

The education proposals which have come under discussion are intensely controversial within the education community. They are bound to be if, as Kenneth Baker told the House of Commons in opening the Second Reading debate, they spring from the conviction that the education system has become 'producer dominated'.

Many of Mr Baker's respondents are drawn from the producers' lobbies – from the hydra-headed educational establishment he holds responsible for past mistakes. But this was not an exercise confined to organizations or pressure groups: there are responses from outside the education service – from parents and business, as well as from teachers and administrators. Populism is not enough: the people who will have to make Mr Baker's plans work are already working in the schools.

1

Schools in the Political Arena

The main proposals for change in English and Welsh schools are discussed separately in the next five chapters, each consisting of responses to consultation papers published by the Government in July 1987. Most respondents followed the Government's lead in answering each document in turn. The related proposals for a national curriculum and national assessment arrangements were put forward in a single booklet, *The National Curriculum, 5–16*, which was seen as the most substantial and far-reaching of more than a dozen Government papers and drew about half of more than 20,000 responses received in Whitehall by the time this book went to press.

Some respondents complained that the Government's pattern of consultation denied them an opening – which many none the less found – to comment on the likely effect in combination of the various changes proposed for schools: a national curriculum and pattern of assessment; 'open enrolment', intended to give parents more scope for choosing their children's school; financial delegation, giving heads and governors responsibility for school budgets; and grant-aiding or 'opting out', the right of parents to take a school out of local-authority control so that it may be run with a State grant.

Although these next chapters contain plenty of political as well as practical matter, the wood is sometimes obscured by the trees. Yet the political arguments for and against the schools reforms as a whole are important. They have been heard loudly since before the general election of 1987, and seem likely to continue long after the passage of the Bill and of all the secondary legislation which is to follow. If the Government's view of its reforms prevails, they are more likely to be accepted by the schools and their communities. If the Government loses the argument, even though it will win most of

the important votes, then ministers must be less confident of
securing the goodwill and support of the professionals and laity
without whom, as they have recognized, their hopes of raising
school standards will not be realized.

This chapter offers, as a curtain-raiser, first a statement of the
Government's political case and – in one fiercely argued but not
unrepresentative document – the case pressed by its most uncom-
promising opponents. The case in favour of the school reforms is
taken from the official report of Kenneth Baker's speech in the
debate on the second reading of the Bill in the House of Commons
on 1 December 1987:

Our education system has operated over the past 40 years on the basis of the
framework laid down by Rab Butler's 1944 Act, which in turn built on the
Balfour Act of 1902. We need to inject a new vitality into that system. It has
become producer-dominated. It has not proved sensitive to the demands for
change that have become ever more urgent over the past ten years. This Bill
will create a new framework, which will raise standards, extend choice and
produce a better-educated Britain.

The need for reform is now urgent. All the evidence shows this –
international comparisons, the reports of Her Majesty's inspectors and,
most recently, the depressing findings on adult illiteracy. It must be a
matter of regret for all hon. members, on both sides of the House, to see the
figures issued last week which suggested that 5.5 million of our people –
three per cent of our population – had difficulty in reading and writing.
There is no doubt that people who have problems in such simple communication skills are more likely to be unemployed, and, alas, likely to remain
unemployed for longer than those who have the skills. This is something
that we should not tolerate in our society today.

If we are to implement the principle of the 1944 Act that children should
'be educated in accordance with the wishes of their parents' we must give
consumers of education a central part in decision making. That means
freeing schools and colleges to deliver the standards that parents and
employers want. It means encouraging the consumer to expect and demand
that all educational bodies do the best job possible. In a word, it means
choice.

The purpose of the Bill is to secure delegation and to widen choice. We
want to see more decision making in the hands of individual schools and
colleges. When governing bodies and heads control their own budgets,
decisions will be taken at a local level. Schools and colleges will be free to
make their own decisions on spending priorities and to develop in their own
way. Grant-maintained schools will give parents and governors a new
opportunity, should they wish to take it, to run their schools themselves.
Grant-maintained schools will be subject to less control, not more control.
They will have more freedom, not less.

I am glad to see the growing consensus for many of the measures in this
Bill. The opinion polls also clearly show its popularity with the people who
count – the parents. That applies, above all, to the national curriculum,
which is the bedrock of our reform proposals.

I shall quote from clause 1(2) of the Bill. We are proposing a curriculum which

(a) promotes the spiritual, moral, cultural, mental and physical development of pupils at the school and of society; and
(b) prepares such pupils for the oppurtunities, responsibilities and experiences of adult life.

Clause 1 provides the framework and the essential purposes against which the House should measure our proposals.

I want to deal first with the content of the curriculum and with religious education. Religious education in our schools is secured in statute by the Education Act 1944. This Bill reinforces the position of religious education as a compulsory subject.

After religious education come the three core subjects of English, maths and science, and the seven other foundation subjects – history, geography, technology in all its aspects, a foreign language in secondary schools, music, art and physical education. In Wales, Welsh will have a firm place in the curriculum. We do not intend to lay down, either on the face of the Bill or in any secondary legislation, the percentage of time to be spent on the different subjects. This will provide an essential flexibility, but it is our belief that it will be difficult, if not impossible, for any school to provide the national curriculum in less than 70 per cent of the time available. The remaining time will allow schools to offer other subject – among them home economics, Latin, business studies, careers education, and a range of other subjects.

We want to build upon the professionalism of the many fine and dedicated teachers throughout our education system. The national curriculum will provide scope for imaginative approaches developed by our teachers.

Another aspect about which concern has been expressed has been our proposals for assessment and testing. We seek a balanced package of assessment arrangements including national tests. It has three purposes: first, to tell a parent or teacher what a child knows, is able to do and is able to understand; secondly, to identify problems which need further diagnosis and whether the child needs extra help or more demanding tasks; thirdly, to indicate through the results of assessment the achievements of schools and local education authorities generally. Parents are entitled to know how their child is doing and how their school is doing. It is not intended that the results showing a child's performance should be published, although they will remain available to the teacher and to the child's parent. Published results will be on a class or school basis. We do not want the discrimination that publishing individual results could produce.

Some people are concerned that our proposals give too much power to the holder of my office. I understand that concern. It would be constitutionally unacceptable for the Secretary of State for Education and Science to write on after the national curriculum at his will or whim. The Bill provides a series of checks and balances. Before any orders can be made, the Secretary of State must first put proposals to the National Curriculum Council, which will be under a statutory duty to consult widely. It will then give advice –

which will be published – to the Secretary of State. He will bring forward draft orders which are subject to a further period of statutory consultation, and publish any reasons for departure from the council's advice. At the end of that very open, public process, it will be for both Houses of Parliament to decide.

Chapter II deals with more open enrolment. The proposal is a natural extension of our concern to maximize parental choice. There are some 10,000 appeals every year by parents who do not get their preferred school. I do not claim that all parents will get their first choice of school under our proposals but I believe that we can remove some unnecessary barriers. At present, many schools have to turn away children because their local authority has decided to spread intakes evenly between popular and less popular schools. This means empty desks in popular schools, which cannot be right.

The clauses on financial delegation in chapter III will give all larger schools in the next few years responsibility for their own budgets. This has been widely welcomed. It is not surprising because many local authorities have already moved a long way down this road. The Government are responding to a healthy trend by prompting all authorities to follow the pioneers. With delegated budgets, governors will be responsible for the selection and dismissal of staff. These powers are closely modelled on those that the governors of voluntary-aided schools now exercise. The Bill will ensure that the professional advice of the chief education officer and his staff will be available to governing bodies in matters of appointment.

Chapter IV deals with the establishment of grant-maintained schools. Our proposals will allow all secondary schools, and primary schools with more than 300 pupils, to opt out of local authority control and to apply for direct funding. This will widen choice for many parents in the State-maintained sector for whom all too often the only choice is take it or leave it. This wider choice will help to improve standards in all schools as we introduce a competitive spirit into the provision of education – and at no extra cost to the consumer.

The final clause in part I of the Bill enables the Secretary of State to enter into long-term agreements with the bodies that will run city technology colleges. This is another important element in our plans to create an education system that is better geared to the needs of a rapidly changing world. City technology colleges will increase choice for parents, particularly in the inner cities.

The proposals which I have outlined to the House today constitute a major change. I would sum up the Bill's 169 pages in three words – standards, freedom and choice. I have no doubt that the Opposition parties share our wish to improve standards. But what they fail to understand is that one cannot improve standards without at the same time increasing choice and freedom. The people of this country understand that. They showed their understanding at the general election. The Opposition parties went to the country with a prospectus of no change. They lost the election. The Conservative Party went to the country with a programme of radical reform, and we won. I now invite the House to give effect to the people's choice and to give a Second Reading to the Bill.

The political case against the Government's main proposals for English and Welsh schools is taken from a submission sent to Mr Baker's department by the Ealing branch of CASE – the Campaign for the Advancement of State Education:

The presentation of the proposals in the form of separate documents is intended to mask the inconsistencies and anomalies, which abound, and to disguise the cumulatively devastating effect the changes will have. None of the discussion documents contains any detail (in fact the one on financial delegation almost makes this a virtue) and we believe that this so-called 'consultation' exercise is a disguised means of ensuring that the education community provides the Secretary of State with an indication of the level of these proposals. These proposals are wrong in principle and we oppose them utterly.

None of the documents makes any mention of the effects the proposed changes will have on present pupils of our schools, their teachers or on the role and responsibilities of headteachers. None draws on either experience or research to inform the ideas contained in them. There is a fundamental inconsistency in the proposals which is so blatant that we must look to the political philosophy which has generated them to find an explanation. Our question is: if the Government believes that a national curriculum will meet the declared aim of uniformly high standards, why does it also need revised admissions criteria, financial delegation and grant-maintained schools, all of which are avowedly designed to increase 'diversity'? Our answer is: the Government wishes to create a polarized education system in which the national curriculum will deliver 'academic success' in the minority of schools whilst underfunded schools, which will form the majority, will be shackled with a narrowly based, high controlled and inappropriate curriculum which uses frequent tests to demonstrate to pupils their 'failure'.

Funding levels will not be increased to meet the cost of implementing the national curriculum. Therefore the proposals for open enrolment, financial delegation and opting out are intended to provide the means by which a minority of schools can be allocated sufficient resources to deliver the national curriculum at the expense of all the others. The change in the admissions procedures to open enrolment is designed both to give the appearance of extending parental choice by increasing the number of children admitted to 'popular' schools and to concentrate resources in larger, more 'economic' units. The corollary (not mentioned in the document) is that other perfectly good schools will be allowed to deteriorate due to loss of revenue and resources in an increasingly underfinanced situation. The delegation of financial powers to schools will have the effect of shifting the responsibility for inadequate financial provision from the Secretary of State on to the governing bodies.

However, these changes will still be insufficient to ensure the success of the Secretary of State's plan for the 'elevation' of some schools at the expense of the majority. The Government finds it unpalatable that LEAs will still own the school land and buildings and employ the teachers. The Government will give opted-out schools the assets which belong to the community. Teachers' contracts will be summarily rewritten to allow the governing bodies to be their employers. Teachers will receive no compensation or redundancy pay if they do not wish to be so employed and the LEA is unable to redeploy them. To protect the Government from the charge that schools are suffering financial distress, all will be expected to raise additional funds from both parents and business interests. This will result in ever-widening differences between the quality of education possible in those schools with high-income parents and those in poorer circumstances.

The proposal for a national curriculum is the only one of the four which has been the subject of debate in political and educational circles in recent years. However, the emerging consensus (around the need to ensure that all pupils have equal access to a broad and relevant education using nationally agreed objectives and guidelines) has been ignored. Instead the proposal is for an imposed, prescriptive and outdated content-specific curriculum. With this national curriculum, the Government has failed to seize the opportunity to make schooling more relevant to all children, to broaden its appeal and free it from the stigma of examination failure. The Secretary of State plans to enforce an inflexible grammar-school-type curriculum with a narrow subject orientation. No mention of multiculturalism is made, nor does it address the inequalities of sex or class. It makes no reference to any of the perspectives that should permeate the curriculum.

The principles which underpin the new GCSE courses apparently go unrecognized since they are totally incompatible with the imposition of norm-referenced standardized tests. No tests of the kind envisaged by the Secretary of State have yet been devised. Deciding how to take account of the enormous social and cultural variations in the school population has proved too difficult. Such tests, which have been used in more local situations, are limited in their application and therefore say nothing about social goals, which are just as important as cognitive ones. Nor can they be broad-based enough to indicate what a child actually knows. This anachronistic and sterile national curriculum with teachers 'teaching to the test' will not provide our children with the skills they will need in the fast-changing world of the 1990s and beyond.

2
A National Curriculum

THE PROPOSALS

The Bill provides for the establishment of a national curriculum for schools in England and Wales, consisting of three core subjects (English, mathematics and science) and seven other foundation subjects (history, geography, technology in all its aspects, a modern foreign language in secondary schools, art, music and physical education). All maintained schools are required by the 1944 Education Act to provide religious education to all pupils, unless their parents withdraw them, in accordance with an agreed syllabus in county schools and with the trust deeds of voluntary schools.

The amount of time spent in studying foundation subjects will not be laid down by law; so schools will have scope, as now, to offer other subjects like classics and home economics.

The national curriculum will establish the content of much of what is learnt but will not specify a school's timetable, teaching methods or textbooks. The aim is to build upon good practice.

A National Curriculum Council (for England) and a Curriculum Council for Wales, whose members will all be appointed by ministers, will be required to keep the curriculum under review, work on curriculum development and advise on changes which will be subject to Parliament's approval.

With few exceptions, the national curriculum will be followed by all pupils of compulsory school age from 5 to 16 at county, voluntary or special schools maintained by education authorities or at the proposed grant-maintained schools. It will apply to every child with a statement of special need, but the statement may set out any changes needed to suit that child. Independent schools will not be required to follow it. It will be a condition of the grant paid to the proposed city technology colleges that they follow the substance of it.

The Government expects the national curriculum and associated arrangements for assessment to be implemented broadly within the planned level of resources. It will take a number of years to implement the national curriculum fully. The Government envisages that new arrangements will be introduced first – for maths and science – at the start of the school year 1989–90.

The above outline of the Government's proposals, like the outlines at the beginning of each of the next four chapters, follows closely the description given in the pamphlet 'Education Reform, the Government's Proposals for Schools' published by the Government after the second reading of the Education Reform Bill on 1 December 1987.

Many responses to the curriculum proposals, including several printed below, were based on the belief that the Government would want teaching of the ten 'foundation subjects' to occupy 80 to 90 per cent of the timetable – a figure which was prominently put forward in the July consultation document as a criterion of 'good practice' in schools. When the Bill was published in November, Mr Baker revised this figure and has since said that it will be 'difficult if not impossible' to teach the curriculum in less than 70 per cent of the time available.

THE DEBATE

Curriculum and market: are they compatible?

John Tomlinson
Professor of Education, University of Warwick

The Education Reform Bill is designed to be a radical break with the past. Once it is in place, the principles underlying the provision of public education in England and Wales will be fundamentally different from those of the 1944 settlement and earlier.

The objectives are to create a 'social market' in education, establish a national curriculum and testing system, make education more responsive to economic forces and attract more non-public funding. It is asserted that if achieved these mechanisms would raise standards, increase consumer choice and make the whole system, including higher education, more accountable.

To establish a social market in education it is necessary to break down the notion and system of a publicly planned and provided education service. The local education authorities which now have this duty to provide education have interpreted it within the tradition developed since 1870. They have seen access to educational opportunity as a right of citizenship rather than a privilege conferred or constrained by accident of birth, geography, class, sex or race. In so doing they were reflecting the intentions of Parliament: the new Education Act 'will have a very big social effect apart from educational. It will weld us into what Disraeli described as "one nation"', as R A Butler put it in 1944 (quoted in the *Listener*, 1988). Education has been seen as one of the processes by which more and more individuals and groups in society might be enfranchised and drawn into full membership of that society.

A market, however, works on different principles. Education needs to be seen as a commodity to be purchased and consumed. There must be significant differences between goods on offer to make choice apparent. The consumer (the parent for the child) must be assumed to know his or her best interest. Hence different kinds of school need to be created, to replace free, universal provision and access based on principles of equity. Hence also 'objective' information for parents, regular monitoring and a complaints procedure must replace the professional–client relationship and its overtones of producer control.

The means by which the duty of the LEA to provide (now characterized as a monopoly) is to be replaced by the market are: open enrolment, financial and managerial delegation to schools, grant-maintained schools ('opting out'), city technology colleges and the assisted places scheme. Were all these mechanisms to be effective to the extent evidently intended there would be no sense in which the local education authority could any longer be held responsible for the strategic planning of educational provision in its area. The responses necessary to meet demographic change (such as the response to the recent impact of falling rolls), economic cycles and changes of educational policy would be effectively in the hands of 'the market', that is, the schools themselves, organized as semi-autonomous, competitive units, and of the macro-financial policies of government. The responsibilities for the variety and quality of provision would have been shifted also – from the elected LEA to the appointed governing bodies and the central government.

Will this radical departure in the way school education is provided achieve the objectives intended? Is it likely, for example, that there will be more choice, higher standards and more accountability? The many contradictions to be found in the Bill, especially between ends and means, must raise serious doubts.

Consider the objective of a national curriculum. The idea of a broad but differentiated curriculum being the entitlement of all children has general political and professional support. Its attraction lies in the implied promise of continuing the attempt to improve equality of opportunity. However, the market will offer different kinds of school. Markets are about differences. The LEA-maintained schools and the 'opted-out' schools will have to 'deliver' the national curriculum. The city technology colleges will have to 'have regard' to it. But it will not apply to independent schools or to pupils in them supported by public funds. It seems an inescapable conclusion that different categories of school will attempt to differentiate themselves by what they offer beyond the national curriculum, and that a hierarchy of status will emerge, backed by additional funding from parents and industry and differential selection policies. A national curriculum and a market in education cannot be compatible in any logic we understand. Perhaps the national curriculum is meant as a safety net for the least favoured maintained schools; or perhaps it is a façade behind which differences can multiply. In either case it becomes a curriculum for other people's children.

Even within the proposal for the national curriculum itself there are contradictions. As Sheila Browne, a former Senior Chief Inspector, put it:

If only one could be sure that, in the Bill, the over-riding sub-clause 1(2) would dominate. This reads:
'The curriculum for a maintained school satisfies the requirements of this section if it is a balanced and broadly based curriculum which (a) promotes the spiritual, moral, cultural, mental and physical development of pupils at

the schools and of society; and (b) prepares such pupils for the opportunities, responsibilities and experience of adult life.'

That is light-years away from Clause 2 with its itemized requirements for attainment targets, programmes of study and assessment arrangements.

(Browne, 1988)

The consultation document spoke with the same two voices, the one that understood the need to set a framework within which individuality and innovation could flourish, and the other which went into self-defeating detail. No justification is offered for expressing the curriculum in subject terms or for the choice of subjects. No acknowledgement is made of the differences in teaching and learning between primary and secondary education. Perhaps most worrying of all, Clause 9 of the Bill apparently forbids all innovation without the express approval of the Secretary of State, and that by a cumbersome procedure.

Is it likely that the proposals will widen choice, at least for more than a few? Within the LEA, the present rules will continue to apply, that if a school other than the nearest to the home is chosen, the difference in the cost of transport is met by the parent. So choice in that sense will be no wider and still available only for those able and willing to pay that extra cost. Moreover, surveys suggest that, within those constraints, more than 90 per cent of parents already get their first choice of secondary school. At grant-maintained schools and city technology colleges the governors will control entry. Again, choice will be available only for the few, and those only in areas where such schools appear – another unknown factor. The very act of choice will, of course, affect the schools chosen or avoided. Unpopular schools will continue to serve many, while declining in resources and morale. Those choosing a popular school may find its character changing as it gains in size. (It is noticeable that established independent schools do not as a matter of policy choose to oscillate in size.) Thus the choices made by the few in the market may affect the educational opportunities of most, themselves included. A more ominous aspect is that parental and community choice may come to be exercised on grounds of social and racial prejudice. 'Ghettoization' is the ugly word applied to this ugly prospect (Campbell, Little and Tomlinson, 1987).

It must also be open to question whether the new-style governing bodies and the responsibilities to be devolved upon them will be attended with the success necessary to achieve the Bill's objectives. The delegation to governors of powers of staff appointment and dismissal is problematic (especially while retaining the LEA as employer). The consequent loss of opportunity for strategic deployment of teachers by the LEA is unproven as a better way to optimize the use of scarce human resources. And the prospect of school appointments being decided at the scale of the parish pump is not encouraging. The retreat from such procedures has been part of the development of the LEA this century. The schemes of devolved financial management remain to be constructed still less implemented and proved. The procedures and systems needed to support grant-maintained schools do not yet exist and those for city technology colleges are yet elementary.

Parents are being asked to adopt a significantly new and different role in their relations with teachers. Research over the last generation has shown the advantages to children's education of their parents being involved as collaborators with teachers. That insight is slowly, through a realignment of relationships, being used in schools. Under the new proposals parents are being asked to adopt the role of inquisitor and monitor of teachers and schools, and to use the new complaints procedures, all in the exercise of consumer sovereignty. It remains uncertain, if we are also to try to continue to pursue the advantages of partnership and collaboration, how many parents and teachers will find it possible to assume the two roles simultaneously and avoid the inherent conflict. Alongside this sits the uncertainty as to whether the larger number of school governors, each bearing greater financial and managerial responsibility, can be recruited from the economic and social communities around the schools. The Bill's ambitions in this respect imply the existence of a 'political nation' whose actuality remains to be proved.

These uncertainties deriving from so much novelty need to be set in the context of a significant redistribution of existing powers and the attribution of many new powers – estimated to total 182 – to the Secretary of State. In the transfer of so much responsibility, from the LEA to the school governing body and the Secretary of State, the loser is local government. That must mean that the structure of elected representative government will be weakened. No discussion of this issue was invited in the consultation documents, and at first its significance was denied by the Government; however, in January 1988 the Secretary of State entitled his address to the North of England Education Conference, 'The Constitutional Significance of the Education Reform Bill'. He argued there was none that mattered. Yet the change in the intentions and in the language of government is stark. It is necessary to go back only as far as March 1985, to the Government's White Paper *Better Schools*, to see the differences. That considerable State paper opened: 'The quality of school education concerns everyone. The Government has reviewed, together with its partners, its policies for school education in England and Wales. This White Paper sets out its conclusions' (DES, 1985). Fifteen months and a general election later the talk of partners had disappeared and the conclusions were radically different.

The anxieties raised by the consultation documents and the Bill remain. Is it reasonable to expect the reforms to achieve their putative aims in the light of the internal contradictions of the Bill and the incompatibility of a market approach with a national curriculum? Is the degree of institutional and political innovation likely to be capable of realization? And, if the answers to these questions must be in doubt, can the slide into authoritarianism be justified? Behind all these questions lies the fundamental issue for a democracy: how the power of the State should be directed so far as the public funding and provision of education are concerned. Should it be directed towards a secular process of enfranchisement, or to reinforce and widen differences? Most of all, if a decision has been made to move from the former objective to the latter, should not that be the true subject of public debate, rather than the rhetoric about choice and standards?

References
Baker, K. (1988), Address to the North of England Education Conference, Nottingham, 6 January 1988.
Browne, S. (1988), Presidential Address to the North of England Education Conference, Nottingham, 4 January 1988.
Campbell, R.J., Little, V. and Tomlinson, J.R.G. (eds) (1987), 'Public education policy: the case explored' *Journal of Education Policy*, 2, 4. (1987)
DES (1985), *Better Schools* (Cmnd 9469), London, HMSO.
Listener (1988), 7 January, p. 27.
Tomlinson, J.R.G. (1986), 'Public education, public good', *Oxford Review of Education*, XII, 3.

THE ADVICE

The Royal Society of Arts Examinations Board lends its support to the concept of a national curriculum, seen as the entitlement of all pupils. Such a curriculum must enable pupils to cope with the demands of adult and working life by developing their competence, their confidence and their ability to co-operate with others in a range of contexts. A broad, coherent and balanced curriculum, developing abilities in significant areas of human experience and setting clear objectives, should be available to all. It is right, too, that society at large should have the major say in determining the nature of the curriculum. RSA believes that there is a developing consensus as to what competences should be developed and in what curriculum areas. It does not believe, however, that such a curriculum can be described in terms of particular subjects (although it *may* be possible to *deliver* it through such an approach). The place for particular subjects should be determined once the overall curriculum objectives have been established: the design process must not start with individual components.

The consultation paper offers no philosophical or other justification for the list of foundation subjects proposed (or even for a subject-based approach). Historical divisions of knowledge do not necessarily provide a satisfactory way of describing curriculum needs for the future, given the rapid change in society. There is a danger too that such an approach will accentuate an emphasis upon knowledge itself rather than upon its application. Any list of subjects immediately raises the question of coherence within the curriculum, as well as highlighting important areas that have been overlooked or undervalued. Where is the place for careers education, for moral and political education for economic awareness? Is enough emphasis being placed on art, music, drama and design? Much recent experience, including that of TVEI, shows the value of an integrated approach rather than a single subject approach. In the consultation paper, an integrated approach seems to be illustrated for combined sciences and for history/geography. Taking the latter as an example, what is it about them that qualifies them for inclusion in the foundation subjects in years 4 and 5, what is it that they develop that could not be developed by other curriculum experiences?

RSA has no doubt that skills, abilities and competences in numeracy, in communication and English, and in scientific and practical processes are essential for all and therefore that their development must form the core of the curriculum. It is right that these skills, abilities and competences should be assessed and certificated, but their importance across the whole curriculum may be obscured if it is suggested that they should be treated entirely as independent and separate subjects. 'The clear objectives for what pupils should be able to know, do and understand' should be framed for the curriculum as a whole: guidance could then be given by various agencies, of which RSA Examinations Board would be pleased to be one, as to ways in which that curriculum could be delivered and assessed. Assessment here should be integrated with teaching.

The emphasis on subjects is consistently unfortunate. For instance, the document states that 'the foundation subjects commonly take up 80–90 per cent of the curriculum in schools where there is good practice'. This seems to imply that in many TVEI schools there is not good practice, yet TVEI is a Government-sponsored initiative. It also suggests that other subjects or themes such as health education and the use of information technology should be taught through the foundation subjects 'without crowding out the essential subjects'. But themes such as information technology, health education and economic awareness, and teaching approaches involving drama and role-play, are themselves just as essential in the development of young people and should not be relegated to second-class status. This again suggests that objectives should be framed for the curriculum as a whole: various combinations or aggregations of those objectives into subjects or modules can then be accepted, rather than starting with a limited and inflexible list of subjects.

RSA foresees serious dangers in setting out the foundation subjects in the main legislation. Such an approach could lead to excessive rigidity, as the environment within which schools operate changes.

RSA supports the creation of a National Curriculum Council, and trusts that its membership will be sufficiently representative of an appropriate range of interests to ensure that its decisions and advice carry authority and command widespread support. While it is regretted that NCC and SEAC cannot be combined into one organization, it is regarded as important that there should be the greatest possible collaboration between the two bodies. Such collaboration will be particularly necessary to ensure that curriculum and assessment development can proceed in a coherent manner. RSA supports the proposal for cross-membership. It particularly wants to see in membership of SEAC people with experience of criterion-referenced assessment and people with experience of bringing together NCVQ-related certification and certification for those of compulsory school age.

Roman Catholic Bishops' Conference of England and Wales – There are many valuable elements in the proposals. In particular we welcome attention being drawn to the need for broad and balanced studies, for setting so far as possible clear objectives for pupils and for schools, for facilitating equal access to the curriculum, for assessment and for accountability. Attaining these objectives would bring about many improvements in the pattern of our education system, which would have a sharper, more professional style. However, we believe that the proposals in the consultative document are open to a number of criticisms.

The general flavour of the proposals is utilitarian, pragmatic and competitive. This is not of course to say that a curriculum should not be constructed with its practical usefulness in mind, nor that an element of competition is necessarily unhealthy, but that utilitarianism is a poor and hazardous basis for the design of a curriculum. The proper basis for a curriculum as indicated in the 1944 Education Act is the 'physical, intellectual, emotional and spiritual development' of children. The reference in the document to 'competitor countries' sits uneasily with any acceptable understanding of education for international co-operation, tending more to the concept of a selfish society than to the kind of society we would all wish to promote.

The consultative document makes little or no reference to the role of the curriculum in developing attitudes, relationships, and moral and spiritual values. A national curriculum which effectively ignores beliefs and values, and which neglects the formation of relationships and their proper care and concern, is dangerously inadequate. The idea of 'education for responsibility' seems to be wholly missing. There is no moral dimension to the programme, though moral education is just as crucial as – indeed more so than – 'meeting the challenges of employment'.

The separation of the secular from the religious curriculum adds to the coherence in the idea of education and to the fragmentation of the concept of the human person. One effect of the marginalization of religious education will be a further decrease in the number of teachers able and willing to specialize in this area of study. It seems likely that the lack of attention to religious education in the consultation document has already led people to suppose that, whatever are the requirements in the 1944 Education Act, this subject does not really matter.

The selection of mathematics, science and English as 'core subjects' seems arbitrary.

It does not appear that due account is taken in practice either of the true range of ability, or of the range of different needs to be found among children of any of our schools. It is, for example, quite unreal to propose that during compulsory secondary schooling 'all pupils should continue with some study of all the foundation subjects', and that 'most pupils should be able to take GCSEs covering seven or eight of the foundation subject areas, and (including) all the core subjects'. Such demands would, we consider, for a significant proportion of pupils simply not be educational, because it would be beyond their capacity. Such anomalies are inevitable if the curriculum is solely subject-centred and not in any designed way child-centred.

A general flavour of the document is of inflexibility. Although the whole spectrum of pupils is here and there mentioned, the impression given is that virtually everyone, everywhere, must broadly do the same thing, as if there were a fear that to take account of differences would be a sign of lack of conviction. There are differences arising out of people's innate interests and needs, where they live, whether they belong to a rural or to an urban community, whether the area is one of high employment or otherwise, whether their family culture is foreign to our countries, whether their religious background is Christian or not. It is necessary within such a curriculum for there to be sufficient flexibility to ensure that these differences can be properly accommodated. Otherwise what is intended to be educationally liberating will in fact be cramping and restrictive.

The document appears to pay little attention to the needs of primary schools. The orientation is towards secondary schools. Each stage in a person's growth has its own proper area of education. There is no a priori reason why core and foundation subjects suitable at secondary-school level should be equally suitable at primary-school level. We consider that the proposals as they stand are so inadequate that a substantial redrafting of them is necessary if the national consensus necessary for their implementation is to be achieved.

Church of England Board of Education – The current proposals for legislation pre-empt and foreclose many crucial areas of discussion, notably whether one can establish curricular objectives on the basis of subjects, or whether it is better (as HMI have done in the past) to work from areas of experience; and, even if one were to find a broad consensus in favour of a subject base, precisely what the list of subjects should be. We believe it is precipitate to rush towards legislation based on a list of named subjects. It may be argued that public discussion has now been in process for over ten years, ever since the then Prime Minister's speech at Ruskin College. There may even be a considerable measure of public agreement over general characteristics of the educational process, but that is a far cry from saying that there is a national agreement over a list of subjects to be embedded in primary legislation, or even over the general approach to legislation that that exemplifies. There is still a great deal of careful thinking to be done over the basic structuring of the school curriculum. We wish to draw attention to just two important areas of unresolved thinking, signalled in the document by the use of the phrases 'cross-curricular themes' and 'the secular curriculum'.

The potential importance of cross-curricular themes is indicated, but the actual significance of this two-dimensional approach has not been consistently realized.

Foundation subjects and cross-curricular themes form the warp and woof on which alone a broad, balanced curriculum can be woven. If one tries to concentrate solely on foundation subjects one is either forced back into a narrow, potentially one-sided curriculum, or one has a constant battle for time between a wide array of competing claimants – the very situation from which we are rightly seeking to escape. What is needed is a fuller acknowledgement of the wide support given to the HMI approach to curriculum building through the identification of 'areas of experience'. Where these are not represented through 'subjects' it is essential that they be woven into the curriculum through 'cross-curricular themes'.

The current implication that a national curriculum must perforce be a secular curriculum is one which cannot be allowed to persist. Such an implication is unfortunately strengthened by the ambivalence of the consultation document over the place of religious education within the curriculum. It is not surprising that many people have seen the recent moves by the Secretary of State to introduce more flexibility into arrangements for school worship as a first step towards its removal. The cool statement, 'Religious education . . . is already required by statute, and must continue to form an essential part of the curriculum', in no way matches the Secretary of State's own assertion that 'religious education should be given the significance it deserves within the curriculum'. That significance can only be properly reflected by the placing of the subject among the foundation subjects. It is not only for the sake of present pupils that this must be done. Anything which makes it less likely that GCSE candidates will include RE among the subjects they might offer will have a major adverse impact on the already inadequate supply of RE teachers, in both primary and secondary schools. It must be included within the range of subjects which are expected to be available in every school, at least for GCSE and preferably for A-level as well.

We welcome the assurance that 'there will not be any general provision for the exemption of individual pupils attending county, voluntary or grant-maintained schools' [from the national curriculum] and would invite the Secretary of State to take this opportunity of applying that principle to religious education as well (if it is truly to be part of the national curriculum and not remain as a barely tolerated, quasi-educational hangover from the past).

When we turn to the question of resources, we find ourselves predictably disappointed at the lack of realism shown. There is to be no 'new' money at the local level, and yet somehow a whole new range of required provision will have to be paid for. What will the LEAs (and consequently the schools, under the new delegation arrangements) have to do without, in terms of time available as well as cash available? The situation appears to be little better at national level. The Secretaries of State are taking on new financial responsibilities, yet there is again no indication that there will be any 'new' money to meet these. What will the Secretaries of State stop doing, in order to pay for the NCC and the whole apparatus of national testing?

Money is not the only problem. Have any calculations been made as to the number of, say science teachers needed if the current proposals were to be implemented? Will that number of teachers be available by September 1989? Or even by 1995?

The 'continuing discussion' of the curriculum which is promised over the next few years must be real discussion, with the Department of Education and Science not merely asking questions but giving time for those questions to be adequately answered and then listening to and acting upon the answers that they receive. Neither simply bureaucratic nor purely political reasons for wishing to hurry the process should be allowed to jeopardize the serious endeavour of trying to get our education system right for the future.

We entirely agree that the 'commitment of the education profession' needs to be thoroughly engaged if the desired improvements are to be brought about. What needs to be looked at in this context, however, is not just the impact of the proposals in the curriculum document alone but the impact of the total package of proposals. The way some of the other documents imply lack of trust in the profession generally, the expectation that teachers (and especially heads) will all 'work much harder', plus the speed with which the current proposals are being rushed through, do not combine to provide a firm base on which the required commitment is likely to grow. The Church will certainly find its own role as employer of staff in aided schools made more difficult by the Government's present intentions. It believes other employers will find equal difficulties.

National Union of Teachers – It is not possible to have a national uniform view of the curriculum. The Welsh, the Scots, the Northern Irish explicitly cannot be accommodated in a 'national uniform curriculum': but we would argue, neither can the Cornish, the Cumbrians, the Asians nor the Afro-Caribbean English pupil, the Muslim and the Christian pupil, be taught in a nationally uniform way. When *Better Schools* said 'even initial agreement will need years to accomplish', the union had hoped that what was envisaged was the kind of local consultation which could have led to a building, in curriculum terms, on the agreement already achieved.

In the document's elaboration of the foundation subjects and, despite the Secretaries of State's declared intention not to prescribe in legislation how much time should be allocated to each subject, it attempts to quantify in percentage terms the time elements involved. The consultative document shows how little its authors have understood the nature of the debate from which any consensus has emerged. Our belief in 1985 that the 'Government's attempts to define the curriculum nationally is misconceived' arose from the knowledge that the attempt was wrong-footed because it broke with good curriculum practice, i.e. it undervalued the teacher.

It is difficult to make a comment on the components of the proposed national curriculum because of the level of generalization. What is particularly difficult to understand is the use of the terms 'core' and 'foundation' in the context in which they are used. Teachers will need to know very much more about the Secretaries of State's intentions for the teaching of science, in particular the relationship of the combined sciences as a single subject. It is extremely doubtful that there is sufficient evidence available on the practicality of teaching a double GCSE award where teachers feel inadequately qualified in other than their main science subject. There is abundant evidence of the shortage of qualified physics teachers, which must severely restrict the schools' capabilities of offering a double GCSE award in science.

The suggestion of a combined course covering art, music, drama and design, working with roughly 10 per cent of the available curriculum time, is novel. These 'practical' subjects make specific demands upon space. Secondary schools have struggled to provide for these in the early years by the so-called 'circus' arrangements. These have usually been severely criticized by HMI. The union cannot believe that what is being proposed is an extension of the circus arrangement in years 4 and 5 of the secondary schooling, yet finds it difficult to imagine how a combined course can be serviced. Some form of modular course is presumably in mind but we must quesiton the practicality of this, given the demands upon staff and accommodation.

There can be little justification for the insular attitudes which have often made the task of teaching modern languages in especially English, but also in many Welsh, schools difficult. Modern-languages teaching created its own problems by working too long to elitist ideas about the nature of languages. We therefore welcome the inclusion of modern languages within the foundation subject. Many of our young people now have access to a range of languages other than English, and the pool of modern languages created has greatly enriched our capacity to trade in the world communities. Central resourcing, and particularly the political voice, has been ambivalent in its response to these developments. A national curriculum, which fails to take account of the demographic changes which have occurred and will accelerate, will not fit the needs of the future. The inclusion of modern languages in the foundation subjects has huge implications for schools, LEAs and central government. It will call for a development programme, itself based on wide consultations with many different interests and requiring increased teacher recruitment with a corresponding demand upon teacher training and in-service education and training.

The document has tried to ride the two horses of rigour and

breadth in a naïve way. In effect the document is saying that what the curriculum must do is to provide easily testable attainment targets in key areas – English, mathematics and science; and so that teachers do not cheat the system by teaching only these, we will make them teach other subjects for certain minimum times. Conversely, to make certain that teachers should not introduce dubious material, we will prescribe what is to be taught for 90 per cent of the curriculum time. It is unfortunate that the document should choose to illustrate only the curriculum of the fourth- and fifth-year secondary pupils. The result is that much of the thinking of the Secretaries of State about the primary school curriculum has to be gleaned from negative allusions.

There can be no confidence in the intentions concerning the programme which pupils will follow. The working groups' recommendations are expected to 'reflect the attainment targets' and describe 'the overall content, knowledge, skills and processes relevant to today's needs'. They must also specify the 'minimum of common content for all pupils and any cross-curricular areas to be explored'. Experience has been that such exercises have tended to produce crowded curricula. The references to 'flexibility' and 'space to accommodate enterprise' in paragraph 37 tend to ring hollow in these circumstances. It will need the exercise of the Secretaries of State's powers to suspend the requirements of the national curriculum for innovation and development work to take place. The union finds this last perhaps the most offensive manifestation of the proposed legislation. It is difficult to understand why the Government and its advisers should so discount the enormous innovative work done by schools in the last 20 years. How can the education service afford to throw away this kind of development and expertise?

Special needs receive the most cursory treatment in the consultation document. The emphasis is upon conformity, with an almost casual indifference to the needs of pupils who are currently disadvantaged or, who, for whatever reason, need special provision. The interests of such pupils have always required protection, yet the document is silent. The dangers for these pupils in the proposals about attainment testing and assessment are that they will be even further disadvantaged and alienated from a system of education which is not for them. To reconcile the spirit of the 1981 Education Act with the uncompromisingly competitive ethos of the proposed legislation is impossible. Modern educational practice for special-needs children emphasizes that every effort should be made to give access to the full range of the curriculum, modified or adapted if necessary to meet their needs. The last thing these pupils need is to be measured in a deficiency model which seems to run through most of this document.

The requirements of the national curriculum are likely to be seen in assimilation terms. This is almost the *raison d'être* for common curriculum approaches. The document does not address the needs of the multi-ethnic and multicultural community which Britain has become. This, again, is a pointer to the conformist thrust of a national curriculum approach. Where in a syllabus of minimum content is there space for that which is not English, white and Christian? The union would wish to see some emphasis on the development of curricular approaches which educate all pupils for life in Britain as it is. Much curriculum development work has been done, in various subject areas, on making those subject relevant to our multicultural society, and this work should find a place in any national curriculum framework.

There is already a very considerable measure of agreement about what the curriculum 5–16 should contain. Unevenness of delivery is far more a consequence of the availability of resources, particularly suitably qualified teachers but, also, basic requirements of specialist accommodation and equipment. Where these have been provided they have offered a satisfying return. It is in addressing this issue that the Government could do most to lift expectation.

The document quotes HMI reports about the failure to stretch young people, especially the middle-ability youngsters, and the fact that expectations are frequently too low. The reports do not support these statements in any but a partial sense. The reports also speak of the satisfactory achievements of the large majority of our schools. So, too, does the other evidence, particularly that which relates to the examination achievements of young people, which have consistenly risen in the last 20 years. Of course, there are problems but these are specific and identifiable. Many of these have curricular implications, and it is these which we should now be discussing.

We have drawn attention to the restricted view which the consultlation document has expressed about the purposes of education. It constructs a curriculum from subject packages of 'minimum content' to fill up to 90 per cent of the teaching time and of attainment targets which are susceptible to testing across the ability range. Pupils will be described in ranked order and, it is thought, be driven to perform better by some competitive urge, and the success of the school will be measured on how successful the pupils have been in these terms. It is a mean view which distrusts the professional competence of teachers, of local authority advisers and administrators and denies the opportunity of developing curriculum best suited to the needs of the children and the community.

The National Association of Schoolmasters/Union of Women Teachers regrets that the Government has, in such a short space of time, departed from important principles underlying the aims and objectives for the curriculum outlined in *Better Schools*, in particular the principle that all pupils should have access to a broad, balanced, relevant and differentiated curiculum. The NAS/UWT is not opposed in principle to the establishment of a national curriculum. It is essential, however, that before the Government legislates it demonstrate that a broadly based curriculum can be available to *all* pupils, regardless of where they happen to go to school. This is dependent on the provision of added staff and resources.

Where the NAS/UWT differs fundamentally from the Government is over the means by which such a curriculum can be implemented. In particular the association is strongly opposed to the introduction of a prescriptive curriculum and to national tests for pupils aged 7, 11, 14 and 16, as outlined in the DES document.

The NAS/UWT also doubts whether the Secretary of State has given proper attention to the practical implications of a national curriculum. According to the recent (July 1987) HMI report on LEA provision, only three authorities in ten in England would at the moment be in a position to cope with the demands of a national curriculum consisting of ten foundation subjects. It will take more than legislation to bring the vast majority of LEAs into line, and to remove the unacceptably high variations in staffing levels, described by HMI, which have turned state education into a lottery.

It is less than a year since the Education (No. 2) Act 1986 received the Royal Assent, section 18 of which gives school governing bodies the power to modify the curricular policies of LEAs so far as these policies relate to individual schools. This is unfortunately typical of the Government's lack of foresight and coherence in developing its policies for educjation. The Government has painstakingly developed a framework for the organization and management of the school curriculum and the machine to deliver policies for the curriculum at local and school level. The plans for a national curriculum threaten to destroy this machinery, and the ability of LEAs to assume responsibilities for the curriculum has been seriously weakened as a consequence of the 1986 Act. In the absence of established administrative machinery, we ask how the Government will introduce and maintain a national curriculum.

The NAS/UWT is not against the idea of establishing a range of foundation subjects to be followed by all pupils to age 16, but it is absurd to believe that no additional resources will be needed to implement a policy whereby most of the foundation subjects will be studies to examination level. The NAS/UWT is concerned that non-statutory guidelines for the organization and management of the curriculum in schools will be followed by a directive that 90 per cent of curriculum time shall be devoted to a study of the foundation subjects; that a curriculum defined in terms of traditonal subjects

will make it more difficulty to promote the development of modular
courses, and cross-curricular themes; that such important elements
as careers teaching and minority subjects such as classics, now
enjoying something of a resurgence, will be squeezed out of the
curriculum; that, contrary to what the Secretary of State has to say,
the list of essential subjects comes very close to describing the whole
curriculum, leaving little or no room for innovation.

The NAS/UWT finds it deplorable that the Secretary of State
persists in refusing to invite nominations from the recognized
teaching organizations for places not only on the NCC, but also on
the key subject working groups. The NCC will act under the
direction of the Secretary of Sate. If the NCC is to be seen as offering
independent advice, it must represent a cross-section of educational
interests and should at least in part therefore be nominated and not
an appointed council. The Secretary of State proposes to take
substantial powers, underpinned by legislation, in respect of the
curriculum, attainment targets, qualifications and examinations. It
is very important that the bodies set up in connection with his
exercise of these powers should be able to exert real influences over
the Secretary of State. Members will find this difficult if they owe
their places on these bodies to the grace and favour of the Secretary
of State. The above comments apply equally to the proposed setting
up of the SEAC. The NAS/UWT contends that serving teachers
should be in the majority on any bodies set up to devise, administer
and moderate the national tests.

Legislation and an expanding bureaucracy go hand in hand; and
LEAs will so find that they have their hands full in dealing with
complaints about the manner in which governing bodies and heads
are discharging the responsibilites for the curriculum. Is it reasonable to impose this burden on LEAs when it is clear that the real
power and responsibility lie with the Secretary of State and the
DES?

The new Education Bill represents the most radical piece of
educational legislation to come before Parliament in more than 40
years. It is the height of irresponsibility to move towards such
legislation with a speed which makes full and genuine consultation
impossible.

National Association of Head Teachers – Has the Government
fully considered the implictions of legislating a national curriculum,
on the one hand giving parents and others the opportunity to
complain and safeguard their rights without, on the other hand,
providing the resource framework to enable the legislated curriculum to be delivered? It is quite wrong to talk about a national
curriculum let alone legislate for one without ensuring that the

teaching force is available in sufficient numbers and suitably trained to deliver that curriculum. Will parents really be able to take legal action if because of the scarcity of foreign-language teachers their child is being taught by a non-specialist with a deplorable accent?

In addition to allowing time for adequate preparation, the commencement of the national curriculum should take account not only of the resource needs but of the serious consequences of introducing too many things at once. Headteachers will need to carry their teachers with them. There has to be full and adequate training of those teachers, but there is a limit to how much in-service and retraining they can take. There is a limit, too, on the amount which can be fitted into initial training. The Government must be aware of all the other initiatives it has introduced and the demands for changes in the CATE criteria.

We would also remind the Secretary of State that we have to carry on running the existing system in the wake of unparalleled disruption and dissatisfaction in the profession whilst facing all the challenges of the new conditions of service packages and the prospect of financial devolution.

We cannot understand how the Goverment can continue with the discredited practice of attempting to bring about major changes whilst maintaining they can take place within the planned level of resources. We have been through all this before with the introduction of GCSE which demonstrated the folly of such an approach. There will be no support for the national curriculum until the resources are seen to be available and either the supply of teachers assured or, if not, changes made to the national curriculum to mirror exactly the shortfall. We require a detailed statement from the Secretary of State on the supply of teachers. We have calculated, using figures from the *DES Statistics of Education: Schools* and the draft statement of policy *Foreign Languages in the School Curriculum*, that an extra 3,000 teachers of a foreign language are required to fulfil the national curriculum requirements of a foreign language for all until 16. The calculations need to be done for all subject areas and published by the DES to demonstrate to parents that, wherever they are in the country and in whichever type of school, their children will be 'entitled to the same opportunities wherever they go to school'. The proposals for timing of implementation have no meaning unless the resources are made available.

The Secondary Heads Association warmly welcomes the Government's commitment to establish an 'entitlement' curriculum for all our children; to continue the rise in education standards in our schools; to continue the existing progress towards agreement on a curriculum offering progression, continuity and coherence; to raise expectations for our pupils' achievement; to adopt a non-statutory approach to time allocation in the curriculum, thus enabling professional flexibility in its delivery.

We believe that the present prescriptive proposals will severely limit pupils' opportunities to develop the qualities listed in paragraph 68 (self-reliance, self-discipline, enterprise and problem-solving in the real world), principally because they have too narrow a view of what education must provide to prepare young people for adult life.

SHA is strongly opposed to the following elements of the present curriculum proposals:

(a) The prescriptive nature from 14+ onwards because many pupils by that age need more choice than 10 per cent.

(b) The proposed reduction in time allocation for basic subjects like English, maths and PE.

(c) The narrow definition of the curriculum on a single-subject basis.

(d) The failure to offer a curriculum necessarily appropriate to the aptitudes and abilities of all pupils, as required by the 1944 Act. As one example we believe that a more flexible approach to the place of modern languages in the curriculum would be advisable.

(e) The failure to acknowledge that many topics essential for preparing all pupils for adult life are best developed through non-examined general education programmes comprising PSE, careers education, education for economic awareness, RE, health education etc. The latter, for example, involving among other topics AIDS and drugs education, is not suitable for a GCSE examination course.

(f) The total devaluation of the arts in reduced time and the notion that pupils can undertake a combined GCSE course in art/music/drama/design.

(g) The divorce of design and technology.

Although we recognize that very many parents are actively concerned and interested in the curriculum and progress of their own children, we believe that comparatively few have the time and interest to become as involved as the Government envisages with the overall curriculum strategy of the school, bearing in mind the considerable time that will be necessary to gain sufficient understanding. As evidence we cite the recent attendances at governors' annual meetings for parents.

Parents are often not the best judge of their own children's potential. There will therefore be unjustified disappointment with 'the effectiveness' of the school. Parents will not wish to see their children struggle with a curriculum inappropriate to their aptitude and ability nor will they wish to have their children identified as failures. (Will parents have the right to 'opt out' of national tests?) The welcome that parents are giving to current pilot records of achievement shows that they want to know what *skills*, knowledge and abilities their individual children have and *not* simplistic grades, test results and positions.

Teachers for the national curriculum especially for science, technology and foreign languages are already in short supply. The effect of devaluing the contribution of many teachers in PE and the arts will leave them disheartened and redundant. Even if it were possible, they might not wish to retrain to teach science, technology or languages. The timetable for teacher training looks as inadequate as for GCSE, unless the slow start, primary only, is implemented. Good teachers, if they have to teach second, third or even fourth subjects because of the new curriculum demands, could be pilloried by parents. High-calibre teachers will not be recruited to a profession where the total climate is dominated by consumer pressure, fear of unjust comparisons and league tables, even within a school.

Assistant Masters' and Mistresses' Association – We welcome the Government's recognition that pupils with statemented special needs should not necessarily be subject to all the requirements of the national curriculum. We strongly urge that statements of special need should also specify any programmes of study, attainment targets and assessment tests which would be inappropriate, having regard to the nature and severity of the pupil's special need(s), and therefore need adjustment. The national number of statemented children falls far short of the estimate made by the Warnock Committee of Inquiry of the number of pupils likely at some time during their schooling to demonstrate special need. We suppose that there are far more pupils with such needs than have been statemented. We urge the Government to establish a working group to inquire into the matter and to take account of its findings when determining the circumstances in which the requirements of the national curriculum might be modified.

The National Curriculum 5–16 makes no mention of unstatemented pupils who, temporarily or over a sustained period, display behavioural problems which severely inhibit or arrest their educational progress. We consider that where a pupil displays behavioural problems which have been notified to his or her parents, the school or unit at which he or she is enrolled or the the local education authority, as the case may be, should be able to specify any national curriculum requirements which should not apply to the pupil or should be modified until such time as his or her behavioural problems have been overcome.

We strongly reject the Government's suggestion that there should be nationally required programmes of study. Schedule 1 of the Education (School Teachers' Pay and Conditions of Employment) Order 1987 made headteachers statutorily responsible for 'determining, organizing and implementing an appropriate curriculum for the school, having regard to the needs, experience, interests, aptitudes and stage of development of the pupils and the resources available to the school'. Schedule 3 of the same order confirmed the contractual and professional responsibility of assistant teachers for 'planning and preparing courses and lessons'. We find it quite inconsistent that the Government should now propose the statutory confiscation of a professional role which, only months ago, it recognized and was anxious to confirm and secure in other legislation.

Institute of Economic Affairs – The debate over a Government-imposed national curriculum is regrettably diverting attention from what really matters in the Government's current proposals, devolved management to schools.

The most effective national curriculum is that set by the market, by the consumers of the education service. This will be far more responsive to children's needs and society's demands than any centrally imposed curriculum, no matter how well meant. Attempts by Government and by Parliament to impose a curriculum, no matter how 'generally agreed' they think it to be, are a poor second best in terms of quality, flexibility and responsiveness to needs than allowing the market to decide and setting the system free to respond to the overwhelming demand for higher standards. The Government must trust market forces rather than some committee of the great and good.

Uniformity between schools is not only unnecessary, it is potentially damaging. The picture of children constantly roaming the country, changing schools frequently, is a false one. To the extent that an enforced change of school interrupts a child's education, that will always be so, with or without a centrally imposed national curriculum. Any attempt to prescribe the curriculum in such a detailed way is the very strait-jacket that the government professes to want to avoid. It would actually reduce standards in the best schools, whilst doing little or nothing for the poorer ones.

It is a fallacy to suppose that setting a crowded curriculum of worthy subjects will crowd out the unacceptable peace studies, homosexual studies and the rest. It is naïve to suppose that the bad teacher and the bad LEA will cease to introduce such dangerous nonsense into the classroom just because Parliament has legislated a national curriculum. If they have a mind to abuse children in such a way, they will continue to do so, whether in the period marked history or in that called health education.

Section C outlining the provisions of the Bill portrays a frightening degree of secondary legislation and bureacracy for years ahead. Such detailed control would set the curriculum in stone for 20 years or more, not even responsive to the higher standards of skill and knowledge which the Government itself expects will be seen in future generations of children. Such legislative detail is a lawyer's dream but a teacher's nightmare. The Government must start treating the teachers, or most of them, as professional people.

By what right do national curriculum subject working groups impose their views upon the teaching profession and upon the consumer market of parents and children? One historian's view will prevail against that of another merely because the one was chosen by the Secretary of State to serve on a committee whilst the other was not. All the Government needs to do is to issue an updated and improved version of *Better Schools* and to say that, henceforth, inspections and judgements on schools registering and deregistering by HMI, will use these criteria. They would soon become the norm, but they could at least be constantly updated. If the Government wants to impose its view, and we doubt that it should, it does not need legislation.

The Confederation of British Industry believes that the proposed national curriculum, with its broad base and avoidance of premature specialization, will make an important contribution to the raising of standards. Employers must be confident that new employees who have recently left full-time education are able to: handle numbers, both directly and with the use of mechanical or electronic aids; transmit and receive ideas accurately, both orally and in writing or by the use of graphics; weigh up situations and problems and apply knowledge and skill to their solution; exercise self-discipline; appreciate norms for behaviour in working situations; and take an open and positive attitude to self-development and change.

The CBI is in agreement with the foundation subjects given in the consultation document. However, we would like to reaffirm the concerns expressed by the industry and commerce regarding the important need to inform these traditional subjects with cross-curricular themes that relate to life after school and the world of work in particular. The DBI is concerned that the document does not contain any specific reference relating to economic awareness and understanding, or careers education. It is important that the national curriculum allows sufficient scope for adequate coverage of aspects of educational experience outside the narrow confines of the traditional individual subject disciplines, for which the Technical and Vocational Education Initiative (TVEI) has proved a particularly valuable and relevant example.

We note that the subject working groups are asked to take account of 'the need for attainment targets and programmes of study to reflect cross-curricular themes and subjects'. We appreciate that this will not be achieved easily, but it is vital that it is. Otherwise there is a serious risk that much of the good work done in recent years to relate the curriculum to life after school will not be sustained in the future.

The CBI welcomes the provision of more information at every level of the education service to facilitate comparisons between schools. Though aware of the problems in making such comparisons, we share the Government's view that more openness about performances and objectives can contribute towards raising standards.

The British Institute of Management has pressed for the time-scale for curriculum change to be shortened and for the Department of Education and Science to provide direction at national level to ensure that change is successfully implemented and that uniformly high standards are achieved. In a recent consultation of BIM's membership, 95 per cent of respondents approved the principle of a national curriculum, which would better equip pupils in maintained schools with the knowledge, skills and understanding required for adult life and employment. In ensuring that pupils would be entitled to the same opportunities wherever they go to school, a number of respondents felt that a significant point in favour of the national curriculum was that their own mobility in the job market would be helped because their children's education would not suffer from changing schools.

The intention that schools would be made more accountable was equally welcome to BIM members, and seen as a contribution to raising standards. Greater regulation of teachers and teaching standards was similarly welcomed.

Employer input into curricular development is as important as that of educationalists. 62 per cent of respondents believe that the current level of employer input is insufficient. To this end, BIM recommend that the proposed National Curriculum Council should involved representatives from industry and commerce as well as from education. BIM recognizes the responsibility of managers for support to education. 85 per cent of respondents believe that insufficient links have been made between industry and schools. If syllabuses are to be relevant to the world of work, and industry provided with a skilled workforce, these links will have to be much more active and regular, preferably aided by an increase in school/industry liaison officers. Work experience could to advantage form part of the foundation element of the curriculum.

Manpower Services Commision – In terms of TVEI, the proposals for a national curriculum are of the greatest potential significance. Key points which the MSC believes the Government should take into account in developing its plan for educational change:

The importance of enhancing the whole curriculum's relevance to adult and working life and the acknowledgement of TVEI's important role and experience in this is welcomed.

The emphasis in the guide lines on a framework rather than a strait-jacket is welcome. Experience in TVEI has demonstrated the importance of giving teachers 'space to accommodate their enterprise' and room for creativity and flexibility if effective delivery is to be achieved.

The common core curriculum to 16 is welcomed, particularly in ensuring equal opportunities in terms of gender and race; science and technology for all to 16 are particularly welcomed here since too may girls still drop out of these subjects if given a choice.

The working groups will have an important role in setting a framework of learning objectives which achieve the overall aims and motivate both teachers and pupils to successful achievement. This part of the process needs time if implementation is to be successful. The TVEI unit could provide useful input to these groups based on experience. Consideration should therefore be given to including TVEI representation on the various working groups.

In terms of specific subjects and the allocation of time and space to them, it is hoped that the curriculum framework will give scope for imaginative integrated and/or cross-curricular schemes. Particularly important across the curriculum are those subjects which are not given specific time, such as economic awareness, careers guidance, health education and personal development.

The supply of suitably qualified teachers to deliver this curriculum – particularly in science and technology – needs consideration and action.

Curricular developments in Scotland could be helpful to the national curriculum, particularly in the emphasis they give to process rather than content. TVEI experience is that changing teaching and learning styles is crucial to the effective implementation of curricular change.

Coherence post-16 needs careful consideration. TVEI experience of 14–18 could be helpful, as could experience in work-related NAFE planning. Collaboration between institutions within LEAs has proved to be important and effective.

British Petroleum Company – The education service has been the victim of recent years, and the Government's reforms will make many new demands. To achieve the national objective will require proper resourcing, effective leadership and a determined effort to restore morale. UK industry has learnt enough about the management of major and often painful change in recent years to know that it cannot be done in a negative or critical spirit and it cannot be done on a shoestring. Many of the Government's plans for the future management and development of the education service depend on increased involvement and participation by industry and commerce. The government runs the risk of overestimating the capacity of industry to respond. The spirit is willing – we believe increasingly so – but the physical ability to support the commitment is limited.

We particularly welcome the importance attached to maths, science and technology, which we believe is an essential corrective to the anti-science prejudice so embedded in modern British culture.

There are dangers in an approach based on a popular appeal to 'getting back to basics'. It will be important to guard against insufficient attention being paid to areas of knowledge and skill which require a contribution from, and co-operation between, the teachers of many different subjects. As a major sponsor of economic awareness initiatives, and as a company with strong interests in design and technology, BP is well versed in the problems of areas of knowledge which cut across traditional subject boundaries. As employers we know that, in addition to requiring people who are numerate, literate and possessed of whatever skills or knowledge we require for particular jobs, we are also looking at the 'whole person', and in particular seeking that range of personal transferable skills (e.g. communication, problem-solving and team-work skills) which is so essential to effective participation in business life.

It is important that teachers of science recognize their common responsibility with those of English to promote effective communication skills and teachers of English, along with those of maths and humanities, accept their responsibility to contribute to themes such as economic awareness. We believe that it should be an absolute requirement of the national curriculum that LEAs, governors and teachers plan the delivery of the cross-curricular themes and skills properly.

Association of British Chambers of Commerce – We are especially concerned that the proposals make no specific reference to work experience and careers advisory activities. Since experience demonstrates that activities which are not timetabled generally receive scant attention and resources, we believe that these activities should be given a specific place in the curriculum for the relevant age groups.

National Confederation of Parent–Teacher Associations – Although we are aware that there has been much debate on this topic within educational circles in recent years, the public at large and parents in particular remain largely unfamiliar with the issues involved. We hope that parents as well as others will be given an opportunity for the fullest possible discussion as detailed content of the national curriculum is determined.

The declared aim of the Government is to equip every pupil with the knowledge, skills, understading and aptitudes to meet the responsibilities of adult life and employment. NCPTA fully supports these aims, believing them to be a cogent summary of what any parent would wish their child to gain from his or her time in school. NCPTA has always maintained that every child has a right to equality of opportunity and should not be disadvantaged by reason of finance or geography. There is likely, therefore, to be substantial support among parents for a national curriculum because it would seem to offer the possibility of equality of opportunity. It is in the classroom that the curriculum is delivered to the pupil, and equality of opportunity also implies equality of access to sufficient appropriately trained and well-motivated teachers. Particularly at secondary level a lack of specialist teachers and facilities will perpetuate discrepancies between schools.

Legislation to impose a national curriculum will be seen by many as an undesirable move towards central control of the education system. It also seems contrary to the spirit of the 1986 Education Act, which has just given to school governors the responsibility to consider the LEA policy for the secular curriculum and to decide whether it should be modified for their particular school.

NCPTA is not convinced that a national curriculum, as outlined, is the best way to achieve the improvement in opportunities and standards desired by parents. There are problems, particularly in certain LEAs, but great care must be taken not to lose beneficial initiatives in the endeavour to raise levels of attainment for all pupils. The document acknowledges the vital part that the teachers' professional contribution will have to play in achieving higher educational standards yet seems at the same time to show an underlying mistrust of teachers and schools.

NCPTA welcomes the emphasis on the need for better information about education to be made available to parents and other 'consumers'. We are anxious that this information should be meaningful and helpful to all concerned.

Whatever objectives are set, unless schools are to be given the means to achieve the objectives there will be no overall improvement. It could be argued that, given better resources, more teachers (particularly in the shortage areas) and smaller teaching groups, a marked improvement could be achieved in the majority of schools, without new legislation.

National Assocation of Governors and Managers – NAGM's policy has always been that schools should be accountable to the governing body for the way in which they organize and deliver the curriculum, though this is still a new idea in many schools. Clear guidelines about appropriate work for different ages is to be welcomed, as long as this does not prevent the school from responding to local needs. NAGM is not sure that these new proposals will help governors to judge how far the school is meeting the needs of its pupils and its local community. This is, after all, the main task of the governing body. We are particularly worried about the effect on children with special educational needs in ordinary schools, and on the special school curriculum.

Advisory Centre for Education – Much of the argument for introducing the 'reforms' in the proposed new Education bill rests on the belief that they will give parents greater choice and power and thereby raise standards. We believe that recent educational reforms incorporated in the 1980, 1981 and 1986 Education Acts have gone a long way towards meeting these aims. Schools, governing bodies and local education authorities are all more open, more accountable and more democratic institutions as a result of this legislation. Much of our advice work is taken up with advising parents of their rights in situations where they feel they are not being listened to or justly treated. But most of the problems that arise cannot be legislated against. They arise out of unprofessionalism, poor communication and misunderstandings. As part of ACE's work, we explain to parents how they can be most effective in the role they have to play in the education of their children, and encourage schools, governing bodies and LEAs to establish positive and constructive strategies to ensure that a genuine partnership exists between parents and schools. The legislation exists to enable this partnership to develop – all that it needs is the will and determination to put it into practice.

ACE would like to see the consensus that already exists on a core curriculum developed, using the examples of best practice from LEAs across the country as the basis for the debate. A child's entitlement to the curriculum has, of course, to be backed up by an entitlement to resources. Other consultation documents clearly show this entitlement will not exist, and the national curriculum, we are told, will be introduced within existing resources. For these reasons alone it will not work.

ACE would like to see published the whole range of responses the DES has received on its proposals, so that a genuine public debate can then take place on desirability of these 'reforms' and the direction a new Education Bill should take.

National Consumer Council – We welcome the proposal on complaints procedures for parents who feel that their children are not getting the curriculum to which they are entitled.

The consultation document puts very little stress on the importance of parental views in developing the national curriculum. Parent representatives should be included on the key bodies – the National Curriculum Council, the Welsh Curriculum Council that we have proposed, the School Examinations and Assessment Council and the subject working groups. The Government should explore ways of supporting the creation of a representative parent body for England and for Wales so that the parental view can inform the continuing work of these key bodies.

The Government's proposals imply new responsibilities for parents. It should commit itself to a programme of research and development of means of informing parents and supporting governing bodies. The Government needs to make resources available for governor training so that governors can fulfil the range of their new responsibilities.

Association of County Councils – The extent of the prescription which the consultative paper appears to propose gives rise to extreme doubts that the flexibility implicit in the Secretary of State's words will be realized. The paper places too much emphasis on subject compartments (each allocated a slice of school time) and too little on the need to present a coherent programme to children and to integrate their work.

Despite the title of the document, its content is heavily weighted to the teaching of the 14–16 age group, and seems to have been widely influenced by the recent developments in 16+ examinations. The wisdom of relying too heavily upon an examination (GCSE) which is still in its infancy, and which is likely to develop significantly over the next few years, must be questioned.

' The illustrative percentage/time allocations proposed could too easily lead to an oversimplification to achieve statistical convenience. There is a need for a more sophisticated and flexible allocation of time. The fact that another far-reaching package of legislation is being prepared even before the 1986 Act changes are all implemented does suggest a lack of coherence in the overall development of policy and that too much is being attempted too quickly.

The proposal that the foundation subjects should take up 75–85 per cent of the timetable for fourth and fifth years (the 10 per cent variance being dependent on how much time is allocated to combined science subjects) is too restrictive. It is not always appropriate for every pupil to study, for example, a foreign language up to the age of 16. Schools will find it more difficult to accommodate pupil (and parent) choice.

The proposal that the headteacher is to be responsible for securing implementation of the curricular policy does not provide a sufficient safeguard unless the overall responsibility of the LEA is recognized. There should be a provision whereby the authority can take action if it is advised, either by the headteacher or by one of its inspectors or advisers, that a governing body's modifications to the curriculum go beyond or are at odds with the policy determined by the LEA.

Both HMI and LEA inspection and advisory services will need substantial strengthening if they are to have responsibility for monitoring the delivery of the national curriculum in LEA-maintained schools. It is essential that LEA inspectors and advisers should remain accountable to the LEA, through the Chief Education Officer, if authorities are to be able to discharge the responsibilities which are still assigned to them. The paper emphasizes the inspecting and monitoring role. At least equal emphasis needs to be laid on advisers and inspectors offering support to schools. Judgement of performance is essential; if poor performance is to be improved, advice and assistance are as important – and more valuable in the long run – than the simple and sometimes negative act of judgement.

There is an interesting reference to 'action by parents'. The consultative paper does not explain what sort of action it foresees and, more important, how this could be developed in a way which would help in the improvement of performance.

The setting up of suitable machinery for handling complaints will require considerable LEA resources and there will be a minority of litigiously minded activists who will dominate the system and consume the time of school and other staff. School and curriculum development is not enhanced by formal complaints machinery: there is a danger that the outcome of the introduction of such procedures will be increasingly defensive and cautious behaviour by schools and LEAs, to the detriment of pupils. The new governing bodies as constituted under the 1986 (No. 2) Act, which give parents more representation and influence, should provide adequate opportunities for complaints about individual schools.

There are significant resource implications in the extensive programmes of in-service training which will be needed if teachers are to be adequately prepared for the introduction of a national curriculum. Most LEAs would need to increase the number of advisers if they were to be able to provide teachers with adequate support and discharge their general responsibilities.

The association believes that the sum of the proposals will cost much more than the paper recognizes. Unless met, the national curriculum initiative will fall far short of Government expectations and lead to frustration and resentment. The power of LEAs to direct resources will be diminished by the introduction of the proposals set out in the consultative paper on financial delegation.

The introduction of a national curriculum would represent the largest single change in the provision of education in schools since the implementation of the 1944 Act. It is essential, for the good of successive generations of pupils and the nation as a whole, that it should be based on a genuine and informed consensus, that it should be broad enough to permit development and variation, and that it should be introduced only when the training and resources which it will require can be made available.

Association of Metropolitan Authorities – All pupils are entitled to a curriculum founded upon broad agreement. National syllabi, however, would be inflexible. A better approach is to secure agreement on philosophy and good practice across the whole curriculum. The nationally agreed curricular arrangements should apply as fully in any city technology colleges and to all pupils in assisted places as to maintained schools.

The resource implications of the Government's proposals are enormous. They include meeting parents' expectations of extra help for particular children and particular schools as a result of the testing process.

Hertfordshire County Council – The Secretary of State's initiative is welcome. This welcome is, however, qualified for these reasons.

There is a danger in expecting too much of a national curriculum; it could be an important part, but only one part alongside other important parts, in raising standards.

The important advances made by many local authorities in promoting progression, continuity and coherence between the different stages of the curriculum have been achieved despite the difficulties in this regard created by the existing autonomy of schools and the influence of parental choice. A national curriculum will clearly reduce the curricular autonomy of schools and, by achieving greater uniformity, largely reduce the parental choice of schools to non-curicular aspects. These developments are welcome, but the previous emphasis presented considerable obstacles to the achievement of the goals which the Secretary of State is now promoting and which LEAs have long wished to promote. In so far as the Government has promoted greater autonomy for schools, it has reduced the ability of local authorities to promote quality in their schools.

The desire to quicken the pace of raising standards to at least those of our 'competitor countries' might lead us, whilst recognizing the folly of transferring the approaches of one country unthinkingly to another, to inquire whether any of our competitors considers it necessary or effective to set up national examinations, controlled and monitored by organizations outside the schools, at the age of 16. To do so at 7, 11 asnd 14 as well is to adopt an approach not thought to be necessary in any major Western industrial nation. Britain is ahead of its competitors in the introduction of technology, modern business education and the use of the microcomputer, and this has been achieved under existing arrangements. The freedom from the need to obtain national agreement has enabled Britain's educational system to respond more quickly than that of its competitors.

The fact that some schools do not offer an adequate curriculum, as defined throughout the document, is as unacceptable to local authorities, which have had no more power in the past than the Secretary of State to require a particular curriculum, as it is to the Government, parents and 'others in the community'. However, such schools are often very popular with parents whose children they recruit – indeed are often oversubscribed and owe their success, as they perceive it, to their offering a curriculum which gives a great deal of choice and often owes little to the concept of balance and breadth. It is also of note that as recently as the 1986 Education Act the local authorities' role in influencing schools' curricular policies was weakened rather than strengthened by the combination of section 18 with section 17.

The objectives set to the subject working groups are welcome. The absence, from the list of examplar qualities to be encouraged in pupils, of co-operation with others and functioning effectively in a group is regretted. The list consists solely of self-reliance, self-discipline, an enterprising approach and problem-solving abilities, all of which are desirable, but there is an exclusive concern with the individual. Employers seek youngsters who can co-operate with other people and serve as a member of a team. They should be listened to.

There is in section 51 a suggestion that, in order to carry out development work on the curiculum, some LEAs and schools may be relieved of the need to follow the national curriculum. This undermines the confidence engendered by earlier statements that the national curriculum will not be 'a strait-jacket'. It is difficulty to reconcile the view that on the one hand the national curriculum is essential but not inflexible and on the other that some pupils may have to forgo it in order for curriculum development to take place. The early and widespread use of the microcomputer in British schools also illustrates the compatibility of traditional values and innovation under present arrangements.

Derbyshire County Council – The general tone of the document is one of disbelief in the teaching profession, a disbelief that the teacher can be anything more than the conveyor of given information. It suggests also that teachers cannot be relied upon to do this efficiently unless carefully monitored. There is an extraordinarily heavy emphasis upon the importance of assessment and testing. It presents a quality control system based on a model already rejected by industry; top-down with no trust displayed in the workforce. This contrasts with some successful competitor countries such as the USA, France and Sweden who are coming to recognize that a successful education system depends upon well-motivated teachers. Young people of calibre and initiative will not be encouraged to join a profession which is viewed in this way.

The document proposes a system in which control of the curriculum is vested totally in the Secretary of State. Any advisory body set up consists totally of his nominees. He is under no obligation to accept any advice that any of them give him. This negates the principle of partnership.

There is in the world at large a consensus that schools need to be able to adapt their curriculum to meet the rapidly changing circumstances of the world outside. This document proposes a system designed to make rapid responses to changing circumstances impossible, so that tomorrow's needs will be met by yesterday's vision.

If it is really intended to 'secure that the curriculum offered in all maintained schools has sufficient in common to enable children to move from one area of the country to another with minimum disruption to their education', this has enormous implications. We must have not only a national curriculum but in every subject a national syllabus which is universally followed in the same sequence. If this is intended, then it is wrong to say that the curriculum can be implemented without extra resourcing, since much of the material and equipment now in use will be useless.

Surrey County Council – A point of concern must be the omission of any mention of careers education. One wonders how the Department of Education and Science can give a high profile to the launch

of the booklet *Working Together for a Better Future* and yet within
weeks publish a consultation document with no mention at all of
this crucial area of the curriculum. Presumably had it been
mentioned at all it would have been included with health education
as a non-essential subject to be taught through other 'essential'
subjects.

It is unrealistic to see a complaints procedure as a means of
securing that the national curriculum 'is implemented in LEA-
maintained and grant-maintained schools'. It reveals the same
departmental attitude which relies on case law to clarify poor
legislation. There should be well thought out procedures and
accountabilities to ensure curriculum delivery.

The proposals raise major management and resource issues.
Additional resources will be required *inter alia* for programmes for
in-service training including inspectorate support, retraining,
altering the balance of the teaching force, providing appropriate and
sufficient specialist accommodation, external moderation of testing,
introducing records of achievement and administering new
complaints procedures. Unless these needs are recognized and met,
the national curriculum initiative will fall far short of Government
expectations and lead to frustration and resentment.

Oxfordshire County Council – The background described in the
consultative document is selective. There is no mention of existing
national curriculum policies nor of the time it has taken to fashion
such agreement: for example, the 'Science Policy 5–16' (1985) and
the recent draft on modern languages. It is surprising that a task
group has been set up to consider science when a policy exists.
There is no mention of the previous documents on the curriculum,
for example the HMI series ('Curriculum Matters') launched and
commended by Sir Keith Joseph, of which only a handful have so
far been issued.

Nor is there reference to the care with which governments, since
the Second World War, have avoided imposing by law – and with
the power residing in one Government minister – a national curriculum. Memories of pre-war Germany, of a Napoleonic France and
of examples of totalitarian regimes of East and West were very
strong in governments. There is no sense of continuinty in the
proposals – even the recent 1986 Act will need substantial amendment to accommodate the sudden change of direction.

If there is to be a national curriculum, it should by law apply to all
schools: after all, the document itself says 'pupils should be entitled
to the same opportunities wherever they go to school'. Moreover
there ought to be some fetter on the power of a single individual,
namely the Secretary of State. A set of commissioners, along the

lines of the BBC, could supply such a check on the growing executive power of this or any subsequent minister.

That sentence – the pupil's entitlement – is the origin of much. Yet there is little in the document, or the other consultative documents, which addresses the issue of equal opportunity. To secure that requires an analysis of the resources available in different schools in different parts of the country. It requires a reconciliation of the issues surrounding private and public education. It demands consideration of the respective fate of children in either grant-maintained or other schools. These issues are simply not addressed.

It is unclear why there needs to be a national *legislated* framework: it will inevitably lead to more work for lawyers.

The Conservative Education Association supports the principle of a national curriculum. We agree that parents should know what their children should be taught. We have some reservations about the details. The curriculum should not run counter to new initiatives like GCSE, TVEI and CPVE, nor become narrow and prescriptive, which we fear could easily happen under the proposals.

State primary education in Britain, at its best, is the envy of educationalists the world over. The integrated curriculum, the practical involvement of pupils in problem-solving activities, and the interest and enthusiasm for learning engendered in the pupils are achievements which require to be acknowledged and built on. There is a tendency for debate on the curriculum to focus on the secondary years. It is important to be clear about the different requirements of primary education. It would be regrettable if the proposed national curriculum were to be interpreted as curtailing, rather than encouraging, the good practice existing in our best primary schools. In particular, the issue of assessment at about 7 needs to be most carefully considered. Anything that narrows the curriculum and leads to mechanical tests, in a mistaken nostalgia for a return to concentrating on basic skills, would be opposed by us.

National Assocation for the Teaching of English – We share many of the intentions expressed in the document. Our objections concern the proposals for their realization. We take particular exception to close specification of the secondary English curriculum. English is a complex subject area. It concerns the interaction between thought, word and creative imagination. To shackle it to a predetermined set of objectives in content and skills would not promote what is necessarily an individual development process for each pupil. The recommended pattern of compulsory foundation subjects, if adhered to, would markedly reduce the time given to English teaching in secondary schools. It is highly likely that both the Kingman Committee and the subject group of English will recommend an extension of the English syllabus at secondary level. Already English teachers are finding it extremely problematic to meet all the demands of the GCSE syllabus within the existing time allocation. To ask them to do more in a shorter time in the name of raising standards would be a fruitless or cynical exercise; it would mean that in many schools literature would no longer be taught to examination level within the mainstream of core subjects.

Education is not an industrial process. Teachers are not workers on an assembly line. Neither children nor the curriculum are products to be delivered. We find the industrial metaphor that pervades the consultation document, and the thinking it represents, to be seriously distorting of the educational process.

The detailed arrangements proposed for the national curriculum, including fixed programmes of study in the foundation subjects, conflict sharply with those embodied in DES and HMI pulications of recent years. Thus, for example, the DES stated in *Better Schools*:

It would not in the view of the Government be right for the Secretaries of State's policy for the range and pattern of the 5–16 curriculum to amount to the determination of national syllabuses for that period.

The establishment of broadly agreed objectives would not mean that the curricular policies of the Secretary of State, the LEA and the school should relate to each other in a nationally uniform way. In the Government's view, such diversity is healthy, accords well with the English and Welsh traditions of school education and makes for liveliness and innovation.

How does what is 'healthy' in 1985 become so unhealthy in 1987 as to merit such drastic and precipitate action?

Joint Association of Classical Teachers – These curriculum proposals, if implemented as they stand, will mean the end of any teaching and learning of classics in maintained secondary schools in the very near future. The exclusion of Latin from years 1 to 3 will remove the necessary base for examined courses in years 4 and 5. The absence of any non-linguistic teaching about the classical world in these years will further damage the subject by removing one of the natural stimuli which leads pupils to take up Latin. These are tried and tested subjects and must not be abandoned until it has been demonstrated that they are to be replaced by something clearly superior to them. If they were lost, the damage to the study of English, medieval history, theology, philosophy and a number of other subjects would be enormous. The fact that we should effectively be cut off from the core of Western civilization and the basis of much of our own culture is frightening. We therefore strongly urge that classical studies should be accorded a position within the foundation subjects in years 1 to 3 of the secondary curriculum.

The Historical Association is very concerned that one interpretation of the consultation document would seem to make it possible for pupils to exclude all study of history from their national curriculum work. A particular concern is that the national curriculum might allow pupils to omit any study of British national history. Such an omission would mean a remarkable contradiction within a curriculum which is labelled 'national'.

Mathematical Association – The Cockcroft Report argued for a mathematics curriculum developed from the 'bottom up' rather than the 'top down'. The association of the GCSE examining groups with assessment in primary education will inevitably convey the opposite impression, of a primary school curriculum which is subservient to the requirements of secondary schools. This would be most unfortunate; it would be preferable to assign the administration of any nationally set tests to some other organization to which this objection could not be raised.

The Microelectronics Education Support Unit was set up by the Secretaries of State to promote and spread good practice in the use of new technologies in the curriculum. We have used the term 'new technologies' in preference to 'information technology', because we are concerned with the use across the curriculum of a broad range of microprocessor-based equipment. The contribution of new technologies has been proven, and should be further exploited, in most subjects.

It is important for pupils to encounter new technologies in schools in order to prepare for employment and citizenship. The value of the new technologies is best learned where they are encountered as a natural and supportive part of learning in every subject. New technologies can improve the quality of learning by freeing pupils to engage in higher order activities.

The unit agrees that information technology can be taught through other subjects, but strongly recommends that two actions could be taken to ensure that it is: each subject working group should, if possible, dedicate at least one of its meetings to the contribution of new technologies to the subject, in terms of both content and delivery; in turn, MESU should commission a group to produce a clear illustration of the potential experience that pupils should have of new technologies as they progress through school. The importance of systematic study, subject by subject, of the impact of new technologies on the curriculum should be promoted by the National Curriculum Council and MESU, as well as other agencies. Scope should be made for pilot schools to develop new opportunities and methods.

Public Information Office, House of Commons – We are concerned about the absence of any explicit reference to education for citizenship in the proposed upper second curriculum. The Public Information Office deals with 70,000 queries each year from members of the public. It is striking how ill equipped many adults are, despite their years spent in school, to exercise their rights or carry out their duties as citizens and how ignorant a large proportion of the population is about how the country is governed. There is a common misconception that the country is governed from the House of Commons. A significant number of calls have to be redirected to a Whitehall department.

The Education Officer each year either meets or corresponds with several thousand senior schoolchildren. Many of these, too, lack both knowledge and understanding. Colleagues in the information services of foreign parliaments are often surprised to learn how patchy citizenship education is in Britain. In many countries, it is a compusory subject for some years. There is universal amazement that it goes by default in the home of parliamentary government. With the introduction of a national curriculum, there is now a unique opportunity to ensure that all young people are properly prepared for this aspect of adult life.

The Economics Association believes there to be a general consensus on the need for economic awareness as part of an entitlement curriculum.

National Association of Inspectors and Educational Advisers drama section – The consultative document appears to suggest that, although drama may be used as a teaching method in primary schools, it should not appear in the secondary curriculum until year 4. Drama ought to be given equal status with the other arts throughout the 5 – 16 curriculum. NAIEA drama section considers that 20 per cent of curriculum time should be made available for the study of the arts as a whole. Of all the art forms, British theatre is famous throughout the world. It is important not only to the cultural life of the nation, but also in it's economic life.

Joint Council of Language Assocations – Language teachers are fearful of the effect of the suggested curriculum on a second foreign language. With only 20 per cent of the time available outside the core and foundation subjects, the numbers of children taking a second foreign language would be small and they would be limited to the most able pupils. We have found, through our graded test schemes, that many more young people are capable of acquiring skills in two or more languages. The long-term effect would be that fewer language students would come into the teaching profession, as the strong tendency now is to encourage all prospective teachers to be dual linguists. These proposals could reinforce the hegomony of French and there would be a danger that the position of so called 'minority' languages would become untenable.

National Association of Teachers of Home Economics – Information technology is utilized in a variety of situations in home economics from diet analysis to creative design of fabrics. Many home economics departments are being provided with computers by local authorities as an aid to curriculum development. Despite the large influx of funds into CDT and science, the numbers of pupils, particularly girls, studying these subjects at examination level is not increasing to any market effect. To ensure equal opportunities, home economics can provide a context where technological skills can be developed without the alienation of the pupil. Technology as a subject would be a real choice for many boys and girls if home economics were part of the foundation curriculum, rather than an imposition to be endured.

The Sports Council – The School Sport Forum, established by the Sports Council at the request of the Department of Education and Science and the Department of the Environment, has already expressed concern at the time currently available to physical education for older pupils. In view of the growing recognition of the importance of adopting an active and healthy lifestyle, the proposal virtually to halve this time will be received by our members with dismay. The change in the balance of the curriculum for all 14- and 15-year-olds to 5 per cent physical, 10 per cent aesthetic and 75 per cent academic subjects, with only the remaining 10 per cent offering scope for adjustment to individual need, is likely to result in a drift into inactivity during those crucial years for physical development and the formation of habits and attitudes to carry over to adult life. There is evidence that a lack of physical activity during the school day leads to inattention and disruptive behaviour, especially among those with little aptitude for academic study.

The King's Fund Institute for Healthy Policy analysis regrets the perfunctory attention given to health education in the consultation document. Two-thirds of secondary schools and one-third of primary schools now have written health education programmes to which Health Education Officers and staff from NHS community and school health services contribute in the classroom. Nevertheless, education on healthy lifestyles in British schools still has far to go if it is to match the programmes currently available to children in the United States and other countries. Recent improvements are put at risk by the current proposals for the inclusion of health education in the national curriculum. While it is appropriate to teach health education through other subjects, it is distinctly inappropriate to see health education solely as an adjunct of other scientific subjects such as biology. The essence of health education is that it is education for healthy living. It necessarily cuts across subject boundaries, and needs systematic, planned attention in its own right by members of staff with specific responsibility for it as a subject area.

Assocation of LEA Advisory Officers for Multicultural Education (ALAOME) – The consultative document makes many assertions about the failures of schools and LEAs but offers no evidence to substantiate them. These assertions are often simplistic and generalized. They do not merit a place in a serious document written for an informed and critical audience. Similarly, the claims made for a national curriculum and nationally determined assessment arrangements are expressed as simple certainties, when educationalists know that neither children nor organizations respond predictably to a series of prescriptions.

A second general comment concerns the values which are often explicit in this argument. There appears to be an obsession with comparing LEAs, in schools and, by implication, teachers. The inference is that schools will only perform to the satisfaction of parents if they constantly look over their shoulder to see how they are doing compared with the competition, and that all criteria of success are measurable. Yet many qualities that make for a good school or class do not lend themselves to league table measurements. If they did, Her Majesty's Inspectorate would have been replaced by auditors a long time ago. We are concerned that the emphasis on self-reliance and self-discipline, highly important qualities in young people, is not accompanied by any value placed on concern and respect for others, co-operation and collaboration.

Our major concern is that the consultation document fails to display any recognition of ethnic diversity or any appreciation of its educational implications. Access is to be available 'regardless of' ethnic origin. ALAOME believes, along with a great many teachers, local authorities, parent groups, the Swann Committee and numerous previous DES statements, that schools should be *mindful* of ethnic origin. The expression 'regardless of' may indicate a policy of equal opportunity but it also suggests that no account will be taken of pupils' backgrounds and experiences. The document is inexplicit and there is a danger that this inexplicitness will reappear in the terms of reference of the subject working groups, the NCC and the SEAC. The starting-point of those seeking access to an entitlement curriculum differs from child to child. We have looked in vain in the document for recognition that the starting-point of many young children is communicative competence not in English (or Welsh) but in a language of one of the ethnic minority communities. Real access for such children is through a process of bilingual teaching in the early years. Any assessment arrangements at 7 should take account of this and should assess and value those communication skills and concepts which a child may possess in another language.

References to parents in the document imply that they share broadly similar feelings of dissatisfaction with schools. No evidence is produced in support of this. Some parents want greater attention to 'the basics', some want more music, others want school to teach a community language, some want a multi-faith approach to RE, others believe a school should only teach about Christianity. Yet the consultative document fails to recognize this wide variety and consequently avoids grasping the nettle of conflicting parental views and expectations. Whose voices are to be heard in Dewsbury: the dissatisfied but vocal few or the quietly satisfied majority?

Members of ALAOME are conscious of the imprtant role of community languages in education. We have looked without success in the document for any hint of the DES's views on community language teaching. The long promised consultative paper on this subject shows no sign of appearing. It is not clear to us whether in his proposals the Secretary of State regards community languages as modern foreign languages. If he does, the subject working groups must include working groups on Bengali, Gujarati, Punjabi, Urdu, etc. If he does not, and if therefore a foundation modern language must be a European language, he should explain and justify this Eurocentricity. Working groups on the teaching of community languages will need to distinguish between the different situations of those who already have some knowledge of what may be their mother tongue and of *ab initio* learners in the rest of the community. Community languages are beginning to appear as timetabled subjects in the upper years of primary schools and in middle schools. Does paragraph 14 of the consultation document imply that they have no place before secondary schooling? Such a view will conflict with much parental and professional opinion.

The Commission for Racial Equality is extremely disappointed that the consultation document makes no mention of the need for a curriculum that reflects the multicultural nature of British society. The need for such a perspective as part of the framework of any national curriculum was clearly established by the Swann Report and the curriculum implications of its philosophy of 'education for all' now command a degree of consensus among educationalists. Such a perspective should now be incorporated, as a matter of course, into the framework for the planning and design of the national curriculum and in the programmes of study of individual subjects. If the pluralist nature of our national culture is not reflected in the criteria for curriculum selection we cannot see how the proposed national curriculum will be able to achieve its stated objective ' to develop the potential of all pupils and equip them for citizenship'. In determining the composition of the subject working groups it will be important that people with practical experience of multicultural and anti-racist curriculum development are included.

The commision is concerned that the term 'modern foreign language' in the consultative document may exclude the home languages of children from ethnic minority familes and that there will be no place for their languages in the timetables for foundation or additional subjects. Curriculum recognition of multilingual diversity is long overdue. Community languages in many parts of the country constitute a rich educational resource which we cannot afford to ignore. Furthermore language is important for the self-respect and self-identity of minority groups, and a level of 'language awareness' is recognized as being important to all pupils regardless of ethnic origin. Thus there are sound educational and social reasons for the recognition of community languages in mainstream schooling.

The Equal Opportunities Commission has a statutory duty to work towards the elimination of discrimination in the context of the Government's emphasis on maths, science and technology, the commision's experience is of particular significance; these are the areas of the curriculum from which many girls are discouraged and to which some are denied access. The problem with respect to physical science and technology is exacerbated in those single-sex girls' schools which have only limited facilities. Cumulative discrimination is faced by many girls from ethnic minority groups.

The commision is confident that the national curriculum will be welcomed by those who have a commitment to equality of opportunity. The commision continues to be concerned that different patterns of education and different educational experiences are identifiable for girls and for boys; and that the outcome of the education system, in terms of subsequent training and employment opportunities, is less favourable for girls, regardless of their ability.

Arrangements for a national curiculum should ensure that girls and boys have *equal access* to the *same* curricular opportunities. Attention should be paid to the existing differences between the participation and performance of girls and boys in the proposed core and foundation subjects; remedial or 'booster' courses may be required if attainment targets are to be reached.

Access to the proposed city technology colleges should comply with section 22 of the Sex Discrimination Act. It would be unlawful to implement any system of quotas in admitting girls and boys. The commision fears that admission on the basis of technological potential may prove to be indirectly discriminatory and lead to a predominance of boys. 'Technology' is a word which regrettably still has a masculine connotation, and many girls, therefore, will need special encouragement in order to apply for a city technology college.

Methodist Church Division of Education and Youth – We looked forward to a further statement on the organization and content of the curriculum as promised in the White Paper, *Better Schools*, anticipating the recommendation of a broad national framework which took account of the need for local initiative with regard to detailed content, organization, teaching and testing within schools. We are, therefore, deeply disturbed that the nation has been presented with proposals far removed from the substance of the White Paper. The proposals contrast sharply with the promises of the White Paper that 'The Government does not intend to introduce legislation affecting the powers of the Secretaries of State in relation to the curriculum' and 'The Government believes that the action now necessary to raise standards in school education can in the main be taken within the existing legal framework.'

There are glimmers of hope in paragraphs 10 and 22 but these are obscured by the weight if the remainder which provides a firm basis for present uniformity and future exploitation by any government which wishes to condition the minds of the nation's children. The proposals are ill founded and inadequate as a basis for reform; to fix them in legislation will stultify educational development and provide a means by which democracy may be assailed.

Free Church Federal Council – The primary curriculum is not given adequate attention and phrases like 'the majority of curriculum time at primary level should be devoted to core subject' ignore the common experience frequently reported by HMI in their inspections of primary schools and in the national primary survey that the base skills are best encouraged in a broad and varied curriculum. There are many successful examples of integrated primary education. In general we feel that children's learning needs, their stages in development, their motivation and how they can best be helped have been ignored.

We are concerned that the role of the local education authorities would be severely undermined if the proposals in this and other current documents are implemented. While we recognize that there have been a very small number of extremist councils who have attempted to influence the curriculum in unacceptable ways, the safeguards which the current diversified system provides are considerable. A nationally centralized curriculum could in the wrong hands create a much worse danger of indoctrination and bias.

The Muslim Educational Trust – The MET believes the principles underlying the formulation of the national curriculum to be clearly secular and materialistic in their policy implications. The MET is strongly of the view that religious studies should be included in the core subjects along with English, maths and science.

The MET notes with concern the trend towards the centralization of education, which will undermine local involvement and deprive already disadvantaged ethnic and religious minorities of their ability to contribute to and benefit from local efforts through LEAs.

The inclusion of music and drama (in their current meaning and practice) in the foundation subjects will also place Muslim pupils at a serious disadvantage as they violate the teachings of Islam. Some aspects of art are also against Islamic teachings. The MET, therefore, suggests flexibility in the choice of foundation subjects.

The proposed curriculum must truly reflect the multilingual and multicultural richness of the society. The special position of Welsh language has been rightly emphasized. Similar emphasis should be given to Arabic, Urdu, Bengali, Punjabi, Greek, Turkish and Persian.

Salvation Army – We wish to record the Salvation Army's general concurrence with the direction indicated in the consultation document, believing that the measures proposed will minimize the worst effects of what we might call the eccentric policies adopted by certain local education authorities.

It would appear essential to us in any worthy educational system to include provision for the promotion of the basic concepts of honesty, truthfulness, family life and integrity, sexual morality expressed in fidelity and commitment on a lifelong basis, respect for persons and for property, and a proper love of country. Would there not be virtue in convening a subject working group in this field as well as in the strictly academic or technical fields?

National Association of Inspectors and Educational Advisers – It is essential to retain the co-operation and mutual support of all the partners in education. In particular, teachers must feel that they are responsible for, and 'own' the curriculum. Without this we should be in danger of losing the richness and excitement in children's learning which so many of our foreign visitors envy.

It should be remembered that there are more 4-year-olds in primary schools than in nursery schools. We would wish all children of the same age to be treated in the same way and recommend that all 4-year-olds should be exempt.

At primary level there is overwhelming evidence that the basic skills are most successfully learnt when applied across the whole curriculum. We, therefore find it hard to accept that 'the majority of curriculum time at primary level should be devoted to the core subjects' (paragraph 14). We commend the breadth of the primary curriculum as set out in section 61 of *Better Schools* which aimed not only to place emphasis on language, mathematics and science, but also to: 'lay the foundation of understanding in religious education, history and geography, and the nature of and value of British society; introduce pupils to a range of activities in the arts; provide opportunities throughout the curriculum for craft and practical work leading up to some experience of design and technology and of solving problems; provide moral education, physical education and health education; introduce pupils to the nature and use in school and in society of new technology; give pupils some insight into the adult world, including how people earn their living'.

The proposals for the secondary curriculum are broadly in line with the direction in which schools are already moving, from a pattern of subject options to an extended common curriculum. We welcome the commitment to a 'balanced' science provision, but seek further clarification on a number of issues: why is religious education not included as a foundation subject? why is its place in the curriculum justified solely in terms of the legal requirement? What is 'technology'? How does it relate to design? Does it include information technology? Why is little time or attention given to the arts? Why is there no mention of drama in the primary or early secondary years? Why is home economics undervalued? Should it not be regarded as an aspect of technology and an important foundation subject for boys as well as girls? Is the time allocated for a modern foreign language also intended for community languages?

The consultation document makes only passing reference to health education and information technology but entirely omits other cross-curricular themes which in *Better Schools* were described as 'essential curricular elements'. These include, for example, personal and social education, careers education, moral education, political education, economic awareness, preparation for life in a multi-ethnic society. We are concerned that the importance of these cross-curricular issued has been seriously undervalued.

Society of Education Officers – The proposed new National Curriculum Council (NCC) and Schools Examination and Assessment Council (SEAC) are welcomed as they provide opportunities for proper involvement of professional and other interests. Whilst the SEO agrees that the ultimate decisions should be made by Parliament it considers the proposed procedures are inadequate to deal with those circumstances, likely to be rare but significant, when the Secretary of State, having had regard to the recommendations of a subject working group, appointed by him, and having received the advice of the NCC, also appointed by him, intends to depart from this advice. A requirement for a debate in Parliament should exist on these occasions. The SEO recommends that where the Secretary of State proposes to lay draft Orders before Parliament which depart from the advice of the NCC or the SEAC he should be required to proceed under the affirmative resolution procedure.

The Government intends that the national curriculum should apply in all maintained schools; country, voluntary and grant but for the 'substance' to be a condition of grant for city technology colleges. As the Secretary of State would be empowered to suspend the requirements of the national curriculum to promote development work, the SEO considers there is no case at the outset for treating CTCs differently from other schools. The SEO understands the importance which independent schools attach to their freedom from external direction. Nevertheless the SEO considers that where independent schools have, of their own volition, chosen to receive public funds through the assisted places scheme they should be required to provide the national curriculum.

LEAs will have an enlarged duty (paragraph 57) to provide education in their area and to monitor the delivery of the national curriculum (paragraph 61). In the event that a school, county or controlled, which the LEA maintains, fails to fulfil its obligations with respect to the national curriculum, the LEA must be empowered to intervene in order to fulfil its statutory obligations. The SEO recommends that a specific reserve power be provided in the proposed legislation similar to that in section 28 of the Education (No. 2) Act 1986.

Department of Education, University of Liverpool – As a department with a large interest in the education of teachers, both pre-service and in-service, we consider that insufficient attention is given in the document to the implications of proposals for teacher supply and for the nature of training courses. We fear, for example, that the supply of teachers in modern languages will be inadequate to teaching 10 per cent of curriculum time for all secondary pupils in years 4 and 5 and similarly for diversification of modern language provision. We are concerned that implementation of the proposals, however modified in consultation, will have, and indeed must have, an impact on the content of teacher education courses. We wish to prepare teachers as well as possible for the future roles but there is insufficient time to reflect upon the proposals and their implications and to prepare appropriate teacher education material.

Some members of the department consider the philosophical base on which the curriculum is designed to be limited and suspect. There is, for example, no rationale for 'core' and 'foundation' subjects. It undervalues whole areas of human experience which a well-balanced curriculum ought to include (e.g. aesthetic, cultural, political and social issues). It appears to want to fit pupils into their place in society rather than educate them. Little attention has been paid to the range of adult roles which pupils need to be prepared for (e.g. consumers of goods and services, parents, members of communities, governors of schools).

Many of us are not opposed to the principle of legislation to introduce a national curriculum which lays down a basic, balanced, wide-ranging and carefully thought out programme, which takes into account the varying backgrounds, abilities and motivations of pupils and does not expect all schools to be able to help all their pupils to reach the same levels of achievement. We return to our concern for teacher education. A qualitative difference in education is more likely to be achieved by investing in personnel, i.e. putting resources into in-service education in sufficient quantities to give every teacher substantial opportunities for refreshing their knowledge and keeping up to date.

The Audit Commission – The paper points to the reduction in overall pupil to teacher ratio since 1979 and the planned continuation of that reduction until 1990. The Secretaries of State expect the developments described in the consultation paper to be carried out within the increased resources which this reduced ratio represents. But a low pupil-to-teacher ratio by itself is no guarantee that a particular curriculum can be delivered. Small schools need lower ratios than larger schools. If the planned level of resources is indeed to be sufficient for the implementation of the national curriculum, schools will need to be reorganized to reduce the prevalence of small schools. Although the Government has recognized the need for schools reorganization and has impressed this need on LEAs, the proposals in other consultation papers make reorganizations both more necessary and more difficult.

The paper states that pupils should be entitled to the same opportunities wherever they go to school. It follows in particular that the opportunities should not vary with the size of school or be affected by falling rolls. In areas where constraints of geography or Government policy (on for example single-sex or denominational provision) limit the scope for closing small schools, rate support grant should be increased to permit the implementation of the national curriculum. Curriculum-led staffing models (as advocated in *Teaching Quality*) can quantify the requried extent of this.

A reduction in pupil-to-teacher ratio represents an increase in only one resource, teachers, even if it is the largest resource involved. Given the need for assessment and testing of every pupil, the involvement of LEA inspectors in monitoring the delivery of the national curriculum and the complaitns machinery described in paragraph 63, additional resources other than increased teacher staffing will have to be applied. It might be useful for SEAC and NCC to take on the assessment of the resource implications of substituting new activities for old.

Chartered Institute of Public Finance and Accountancy – The consultation paper states that implementation of the national curriculum will have to be done 'broadly within the planned level of resources'. No detailed assessment of the likely costs involved is provided. Some funds will be made available, it is understood, via education support grants and LEA training grants, where emphasis will be given to supporting the national curriculum, but whether at the expense of other specialist areas is unclear. The concept has a potential for significant additional resource requirements. These will include training, both of teaching and non-teaching staff, to cover such areas as pupil assessment (and its moderation), the compilation of records of pupils' achievement, and in monitoring the implementation of the national curriculum. There is also the requirement to produce and publish additional information, including the governing bodies annual report to parents.

The institute regrets that no indication of the size of the additional requirements, or the implications thereof, have been given.

School Curriculum Development Committee – In principle a national curriculum will, we believe, be received favourably by the teaching profession, by parents, employers and school governors. At the same time the scale and extent of the change should not be underestimated. The idea is unfamiliar in the British educational system and is contrary to a tradition of school autonomy in curriculum planning and implementation which has lasted for over 40 years.

The specification of the national curriculum is in terms of *traditional subjects* throughout the years 5–16 and the recommendation of programmes of study will be the responsibility of subject working groups. By contrast there has been recognition in recent years that traditional subjects alone are not an adequate vehicle for conveying the knowlege, concepts, skills and attitudes required by pupils in the last years of the twentieth century and the early years of the twenty-first. New subjects and themes have entered the curriculum in recent years to meet new needs and insights. There appears to be no place for some of them in the national curriculum. The national curriculum allows little room for pupil choice and is more prescriptive than has been customary.

The introduction of the national curriculum cannot be divorced from the resources needed to implement it. SCDC believes that these should be quantified realistically and incorporated into a planned programme at an early date. A substantial programme of in-service training for all teachers will be required. In some subject areas, for example modern languages, technology and the sciences, there will be a serious shortage of qualified and trained teachers. Additional workshops, laboratories and specialist facilities will be required.

We pose three questions about the proposals in their present form which require further consideration:

(a) Should the national curriculum be specified by means of the same compulsory foundation subjects for pupils through the age range 5–16? Some would argue for example that developing competencies in the early years fits uneasily into a compartmentalized subject curriculum. Others would claim that there should be a significant element of choice in the later secondary years even though breadth and balance must be ensured. These would be useful areas for early discussion by the shadow (NCC).

(b) How should the national curriculum be specified so that the needs of pupils of all abilities and aptitudes are fully met? It is envisaged that pupils with statements of special educational need under the Education Act 1981 could be exempted from some parts of the national curriculum. In the board's view this principle may extend further and apply positively as well as negatively. Some pupils' needs may be better met by the inclusion of elements not apparently in the national curriculum in place of some that are.

(c) How can the national curriculum combine a firm framework with the degree of flexibility which the Secretaries of State envisage? The national curriculum is intended to provide for all pupils 'access to broadly the same good, relevant curriculum and programmes of study regardless of sex, ethnic origin and georgraphic location'. It is clearly of great importance that there should be a common entitlement. There is however also need for different emphases to enable pupils to relate learning to their own experience.

SCDC recommends that adherence to the national curriculum should be required of independent schools. It would be regrettable if introduction were to lead to greater disparity between the maintained and independent sectors. In particular independent schools might alone be able to make full provision for the teaching of classical languages and for a second foreign language below 16.

In the view of SCDC there is need for a curriculum framework whose relation to the foundation subjects might be compared with that of GCSE general criteria to GCSE subject criteria. SCDC recommends that a task group on the national curriculum framework should be set up. This would be an important early assignment for the shadow NCC. If however work does not begin until the shadow NCC is set up some subject working groups will be operating without this framework and there must be a danger of contradictory requirements. The framework might include:

1   A statement of the purposes of learning and of fundamental curriculum principles.
2   Principles which run through all foundation subjects, for example consideration of special educational needs, cultural diversity and equal opportunities.
3   Consideration of cross-curricular themes and the subjects through which they are to be realized.
4   An examination of curriculum goals not likely to be directly achieved through a subject-based curriculum.

The consultation document refers to 'subjects or themes' which are additional to the foundation subjects. It includes health education and information technology as examples. It proposes that these should be taught 'through the foundation subjects'. There are many such themes taught in schools employing a variety of organizing devices. They include health (incorporating alcohol, drugs and sex education), economic awareness, political education, law and relations with the police and values education. Almost all schools have well developed careers programmes to which the consultation document makes no reference. Some of these themes can be developed through the foundation subjects. The difficulty of doing this adequately through single subjects has, however, been demonstrated by TVEI which has found it necessary to make extensive use of new cross-curriculum courses and modules. SCDC is aware of excellent work which has gone into the development of personal and social education. It recommends that the national curriculum should provide for this to be continued as an identifiable element in the curriculum and not only at 14–16, even though suggested time allocations for other subjects will need to be adjusted.

The national curriculum makes no reference to humanities or social science as a generic title. Yet social science is one of the twenty GCSE subject for which national criteria have been drawn up and many schools have humanities programmes operating throughout the secondary curriculum 11–16. It is an area which often includes, in addition to history and geography, economics, social studies, religious studies, classical studies and government and politics. This area of the curriculum has as its main aim providing pupils with the means to understand the world in which they live through a number of related disciplines. The national curriculum specifies history and geography as foundation subjects and makes no reference to any other subject (apart from religious studies which is considered in a different context) from this curriculum area. This is not in our view an issue which can be left to subject working groups in history and geography. There is a need for an additional working group on the humanities/social science area.

The arts require fuller and more flexible provision than is suggested in the consultation document. The inclusion of art and music as foundation subjects will be widely welcomed. Opportunities in other disciplines are also essential to make the most of individual aptitudes and abilities. However, it is only at 14–16 that drama appears among the foundation subjects, and then as a limited option. Dance and verbal arts are omitted. It is not necessary for all pupils to work in all of the arts from 5–16. It is necessary that they should have a broad base of arts experiences in the primary school and that in the secondary school they should have opportunities 'on a worthwhile scale' (*Better Schools*, paragraph 67) to work in arts disciplines which best accord with their aptitude and abilities. The arts, like the sciences, should be seen as a generic curriculum area and an additional working group should be appointed to coordinate planning across this area from 5–16.

Secondary Examinations Council – The SEC operating largely on the basis of argument and persuasion, has managed to give effect to the GCSE national criteria up to a certain point. We have experienced a number of problems in our attempts to avoid pupils being subjected to unduly narrow examined courses within the GCSE framework. For example, with the Secretary of State's support, we have ruled that to offer 'arithmetic' syllabuses would be to limit unacceptably pupils' educational experience. We have required that such proposals be extended to place the work in the practical context required by the GCSE mathematics criteria. Similarly, we have concluded that 'English as a second language' should not be offered as a GCSE subject, believing that the aim of support for pupils whose mother tongue is not English should be to provide full access to a high status GCSE English certificate. Having said this we of course accept the need to provide suitably certificated short-term targets for such pupils as they progress towards their GCSE certificates. There are other examples; thus, as we work to ensure that design becomes an essential part of studies concerned with skills of hand and eye, others still insist that tests with no design element should be on offer, thereby characterizing pupils who undertake craft courses as incapable of thoughtful action. We do not consider such provision to be in pupil's best interests.

Conversely, and just as frustratingly, there are excellent developments which could enrich the GCSE but for their initiators' insistence that they should be associated with separate certification.

In the light of this experience, we would argue that it is vital to ensure, when the national curriculum with its attendant attainment targets and assessment procedures is introduced, that powers be included to control all qualifications on offer during statutory schooling – irrespective of their sources – so that pupils receive their curriculum entitlement and full recognition of their achievements.

We believe that the status of pupils' hard-won qualifications is undermined by the present proliferation of certificates, syllabuses and subject titles. Some diversity is needed to allow reasonable choice, to avoid ossification and to provide routes for innovation; however, there is in general no case for syllabuses which duplicate or are not sufficiently distinct from existing provision, or for subject titles which mystify potential users.

We therefore believe that the Government and the new SEAC when considering how to exercise their respective suggested powers to approve qualifications and syllabuses should give careful thought to the rules necessary to permit reasonable diversity without extravagant proliferation. Further, we consider it important that the opportunity be taken to consider whether certain subjects are appropriate for GCSE certification or, indeed, the compulsory period of schooling.

Further Education Unit – The national curriculum framework is currently presented as if the whole was no more than the sum of its parts. There is no overall view presented which explains this particular selection of foundation subjects, or would justify the inclusion or exclusion of another area as a cross-curricular 'theme', or help allocate the remaining 10 per cent of time in years 4 and 5. This is in contrast to many recent developments affecting FE colleges, where what is to be assessed, and/or the selection of areas of learning, and/or design of the learning activities is measured against clearly specified overall aims or criteria. In so far as the rationale can be deduced, the approach of the consultative document seems to differ from that adopted by the MSC (via YTS and to some extent TVEI), NCVQ, CPVE, and the FE examining and validating bodies. Although these all differ one from the other, certain common features may be discerned – such as a move towards testing competence on multidisciplinary tasks, an emphasis on the integration of learning, individualized learning programmes and personal effectiveness as a curriculum objective in its own right. We are not commenting on the appropriateness or otherwise of these principles to the school curriculum, but any divergence in approach between 'academic' and 'vocational' provision needs to be watched with care. Otherwise progression may be hindered, the status of one form of provision may suffer compared to the other and there will be difficulty for FE colleges operating both forms in parallel.

The most serious implication, however, would be the danger of undermining efforts to promote coherence within the 14–18 curriculum. We would advocate the further development of a set of aims which would define the educational purpose of core or foundation studies throughout the whole 14–18 curriculum, and against which the existing FE curricula and developing national curriculum could be tested. As well as promoting coherence and equality of treatment, it would also avoid the danger of important areas of learning which do not fall naturally under subject headings being neglected in the national curriculum.

The document argues that pupils should be entitled to the same opportunities wherever they go to school. Whilst fully agreeing with this, we are concerned that there is too great a tendency to equate this to an entitlement to a minimum number of hours of teaching, and to teaching of given subjects according to standard programmes of study. This may be in conflict with paragraph 8(iii) which emphasizes the importance of 'ensuring that all pupils, regardless of sex, ethnic origin and geographical location have access to broadly the same good and relevant curriculum'. Different learners need to be helped to reach the same objectives in different ways. It seems very likely that cultural differences between pupils, whether a factor of their sex, ethnic origin or geographical location, will require differences in 'programmes of study', however defined.

Nor do all learners benefit equally from the same balance of 'teaching' to 'tutoring'. Some older schoolchildren, at least, learn more effectively when proportionately more time is spent on their personal and social development, thus providing them with greater autonomy and learning skills, from which their whole learning programme benefits. There is no mention in the document of entitlement to tutorial support or educational counselling. Mention is made of 'personal qualities which cannot be written into a programme of study or an attainment target'. We would argue that this is only the case when the curriculum objectives are framed solely in subject terms. Many examples exist, in school and FE, of programmes which do plan to develop some personal qualities, and of assessment procedures which report on their achievement.

One aspect of curriculum design which can fundamentally affect the learner's motivation is the degree to which the programme seems relevant to them and the extent to which they have been able to choose and influence their own programme. This factor becomes increasingly important as the learner gets beyond 14.

The Rathbone Society is a national voluntary organization established to work with and on behalf of children, young people and adults who experience educational disadvantage. It is particularly concerned with the needs of those who have moderate difficulties, identified in the Warnock Report of 1978 as by far the largest group of those with special educational needs but yet the least recognized by the public at large. According to Warnock, one in five children have special educational needs at some point in their school career. They are virtually ignored by the consultation document. The society believes this to be a major deficiency. A 'national' curriculum can only be that if it is a curriculum for all children. A child's progress in school depends upon a complex interaction of the child's intellectual skills and the child's environment at home and in school. The likelihood of progress is not measured by ability to achieve a particular score in a test. The standard of attainment of pupils depends primarily upon the skill training and conscientiousness of their teachers and their relationship with them. Significant discretion as to the content of what is taught to any particular class should be available to the classroom teachers, subject to board guidelines. Teacher discretion in identifying and dealing with the educational needs of pupils at any given time is particularly important for the disadvantaged and those with moderate learning difficulties in mainstream or special schools.

It is proposed that a statement of special need under the Education Act 1981 should specify any national curriculum requirements which should not apply. While some children who are disadvantaged or have learning difficulties are subject to a statement, many are not and need not be. There should be arrangements to permit schools the discretion to modify national curriculum requirements for such pupils when this is thought to be in their best interest.

Voluntary Council for Handicapped Children – We are very concerned at the implications of testing and a national curriculum for children with special educational needs. If the curriculum is modified by agreement for these children, we would want assurances that their academic achievements would not be downgraded by such modifications. As the population of special schools appears to be changing, with children becoming more 'special' and with multiple handicaps, it will be absolutely essential to be (a) flexible about the age at which any testing is carried out; (b) specific about the nature of any modifications to the curriculum; (c) aware of the curriculum development which has been a feature of recent progress in working with children with special educational needs and (d) determining what the relationship of testing and the national curriculum will be to the formal assessment procedures of the 1981 Education Act and the statement.

Special Educational Needs, National Advisory Council – The major developments from which we have drawn encouragement during the past decade include the Warnock Report (1978), the Education Act (1981), and the Third Report of the Committee for Education, Science and Art (1987), together with the positive response to these of many LEAs and individual schools. Although the unevenness of responses and the inadequacy of funding for improved teacher–pupil ratios and in-service education leave much to be achieved, there was reason to hope that progress required by law would continue. However, our reading of the consultative document leads us to fear that the interests of children with special educational needs could suffer a setback. The consulation document makes only one reference to the Education Act (1981) and then only to the minority, namely those individuals with LEA statements of special educational needs and provision. We ask that the existing legislation and related recommendations, together with the philosophy which underlies these, are taken fully into account in legislation for a national curriculum and for the management of schools.

Royal National Institute for the Blind, Shaftesbury Society, Spastics Society, Dr Barnado's and National Children's Home – We write as Directors and advisers employed by voluntary organizations making direct school provision for a range of pupils with special needs. We make no claims to be an 'official' group. What has brought us together is a shared concern about proposed changes and the effect these are likely to have on the schools and other educational establishments administered by the voluntary organizations, in addition to the implications for a large group of pupils with a range of special needs which are currently being met in mainstream LEA schools. In all the [consultation] documents, pupils with special needs are at best considered as an afterthought or at worst ignored as a group who don't fit neatly into predetermined structures. Over the last decade or more, and certainly since the publication of the report of the Warnock Committee in 1978, the special needs of a wide range of pupils have been well to the fore on most educational agenda: the present proposals seem to relegate them once more to the realm of the unconsidered. Our concern is that pupils with a wide range of special needs receive a diluted version of the mainstream national curriculum which would in no way be tailored to suit their needs.

The consultation document refers specifically to pupils with a statement, but does so in relation to the possibility of exclusion and exemption rather than in the light of any positive attempt to provide a needs-related curriculum. Many of the pupils in schools run by voluntary societies are multi-handicapped, often profoundly so, and the concept of 'subjects' is hardly relevant. An acknowledgement of the importance of a developmental curriculum would be welcome, as would the need for a modified curriculum, without the constraint of enforcing an eighty to ninety per cent take-up on foundation subjects, for a large number of pupils with special needs both in mainstream and special schools.

National Deaf Children's Society – Unless legislation starts from the assumption that all children are of equal potential, but that the judgement of potential is necessarily arbitrary, deaf children and other special-needs children will not be able to benefit from the proposed changes. A more positive approach would be to permit flexibility within the national curriculum to *include* children with special educational needs rather than to exclude them. Exclusion of these children from some areas of the national curriculum could have a regressive effect on the implementation of the Education Act 1981. The level of integration could be determined by the ability to follow the national curriculum and to reach the required attainment levels.

The apparent inflexibility of the national curriculum is a particular cause for concern, with the accompanying emphasis on modification rather than the acknowledgement of the need for a developmental curriculum for special-needs children. Such acknowledgement is important because some deaf children may have severe difficulties in English and may benefit from the introduction of sign language. However, a *delay* in the introduction of sign language may be detrimental to the child's general education. This issue goes beyond the boundaries specified by the consultative document. The rigid specification of the national curriculum does not allow for the recognition of sign language as a modern language. The society's education subcommittee suggests, therefore, that the modern languages regulations be modified to include specific reference to any language which will aid the development of potential.

The National Association for Gifted Children has examined the proposals with the special needs of talented and gifted children [in mind]. Such children frequently demonstrate one or more of the following characteristics: they can learn more quickly than others; they can have very retentive memories; they can induce general principles from comparatively few particular examples; they can see connections that may escape many adults; given the chance to choose for themselves, they can concentrate for a long time on particular favourite activities; they are often original and creative; they often excel in games, music, art, and in mechanical crafts.

If their school needs are not met however, they may become anti-school, orally knowledgeable but poor in written work, bored, absorbed in a private world, excessively self-critical, unable to make good social relationships with peer group or teachers, emotionally unstable and very skilled at deception.

They need the company of their intellectual peers for some part of the day or week (not necessarily of their own age group); access to suitable books and learning experiences; and time for work in depth on individual interests. A major concern, from bitter experience, is that many teachers make a generalized provision for classes aimed at a theoretical 'average' child with an age-locked system. Such provision rarely provides a suitable challenge to the very able. Nor does it present opportunities for failure, which are very important for the psychological and moral welfare of the gifted. Any curriculum proposals that tend to reinforce a standardized, generalized approach to teaching will militate against the interests of the most able (and the least able) individual.

It is proper that due attention be paid to the core subjects, English, maths and science. Whether the majority of curriculum time at primary level should be devoted to them is however debatable. Many able children are already fluent readers and advanced in number before they begin statutory schooling. If such children are required to drag through graded readers or workbooks, or to repeat examples of mathematics long since mastered, in order to complete a specific quota of time to be spent on any core subject, the result will be counter-productive. The needs of gifted children, who wish to develop talents and interests not sponsored by the national curriculum, will be ignored in many schools unless the Secretary of State makes a positive declaration of intent to encourage the provision of such needs.

Association of Workers for Maladjusted Children – Not all children with emotional and/or behavioural difficulties are educated in special, separate provision, nor hold a statement of special educational needs (SSEN). These pupils do not fit neatly into any one part of the spectrum of difficulty from mild to extreme. It is of concern that the requirements of a national curriculum as set out will inhibit the established and continuing trend for those for whom it is appropriate to be educated in the least restrictive setting possible. This is important, not only for those who hold an SSEN but also for those who require special educational consideration but whose needs can be met without that formal protection. In broad terms, this includes the Warnock 18 per cent, the low attainers and the disaffected, most of whom suffer from low self-esteem and for whom comparison of personal attainment with established norm-referenced assessment can only further depress perceptions of personal and academic worth.

In social priority areas where there is a high proportion of pupils with special educational needs that have not been formally assessed but have been identified by the statutory school-based assessment procedures, in the absence of significant additional resources the school will find it impossible to maintain the requirements of the national curriculum, to give equity of opportunity to those both within and without the regulations.

British Association for Early Childhood Education – It is accepted that there are 4-year-olds in reception classes in primary schools. To begin the national curriculum at four may ignore the developmental needs of these children in favour of the early introduction of the basic skills. Criticism of the emphasis on core subject teaching, with the implication of a return to didactic teaching methods, applies equally to all children in the primary sector of education; however, the youngest children are most vulnerable. Other vital aspects of their development, such as self-concept, emotional expression and control, social behaviour, imaginative representation through creative, constructive play, art and craft, music and drama, being difficult to measure objectively will inevitably be reduced in time and value. This will certainly prove detrimental to the primary curriculum. The amount of time to be programmed for teaching of the basic subjects may well impoverish the development of the imaginative faculties including logical reasoning and problem-solving qualities of mind which are essential to more advanced learning.

Education Otherwise – Under the 1944 Act it is the parent's duty to see that the child is suitably educated 'by regular attendance at school or otherwise'. Certain parents choose to exercise their right to educate otherwise than by sending their children to school. Education Otherwise aims to support these parents. It is not unusual in our experience for LEA officers to react to this kind of provision with unwarranted hostility and prejudice. The constraints imposed by the proposed national curriculum, if they were to be applied to home education, would make the self-directed approach unworkable. We are aware that these proposals apply to maintained schools only, and we have been assured that there is no possibility of extending them to home education. Nevertheless we see a real danger that LEAs will attempt to apply the criteria of the national curriculum to home educating families. For this reason we feel it is essential that legislation relating to a national curriculum should quite explicitly exclude children educated otherwise than by attendance at school.

National Association of Teachers of Travellers – The life-style of the gypsy/traveller community does not appear to have been taken account of. Often children have complete stages of school-based education missing. Provision across authorities is, to say the least, *ad hoc*. The gypsy/traveller community has been identified in the Plowden and Swan reports, and consistently by HMI as probably the most severely disadvantaged children in the country. Traveller children do not have learning difficulties *per se*: they lack the opportunity to receive school-based education. The membership of NATT emphasize the need for Government to consider the life-style of the gypsy/traveller community and make appropriate provision in terms of resources and teachers.

Chairman of Governors, **Dr Challoner's High School, Little Chalfont, Buckinghamshire** – The governors of this school express their very deep concern at the implications of these proposals for the pupils of this selective girls grammar school. As governors we have a statutory duty to oversee the curriculum of this school. We have not been shown the consultation document by you or by anyone on your behalf. We ask you to advise the Minister that the decisions he may now take are not informed by direct consultations with governors, and in any public announcement he ought to say so.

We have always offered a broad and balanced curriculum. It has benefited scientists, linguists, classicists and others in the liberal arts. Our present timetable enables us to produce doctors, research scientists, academics, lawyers, business and industrial leaders, because it allows for choice, specialization and well-directed teaching. The proposals in the consultation document would narrow choice, inhibit teaching and limit the pursuit of excellence. We believe the educational opportunities we offer, to a number of competent and gifted children, are essential for the nation's future. They will be damaged by the present proposals.

Dr K. J. Funnell, headmaster, Eastfield County Primary School, Thurmaston, Leicester – The emphasis on 'delivering the curriculum' (a term at variance with the highest principles of education, which place the pupil and the teacher at the centre of the process) takes no account of the absolutely vital work going on in each classroom to meet the individual needs of each child. These needs are not merely intellectual; indeed, it could be argued that emotional, social, medical and developmental needs should take precedence. Almost all children already suffer some stress and anxiety for a variety of reasons. Frequent and rigorous testing can only add to their emotional burdens. Teacher stress, too, will also be intensified.

It is worrying that the proposed system will ultimately be under the guardianship, not of elected parents or governors, but of any and every parent. Every teacher will have a hundred watchdogs, often basing their criticisms on very narrow interpretations of what is seen as 'delivering the curriculum'. A system of protest needs formalization, with safeguards for all involved. There is something Orwellian about the statement that 'another essential part of the monitoring arrangements will be action by parents, who will be able to pinpoint deficiencies in the delivery of the national curriculum'.

It is said that under the proposed system the role of the primary school teacher will be enhanced. This cannot be so in so far as a kind of dubious prestige will accrue to those teachers whose children have 'done well' in the tests. There is precious little opportunity for 'professionalism' when teachers are required (ultimately by law) to 'deliver' a national curriculum devised and imposed by those remote from the classroom. 'Delivering' suggests the task of the milkman in supplying pre-packaged materials regularly to individual doorsteps and is a concept which has no place in education.

Twenty-six members of the staff of The Minster School, Leominster, Herefordshire – We express our extreme concern. For a decade or more an enormous amount of time and effort have been devoted to the development of a sound curriculum framework. The culmination was the publication of *The Curriculum from 5–16* by HMI in 1985. This was in response to the Secretary of State's requirement that broad agreement about the curriculum should be sought. Whilst a good deal of fine tuning was necessary to those proposals, the basis was sound, well thought out and generally agreed by the profession to form the basis of a national curriculum framework.

The proposals [for a] narrow, simplistic curriculum represented by a list of subjects – with or without time allocations – neglect all the good work that has already been done. Can we please have a national curriculum framework which looks less like something quickly concocted by an office junior trying to recall his old school timetable, and more like a well thought out piece of educational development based on all the good work that has gone on over the past decade?

Parochial Church Council of the Bedminster [Bristol] Team Ministry (churches of St Aldhelm, St Dunstan, St Francis and St Paul) – We approve the general idea of the core curriculum for schools, but deplore in the most vehement way the failure so far to include religious education/studies. If the law at present is widely and openly flouted when religious education is the only compulsory subject, you cannot claim with any credibility to recognize its importance (for those of any religious tradition, or of none) if you now propose to exclude it from the core. We call upon you to remedy this grievous fault.

British Housewives League – We are perturbed to see that in your suggested allocation of curriculum time only ten per cent is given to English and 20 to 30 per cent to science and technology. This would give us illiterate scientists – and not all children are scientifically inclined. Could it be that we are being chivvied into technological education by Lord Cockfield? Teaching of grammar, correct spelling and punctuation must be restored. Children must again be acquainted with the traditionally accepted best in English literature. Children have been served dross in the name of modernity. Logical thinking is impossible if language knowledge is poor.

We would also welcome the reintroduction of learning by heart – poetry, important passages from the Bible (Authorized Version), speeches from Shakespeare. Memorizing is good training for the mind.

If people had a larger vocabulary they would have less need of profanity.

(The consultative document did not propose a separate Curriculum Council for Wales. Very many responses to the Secretary of State for Wales criticized this omission, and it was made good when the Bill was published. But there were other anxieties about the prospects for the Welsh language and culture.)

Headmaster, **Duffryn Teifi Comprehensive School**, Llandysul, Dyfed – At a meeting of the staff of the above school on 3 November 1987 it was decided that I write to urge you: that a Welsh Curriculum Committee be established corresponding to the National Curriculum Committee in England; that separate subject working parties be established for Wales; that county councils be given the right to establish Welsh as a foundation subject within their territories or in specific areas/schools; where county councils choose not to take advantage of this right, that it be given to school governing bodies; that the Government declare that its long-term aim is to make Welsh a foundation subject throughout Wales; that particular arrangements be made for the assessment of achievement in English for children from a Welsh-language background and/or who are being educated through the medium of Welsh. In addition to the above, the staff expressed their general objection to the principle of assessing according to standard guidelines at ages 7, 11 and 14. The teachers believe that development can be satisfactorily assessed within existing arrangements. Also, the addition of standard assessment at 14, on top of all the new demands now being placed on teachers, will constitute an unacceptable additional burden.

The Welsh Consumer Council welcomes any proposal that is likely to help raise standards in schools. We share the Government's concern that all pupils have access to broadly the same good and relevant curriculum, and that schools should be more accountable for the education they offer their pupils. However, we are not convinced that a prescribed statutory national curriculum is the only way of achieving these objectives, or indeed a good way.

There are likely to be difficulties in providing for the distinctive characteristics and culture of Wales in such a curriculum. Provision for the teaching of Welsh poses problems in a tightly defined framework in which 80 to 90 per cent of curriculum time will be spent on prescribed foundation subjects. In some counties of Wales, Welsh will be a foundation subject, but it is not clear whether this will be achieved by substituting it for another foundation subject or by Welsh cutting into the small amount of time left for optional studies.

We recommend that, to safeguard the Welsh interest, there should be a Welsh Curriculum Council comprising representatives of educational interests (including parents) in Wales, which would, of course, work closely with the National Curriculum Council, and that there should be separate subject working groups for Wales.

Clarification is needed on the process for deciding whether or not Welsh should be a foundation subject in individual Welsh counties, or who within Wales will make those decisions and how such decisions should be implemented.

School Curriculum Development Committee – The development of a national curriculum, with a specification of 80 to 90 per cent of time for foundation subjects, raises specific issues for schools in Wales. Three, in particular, need further clarification.

Welsh as a first language: In Welsh-medium education, and also in parts of Wales where it is deemed appropriate for English-medium schools, Welsh will be an additional foundation subject. This will presumably be achieved either by using the percentage time available for optional subjects or by altering the time allocation for other foundation subjects. These implications need to be considered in more detail.

Welsh as a second language: The document notes that it would not at present be appropriate to require the study of Welsh throughout the period of compulsory education for pupils who study through the medium of English. This has implications for existing LEA policies for the teaching of Welsh as a second language which need to be explored further. It also places Welsh in an anomalous position *vis-à-vis* the proposed statutory modern language provision.

Subjects other than Welsh: Reference has already been made to the perturbating effect of Welsh as a subject on the percentage time allocation for other subjects. Irrespective of this, however, it cannot be assumed that programmes for foundation subjects other than Welsh should be the same in Wales and England. The means by which these Welsh dimensions are to be identified and developed need to be considered more carefully.

National Union of Teachers – The Government's stated intention is to make Welsh a foundation subject in some parts of the principality while in other areas it is to have no significant part. The document rightly states that the linguistic pattern of Wales is complex. The Government's proposals, far from recognizing that complexity, set out two courses only; to recognize the just claim for Welsh within the curriculum in some areas, and to withhold recognition of its place in schools elsewhere. There has been a growing demand for Welsh-medium education in the more anglicized areas of Wales, leading to the establishment of may successful schools. The union foresees a check in the momentum of these developments when English-speaking parents are faced with the prospect of testing in core subjects for their children. This course of action will put in jeopardy much of the teaching of the language in primary schools in most LEAs and fails to recognize and support the work which has taken place to establish sound second-language teaching. The complexity of the linguistic pattern in Wales has not prevented a renascence of the language in many areas.

The intentions of the Government on the place of Welsh in schools are contrary to one of the principles which it claims a national curriculum will fulfil 'that the curriculum offered in all maintained schools has sufficient in common to enable children to move from one area of the country to another with minimum disruption to their education'. What would happen if a child were to move from an area where no Welsh was required to one in which Welsh was a compulsory element in the curriculum? The answer which is not acceptable is that such a situation could arise at present: a national curriculum is intended to obviate such disadvantage. The language is the heritage of all children in Wales. In some areas Welsh should have accorded to it the same status as that given to English in England. In other areas, in keeping with the sharing of a common heritage, it should find a place in the curriculum of every child. The extent to which this should apply would best be left to the sensitivity of LEAs and schools in respect of the communities which they serve.

3

Testing and Assessment

THE PROPOSALS

In association with the proposed national curriculum, the Bill provides for attainment targets to be set for each of the ten foundation subjects, stating what pupils with different abilities can be expected to know and understand at about the ages of 7, and at 11, 14 and 16. There will be four formal assessment points at these ages, and national arrangements to assess what pupils have learned will include nationally prescribed tests.

A coherent national assessment system will offer better information about how schools are performing. An independent task group, appointed by the Government, has recommended a new system, combining teacher assessment with a mixture of oral, written and practical tests. The aim is to give a clear picture of how pupils are faring by comparison with attainment targets agreed for each age point. There should be an appropriate range of methods to assess how children are getting on and to record the results.

The tests are intended not to stigmatize children as failures but to measure their progress. Assessment will allow schools to begin diagnosing pupils' strengths and weaknesses so that teachers and parents together can decide what may need to be done.

A new School Examinations and Assessment Council will advise ministers on all aspects of examination, assessment and testing, approve examination syllabuses and monitor examining bodies' procedures.

THE DEBATE

Will the tools help the teacher help the child?

Norman Thomas*
HM Chief Inspector of Schools, 1973–81

Teaching depends on having views about what a child already knows and can do, and on what he or she might usefully learn. Why, then, should there be any worries that the Government intends to include a system of assessment in the arrangements for the national curriculum?

Some doubts flow from the past and current practices in assessing children and the purposes to which the results have been put.

Assessments to distinguish between children

There are still areas in England and Wales where children are assessed at about 11 or 12 years of age to decide which kind of secondary school they should attend. Various aspects of children's educational development are assessed and the results combined to produce a single list of marks. The children are separated into two groups: those above and those below a point in the list. All measurement is subject to some degree of uncertainty, and that is increased when marks in unrelated or hardly related aspects of learning are combined. It is not possible to separate children out into two quite distinct groups one of which is educationally more able and the other educationally less able in every respect. Some children in one group might, given small shifts in the assessment procedures, have been exchanged for children in the other group – even if the shift was simply to take a test on a different day.

Tests to compare children are used more widely than for the purpose of allocating secondary-school places. Many are set on a school's own initiative; a substantial number of local education authorities also require their use. Tests of reading and mathematics of this kind were originally taken by a sample of children chosen as representing their age group. The performances of children subsequently given the test are then compared with the original sample. These are norm-referenced tests. One test usually calls upon a group of related skills, and so the problem of combining results in different skills is slight. However, the content of the test may have only a general connection with what the children taking it have been taught.

Assessment procedures that determine what is taught

On the other hand, the programme of work may be constrained by assessment procedures. Some things are easier to assess than others.

It is simpler to judge whether a child can find the difference between 60 and 52 than to discover whether he or she always knows what change to expect when buying articles costing less than £1. It is still more difficult to determine whether a child's language is adequate for describing the feelings associated with a range of experiences. Pencil-and-paper tests are quick to administer and can be made relatively easy to mark. When work is geared to them, too little attention may be paid to practical experiences leading to wider understanding and the application of ideas and skills. Assessment procedures should be built into the curriculum, but not determine it.

Were minimum levels of attainment to be defined, many fear that these would be regarded as sufficient. Children and schools reaching them would be thought to have done enough, and ambition be discouraged. But if every child must go through the standard assessment procedure, some may find the experience dispiriting.

Reporting the results of assessment

Parents want to know how their children are getting on. It is difficult for a school's governing body or a local education authority to judge what a school requires without some information about children's attainments. The Government and the public at large are also properly interested.

Many teachers of young children fear that comparative assessments of children lead many parents to put children under undue pressure to do better. They prefer to tell parents whether the child is doing as well as can be expected. They may resist making any statement about how, broadly, a child is doing for his or her age. Yet most teachers who are parents would probably form such a view about their own children.

It is widely accepted that, on average, children from families in poor socioeconomic circumstances do worse at school than children from more affluent homes. If schools have to report the aggregated attainments of their pupils, those in the poorer areas may be unfairly castigated because, in absolute terms, their results are inferior.

Are there any solutions?

One attitude towards assessment is deeply ingrained: its purpose is to compare children. An act of will is necessary to replace that attitude. Assessment should be for determining what children know so that the best decisions can be taken about how to help them forward. Assessment should be formative.

The common presumptions about tests are: they are done by whole classes of children together, and require the use of pencil and paper; they are intended to put pressure on children to do their best. Yet tests are already available that engage children in practical activities and discussion. If their purpose is to aid assessment and to help in calibrating one teacher's judgement against others, tests need not be fearsome. Children who would be distressed by a test because they do not yet have the necessary skills or knowledge need not be made to take it. The tests should be designed to show what children can do, not to compare them: they should be criterion-referenced.

Assessments and tests suited to this system must relate to clearly defined attainment targets. The targets used by teachers are too numerous to be reported individually, and some clustering is required if reports on individuals and on groups of children are to be comprehensible. On the other hand, care must be taken to avoid bundling together results about disparate aspects of the curriculum. It is not helpful to divide children into five or six grades year by year so that some are permanently to be in the bottom grade – or the top, for that matter. The labelling of levels of attainment needs to give a proper sense of the progress that children make.

It is more difficult to devise a system that is fair and provides useful information on the results for a school as a whole. Maybe the best thing is to set them in a general statement about what the school is doing and its circumstances.

The first of the Secretary of State's working groups to issue a main report is the Task Group on Assessment and Testing. It has attempted to address the difficulties and worries about assessment as well as searching out any advantages there may be in a system aimed at enhancing the learning of children and placing assessment tools in the hands of the teachers. It remains to be seen whether the proposals will prove acceptable and, if so, accomplish what they intend.

The writer was a member of the Task Group, which reported to the Secretary of State on 24 December 1987.

THE ADVICE

Joint statement by the **Association for Science Education, Association of Teachers of Mathematics** and **National Association for the Teaching of English** – While there are aspects of the proposed national curriculum which we would support, we consider that to involve all pupils in nationally prescribed tests at the ages specified would be counter-productive to this endeavour.

Conflict of purposes
We have grave doubts concerning the number of different purposes

which the tests are expected to serve, which we list as follows: *diagnostic assessment* to probe individual children's understanding and competences in a way that can inform teaching and enhance learning; *reports to parents* to describe the achievements of the individual child and also the range of achievements both within the school and nationally, so that parents may see how their child stands in relation to others; *summative assessment* to provide information at the final point of compulsory education, for students and prospective employers; *the national monitoring of attainment* to collect comprehensive data on learning in the chosen curriculum areas, and thus to permit comparisons over time, and also between different types of school and different parts of the country.

These are all achievable purposes for assessment, but we do not believe that any one set of instruments can achieve all these aims, since they require different types of information, gained in different ways, at different times. Even if such a complex and expensive apparatus were produced, for reasons we state below, this would not fully meet the needs of summative assessment or reporting to parents.

Timing

Our associations have severe doubts about the suitability for these different purposes of the proposed assessment points, namely [ages] 7, 11, 14 and 16. While summative assessment is clearly appropriate at 16, the ages of 7, 11 and 14 are not suitable for this purpose. Nor are they for reports to parents, who require far more frequent information than the four age points would provide. For the purposes of national monitoring, the chosen points seem at best arbitrary and at worst disruptive. For diagnostic purposes, what are traditionally the end points of the infant, junior and early secondary phases seem particularly inappropriate, since in most cases it would be impossible for the child's teachers at the time of the testing to make constructive use of the information gained.

Validity and its cost implications

The development of new forms of examination and testing by GCSE boards and by the Assessment of Performance Unit has vividly demonstrated that, to be valid, assessment must inevitably be expensive. While at 16 many of the skills and abilities relevant to the core curriculum can be demonstrated on paper, such skills form a less significant part of the curriculum at earlier stages. The APU has pioneered good practice in valid assessment across a wide range of skill areas. In many cases their testing necessitates delicate and time-consuming observation of individuals or small groups of children carrying out a range of practical tasks, which make heavy demands on teacher/assessor time. In the case of the APU, such observation and testing is made feasible by being administered on the basis of light sampling of a given age group, a practice that yields sufficient information for the purposes of national monitoring. It is impossible to see how assessment of this quality could be accomplished on the scale envisaged within the proposed resources. To reduce the range of objectives, particularly to those which most readily lend themselves to inexpensive testing, would imperil validity and have serious consequences on the width and depth of the curriculum as it is taught.

Negative and positive approaches to assessment
Any centrally devised national test would be in serious danger of focusing attention on what children cannot do rather than what they can. In our present rapidly changing technological world, the ability to cope with new and changing skills and knowledge could be limited by a narrow concentration on such pre-set tests. A much wider model is required. In the upper years of secondary education, pupil profiles and records of achievement are finding general acceptance, especially at 16, and could profitably be developed for children of younger ages. Such a descriptive approach has been widely welcomed by parents and employers since it provides a better indication of attainment than a mark of (say) 50 per cent, which can show neither what the child has succeeded in, nor where the failure lies.

Current studies on these forms of assessment, particularly in relation to the Technical and Vocational Education Initiative and the Certificate of Pre-Vocational Education, have found the inclusion of self-assessment to be a powerful tool in providing a fuller picture of achievement and in improving pupil commitment and motivation. It deserves an honourable place in the learning and assessment process.

Testing as a means of raising standards
There is now a considerable body of evidence to show that, far from raising educational standards, repeated testing has precisely the reverse effect. Lower-achieving pupils are particularly at risk.

The effect of testing on the curriculum taught
All the evidence to date suggests that the tests themselves would quickly come to dominate and constrain the curriculum to such an extent that teachers would, rather than using the tests to show what the children have achieved, find themselves teaching for the test, just as they did with the 11+ selection test. In such circumstances the curriculum would, to all intents and purposes, become test-driven and thus lose the very qualities of breadth and variety which HMI surveys have associated with high achievement in the core areas.

The nature of learning

Learning, particularly at the primary stage, does not proceed at an even pace, or in linear progression. In our curriculum areas as in others, progress involves the understanding of fundamental concepts and the development of strategies, such as the ability to recognize a general rule from specific instances – a facility needed in language work as well as in mathematics and science – and the ability to formulate and communicate these perceptions effectively in spoken or written language. Children acquire expertise in different areas in different orders, at uneven rates and often in response to different experiences. Valid assessment of achievements of this kind requires sensitivity and subtlety. A written test designed to be taken by every child of a particular age cannot pinpoint the child's position on the complicated and idiosyncratic route toward understanding and competence. It would be particularly misleading to use evidence from such test to make comparisons between children in terms of their success as learners in a given area.

Conclusion

The terms of reference for the subject working groups, laid down in the national curriculum document, request that they take account of 'best practice and the results of relevant research and curriculum developments'. However, the history of educational research and curriculum development over the last 15 years shows that, as we have grown in our understanding of how pupils' learning advances, we have found it increasingly necessary to move away from the very forms of assessment which the Secretary of State proposes to introduce. Meanwhile, in West Germany, Belgium, France and other West European countries that share a concern for educational quality, there is a consistent trend away from such national testing and towards teacher assessment.

In the name of improved standards it is intended to impose on our schools a system of testing that we are convinced will militate against the maintenance and enhancement of quality in education.

The Royal Society of Arts Examinations Board is not convinced of the practicability or desirability of 'established national standards' at ages 7, 11 and 14. Much evidence exists of the very wide spread of achievement at these ages, of the very varied rates of progress made by individuals at different stages of their school careers and of the effects of cultural, linguistic and socioeconomic factors.

It is recognized, however, that if 16 is to continue to be the official school-leaving age, then there is a place at that age for certification to national standards. It is important that any such attainment targets be set for the curriculum objectives as a whole and not just for those that have been traditionally associated with particular subjects. It is also important that they be clearly criterion-referenced rather than reverting to notions of rank order within the age cohort.

The document suggests that 'nationally prescribed tests' are in some way to be preferred to other forms of assessment. No justification is advanced for this view, nor is there any indication as to the basis on which such a view could be adopted; are they more reliable, are they more valid, are they more appropriate for assessing particular objectives? Assessment to national standards, with the appropriate degree of national moderation, is what is important, not the format of the assessment. The document refers to the Government's policy on records of achievement for school-leavers. RSA regards this policy area as crucial and believes that it is essential that records of achievement have a clear relationship to the national curriculum and to the qualification system. Indeed, RSA takes the view that it is the record of achievement which should certify individuals' performances in relation to the overall curriculum objectives. This means that statements within such records must have a direct relationship to particular objectives and must have clear criteria for achievement, to national standards. Performances in GCSE can of course serve as such statements in particular curriculum areas. This is the only way in which achievements across and beyond the national curriculum can be pulled together.

RSA supports the concept of certificated courses being required to satisfy national criteria. It has some concerns, however, over the proposal for the Government to take a reserve power to regulate qualifications offered to full-time 16–19-year-old pupils in schools and colleges – 'for use only if experience shows this to be necessary'. What sort of experience or evidence would be regarded as appropriate for invoking this reserve power? RSA's particular concern relates to the possibility of accentuating damaging divisions between the so-called 'academic' and the so-called 'vocational', since part-time students would not find the range of courses available to them limited by regulation. The dividing line between full-time and part-time students can be very difficult to determine. So too the programme followed by a full-time student in college, with appropriate work experience, may be virtually identical to that of a YTS trainee with a commercial concern. Why should Government regulation treat the two cases in different ways?

RSA strongly supports the proposals for the training of teachers. Most teachers have received little or no such training in assessment methodology and practices. Such training forms part of the requirements of a number of RSA teachers' qualifications, and RSA would be prepared to make its experience more widely available.

Godfrey Thomson Unit for Educational Research, University of

Edinburgh – Tests are only one method of carrying out assessment and a very limiting one. The proposed national tests, at approximately three-year intervals, will not help meet most of the aims outlined in the consultation document, and will make it more difficult for other forms of assessment to do so. There are alternatives to the proposal which would ensure a balanced approach to the production of a range of assessment procedures, with beneficial educational effects, and also to their use in schools.

The existence of a national curriculum will make national assessment easier, since it will ensure more uniformity of teaching and learning than exists now in England and Wales, and this in turn will make it easier to design assessment materials. For example, it has always been difficult to produce mathematics tests for primary-school children that would be appropriate in more than one LEA because of the variations in the sequence of introducing the different topics. If the national curriculum is to specify the sequence of topics, then tests with a wider currency will be possible at all stages of school.

The consultation document suggests that the Secretaries of State hold certain beliefs about the role of assessment: good learning can only be assured if accompanied by good assessment; good assessment must provide information which is interpretable outside the classroom as well as within it; such information should be made available to all those who have a valid interest in the standards of attainment reached by a child or group of children. We do not disagree with any of these statements, provided that the meaning of the word 'assessment' is kept broad enough. Problems will arise only where tests which are too narrow in scope or content are used to assess the important results of learning, and interpreted too broadly as evidence of educational outcomes.

We believe that the procedures proposed in the consultation document are inconsistent with these beliefs in certain respects and will fail to achieve the advantages outlined. To achieve the aims expressed by the document there needs to be a national system of assessment which should enable teachers to provide evidence about all of the important objectives that they are trying to achieve, and nor merely about those that are easily measured; frequently updated information about children's progress; and cumulative information that parents and others can understand. In addition, the assessments should be useful to teacher and to children, and integrated into classroom work as closely as possible.

The Secretaries of State are proposing a national curriculum, not a national scheme of work or textbook, in order to 'leave full scope for professional judgement and . . . to try out and develop new approaches'. This is 'framework' rather than 'strait-jacket'. But when they turn to assessment they propose national tests rather than national testing: this is 'strait-jacket' rather than 'framework'.

National tests which must not be unfair to anyone will of necessity be cautious in their approach. At the same time they will tend to squeeze out of the market any independent test producers and publishers. Where will the 'new approaches' be tried out, and at whose expense?

There are alternative approaches to setting up an assessment system which could be usefully explored. Some countries provide collections of questions, tests and other exercises for schools or school boards to use for their own assessment purposes. Probably the most successful examples are the Ontario Assessment Instrument Pools, begun in 1976, which in most subjects are broad enough to have won teachers' professional acceptance, and are large enough to allow unrestricted access by schools without compromising the monitoring functions. The principal problem is that such item banks are expensive to set up and maintain at a national level.

In some countries, notably the United States, commercial agencies provide the tests. In Britain, because of the dominance of the examination systems, commercial tests play a much more limited role. Nevertheless the commercial publishers have had substantial influence on educational practice in some areas. The Edinburgh Reading Tests have profoundly influenced the nature of reading curricula, especially in the upper primary school, since they first appeared in 1972. The Primary Mathematics Item Bank was developed under Scottish Education Department funding. Macmillan Education is now investing the money required to bring this to publication as a bank of calibrated tests for primary school. Each of these developments is having a significant influence. Each depended to some degree on the willingness of a publisher to invest in their creation. National tests would scotch such developments by removing the market. It would be strange if this Government were to stifle initiative by nationalizing educational assessment.

Department of Education, University of Liverpool – Whilst diagnostic testing is an important part of teaching, it is hard to see the value of nationally prescribed achievement tests for all. The status of tests is decribed confusingly as the 'heart' of the assessment process and as a 'supplement' to individual teachers' assessments. It is impossible for both of these to be true. And if, as is likely given their projected use, the tests are to be the 'heart', of the process, they are likely to become a means of moderating teachers' own assessments and ultimately to shape the type of assessments teachers use. Given the artificiality of mass-testing procedures, their notorious unreliability in all but the most narrowly defined circumstances, their unsuitability for obtaining information about highly relevant skills and their power to distort the curriculum, it seems unlikely that reliable information about children's true abilities will be obtained and the curriculum will be in danger of becoming less rather than more like the real life to which it must aspire.

Current progress in assessment, from which GCSE has benefited, has not only consolidated moves away from artificial testing and towards more naturalistic contexts, but has also recognized and made use of teachers' expertise in assessment. This progress is ignored by the proposals, and there is even the suggestion that there will be changes in the GCSE. In this context the claims made about the 'enhanced' teacher's role sound hollow – the role is being diminished in terms of their professional expertise.

School of Education, University of Exeter – While we have no rooted objection to a national curriculum, we are disturbed at the narrow and overwhelmingly utilitarian nature of the present proposals. The narrow view of education underlying the document is intensified and exacerbated by the preoccupation with testing. We do not accept the proposals to test children at around 7, 11 and 14. The techniques for valid and reliable testing on the scale and to the purposes envisaged are not available. The danger of 'teaching to the test' is almost unavoidable. Pointless competition between children, parents, teachers and schools will result. Good teachers have worked hard to reduce these evils while challenging every pupil at their own level. This will be set at naught in a regime which will encourage drudgery and rote learning, however the Secretaries of State may hope otherwise.

University of Southampton Primary School Pupil Assessment Project – We strongly support the attempt to link the proposed assessment system to explicitly stated criteria and attainment targets. We do however feel that the difficulties have been seriously underestimated. We have noted the recommendation from the King's College research that 'nine years would be needed before full national implementation was achieved' and regard this as a realistic time scale for such an ambitious exercise.

The purpose of tests at 7, 11 and 14 [is described as] being for both diagnosis at the level of the learning of individual pupils and for monitoring the education system nationally. We are convinced that it won't be possible to achieve such diverse aims with a single system of assessments.

We can see no sensible justification for linking attainment targets to defined ages. We would strongly urge that this aspect of the brief of the working groups is revised, so that a system of assessment can be devised that encourages all children to work towards and reach attainment targets as quickly as is appropriate to their own individual development and educational progress, regardless of whether this occurs at 7, 11, 14 or whatever years of age.

In this respect we would also strongly urge that the valuable development work that has been conducted by many LEAs and schools as part of the DES funded 'records of achievement' initiative be used as a basis for planning a system of pupil profiling and record keeping that is in harmony with the broad aims of a national curriculum. Such a system should allow all worthwhile achievements to be recorded, regardless of the age when each individual child reaches them.

There is a danger that the working groups may find it impossible to encapsulate all of the worthwhile aims of the foundation subjects in the form of a list of attainment targets. If this type of difficulty leads to certain curriculum being excluded, with the attainment targets focusing on isolated fragments of the curriculum (which have been given the perhaps unhelpful label of 'subjects'), then the exercise could be very damaging in terms of its potential influence on the education system.

Secondary Examinations Council – The consultation document conceives of assessment and reporting having a variety of purposes. These include functions which may be described as diagnostic, formative, summative and evaluative (this last in the sense of allowing evaluation of the work of an individual teacher, department, school or local education authority). In our experience, there are tensions between these goals. It is by no means clear at present how these conflicts can be resolved in ways that will improve the quality of education for all pupils and the usefulness of the information provided for the various audiences. The complexity of the task should not be underestimated.

The paramount role of assessment is as an aid to learning. While the need to provide helpful information to selectors for jobs, courses and training is recognized as a key aspect of assessment at 16, we would hold to the general principle that assessment systems during the earlier years of compulsory schooling should be primarily concerned with promoting better learning through feedback to pupils, parents and teachers from coursework assessment, and through the beneficial backwash of well-developed assessment instruments on the curriculum. We believe that the national curriculum attainment target should be designed first and foremost in a form that will help teachers to make learning goals clear to their pupils. In this regard we support the statement that the main purpose of assessment against the national curriculum attainment targets will be 'to show what a pupil has learnt and mastered and to enable parents and teachers to ensure that he or she is making adequate progress'. The detailed guidance given to science and mathematics curriculum groups is encouraging in identifying the main purpose of assessment as being 'to inform decisions about the next steps'.

The introduction of the national curriculum should reinforce the significant move towards positive and informative assessment which has attended the introduction of the GCSE and the development of records of achievement. The concept of assessment at specified ages will need to be carefully thought through if it is to be introduced in a fashion that does not run counter to the principle of positive assessment, thereby demotivating pupils and suppressing achievement.

We cannot emphasize too strongly, from our recent experience, the importance of appropriate initial and in-service training for teachers. The point is particularly significant given that attainment targets for the earlier years of schooling are to be formulated for the first time. Teachers will need much help if they are to assess their pupils fairly and to nationally agreed standards. Effective moderation will be needed to ensure that standards are comparable across the country. To be effective, the systems adopted will need to place as much emphasis on helping teachers to make good assessments as upon checking the results of their work.

We recognize that Government expenditure of some £8,000 million per annum on education in the statutory years requires some quality control mechanisms. One such mechanism has been the external examinations system at 16 and 18 where the SEC's role is to monitor the quality of syllabuses and their assessment. The proposal that checks on attainment should additionally be made at (7), 11 and 14 extends this mechanism in certain ways but differs in an important respect: assessment at 16 has a significant summative role whereas assessment in earlier years should be formative, leading to action in the classroom on the basis of accurate diagnoses. It is therefore all the more important that the SEAC is properly resourced to see that this new work is performed to impeccable standards and that the data collected is valid and reliable.

We wish to draw attention to an issue which the consultation document fails to address. It is not clear who is to act on the information generated, how and with what kinds of guidance and accountability. Who is responsible for ensuring that appropriate action is taken in classrooms in the light of the evidence arising from assessment within the national curriculum?

The functions of the SEAC need to be spelled out in more detail to make it clear how the efficacy of the school-based assessment and the national tests is to be established and maintained. It is not clear whether the SEAC will take sole responsibility or, if other agencies are to be involved, what collaborative arrangements will apply.

School Curriculum Development Committee – The national curriculum allows little room for pupil choice and is more prescriptive than has been customary. Recognition of the limitations of formal assessment for some pupils has contributed to the development of profiling and records of achievement and it is the Government's policy that a record of achievement following a nationally agreed pattern should be available for all pupils by 1990. SCDC support the development of records of achievement, believing that they will help to emphasize the growth in particular of skills and attitudes. It recommends that their relation to the national curriculum should receive further consideration. The consultation document refers briefly to records of achievement but does not make clear how they are to be harmonized with attainment targets, assessment and testing.

SCDC's main concern with attainment targets, assessment and testing, is the impact which they are likely to have on programmes of study in each foundation subject and on the curriculum as a whole. The relationship between curriculum, assessment and testing has in recent years been a fundamental educational issue. Many primary-school teachers fear that the liberation of curriculum which resulted from the demise of the 11+ examination could be reversed. In practice testing and examinations tend to determine curriculum rather than vice versa. The articulation for the first time of an assessment and testing system in schools will be as important an innovation as the national curriculum itself.

The committee wishes to draw attention to some issues of principle:

The consultation document makes clear that the specification of attainment targets and the accompanying assessment and testing must leave scope for the very able, those of average ability, and for the less able. The range of both ability and aptitude is enormous, and it is hard to see how a single system of testing can serve to extend the able and the average without discouraging those of lower academic ability. The experience of failure neither provides useful feedback for the teacher nor serves to improve pupil performance.

Despite the intensive work done in relation to GCSE it is by no means certain that the art (or science) of assessment and testing is advanced enough to achieve what the consultation document expects it to do.

Testing tends to restrict teaching to what is testable. A programme of testing on four occasions during a pupil's school career may have the unintended effect of placing emphasis on factual content and memory, which are more easily tested, than other aspects of achievement such as the capacity to solve problems, to apply knowledge and to develop concepts and skills.

SCDC is pleased to note that assessment (apart from GCSE at 16) 'will be done by teachers as an integral part of normal classroom work'. However, 'at the heart of the assessment process there will be nationally prescribed tests done by all pupils', administered and marked by teachers but external moderated. If there is not to be a substantial increase in the proportion of school time devoted to assessment and testing, as opposed to teaching, it will be important to integrate teaching, assessment and testing as far as possible. Assessment and testing will need to be the continuation of teaching and learning by other means.

The purpose of assessment and testing needs to be defined. They are in the view of SCDC valuable in school chiefly for diagnostic and screening purposes. The consultation document endorses this view indicating that assessment and testing are intended to enable pupils 'to be stretched fully when they are doing well and given more help when they are not'. Assessment and testing should therefore take place at ages and times when remediation is available and improvement where needed can be effected. This may not be the same in all subjects. Blanket testing at 7 (or thereabouts) 11, 14 and 16 needs to be considered in the light of this principle.

The board has particular misgivings about the requirement of testing at 7 and welcomes the caveat 'or thereabouts'. Determining what a child of 7 should 'normally be expected to know' is particularly problematic when the range and quality of early years experience at home and in pre-school provision gives such varying starting points. This problem is exacerbated by the different ages at which children enter school. In addition, pencil-and-paper testing for young children has indicated the limitations of too early written work for instance in mathematics. At 7 or thereabouts it seems that diagnostic assessment might be profitable for some but that any formal testing of the whole cohort would be damaging.

Testing at age 11 when the majority are changing school reduces the likelihood of adequate remedial work where this is necessary, and in any case the remedial work would be in the hands of teachers at the new school who are unfamiliar with the pupils. SCDC recommends that these issues should be remitted to TGAT.

SCDC believes that the area of special educational needs in relation to assessment and testing requires further consideration. The consultation document provides for the exemption of a pupil who has a statement of special need under the Education Act of 1981 from some or all of the national curriculum requirements. This is however a negative way of viewing the needs of this category of pupil. The committee wishes to reinforce the appeal of the House of Commons Select Committee on Special Education to the Department of Education and Science to monitor the implications for special-needs children of testing. 'The proposal for defining levels of achievement, including testing attainment levels, may present problems about the interpretation of individual results. A major question arises about the prospective relationship between inability to reach the standard set and the identification of special educational needs as defined by the Act.'

Association for the Study of Curriculum – It is ironic that, while the professional expertise of teachers is being denied, that of the tester finds uncritical acceptance. Many of our members would support Maurice Holt's claim that the testers' search for objective certainty is a 'quest for an unattainable goal'. Others would argue that standards of attainment are not synonymous with standards of education. The prospect of nationally prescribed tests at 7 (or thereabouts), 11, 14 and 16 in relation to agreed national targets raises the spectre of an inevitable return to such anti-educational practices as cramming, teaching to the test, rote learning and regurgitation of inert knowledge, didactic teaching styles and streaming.

The National Association of Head Teachers proposes a school – home contract. In arguing the need for a national curriculum it has been said that parents have a right to be better informed, more involved, and have a greater influence over the education of their children. The Secretary of State has stressed the concept of partnership. 'We have here the basis for a particularly fruitful partnership between teachers and parents. That partnership needs to be established for all children. It should be a two-way partnership.'

With this we would not disagree but we do not believe that such a partnership can grow our of a national curriculum which bases the school–home relationship on the results of age-related tests. Such interaction of teacher and parent will concentrate on failure, comparison of pupils, criticism of teaching and the judging of schools. It need not be so. A national curriculum could incorporate within it a school–home contract which would provide the following basis for a positive relationship helpful to school and pupil.

(1) Parents would be informed in advance of the objectives and targets for their children within a given future period. This would be linked to the specific learning goals of the national curriculum guidelines and would include explanations of syllabuses and teaching schemes.

(2) Parents would be made aware of how it was planned to assess children in relation to these targets.

(3) Parents would be invited to a regular review of their child's

progress in relation to previously agreed targets and would further include consideration of the assessments and the evidence upon which they were made, an agreement on future targets, and a discussion on the most effective way in which the parents can best support their child (e.g. there are many excellent schemes of parental involvement in the teaching of reading).

(4) All pupils would have a record of achievement which would span their school careers with a series of formative records being incorporated into summative records at agreed points. This record would give the whole picture of a child's achievement. It would be a key factor in parent–teacher consultations, and a formal recognition that they had taken place.

(5) In schools where a pupil is taught by more than one teacher there should be the opportunity for meeting of all the teachers who teach a particular child to contribute in discussion to the school's views of that pupil. This sharing of views gives all teachers a better picture of the pupils they teach.

(6) A national curriculum would need to recognize formally such a system to make sure that it operates, and to provide safeguards for parents and teachers.

It is our belief that, given adequate resourcing, developments along these lines will produce the 'fruitful partnership' which is called for, and we urge the Secretary of State to explore with us this real, constructive alternative to a home–school relationship based upon public testing.

To measure the needs of the child and to judge whether the attainment at 7 (or indeed at any moment in the child's progress) is acceptable, there has to be some form of diagnostic assessment at age 5 – the statutory entry into education. Up to that point, parents have made by far the greatest contribution to the 'starting base' of their children and know them better than anyone. Parents should therefore contribute to the assessment process.

It would be outrageous to suggest that there should be national tests with published results at the age of 5. Even more than at later ages, no fair test could be set which took into account the immense diversity of pre-school experience between different children.

Once the initial assessment has been done and agreed as the starting point for the home–school contract, the only sensible assessment of children which can be made at age 7 (or at any time in their progress) is how far they have developed in all aspects from their starting base. The true achievement is measured in the distance travelled not by the point reached.

We believe this system would be greatly advantageous to children with special needs. Far too little is done by local authorities and supporting agencies to identify severe learning and other difficulties before the age of 5 or even 7. This prevents teachers, who themselves are aware that these children have serious problems, from offering the support needed by these children from the very beginning.

The Secondary Heads Association is strongly opposed to the introduction of the whole paraphernalia of national external tests at 7, 11, 14 and the additional examinations at 16.

(a) The whole process will seriously reduce teaching time.

(b) In view of the published purpose of testing (evaluation, appraisal, parental choice), schools and teachers will undoubtedly concentrate on teaching for the tests, holding rehearsals, practices.

(c) Testing for 7-year-olds will create an early sense of failure in both pupils and parents. Remember the 11+.

(d) Testing is *not* a proven essential way of raising standards as alleged in the document.

(e) Testing will inevitably curtail the flair and initiative of teachers, as did the 11+.

(f) The publication of test results for comparison by parents (school by school and class by class) cannot take into account all the relevant factors and will generate tension and uncertainty for teachers, parents and pupils.

(g) These proposals contradict the recent positive developments towards records of achievement.

(h) To return to anything resembling 'position in the class' is retrograde – it will not stress individual achievement with regard to potential and indeed, by constantly identifying failure, will depress motivation and achievement.

(i) The administration and marking of the tests will impose an impossible additional workload for teachers unless pupil – teacher ratio is significantly reduced.

(j) Since it is acknowledged that testing for targets is neither appropriate nor valid in art, music and PE, there arise serious questions on the validity of such continuous public testing and reporting on other areas of the curriculum.

National Union of Teachers – With the prospect of testing at 7 looming, the pressures to teach rather than to encourage to learn can be extreme. The emphasis given to testing and attainment will affect parental expectations, and the teacher's professional judgement to resist the demands will be weakened. The strain on the relationship between teachers and parents, especially of very young children, could be damaging.

We have already indicated our scepticism about the credibility of

attainment targets. The union noted that there is considerable
uncertainty about subjects other that the so-called 'core' subjects,
but for art, music and physical education there will be guidelines
rather than specific attainment targets. The union has no doubt that
when these attainment targets are made known they are likely to
prove controversial and we would expect the working groups to
indicate very clearly the evidence for the targets they have fixed.
There are inherent dangers in attainment targets coming to define
the curriculum but can (and have done too frequently in the past)
result in depressed standards of education.

The terms of reference to the working groups seek to establish
attainment targets for the knowledge, skills, understanding and
aptitudes which pupils of different abilities and maturity should be
expected to have acquired. What is not clear is the part that
achievement testing is to play in assessing these. The prominence
given to attainment targets and the uses to which they are to be put
points directly to the political rather than the educational prov-
enance of the Bill. Paragraph 23 refers to 'the range of attainment
targets (which) should cater for the full ability range'. Paragraph 36
seeks to create a hierarchy of ranking systems – inter-child, inter-
class and inter-school rankings – and there can be little doubt that
the result will be that teachers will be increasingly pressured
towards selecting pupils for appropriate levels of testing with all its
consequences for the teaching of children. Again, the proposals on
the curriculum cannot be seen in isolation from the other major
proposals of the new Bill. These will lead teachers to see that a
limited view of children, of their needs and what they need to know
is the safest way to approach their task.

The union's view of attainment testing is that it has a role to play,
particularly in diagnosing and helping to deal with specific learning
difficulties, but also, when used sensitively, to aid teaching and
learning generally. It rejects the view that tests can be used as a
competitive stimulus between pupils or between schools. As indicators of personal performances they have limited usefulness
because they have to be understood within contexts that themselves
require analysis.

We have indicated our view of the proper place of nationally
prescribed tests in the curriculum. That teacher marking and
assessment should be moderated and the tests administered by the
five GCSE examining boards is to introduce an element of farce into
the whole process. Assessments at 7 (or 8 or 9) and 11 administered
and moderated by the GCSE board with freedom of choice by the
school among the boards! Or, is it intended that the primary schools
should not enjoy the same rights as secondary schools? Have these
proposals been discussed even informally with some of the interests
who could be inferred to be centrally involved? The time scale

envisaged is such that we must necessarily ask these questions. Underlying our questions is the worry that this is indeed a hastily cobbled together document with solutions to specific problems floated to see where they bounce. The alternative, i.e. that these solutions represent an advanced stage of consultation with particular interests to which no one else has been party, is fearsome.

National Association of Schoolmasters/Union of Women Teachers – The programmes of study 'will reflect the attainment targets, and set out the overall content, knowledge, skills and processes relevant to today's needs which pupils should be taught in order to achieve them'. It is an indictment of the Government's forward planning that some GCSE syllabuses, which were published only a short while ago, will need to be comprehensively revised to accord with the attainment targets to be set for pupils at age 16.

With the degree of prescription that is inherent in any system of nationally imposed tests, it is difficult to believe the statement that 'Within the programmes of study teachers will be free to determine the detail of what should be taught in order to ensure that pupils achieve appropriate levels of attainment.' It is particularly naïve of the Secretary of State to take the view that 'Attainment targets should not result in an unduly narrow approach to teaching and learning' (evidence to the Education, Science and Arts Select Committee, April 1987). The Government should not be surprised if a disproportionate amount of time is spent in schools preparing pupils for tests and teaching what is testable.

The NAS/UWT fears that the introduction of attainment tests, as proposed by the Secretary of State, means: that it will prove to be impossible to devise a set of attainment targets to cater for the full ability range; that the tests will assume excessive importance and will subsume other, more positive aspects of pupils' learning and attainments; the the test results will be used as a superficial yardstick to compare how standards vary from one school to another; that many children will come to see themselves as failures at any early age. A system of pupil records of achievement, based on continuous assessment and linked to standardized and school-based tests used for diagnostic and other purposes, provides a more reliable method of monitoring and recording pupils' attainments at different ages while at school. The danger is that teachers may be forced into the role of instructors.

Assistant Masters' and Mistresses' Association – We believe that a nationally administered system of assessment – certainly if it included periodic formal testing – and the introduction of records of achievement will substantially increase the work of teachers. We do not think it possible for that increase to be accommodated within the parameters of reasonableness which properly circumscribe the recently introduced conditions of employment for teachers. Since the Government was the author of those contractual arrangements, we call upon them to provide the evidence that it can be. In that the Secretaries of State have wisely seen the advantage of establishing working groups to advise them on other matters relating to the nation curriculum, we think it would be consistent and desirable for them to establish a working group on this issue also, and to consult the affected parties upon its recommendations.

Association of Municipal Authorities – The proposed attainment tests are the cause of several concerns:

(a) that their effect will be to narrow the curriculum taught, and encourage teaching especially for the tests;
(b) that they are likely to depress the results of ethnic minority children; tests without cultural bias are rare, and limited in their application;
(c) that it is unclear to what extent tests will be differentiated according to pupils' abilities and aptitudes, and how (and in which circumstances) the raw scores will be refined to take account of schools' socioeconomic backgrounds;
(d) whether the principal purpose of testing will be to meet national requirements, or to identify children who need particular help;
(e) on their apparent conflict with the painstaking work which has gone on over many years, with DES support, to develop multidisciplinary profiling leading to records of achievement; and
(f) on the consultative document's sketchy acknowledgement of the work done already by the Assessment of Performance Unit and of its potential to assist the national curriculum.

Association of County Councils – Testing has considerable value when the results are used to help teachers plan future work to meet pupils' individual needs. The principle becomes devalued, however, if the emphasis is placed on providing results to be measured against group 'norms'. The information could easily be interpreted to encourage complacency because an artificial 'standard' had been achieved, or alarm where it had not. The results in either case might bear no relationship to the needs or performance of the pupils concerned. One of the major factors that prevents pupils from learning and achieving, and which acts as a significant demotivator, is the need for constant revision and preparation for tests and examinations. Teachers who are understandably anxious that pupils succeed (especially where the results of tests are published as an assumed measure of a school's performance) are likely to spend too much time on teaching the test syllabus rather than offering their classes a broader perspective on the subject (as HMI have recommended).

The proposal that pupils should be asssessed at 7, 11, 14 and 16 will certainly lead to an extension of the examination industry out of proportion to the real business of improved teaching and the support of teaching. The proposals are cumbersome and will be expensive.

It is essential that the effects of testing and the imposition of attainment targets on children with learning difficulties and special educational needs should be thoroughly explored. It would be most regrettable if schools which have increasingly integrated such children as a result of the Education Act 1981 were to find themselves under pressure to reverse the trend.

Many authorities have expressed concern that an overemphasis on tests and assessments will promote an attitude whereby only that which can be tested will be taught, and standards, instead of being raised, will be depressed. Tests alone do not provide an adequate basis for determining a child's needs or achievements.

[The proposal to publish information on the performance of schools] begs the question as to what action the Government would take if it was not satisfied that sufficient progress was being made. Is the implication that schools would be closed? Or would the tests be made easier? Would the pupils who 'fail' the tests be made to repeat a year? Or would the authority be encouraged, and assisted, to spend additional resources to help the school achieve better results?

Hertfordshire County Council – There is evident tension in the paper between the notion of year-group learning objectives and the varying talents or speed of learning of individual children. The Secretary of State's belief that many children are brighter than they are sometimes thought to be is welcome and shared. Underachievement of pupils is recognized in part to be a failure by the educational system. The problem with the document's approach is that it tries to relate the individual child's potential ('each child to develop his or her potential', 'each child, according to his or her ability') to a general (average or very broad?) standard for a year group ('setting clear objectives for what children over the full range of ability should be able to achieve'). This is a problem with which all teachers are familiar. It does not become less of a problem by being made into a national scheme. The document's conclusion seems to be that the assessments of pupils will show that some pupils are doing well and need to be 'stretched further', and that some pupils are not doing well and will need to be 'given more help'. There seems to be little new in that.

There is a similar tension between assessing a school's standards and those of the nation as a whole. There is a desire to allow parents and governors to set their own school's achievements against a national average. The tension in this activity is acknowledged by the escape route which allows the school to be 'taking account of its particular circumstances'. The problem for the school is the same as for some below-average children. Whilst some will, by great effort, go up the league table and perhaps become above average, the odds against some schools and children ever becoming above average will be too great. There are no merits in giving the inevitable position of a school in a national ranking order a stamp of statistical authority, especially a stamp of spurious statistical authority. The rank will not necessarily reflect the merits of the school. A high-ranking school could be letting down its able but under-performing pupils, whilst a low-ranking school might be raising its pupils' standards enormously. The former will become self-satisfied; the latter may despair. Neither state of mind raises standards.

There is a widely held view that the achievements of pupils should be recorded positively in terms of what they know and can do, not how well they perform in comparison with other pupils. Achievement is seen as more important than rank. Confidence is seen as making a more important contribution to raising standards than is denigration. This view is currently being promoted by the Manpower Services Commission (in the Youth Training Scheme and the Technical and Vocational Education Initiative), the Department of Education and Science (in GCSE with the goal of criterion-referenced rather than norm-referenced results; and in the education support grant project for records of achievement). These other Government initiatives show greater understanding of how to promote higher standards than do the present proposals.

There are no grounds for believing that the five GCSE examining groups or any other existing organizations have the capacity to moderate the marking of tests by the pupils' own teachers. The moderation of GCE and CSE papers over the years (a simple exercise by comparison) has left much to be desired. The moderation of national tests, sat by every single pupil in the land four times during their school careers and in most foundations subjects and marked by their own teachers, is an undertaking on a scale which is barely imaginable. It is also bound to be very expensive and it is not clear who is to meet the additional cost. It is very likely that it will be made manageable, both as a task and in terms of cost, by using only a single form of written test, based on factual knowledge, simple recall and possibly multiple choice questions.

What is a well-trained, universally admired, hard-working teacher to do if, year after year, his or her pupils on average are below the national average and known by parents and the local authority to be so? It is recognized in the document that there are other important factors at work in determining the attainment of pupils besides the quality of teaching, yet a single measurement is to be published as a spur to competition between teachers which cannot, in itself, ameliorate any of those other factors. One important factor in a child's performance is his or her ability. It is not, therefore, a valid performance indicator to say, in relation to a school, how many pupils have reached the standard of what an average child of 7 should know and understand, how many have reached the standard which should be attained by children who are 20 per cent above average, and so on.

Inner London Education Authority – The relationship between attainment targets, tests and the GCSE is unclear. The document states that attainment targets for age 16 will take account of GCSE criteria. It is suggested that there will be assessment and testing of pupils at 16 in non-examined subjects. One interpretation of this is if pupils are taking GCSE – which will be modified to take account of attainment targets – they will be exempt from tests at 16. If they are not taking GCSE in any core subject they will be expected to take a test at age 16. It is obvious that there are many practical difficulties associated with this, and further clarification is required.

The argument outlined in support of the Secretary of State's intention to take a reserve power to regulate qualifications at 16–19 is limited, and the implication that there will be restrictions placed on schools, national bodies and other organizations which may wish to devise their own courses and certificates is a matter of concern. The role of the National Council for Vocational Qualifications (NCVQ) is crucial in this respect in devising and maintaining a system of coherent qualifications. It may be appropriate for the Secretary of State's reserve powers to be used to regulate the qualifications where their promoters, recognizing the range of organizations involved and the public funds employed in the preparation of students, are either unwilling or unable to meet the standards laid down by the NCVQ. However, the powers should not be used to inhibit curriculum development to meet other particular needs of students.

British Dyslexia Association – Those who work with children with special educational needs are exceedingly concerned that these proposals may prove detrimental to these children. Many more will need the protection of a statement (e.g. to opt out of a foreign language – which is in itself a negative attitude to take). For the underachiever who is underachieving because of a literacy deficit, the testing merely reinforces his or her inadequacy. There is grave concern that schools which opt out and become grant-maintained may use information obtained through assessments as part of a selection process. Such schools may be in a position to refuse children with special educational needs, and indeed not maintain provision for such children. In the past, O- and A-Level examination boards have endeavoured to ensure that handicapped candidates are able to compete with their non-handicapped peers on an equal basis; the GCSE boards are developing a similar strategy. In the same way it must be possible to afford children with special education needs the opportunity to compete on an equal basis in tests at 7, 11, etc. Discrimination against children with special educational needs has to be avoided in the national curriculum.

National Association for Remedial Education – The worth, status and performance of state schools could soon be linked in the public eye with their test levels on the assessment targets. Children with learning difficulties will depress these levels. There will be a temptation for schools to refer more of these children for formal assessment under the Education Act 1981 in the hope that the ensuing statements will recommend education in special schools or exemption from certain of the national curriculum requirements. The exemption section of the document is potentially most divisive and will deeply disturb many parents of children with special educational needs. It is likely that little value will be given to profiles written on exempted children in 1991.

The Rathbone Society – For the very bright child [attainment] tests are not needed, and for the child with learning difficulties they will serve to reinforce failure. This, in turn, will lead to an increasing lack of self-confidence and self-esteem, qualities which all children need and which are fundamental requirements of employers. Classes or schools admitting the educationally disadvantaged and those with moderate learning difficulties will inevitably compare unfavourably on a basis of national test results with classes or schools having a more highly selective entry.

Association of LEA Advisory Officers for Multicultural Education (ALAOME) – The document states that 'teachers will be free to determine the detail of what should be taught' and 'to adapt what they teach to the needs of the individual pupil'. However, even today the curriculum of many schools pays scant attention to the realities of an ethnically diverse society. If these realities are not reflected in the national tests and assessment procedures, teachers who seek to make their teaching respond to these realities may find that their pupils are penalized. For example, if a humanities teacher believes it important to teach about the effects of racism, and if this concern is not reflected in what is assessed, may not pupils and parents feel that such teaching is a waste of time? If a group of primary-age children learn about the development of their town as a multi-racial community and are helped to develop positive attitudes towards ethnic diversity, will the arrangements for assessment and the benchmarks of knowledge give credit for this? To put it simply, will the freedom and flexibility of the teacher be supported by the assessment process or will teachers who stray from the narrow path of the prescribed programme do so at their pupils', their own and their school's risk?

Commission for Racial Equality – The problem of devising any form of testing that is free from cultural bias, and that will not inappropriately diagnose the level of attainment of ethnic minority pupils, has long been recognized. Given the proposal that such tests will be nationally prescribed, the commission is concerned that any such method of uniform assessment should only go forward if fair and culturally unbiased methods and techniques can be developed. Similar concerns arise regarding records of achievement and pupil profiles. Careful thought should be given to the criteria and methods of compilation of such pupil records to ensure that they are free from subjective racial prejudices. Extensive programmes of in-service teacher training will be required.

British Association for Counselling – We question the atmosphere of competition that will be engendered by national testing. Competition can be helpful, it can motivate, but competition where a large number of our children will be less than average (statistically this has to be so) will lead to young people who believe themselves to be less than average people. It will demotivate them and lead to a withdrawal and lessened confidence. The plan must be to give each child confidence that he or she is achieving his or her potential – that there is still more to be learned, but to be learned for the joy of learning rather than because they must come up to the benchmark of what has been prescribed and considered to be 'normal'. Our children have a diversity of talents which they will take with them into adulthood if that diversity is recognized and sanction given for them to continue to develop their individual talents. When they are confident as individuals then they will be able to contribute confidently to group teamwork and thus to society.

All educators should have within their initial training a basic training in counselling skills since those skills required in education for profiling, negotiated learning and personal assessment have their basis in the discipline of counselling. Under the proposed national curriculum, all members of staff will need the skills to support their pupils and their parents through a system of testing which cannot but be anxiety-provoking.

Confederation of British Industry – Employers set considerable store by the availability of consistent assessments of school-leavers against nationally defined standards of attainment which will help them to evaluate potential recruits from all parts of the country. However, they are concerned that this should not result in an approach which is so mechanical that it would be detrimental to the motivation of many students and teachers. Very careful thought will be needed before a system can be implemented, however desirable its objective, which will enable parents 'to compare their child's progress against agreed national targets of attainment and also to be able to judge how effective their school is', except in the most general terms. Nevertheless, the principle of attainment testing is supported. Where possible, we would like to see authoritative annual international comparisons of attainment.

The CBI has consistently supported the introduction of records of achievement for all school-leavers. We would like to see the associated counselling and profiling used to reinforce and complement the proposed nationally prescribed tests. Ensuring that records of achievement contain references to the foundation subjects studied and standards reached will be of considerable importance to employers. Further consideration needs to be given to how the national curriculum should be applied to those with special educational needs and whether all students should be entered for the GCSE examinations.

Members of the **British Institute of Management** were asked if, as employers, they felt it would be useful to have access to a prospective employee's school attainment records in addition, as is planned, to those of his or her school. Eighty-one per cent were in favour of having such access. The proposal that every school-leaver should have a record of achievement which includes not only formal examination results but other less traditionally academic attainments was even more welcome. Members saw that such a record would complement examination results in assessing the real knowledge, skill, understanding and potential of a young person.

Only 37 per cent of members said that they would rely more on examination results than the record of achievement as an indication of a potential employee's ability, but that this would vary according to the job in question. Attainment targets were expected also to be useful in focusing teachers' attention, throughout a child's school career, on what has been learned, allowing remedial applications at an early stage.

National Confederation of Parent–Teacher Associations – What a plethora of class lists, school lists, teacher lists and league tables will be produced and presumably published! Yes, parents are in favour of higher standards, better opportunities and more information about their children's progress, but we would do well to consider carefully whether such detailed monitoring and publicity would really be in the best interests of the children.

As parents we are particularly concerned to find ourselves caught up in the proposed mechanisms for enforcement of the national curriculum. We have moved on from being the 'partners in a shared task' mentioned in *Better Schools* to being seen now as 'Another essential part of the monitoring arrangements . . . able to pinpoint deficiencies'. Parents wish to be recognized as partners. They will firmly reject the role of snoopers. If this is not what is meant, we can only say that the form of words is most unfortunate. Having worked for years to promote better home–school links, NCPTA is dismayed at this reference to the role of parents, and a number of others in the document, which suggest that consumers and providers of education are to be set against one another. We would be very deeply opposed to any suggestion that parents should be seen as some kind of lay inspectors.

Muslim Educational Trust – Care must be taken while setting attainment targets to see that pupils for whom English is a second language are not unjustly categorized as low achievers.

The Chuch of England Board of Education is concerned that the proposals for the setting up of attainment targets and, within that process, the establishment of national tests will establish a hierarchy of subjects within the curriculum, i.e. (1) the three core subjects; (2) the other 'targeted' foundation subjects; (3) the 'non-targeted' foundation subjects (as being those one need not be too bothered about); (4) everything else (which has no real importance at all). Another concern is that, despite the emphasis placed on 'middle-range' children, the actual focus of attention will centre on high and low achievers. We await with interest to see whether attainment targets can be set which 'cater for the full ability range' and which reflect 'different abilities and maturity' at different physical ages. A further concern is whether the GCSE examining groups are really suitable bodies to moderate and administer tests in the primary schools.

Our most substantial concern in this area, however, [is that] while accepting the principle that parents should know in some detail how their children are progressing, we would not accept that this is best done by the 'publication' of test results in the way apparently being proposed. Those whose success in life have brought them to the position of being policy-makers can have little real idea of the debilitating effect of being publicly labelled a failure at any age, let alone twice within the period of one's primary schooling. If individual children's results are to be conveyed to parents, it must be (a) confidentially and (b) personally, with commentary and the opportunity for discussion. This will necessarily be costly in terms of teachers' time but is essential if the system is to work effectively, i.e. humanely. Testing will call for very sensitive handling – and a significant input of resources.

Methodist Church Division of Education and Youth – We support the setting of attainment targets and testing for diagnostic purposes and are pleased to note that the document values assessments carried out by teachers. Such targets and tests should normally, in the interests of the particular children, be devised by those who are sufficiently close to them to know their strengths and weaknesses. Regular nationally prescribed tests based on attainment targets which 'will establish what children should normally be expected to know, understand and be able to do at around the ages of 7, 11, 14 and 16' do nothing to encourage individual development.

The document looks forward 'to the point where every pupil is studying for and being regularly assessed against worthwhile attainment targets in all the essential foundation subjects'. It heralds a new mediocrity which will dull the classrooms of England from one national assessment to the next.

Roman Catholic Bishops' Conference of England and Wales – In the area of targeting we note that no account is taken of the needs of the slow learner. It is assumed that attainment targets can be standardized, and that 'established national standards . . . will reflect what pupils must achieve to progress in their education and to become thinking and informed people'. It would be quite wrong, however, to label the slow learner who fails to reach the 'standard' either as making no progress or as unthinking or uninformed. The value of standards depends in large measure on the flexibility of their application, a flexibility which seems to be lacking in the consultation document itself.

Appraisal is clearly an important part of education. It is valuable for the pupil as well as for the teacher and parent. It is to be hoped, however, that proper attention be paid to the way in which pupils are assessed. In recent years much has been learned about profiling and about methods of assessment, so that the talents and achievements of individuals can be more accurately recognized. Much care will need to be given to this area; whatever may be the intention one effect of some of the proposals (for example, the publication of aggregated results) will be to weight attention towards easily assessable written tests. If the principal type of assessment to be used is the written test, there will be many pupils who will thereby be unnecessarily disadvantaged. There are other equally valid ways of testing.

The National Association of Governors and Managers welcomes the requirements to give parents (and governors) the right to detailed information about the work going on in the school, but we are concerned that the proposals about testing and the publication of test results could have the effect not of raising standards but of distorting the teaching in order to produce apparently good test results. All the assessment and monitoring procedures appear to be concerned with the need to ensure that the new curriculum is fully implemented, and with judging pupils' performance only in its terms. We consider that governing bodies and other agencies should also have a duty to report on how well the new arrangements are serving the pupils in their school and to what extent the quality of the education provided in their school has been enhanced or diminished.

The Communist Party of Great Britain favours a national curriculum, and the right of all children, irrespective of sex, race, religion or family income, to have the best education available. But the intention is clearly for a rigid and centrally determined curriculum. The policy on testing which is proposed [will] structure the curriculum rather than check it. Assessment of the proper delivery of the curriculum is sensible. Assessment of children's progress (feedback) is an essential component of good teaching and goes on all the time. If there is concern over such assessments, than better teacher training is the answer, not testing from central government. The proposals give the impression of returning to a version of the 11+ examination, which most parents regard with horror – and threaten a subsequent 'go/no go' test for entry to the next class or school. It should be clear whether checking on schools, teachers or pupils is the purposes of a test.

When we consider what could happen in history, which version of historical events will count as correct? The gap between guidelines on the general content of schooling, and the laying down of precisely what shall be taught and when, becomes clearly visible when such questions are asked. We reject the proposed testing altogether.

4
Opting Out

THE PROPOSALS

Any maintained secondary school, or primary school with at least 300 pupils, will be able to apply to the Secretary of State to opt out of local authority control and be maintained instead by direct Government grant. The grant will be equivalent to the amount the LEA would have spent on the school, including its share of the cost of central services. The Government intends that the establishment of a grant-maintained school should leave the LEA in the same financial position.

The initiative in opting out can be taken by governors or by a substantial number of parents petitioning the governors, and an application will need the support of a majority of parents voting by secret postal ballot. Before approving an application, the Secretary of State will wish to be satisfied that the school has a secure future and that the governors and head are competent to run it. If the LEA proposes to close the school, he will decide the application to opt out before ruling on the LEA's plans. The school will not at first be allowed to change its character, size or age range; but, once it has established itself in its new role, the governors could make a public proposal, as LEAs do, to which objections could be made and which the Secretary of State would determine.

Parents of all local children will be able to apply for places. So will those who do not live close, and they will have the same entitlement to help from the LEA with transport. Those refused a place will have a right of appeal.

The foundation or trust at a former voluntary school will continue to own and run it and appoint a majority of governors. At a former county school the governors will become the owners; a new category of 'first' governors, who would have a long-term commitment to the school and would include members of the local business community, would form the majority. The Secretary of State would have a reserve power to appoint governors. The Government means to set up a trust as a centre of advice for governors and to promote the development of grant-maintained schools.

Staff employed wholly at the school will transfer automatically to the governors' employment. Those who work partly elsewhere may also be transferred after discussion with the governors and the LEA. Pay and conditions will be subject to the same statutory provisions. A teacher who did not wish to transfer and could not be redeployed would be deemed to have resigned and would not get compensation. Staff at grant-maintained schools would continue to have rights under employment law. The schools would have the right to appoint a teacher who does not yet hold qualified teacher status; and statutory probation arrangements would not apply.

THE DEBATE

How many schools in the escapers' club?

Jack Straw
Labour MP for Blackburn and principal Opposition spokesman on Education.

No single issue caused more trouble for the Conservatives during the 1987 general election than their manifesto proposal to allow individual schools to 'opt out' of local authority control. Even the *Sunday Times*, whose loyalty to the Conservatives was never in doubt, was forced to publish a major feature under the headline, 'Schools: Tory plan that didn't add up'. The policy failed and still fails to add up, for a simple reason – that it was set in concrete before it had ever been thought through.

The hostility of groups on the Right of the Conservative Party to local education authorities in general and Labour-controlled ones in particular is well documented. These groups have long been concerned about ways in which schooling for the majority of children could be prised away from LEAs, but without offending too deeply the principle that the State should ensure that education for compulsory-aged children should be free. Opting out seemed to provide the answer. The 'No Turning Back' group of Right-wing Conservative MPs published a pamphlet *'Save our Schools'* in 1986 with the proposition that LEA control over schools should be 'devolved down to the schools themselves', which would 'effectively become independent, autonomous units'. This model was the one which actually found some short-lived favour among Scottish Conservative ministers in the proposals for Scottish school boards from Michael Forsyth, Parliamentary Under-Secretary at the Scottish Office, now scrapped in the face of overwhelming public hostility.

For England the idea was refined in the Hillgate Group manifesto written by Baroness Cox. There she proposed that 'schools must be released from the control of local government and financed by direct grant from central funds'.

The Hillgate Group proposals were published in early 1987. In February 1987 the Conservatives leaked to the Sunday newspapers that opting out would form part of their manifesto proposals, but at this point – and who knows why? – serious study as to how this proposal would work seems to have been abandoned, with near-catastrophic results. When Mrs Thatcher was questioned about the proposals at a press conference on 22 May she was unbriefed. She chose to rely upon her instincts. So she told the world that opted-out schools could be selective ('it is up to the school to pursue its own admission policies') and that they would have freedom to charge fees ('so far we have not thought to preclude those schools from raising extra sums of money, and I think it would be wrong to do so. We should of course look very closely if there was any imposition of a fee upon children'). Within a day both statements were contradicted by Mr Baker. There would be no fees, and if a school was non-selective now it would remain non-selective once opted out.

Mrs Thatcher is enthusiastic about this policy. Mr Baker is not. It has been easy to spot the join. Mrs Thatcher has said that she expects 'most schools' to opt out. Mr Baker says that the 'vast number' of schools will stay in. Indeed, on Mr Baker's view it is now difficult to see exactly how a school would change were it to opt out. In a key speech to Chief Education Officers in January 1988 he said of opted-out schools that he was not

in the business of giving [them] an unfair advantage. They will not be funded any more generously than other schools in the neighbourhood. They will have to agree admission arrangements with me, preserve the character they have as local authority schools and ensure that they continue to serve much the same community . . . So schools which apply to opt out will not be doing it in anticipation of special favours.

So he has now said that opted-out schools will have the same funding as other schools in the neighbourhood; they will not be able to change their character; they will have no greater control over their staff than LEA schools under the new arrangement for local financial mangement. Given all this, the big question is: why opt out at all? What exactly is the point? To this, when challenged in the Commons Standing Committee examining his Bill, Mr Baker has chosen to remain silent.

No one can be certain whether opting out will be a damp squib or whether it will take off. That will depend among other things on the general political climate, on how much money the Government decides to put in to sell the idea, on how far LEA schools are put at a direct disadvantage with the new arrangements for local government finance. What is clear is that this ill-thought-out idea, if it does take off, will be 'to the disadvantage of a far greater number of children', for whom the local education authority would continue to remain responsible. That is not my opinion, but that of Mr Baker's own Conservatives in Surrey County Council. As this chapter will show, opting out has generated greater criticism than any other single proposal from Mr Baker. Of 22 Conservative authorities which responded to Mr Baker's document only six favoured the principle, while the 16 others were both opposed in principle and highly critical in detail. It is testimony to the confusion in which this idea was born that Mrs Thatcher has been unable to convince even her own most loyal supporters in Barnet, which includes her parliamentary seat. It was Conservative Barnet which concluded that opting out would end 'with a system loaded against maintained schools in an indefensively inequitable manner'. For once Barnet Conservatives are right.

THE ADVICE

Centre for Policy Studies – Although there are other ways of realizing the basic aim of freeing schools from centralized LEA control (e.g. by the use of vouchers), the Government's proposals provide a realistic way forward. We would, however, like to see the grant-maintained schools become even more like independent schools than the paper proposes, subject of course to the overriding condition that no fees are charged. We are very disappointed that the proposals do not permit the setting up of new schools to satisfy the needs of parents that are not at present being met. We have particularly in mind the need to encourage new Christian and Muslim schools. We strongly recommend that the Bill should enable such schools to opt into grant-maintained status.

Parents have the right to have their children educated in conformity with their own religious and philosophical convictions. The independent sector provides sufficient variety to guarantee this right to parents who can afford school fees; it is a right that should be enjoyed by poor parents too. LEAs, which are monopolies maintaining a 94 per cent share of the market, have for the most part ignored and continue to ignore this right. Some have chosen to use the schools to promote a particular ideology. They have been supported in this by other vested interests. For example, the National Union of Teachers has declared that the wishes of parents must not be allowed to stand in the way of comprehensivization, although it is abundantly clear that parents' objections to comprehensive schools fall under the definition of religious and philosophical convictions of the European Commission of Human Rights. These forces have destroyed pluralism in the maintained sector. Many parents feel that their children are trapped in schools whose values they deplore – manifested in peace studies used as propaganda for defencelessness, gay and lesbian lessons and hostility to Britain and its culture. They feel that the schools are being used for the promotion of secular and socialist values. Opting out offers a way out of this desperate situation.

One of the main differences between the independent and maintained sectors of education is that, in the latter, good schools can be – and often are – closed down. This never happens to successful independent schools. Good State schools are usually closed for one of two reasons. LEAs may embark on a programme of reorganization for socio-political reasons and against the wishes of parents. This happened with comprehensive reorganization, which was also opposed by a large majority of teachers. Or bad planning brings about an unforeseen and hopeless situation, which can only be salvaged by the sacrifice of good schools. For example, the first secondary reorganization led to schools which for the most part had non-viable sixth forms. The planners have been forced to consider stripping such schools of their sixth forms and centring them in a sixth-form or tertiary college. The snag is that all the sixth forms combined are often still not large enough to produce a viable sixth-form college. The planners are therefore driven to propose that schools in the same area that have big sixth forms should be stripped of their sixth forms too, to make up the numbers in the sixth-form college. This mismatch between the visions of the planners and the perceptions of the public is a recipe for a series of major dislocations.

By contrast, independent schools must either adapt to satisfy customer choice or die. Some do indeed go under, but never the successful ones. All have to try to keep up to the mark and, unlike LEA schools, have an immediate incentive to satisfy the public.

In a time of falling rolls, the proposed reform would offer the most effective and democratic way of deciding change and bringing about the closures recommended by the Audit Commission in the interests of efficiency. The commission's report showed that over the next five years there will be excess provision of around 1,000 schools. Some schools, which do not elect to leave LEA control, will have to close: it seems right and proper that these should be the schools that cannot attract pupils.

The proposals are good as far as they go, but we recommend certain extensions and modifications. Grant-maintained schools should not be subject to the legal framework of a national curriculum but should be in exactly the same position in relation to a national curriculum as an independent school. Even if a grant-maintained school were subject to a national curriculum it would still have a great deal of independence – in the very important hidden curriculum; in determining those parts of the formal curriculum excluded from the core and foundation subjects; and in the interpretation of the core and foundation subject syllabuses themselves. We believe, however, that the best way of deciding the school curriculum (mix of subjects, teaching styles, aims and characters of schools) is by the market. This serves the independent sector well. Schools are subject to HM Inspection, but within this limit are free to experiment and provide the variety of choice that a pluralistic society requires. The Government may wish to issue guidelines, but the schools should not be subject to statutory requirements to follow them.

One reason for Government action was to allow parents to escape the stranglehold on education being imposed in some left-wing London boroughs. The fear that left-wing heads might lead their schools to opt out of right-wing boroughs is understood. But to attempt to use the national curriculum to bring such heads back on the straight and narrow would be deplorable. It would betray the spirit of the whole enterprise, which is to restore power to the people, not to central government. Parents must be trusted. It is most unlikely that they would support the left-wing extremism that is much in evidence today. But if they did it would be their right to do so.

There should be no artificial restrictions, relating to size, on schools that are permitted to exercise the right to autonomy. Small village primary schools, for example, are likely to be among the main beneficiaries of an opting-out scheme. They are popular with parents, and many will only be saved if they are allowed to assume grant-maintained status. The Bill should make immediate provision for this.

Grant-maintained schools should have flexibility over their admissions policy. Selection is always required whenever the demand for places exceeds the supply. Even comprehensive schools can be selective. There seems little point in freeing grant-maintained schools from LEA control only to subject them to a control of a different kind. They should be allowed to operate their admissions system in the way that independent schools do, and we see no need for a statutory complaints procedure in respect of admissions, suspensions and expulsions. Governors should, within the existing law, be able to determine their own system of discipline. Since they will be able to ask unsuitable pupils to leave they can make higher demands, both academic and disciplinary, on their pupils. The principle of *in loco parentis* will be strengthened and this will have a beneficial effect on authority, not only in the schools but also in the home.

Grant-maintained schools should be as much like independent schools as possible, without of course being permitted to charge fees. The strength of independent schools is based on three important characteristics which have nothing to do with money or privilege: the ability to offer a distinctive curriculum which gives each school a special ethos; the ability to satisfy parental wishes; and an ability to stand on their own two feet and to be master of their own destinies.

We applaud your determination to take education out of the

hands of planners and return it to parents where it belongs. One thing is certain: the vested interests which have been responsible for bringing the education system to its present sorry state will rise up in fury against your proposals.

Audit Commission – Bearing in mind its statutory remit to review the economy, efficiency and effectiveness with which local authorities deploy their resources, the Audit Commission has considered the proposals against two principal criteria: their impact on value for money in educational provision, and their implications for local accountability.

The commission has consistently taken the view that the best insurance policy against waste and inefficiency is strengthened accountability at the local level. It has drawn attention to the failure of most local authorities properly to address the issues posed by the decline in the number of children of secondary school age. This is one of the principal obstacles in the way of an optimal utilization of resources. The commission is concerned that the proposals may slow down the process of schools rationalization rather than the reverse. There is a risk that local authorities will not propose schools for closure if they suspect that schools so scheduled will then try to opt out of LEA control. There is already some anecdotal evidence that authorites are taking this view and have suspended their rationalization plans. It would be unfortunate, to say the least, if the net effect of these proposals were to perpetuate a wasteful distribution of resources and perpetuate schools which could only provide good education, particularly within the Government's proposals for a national curriculum, at exaggerated cost. Competition can only further efficiency if schools which are demonstrably less successful in attracting pupils are closed. Unless this happens surplus capacity will simply be shuffled around.

The proposals envisage that closure of a grant-maintained school will be a protracted process, lasting at least five years. For LEA schools there is no proposal to improve the present cumbersome closure procedures. And the other difficulties LEAs face – school closures and reorganization tend to cost money in the short term – seem likely to persist. So there is a danger that existing inadequacies will be ossified.

There is no easy solution. Two alternative approaches are possible, but both have significant drawbacks:

(1) To phase in the proposals over a lengthy period, removing the admission limits first, to assist in clearer identification of unpopular schools, which should be closed, followed – after a spate of closures and reorganization – with the introduction of

the grant-maintained concept.
(2) To include in the legislation a tougher, efficiency-driven limit (perhaps including a separate sixth-form limit) below which, in the light of the national curriculum requirements, schools would not be allowed to opt out.

If neither option is acceptable then, unless LEAs can achieve rapid reductions in central costs, it seems likely that, if educational standards are not to suffer while these reforms are phased in, the Government will need to devote greater resources to education. It is difficult to assess these extra costs. But commission research shows that in an individual secondary school, if the annual intake falls from 180 pupils to 150, teaching costs per pupil can be expected to increase by 5 per cent if curricular standards are to be maintained. Other costs (30 per cent of the total) are mainly fixed and therefore, per pupil, increase by considerably more, perhaps 15 per cent in this example. With the pupil population set to fall further, any reduction in the rate of closure of schools is bound to increase total cost. Even a rise of one per cent in total educational spending by LEAs would amount to £120 million.

The future LEA role should be clearly defined. There should be an explicit recognition of the local education authority's duties (which could usefully include an obligation to act economically, efficiently and effectively) and an acknowledgement of the importance of the role it will continue to play. Without some clear assurance from the Government of the continued importance of local education authorities – even with reduced powers and a firm requirement to devolve responsibility – there is a risk of declining morale and a haemorrhage of talent with damaging effects on the quality of educational management.

While no one – least of all the commission – would wish to maintain that the accounting procedures in local authorities were ideal, the auditing and monitoring procedures have much to recommend them. They allow for accurate comparisons of expenditure and provision in different areas. The proposed reforms should not result in a diminution of this oversight. Where schemes of financial delegation are put in place then no formal change is required in the auditing structure. Grant-maintained schools pose a different problem.

It may be argued that where a free market in education provision is created the responsibility for ensuring efficient use of resources can be safely left to the consumer or his or her representatives (in this case the governors). But the 'market' created is far from perfectly competitive. Schools will still be heavily regulated by both central and local government. Their finances will still be closely

linked to those of the LEA through the operation of the per capita
funding mechanism influenced by the size and type of school. The
expenditure will fall to be audited by the commission as it leaves the
LEA. In these circumstances there would be advantage in grant-
maintained schools themselves being audited by auditors appointed
by the commission, with a specific responsibility for ensuring value
for money. This would assist local managers (governors and
parents) in providing them with comparative information on cost
and performance, and allow the LEAs and the DES to monitor the
economy, efficiency and effectiveness of individual schools.

Supplement to Audit Commission response
The establishment of a grant-maintained school involves a vote by
parents. If the school is to thrive after the vote – whichever way it
goes – all concerned must feel able to accept the result. The
proposals leave a number of points unresolved:

(1) The franchise. If both a child's parents have votes, single-
     parent families will be disadvantaged. If not, it will be hard to
     establish rules for one secret vote to be cast in respect of each
     child. Do parents have votes for each of their children in the
     school? Should parents whose children are about to leave the
     school have votes? How many votes would the LEA have on
     behalf of children in the care of its social services department?
(2) The rules for a quorum. The paper implies that a vote of two
     parents for, one against and the rest abstaining will lead to a
     proposal for grant-maintained status.
(3) Information prior to voting. The paper says that the governors
     will provide parents with their proposals, but any parents who
     are opposed to the proposals may lack access to reprographic
     facilities and the address list and therefore be unable to put
     their view. The legislation should provide explicitly for
     parents who oppose grant-maintained status to put their views.

To minimize waste and delay over applications to the Secretary of
State, it is important that there should be: prestated criteria by
which the Secretary of State will judge applications; a specified
maximum time period for him to give his verdict on any application;
a statement of reasons to be given with his decision on every
application. Experience with plans for schools reorganization has
shown that, without these, considerable harm can be done.

Where school rolls are falling, the possibility of an application for
grant-maintained status will tend to deter the LEA from making
closure proposals, even if no application is ultimately made. It is
proposed that 'as a guarantee of continuity', the Secretary of State
will be required to give five years' notice to grant-maintained

schools before deciding to terminate their grant. If LEAs are not to be put at a disadvantage it would surely be reasonable to give the same guarantee to an LEA before transferring one of its schools to grant-maintained status.

The legislation will need to make clear any special rights and duties of governors and any penalties to which they may be liable. Can governors be surcharged for waste of resources? Governors will be responsible for staff performance appraisal and for in-service training. The paper does not indicate where the expertise for these responsibilities will be found.

LEAs formulas for allocating funds to schools are liable to be altered from year to year. As well as alterations due to changes in total budgets, there may be alterations due to changes in the schools which they are funding. If the new, less restrictive admission arrangements lead to an increase in the number of small schools, funds allocation arrangements will have to be changed to ensure that these schools can continue to deliver the national curriculum. Such changes will affect grant-maintained and LEA schools in an LEA area. Grant-maintained schools may find it difficult to plan in the face of alterations in income over which they will have no control.

The presence of one or more grant-maintained schools has further implications for LEAs. The level of funding of grant-maintained and LEA schools is crucial to both. The paper envisages that 'LEAs will in future allocate funds to their schools on a per capita basis.' This contradicts the consultation paper on the delegation of financial management where an 'appropriate formula' is mentioned.

Paragraph 21(ii)(c) of the consultation paper makes clear that grant-maintained schools will be responsible for their own welfare services, but paragraph 25 ascribes to LEAs the duty to ensure that parents cause their children to receive full-time education, a duty for which the welfare service is responsible. The two paragraphs are inconsistent. For all those services currently provided by LEAs, including educational psychology and peripatetic support teaching, it is important that responsibility for providing them should be clearly assigned, either to the LEA or to the grant-maintained school.

The paper restates the duties of an LEA to secure the availability of sufficient schools for their areas. Since the LEA will have no say in parental choice between grant-maintained and LEA schools, admissions to grant-maintained schools or expulsions and suspensions from grant-maintained schools, it cannot predict what size of provision it will need to make. Furthermore, it will not be involved in the procedures which can lead to closure of a grant-maintained school. If it wishes to be sure to have enough places for all pupils who may need them, it will have to maintain a large surplus of capacity in its own schools. This would be extremely wasteful.

Professional Association of Teachers – The proposals in this consultative paper are based on a series of assumptions which we doubt: that there are a sufficiently large number of well-informed, well-intentioned and leisured people to provide suitable governors; that all parents make choices as to the administration of schools which are both wise and informed; that grant-maintained schools will be at least as cost-effective as LEA-maintained schools; that governors and parents are the people best able to improve the education service; that all schools will be improved if some of them acquire grant-maintained status; that willingness to assume responsibility is the same thing as capacity to discharge it. What is not in doubt is that there are many indications in this paper that it has been written in haste, without due consideration of all those important matters which will need to be satisfactorily resolved if grant-maintained schools are to come into being without doing irrevocable damage to the education service. We urge the Government to ensure that these matters are addressed.

We remain totally committed to the principle of equality of opportunity in education. This does not mean that we do not accept that different kinds of school are equally able to provide good education. We have never denied the right of parents to buy education for their children, if that is their choice, nor the right which parents have, and which the Government is seeking to extend, to express a preference about the schools their children attend. We look for safeguards to ensure that no particular kind of school was disadvantaged as compared with any other kind and that no child was disadvantaged because of the type of school he or she attended.

We believe that the parents from whom the Government has received indications that they would welcome the opportunity to run schools are unlikely to prove representative of the majority. While parents have, inevitably, a transient interest in the schools their children attend, the effective management of a school is a long-term task.

We challenge the view that 'the greater diversity of provision' which would result from the proposals would 'enhance the prospect of improving education standards in all schools', for we can see no means by which this would be brought about. How, if one school in an area opts to become grant maintained, will this improve standards in other local schools? We also challenge the view that diversity of educational opportunity, of itself, improves standards. it can produce unjust allocation of scarce resources and it can be divisive.

Initially at least, only schools with 300+ pupils may apply for grant-maintained status. The LEAs, therefore, will be left to run precisely those schools which are the least cost-effective, that is, the very small schools. This will need to be borne in mind when the relative cost-effectiveness of grant-maintained and LEA-maintained schools is considered.

We foresee a danger that, should a grant-maintained school become sufficiently popular, there will be pressure to reintroduce some form of selection as a means of avoiding overcrowding. If selection is to be reintroduced (and that would be a proposal of such importance as to merit a separate consultation exercise) then let it be because there is consensus that such a thing would be in the best interests of all of the children in our schools, not the by-product of a change in the way in which schools are administered.

A simple majority of those parents voting is not enough. to endorse an application for grant-maintained status. A simple majority of those voting could well be – indeed, is very likely to be if apathy runs at the levels revealed by some annual governors' meetings – a very small percentage of the parent body. That small percentage might be unrepresentative in terms of social economic grouping or in terms of race. No resolution to apply for grant-maintained status should be deemed to have been passed which does not have the support of a genuine majority of the parent body.

We wish to see a requirement that the headteacher and staff of a school are consulted after the governing body has published proposals but before the parent body is consulted. No proposals concerning the status of a school which do not have the whole-hearted support of both the headteacher and the staff can possibly bring about an improvement to the education of the children in that school. Our major concern about this consultative paper is the extent to which it assumes that it is governors and parents who determine the calibre of the education service. It is not. The quality of education on offer to the children in our schools is finally determined not by systems, nor by status, nor by economic or management theory: it is determined by the calibre, commitment and professionalism of the teaching force.

The association welcomes the proposal to establish an advisory body, independent of the DES, which will assist the governors of grant-maintained schools. If they are to succeed, grant-maintained schools will need all the advice they can get.

We have the proposals relating to staff. There is no evidence that many aspects of employment law, as it relates to teachers, have been considered. At best, these proposals are simplistic: at worst, they are shabby. An employee in a commercial operation has a number of statutory rights if the employer is bought out. For example, each employee's contract automatically continues on the same terms and conditions after the take-over, and recognized trade unions must be consulted about the change. The legislation must set out, quite specifically and in clearer terms than the current regulations, what the rights of teacher are prior to, and on transfer to, a grant-maintained school. One of these rights must be the right to belong to a trade union of the teacher's choice.

The legal framework of a grant-maintained school should be that the governing body is an 'associated employer' in terms of employment legislation. It is extremely important, and particularly if a grant-maintained school should fail, that the employee's position in terms of the counting of his or her continuous employment should be safeguarded.

It is nonsense to suggest that responsibility for staff appraisal and for in-service training should lie with the governing body if this means that it is believed possible for these things to be provided internally. Governors will have neither the resources nor the expertise for these tasks. A professional system of staff appraisal, and a properly planned programme of in-service training, is indispensable to the education service. Without them none of the Government's planned reforms will improve education in our schools. If grant-maintained schools do not have acccess to professional in-service training and if they do not have an adequate and just system of staff appraisal they will, quite simply, fail. The question, therefore, of who is to provide these services must be addressed. If they are to be bought in from the LEA, adequate funding must be available.

The suggestion that governing bodies will be able to employ teachers who have not taken normal initial training courses is completely unacceptable. Grant-maintained schools can only be justified if they raise standards: this will lower them. In our view the provisions of Schedule 5 (Qualified Teacher Status) of the Education (Teachers) Regulations 1982 should apply to grant-maintained schools. We also find the suggestion that grant-maintained schools should not be subject to the statutory probation arrangements which apply to teachers in LEA-maintained schools unacceptable, indeed inexplicable. Grant-maintained schools must not become the back door into the profession for the underqualified, the inappropriately qualified and the probation-shy.

No teacher should be disadvantaged because of the change of status of his or her school. The association totally disagrees with the proposal that a teacher not wishing to transfer to the new school, and whom the LEA was unable to redeploy, should be ineligible for compensation.

The Welsh Consumer Council believes that the fullest practicable development of community use of schools is in the consumer interest. However, the proposed changes could affect the availability of school buildings and equipment for use by the wider community. Community use of schools is about using school buildings and equipment to their maximum potential for educating children, for adult education and for a wide variety of other purposes by the whole community (including sports use, cultural events and activities, meetings, charitable activities, etc.). Its benefits include: increased consumer choice and, for some people (in rural areas, for example), provision of facilities which would not be available elsewhere and could not be econonomically provided otherwise; value for money for the taxpayer and ratepayers who finance schools; efficient use of resources, and reduced need for providing additional, costly, purpose-built leisure centres; benefits for the curriculum (e.g. contacts with community groups which might help class projects) and for home–school liaison (by making schools less isolated and forbidding places).

The Government supports the development of community use of schools. The DES offers extensive practical guidance to LEAs and schools in a series of papers which it has produced. The WCC is working with the Sports Council for Wales on a project to make more school sports facilities available to the public. The project is demonstrating that school sports facilities can be opened to the community on a wider schale than at present. It is also proving that provision of public sports facilities in this way is efficient and cost-effective and that reluctance to open schools to public use can be overcome.

The consultation paper on grant-maintained schools does not mention community use at all (except in the context of ownership of assets where there is already joint use). This is a major oversight since the transfer of assets from the LEA to a grant-maintained school will mean a change of ownership for an important local public asset.

Funding from outside the school budget needs to be available to facilitate the development and operation of community use. This applies to both GM schools and LEA schools with delegated budgetary responsibilities. At present, the LEA and district councils can put money into developments in schools as part of their respective policies and duties. Under the proposed changes, LEA-maintained schools may have within their school budget monies for community facilities. It is not clear whether capital grants to grant-maintained schools could be for the development or adaptation of facilities for community use. If schools have to find money for community use from their own budget, it will be competing with the eductional requirements of pupils and as a result, may be continually given a low priority. A funding body outside the school may also be in a better position to ensure that the wider needs of the community are not neglected.

The WCC is concerned that charges to the public for using school facilities should not rise to a level that is prohibitive to low-income consumers and local groups and organizations. We believe that poorer consumers and local groups should not be deprived of access to community facilities as a result of these proposals. If schools are required to finance entirely from within their own budgets the development and operation of community use of their schools, they may be tempted to set charges at a high level.

Consideration should be given to putting school governing bodies under a clear statutory duty to develop community use of their school. Clause 42 of the 1986 Education Act gives governing bodies responsibility for the use of school premises outside school sessions, and requires them to 'have regard to the desirability of the premises being made available'. This comes into force for existing LEA schools in 1988. We believe there is a danger that, in some schools, governing bodies' enhanced responsibilities for finance and staffing (and for other matters covered by the Bill, such as monitoring the national curriculum) will leave community use a marginal or neglected issue. Meeting these responsibilities will be vital to the effectiveness of the school, but it would be unfortunate if progress in expanding community use were slowed or reversed.

Social Democratic Party – An unstated objective [of these proposals] is the wish to provide local schools with the ability to opt out of local education authority control because of the activities of certain extreme LEAs. In recent months the activities of local education authorities such as Haringey and Brent have aroused considerable parental anxiety. It is also clear that another unstated objective is to allow the widening of selective education.

We do not oppose the idea of greater parental choice, the need for a plurality of providers of education or the idea of changing the relationship between schools and the LEA. But the context in which the Government is introducing these proposals – preserving grammar schools and extending selection by the back door – makes it impossible to support opting out in its proposed form. We agree that the distribution of power and influence in education between the DES, LEAs, school governors and parents needs to be reformed in the direction of governors and parents. Unlike the Government's proposals on local financial management and the national curriculum, which we broadly support, we do not believe that the opting-out proposals will achieve the decentralization of power or the rise in educational standards which is claimed for them. Neither will they solve the problem of abuse of power by extremist LEAs. Furthermore, we believe that if the proposals were implemented they would cause a number of serious problems, some technical, some very wide-ranging in their effect.

It is an openly stated aim of these proposals to preserve grammar schools by allowing them to opt out of LEA control. We believe that schools which opt out could rapidly turn into selective schools even, if not directly then indirectly – for example, by being the only school with a sixth form in an area which had decided to work on the tertiary college principle. The criteria that will be used in selecting pupils will revolve around such factors as the parents' ability to contribute to the school (financially or otherwise). We may therefore end up with selection socially, if not academically.

Opting out places far too much power in the hands of the Secretary of State and his department. What happens if the standards in a school which has oted out fall dramatically? The DES clearly will not be able to play nearly as effective a role as an LEA can in helping such schools. Equally, the LEA can be held to account much more easily than the DES, if such a spiral of failure occurs. It makes far more sense for the LEA to play a mediating role if relations in the school between governors and head or governors and staff break down.

We are concerned that there is no provision for opting back in to LEA control. It may well be that an enthusiastic group of parents and governors was replaced, over time, by a rather less enthusiastic group who wanted the school returned to LEA control.

We are also concerned that the implications for race relations and equal opportunities have not been thought through. The national curriculum is not enough by itself to ensure that opted-out schools offer equal opportunities to both genders and all races. If the proposals were implemented we would like to see the agreement to give a direct grant contingent upon a commitment to equal opportunities from the schools' governing body.

National Confederation of Parent–Teacher Associations – Recruiting personnel into the classroom who have not had normal initial teacher training will heighten disquiet. A great deal of progress has been made to achieve an all-trained profession, and to revert to the earlier unsatisfactory position may be regarded by many parents (and teachers) as a retrograde step. While parents wish to be assured of academic excellence, the presence in the classroom of a person in charge who has declared a dedication to the education of children by pursuing a prolonged period of teacher training is of equal if not greater importance to them.

The concept of 'first' governors is an interesting one. Clearly the Government wishes to replace what has traditionally been control by the LEA with control of governing bodies by 'first' governors. There can be no doubt that these will be every bit as difficult to find as are governors of a suitably neutral disposition now (the co-opted group). It seems an incredible concept that a school will be placed in the control of individuals who may know nothing of it, simply on the grounds that they are thought to have some necessary expertise. e.g. accountancy.

Since parental contributions will become more or less mandatory as schools struggle to survive, and there seems little doubt that the DES will have little room for manoeuvre in terms of overall funding levels, it must be concluded that this represents an attempt to shift the burden of funding State education much more from the public sector to the private one. Parents will not only pay for State education through rates and taxes but also through support they will have to give to opted-out schools. NCPTA is forced to conclude that the proposals for grant-maintained schools will damage rather than improve State education. These proposals must be resisted by those who are concerned about the majority of the pupils within State education.

NCPTA believes that strengthening the powers of the governing body further, and making major matters of school policy subject to agreement by a majority of parents, will achieve all the Government has stated it wishes to achieve through these proposals, and much more besides.

The Commission for Racial Equality would be concerned if, at some future date, grant-maintained schools sought to change their admissions policies in ways that indirectly discriminated against particular racial groups. The commission therefore welcomes the proposal that governing bodies would be required to publish statutory proposals regarding any changes in admissions policy or character of the school.

The commission is concerned that the development of LEA equal opportunity and multiracial education policies will be restricted if local authority schools opt for grant-maintained status. We estimate that at least 50 LEAs now have such policies and share the Swann Committee's view that they are an essential prerequisite to the development of an education appropriate to a multi-ethnic society. We fear that, if grant-maintained schools are no longer subject to LEA statutory duties under section 71 of the Race Relations Act, important developments in equal opportunities and curriculum development will be limited in their effectiveness. Grant-maintained schools should be encouraged to adopt the CRE's employment code of practice, and their articles of government should include principles similar to those applying to LEAs under section 71. We understand that the first city technology college has declared itself to be an equal opportunity employer and we would like to see this example followed by grant-maintained schools. The commission will be seeking to use the vehicle of the new Education Bill to secure the statutory power to make a code of practice for education.

Liverpool City Council notes with some dismay that the parents of contributory primary schools whose children will be the latter members of the secondary-school community are not to be consulted even though their children are likely to be more affected by any decision to elect for grant-maintained status than the children currently in the secondary schools concerned.

The secondary schools in Liverpool have in the course of the last four years undergone massive reorganization and endured all the disruption which this inevitably involved. They cannot sensibly be asked to cope with further periods of uncertainty and disruption.

If the proposals are implemented, there is a mssive problem of training, both of governors and heads of schools, and the question arises as to who is to provide and fund the intensive programme required. Liverpool sought to broaden the base of its governing bodies as long ago as 1974. Our experience since that time must cast doubt on the bility of governing bodies which may elect to apply for grant-maintained status to manage the schools without a major injection of professional resources to deal with very complex issues of budget, staffing, curriculum, etc.

It seems inevitable that the move towards grant-maintained status will lead to a progressive dismantling of the local authority as an education authority and, if this is the intention, then it is not an objective which should be achieved by stealth but one which should be openly stated.

In Liverpool four consortia have been established involving secondary schools and further education colleges so that they can work in collaboration in providing the best range and quality of opportunity for young people in post-16 education. The withdrawal of an unknown number of schools in the grant-maintained sector would breach these established arrangements and restrict the extent to which the authority can control post-16 provision.

London Borough of Barnet – Grant-maintained schools should be subject to exactly the same regulations as LEA-maintained schools in regard to the employment of qualified teachers. That no statutory probation is proposed implies a sad neglect of professional responsibility.

Should there not be provision for something akin to 'a schedule of dilapidation' in cases where governor wish to cease grant-maintained status so as to avoid the LEA having to take back and recommission a school building in a much worse condition than when it left LEA control originally? The proposals on assets seem underpinned by an unfair principle that schools should transfer from LEAs to grant-maintained status without compensation to the LEAs but that, in the event of the closure of a grant-maintained school and its reversion to the ownership of the LEA, the Secretary of State would be able to secure compensation for capital work undertaken at the school for which he had paid grant. This seems a flagrant case of 'heads the LEAs lose, tails the Secretary of State wins'.

The proposal to pay 100 per cent capital grant to grant-maintained schools seems unfair on voluntary-aided schools and the rationale of this proposal is not immediately obvious. It could provide a powerful inducement to voluntary-aided schools to seek grant-maintained status. (Perhaps this is the rationale.)

On the assumption that grant-maintained schools would become selective in one form or another and would admit pupils from a very wide area, it follows that the average travelling distance for every child in an LEA would increase; consequently transport costs would increase. Since it is proposed that the LEA should continue to bear this charge, this is another reason why the LEA would be in a worsened financial position. Decisions concerning the admission of pupils would effectively pre-empt a budget over which the LEA would have no control.

If these proposals were to result in a very large number of grant-maintained schools (reponsible, say, for educating 60 to 70 per cent of the nation's children), we perceive very grave implications. Everything involved in two of the principal responsibilities of LEAs, i.e. the provision and maintenance of a national system of education, will obviously become very difficult if not impossible. A third principal function of LEAs – monitoring educational standards, 'quality control', developmental work in curricular and related fields – will also become very difficult if not impossible. The ability of an LEA to set up administrative systems according to principles of fairness, reasonableness and the best interests of all schools and all pupils over such crucially important matters as admissions, exclusions and central services provided directly will become impossible.

Contrary to the hopes expressed in the consultation papers, this could result in an invidiously divisive system of perhaps as many as five tiers of schools throughout the country. LEAs could have little more than a residuary function providing education largely for those children who could not gain admission to or who were excluded from the other kinds of school.

Derbyshire County Council – No mention is made in the paper of the special position of pupils who have been the subject of a statement under the Education Act 1981. Governors of grant-maintained schools will have responsibility for admissions and, unless specific arrangements are included in the proposed legislation, it appears that the LEA could not require a governing body to admit a statemented pupil. The additional cost incurred in placing a pupil at an LEA school would fall on the authority, and these factors together would suggest that the 'Warnock' philosophy of integration will be hindered by these proposals.

Association of Metropolitan Authorities – We believe the suggestions in the paper are as much designed to create a demand as to satisfy one. We acknowledge that local policy initiatives in some LEAs have generated a large amount of controversy, but we have also noted that the local political and democratic process has been effective in commenting on, and securing amendments to, those policies. Public debate and the influence of the local community on the determination of local policy seem to us to be a more satisfctory way of promoting the strength of the local education service than encouraging some institutions to opt out.

The argument that permitting schools to opt for grant-maintained status will promote diversity and choice seems to us to be mere casuistry. The choice will be exercised by a particular group of parents at a particular time and will bind future generations of parents and children to a given form of education and type of school.

The provisos that grant-maintained schools would not be able to undergo a significant change of charcter, size or age range would be more reassuring to local authorities if they were more precisely expressed. How long will these provisos retain their strength? Would changes (which might be forced on the grant-maintained schools by population shifts, planning decisions or other developments) be permitted after five years, or ten? Will they be expected to adhere to their existing catchment areas or will they increasingly adopt the arrangements recommended for city technology colleges and have a wider catchment covering up to, say, 5,000 pupils of secondary age?

When considering an application for grant-maintained status there should be a specific obligation on the Secretary of State to consult with the LEA. But the Secretary of State needs to undertake wider consultations. He should seek the views of the head, the staff (especially given the staffing proposals set out in the paper) and of the wider community, especially of parents whose children might be expecting to transfer at the time when the school assumed its new status. We note that the head is likely in any case to be in an invidious position, as both a governor (probably), and therefore bound by governers' decisions with which he or she might disagree, and also as an employee of the local authority.

LEAs are still under an obligation to remove surplus school places, but unless the Secretary of State makes it clear that he would not view sympathetically applications for grant-maintained status which appear to arise largely from a schools' desire to avoid the consequences of reorganizations, rationalization schemes will be inhibited. It would be logical for decisions on grant-maintained status to be taken at the same time as decisions on the LEAs plans and not first, as suggested.

Presumably the Secretary of State will expect the promoters of changed status to produce a detailed prospectus for the school in its new guise. They should be able to demonstrate what experience they have in managing educational resources; that they are fit persons to run a school; and that a succession of able governors is reasonably assured. The Secretary of State will need to consider evidence of the place of the school in overall provision, numerical strength and the numbers likely to wish to transfer. He will also want information on the condition of the buildings, life expectancy of plant and equipment and the planning and development possibilities of the land. There would be a strong case for the local authority to be able to make a charge for providing some of this information because of the time involved and to deter frivolous inquiries.

If the proposals on open enrolment now under consultation are passed into law, grant-maintained schools are as likely to be adversely affected by them as are LEA schools. Grant-maintained status is not necessarily synonymous either with long-term quality or long-term viability.

The paper hints at the responsibilities of governors, but it fails to spell out the full extent of their liabilities, which they will have to discharge with little support. We foresee special difficulties for governors over funding. Since grant-maintained schools will apparently be corporate bodies, governors will presumably be personally liable for misuse of funds; and the degree of skill in financial management required is likely to be significantly greater than would have been expected of schools even under local financial management regimes.

We do not feel that those who have hankered after grant-maintained status quite understand the extent to which they will be on their own, and subject to public scrutiny over whether the claims they make for the new forms of management will be justified. Given those claims, governors of grant-maintainced schools will be expected to provide a better quality of eduction than was made available by the LEA.

We note that if a grant-maintained school became non-viable and ran into increasing financial difficulties, the state of equipment and buildings might significantly deteriorate. If it was subsequently to close, it would clearly become the responsibility of the local authority to provide for its pupils. The authority might incur considerable expense to bring the school back to a reasonable standard. In these circumstances, the Secretary of State should reimburse the authority for any additional expenditure.

If the local authority retains certain duties towards grant-maintained schools, and retains, through the existence of dual use facilities, a role in the mangement of the site, then we feel bound to raise the question of whether the authority should not be represented on the governing body, to the extend of one or two places.

Association of County Councils – In total the effect of the proposals would be the creation of a new sector of independent schools funded by tax- and rate-payers, with little public accountability. The consequences for the education of the great majority who would not be in GM schools could vary widely. Services which have been built up over many years to benefit areas (community education and recreation, special education and so on) would be inevitably disrupted and weakened. An element of seemingly permanent instability would be injected into the provision of public education.

The proposals will reduce effective choice of some parents and the atomization of the system will lead to diseconomies. The association is, therefore, opposed in principle to the concept of grant-maintained schools.

The possibility that the governors of a GM school could seek approval to alter its size, appearance or character at any time in the future in itself would seriously undermine an LEA's capacity to plan rationally for that part of its area.

It would be possible that a proposal in favour of GM status could be carried by the votes of parents who would have no children in the school when it achieved autonomy. It could certainly be carried on the votes of a minority of parents. A proposal to re-establish a school as an independent, publicly funded, institution should rest on a more secure foundation. Since they involve a significant change in the character of the school, proposals should be subject to the same regulations as those with which LEAs have to comply under section 12 of the Education Act 1980. As modifications to a proposal could, like the proposal itself, significantly affect provision in neighbouring schools, the Secretary of State should be required also to consult the LEA, and to consider any other representations and objections.

It is not clear what responsibility the LEA would have for pupils of statutory school age who might be expelled from a GM school. The possibility arises that, as autonomous although publicly funded providers, GM schools would be able to avoid responsibility in respect of some pupils.

There is reference to the Secretary of State's readiness to make a special grant available for approved dismissals or redundancies during the first 12 months of GM status. The proposal appears to encourage governors of GM schools to make decisions leading to redundancy or dismissal within a few months of the change of status and before they can themselves have had much experience of the performance of the staff involved. The proposal that staff who do not wish to transfer to the new employers and who cannot be redeployed by their LEA should be deemed to have resigned could put an unreasonable degree of pressure on the staff concerned. Governors and parents considering making an application for GM status should be obliged to consult staff employed at the school.

Clarification is needed on the position that would arise where a GM school refused admission to a pupil for whom it was the nearest appropriate school. Like the case of a suspended pupil, this illustrates the difficulty which LEAs would have in discharging their responsibilities for all pupils. It could well happen that a pupil did not gain access to a GM school even though it was the nearest and most appropriate, or that parents migh prefer to send a child to a local authority school. If it then fell to the LEA to provide transport to another school, considerable extra costs would be incurred.

Society of Education Officers – The proposals are another example of measures by the Government to weaken and bypass local authorities, and to inhibit good overall management of the education service. That is to be regretted. If there were gains in efficiency and effectiveness as a result, the process might have the beginnings of a defence; but the opposite will be the case. The society, regretfully, must say without equivocation that it cannot find any merit in the proposals.

The proposals will delay rationalization of provision. Decision-making by the Secretary of State on proposals for rationalization is already far too slow, despite constant exhortations from central government that the process be speeded up. The proposed provision that consideration of rationalization proposals will be frozen if an application for grant-maintained status is made will slow down the process even more. LEAs may well feel discouraged from embarking on consideration of rationalization schemes. There is already evidence that some authorities have abandoned consideration of rationalization for this very reason.

The proposals would involve inefficient and ineffective use of available funds and lead to wasteful duplication and loss of economies of scale, together with additional costs for LEAs, such as additional transport, without any benefit to the service. They would make the planning of a coherent, sensible, overall system of education in an area much more difficult, and changes in status or selective methods of operating admissions in grant-maintained schools would unilaterally change the nature of local authority schools.

At the very least, there ought to be a requirement that an application for grant-maintained status could not be made unless the majority of governors are in favour; the majority of staff are in favour; the majority of parents are in favour (and a clear majority of, say, two-thirds); and primary parents in the area can express a view, and that at least a majority are in favour.

Notwithstanding their formal status, for example, as comprehensive schools, the grant-maintained schools could select the pupils they wished to accept, and selection could be with reference to ability, motivation, social class, the level of affluence of the parents or any combination of those factors, so that a divisive system would be created, characterized by diversity of resourcing, esteem and standards, thereby reducing standards for many pupils. Choice for the majority of parents would be reduced, there would be no external scrutiny of the action of governors, parents would have no right of appeal on admissions or expulsions, and many would be put to serious inconvenience.

An LEA's assets could be taken away without compensation, the LEA would continue to pay debt charges, lose control of the asset and have no guarantee that the asset would be returned in due course in a satisfactory condition. The governing body of a grant-maintained school would not be accountable, could be controlled by party political interests and would nevertheless control large sums of public money.

It seems likely that, for future recruitment, the grant-maintained schools will be able to attract the best teachers because they will be offering generally able and well-motivated pupils for the teachers to teach, and that is bound to be attractive (and to the detriment of the LEA-maintained schools, of course). It is interesting to note that grant-maintained schools would be required to have arrangements for the induction of new teachers, such as lighter timetables. That, of course, is a very good idea, which many people have been pressing for a long time. If this means that the Government envisage that LEA-maintained schools can also be resourced at a level to make this possible, that would be very welcome and no doubt reflected in rate support grant arrangements. Alternatively, it could mean that new teachers in grant-maintained schools will have a better deal because the budgeting arrangements there will be better, on account of the 'voluntary donations' which will enable induction to be put on a good basis, and better than in LEA-maintained schools.

The proposal rests on the assumption tht schools are financed on a formula or unit cost basis generally. This is not true. Generally, the amount of money spent on each school each year, is determined by need. The Secretary of State would like schools to be funded in future on a formula basis. However, so far as is known, he does not know on what basis an equitable formula could be arranged, and neither does anyone else. It may well be that in due course a basis can be found. However, there is no guarantee of that, and it would be premature to set up grant-maintained schools on the assumption that formula funding will be a reality by 1989.

Society of Local Authority Chief Executives – Is the proposal not to require statutory probation arrangements going to lead to a lowering of standards? It seems contradictory that the Secretary of State should encourage the establishment of these schools presumably as part of the pursuit of excellence, whilst at the same time forfeiting the controls and safeguard which are designed to ensure the maintenance of standards in LEA-maintained schools. It is almost as if a governing body's belief in itself will be sufficient.

Perhaps the most significant impact of the financial proposals is that the grant system will result in financial preference for these schools. Each time a school opts out the LEA system it will increase the unit cost of maintaining the remaining LEA schools. That unit cost will then operate as a basis for calculating the level of recurrent grant thereby enhancing the finances of the grant-maintained school compared to the LEA school.

Church of England Board of Education – The introduction of grant-maintained schools on anything other than a very limited basis will constitute such a departure from both the letter and the spirit of the 1944 Education Act that the whole partnership between Church and State in the provision of education would be thrown into question. To rush into new legislation of such consequence after such a totally inadequate period of consultation is therefore quite unacceptable.

The consultation paper contains a reference to voluntary donations. We have to express a concern that grant-maintained schools could accentuate the tendency that aleady exists for inequities of provision in such matters as books and equipment to result from increasing reliance on voluntary donations. This would certainly happen in the case of some former voluntary-aided schools with substantial trust funds that are at present used for the 15 per cent contributions.

We are pleased to read of the intention, after consultation, to issue detailed guidance about the procedures to be followed. It is vital that such guidance should give a clear idea of the sort of case likely to impress the Secretary of State, if a great deal of ultimately unproductive work is not to be undertaken by hard-pressed DES and LEA staff, with consequent disgruntlement and disillusionment being felt by disappointed applicants.

Has any consideration been given to procedures relating to appeals against refusal to admit and against exclusions? As governors of aided schools, receiving only 85 per cent grant for certain expenditure elements, have to be subject to an appeals panel with some independent membership, it would appear wrong to us if grant-maintained schools, being 100 per cent supported from public funds, did not have to meet a similar requirement.

With the volatile nature of the education system (current Government initiatives hardly give a promise of stability for some time to come), it would appear to us that mobility of the teaching force should be facilitated. The waiving of the probation requirement could well inhibit a new teacher's moving from a grant-maintained school to a LEA school. The removal of the requirement for QTS in grant-maintained schools would be another barrier to movement between the sectors. (We would in any case, on grounds of quality, have reservations about the removal of this requirement.)

We note the requirement that grant-maintained schools would not only 'account to the Secretary of State for their disbursement of grant' but would also 'provide to him such detailed information as he required'. We foresee this inflicting on the schools the same restrictive controls on cash flow and expenditure which the voluntary- and grant-aided colleges have been experiencing in recent years – a form of control in many ways less conducive to effective management of resources than the controls imposed by local authroities.

The Diocese of Leeds Schools Commission agrees that parents should be able to have considerable influence upon schools and welcomes the enhanced powers which they will derive from provisions of the Education (No. 2) Act 1986 and proposals on financial delegation. But it is opposed to the Government's concept of allowing groups of parents the responsibility of running their schools as individual institutions.

As you will be aware, the Schools Commission acts on behalf of the trustees of the diocese in whom is vested under general trust deed responsibility for 115 voluntary-aided schools maintained by seven different education authorities. In all their dealings the trustees and School Commission have regard to the efficient provision of Roman Catholic education over the diocese as a whole as well as to the best interests of individual institutions. The general trust deed arrangements in the Roman Catholic sector differ from those

historically adopted by the Church of England authorities whose
schools more often have indiviual trusts. The commission feels that
the general trust deed approach leads to much greater efficiency and
is in the best interests of the parents and pupils of the area as a
whole.

In equity and justice the Church believes that the same types of
educational opportunities should be available to children throughout the diocese. Without wishing to appear either too paternalistic
or patronizing, the commission feels that in assisting parents with
their prime responsibility of educating their children the Church
and its commission is best able to assess the degree of support
required not only by individual familes but by groups of families in
different localities. The commission fears that the Government's
proposals will be counter-productive to their declared intention of
enhancing the prospect of improving educational standards in all
schools. Rather they could prove socially divisive and detrimental to
standards of education and pupil achievement in the majority of
schools.

The commission feels that the best interests of the trustees as
owners of the sites and buildings of the schools would not be
sufficiently safeguarded. Parents are a fluctuating and transient
group who might, with the best interests of their own children at
heart, take decisions contrary to the long-term interests of the
maintenance of the site and buildings of the school. If grant-
maintained schools are to be considered, legislation should require
the consent of the trustees before approval for grant-maintained
status were granted by the Secretary of State.

Diocese of Westminster – Cardinal Hume, who has over 200
maintained Catholic schools in his diocese of Westminster, wishes to
emphasize the indivisibility of this provision. By this he means that
a pattern of schools has been established throughout the area as a
result of the 1944 Education Act in order to provide a Catholic
education for every Catholic child, but first and foremost for the
poor and those deprived of family affection. The proposed legislation could have a most serious effect, if not even completely destroy
the provision which has been established over the last 40 years,
unless the new Act incorporates explicitly a provision to safeguard
the rights of a diocesan bishop/trustee with regard to the schools
which have been founded by, or passed into, the trusteeship of the
diocese.

The application of a Catholic school for grant-maintained status
can only be correctly weighed against the interests of other Catholic
schools in the diocese by the ordinary or bishop who has an overall
responsibility for the provision of Catholic education in that area.

Although it may be that a bishop might agree to the wish of a school or schools to seek grant-maintained status in the general interest of itself and the diocese, the only certain way of preserving the Church's position would be to define by statute the need for such an agreement, and we earnestly request that this may be so incorporated in the Act.

Free Church Federal Council – One of the stated aims of the Government's proposal, to make schools responsive to parental wishes, is hardly matched by the proposal's detail. We fail to see how the composition of a governing body, with seven parents out of a total of 18 or 19 governors for a school which might have 1,000 pupils, secures responsiveness to parental wishes.

National Association of Governors and Managers – Governors in grant-maintained schools will be asked to take on many responsibilities and will be responsible for the way in which educational resources, provided by the whole community, are spent in one school. It is not clear to whom these governing bodies will be accountable, or by whom they will be appointed, especially once the 'first' governors' term of office has expired. If these schools are to be the direct responsibility of the Secretary of State it is difficult to see what practical say the local community will have. We also have serious reservations about the suggestion that a minority of parents could oblige the governors to apply for grant-maintained status. At the very least, there should be some quorum required and something more than a simple majority for any decision to apply for grant-maintained status. We hope that a way can be found of recognizing that there is a wider interest in the community's investment in a school than that of current parents.

Universities' Council for the Education of Teachers – There is no indication in the consultative paper that any relevant experience of schools and education will be sought in any governor of a former county school. A governing body composed in this way may be incapable of discharging the role envisaged in the paper. In those circumstances standards of achievement might fall markedly. In the very successful governing bodies of many independent schools new governors are usually chosen with great care to achieve a spectrum of business, industrial and educational expertise. There is usually the inclusion, too, of persons from higher education. It is essential that governing bodies should include persons of experience in education if they are to recruit and retain good teaching staff.

National and Local Government Officers' Association – The proposals assume that the DES has an unlimited capacity to assume responsibility for an unknown number of schools and retain sufficient day-to-day contact with them in order to provide assistance and guidance as required. We very much doubt that this is the case, and indeed question whether the role of the DES should be to act as a surrogate LEA for schools. The indication that the Government will 'assist the creation' of a body to provide advice on opting out and possibly assume some administrative functions actually confirms this.

This particular proposal is alarming on two fronts. It suggests: that the Government does indeed have the resources to opt into the development of the education system – in contradiction of its pronouncements in recent years – but is only prepared to use them in furtherance of one part of that system and specifically to undermine local education authorities; that the Government believes a national body will be able to deliver administrative services effectively to schools scattered across the country. What advantages does this offer over the local delivery of such services by LEAs who are both closer to the schools and know their particular circumstances and needs?

National Union of Teachers – How is it possible for people with other major demands on their time to acquire the experience and expertise to run schools? The demands of a modern educational system will be new territory for many whose experience of schools is limited to their own school days.

The union believes, and indeed so does the Secretary of State, that not many governing bodies will seek to become grant maintained. If this is the case, it is the implications for those schools which will remain in the local-authority-maintained system which should be the major focus of concern. But the paper is largely concerned with the bureaucratic arrangements for the stablishment of grant-maintained schools. This leads to the assumption that what is proposed is really a means of reintroducing in a covert manner an elitist and centrally controlled system of direct grants schools on the lines of grammar schools, under the guise of increasing parental choice. The large majority of parents have expressed support for the comprehensive system and have opposed proposals to reintroduce grammar schools and selection where LEAs have brought forward such plans. We therefore believe there is not a mandate for the proposal as the Government claims, because the full ramifications have not been explained to the public.

Despite the Secretary of State's confirmation that grant-maintained schools would provide free education, the hidden agenda underlying the statement that they would be able to accept voluntary donations from parents and others in the community appears to be that, in the longer term, Government grant could be reduced if the school was well supported financially by donations from parents and other sources. This proposal represents a trend towards the privatization of the publicly provided education service. We would be fundamentally opposed to such a trend.

The Secretary of State wishes to be able to appoint additional governors (foundation or 'first' governors) to assist in the running of grant-maintained schools. In our view, it would be an improper use of patronage for the Secretary of State to appoint governors. The paper envisages that all that would be required of these governors would be 'commitment'; that they should be local people (including the business community). We are sceptical that such people will be willing and able to take on such onerous commitments, particularly in view of their responsibility in delgated financial arrangements.

The union hopes that the proposed model articles of government for grant-maintained schools would enable them (unless they were already selective schools) to discriminate in their admissions policy on grounds of ability, race or special needs. If this were not the case we would be extremely worried that such schools would attract only white, middle-class children of articulate, well-paid parents, thus reinforcing and exacerbating existing social divisions. On the other hand, it is possible that the proposals might be used by groups of parents of one particular religious or cultural affiliation to establish an exclusive school for their own group. We consider that this again would undermine principles of social cohesiveness in a pluralist society. We are against segregation, which would be encouraged by the establishment of such schools, and for educating children together for life in a society which accepts and values differences and does not seek to exclude them or deny them.

College of Preceptors – The paper states that 'The greater diversity of provision . . . should enhance the prospect of improving standards in schools.' In view of the Government's other proposal of a national curriculum for all schools, which in itself is intended to enhance the prospect of improving standards in schools, this present proposal would appear to be unnecessary. Furthermore, it is in national terms unworkable. Only in prosperous urban areas where there is a multiplicity of available schools can this proposal have any chance of being operable. In rural areas where there is no readily available choice of schools, where private financial support might well prove minimal and where the school unit is probably too small to be financially viable without an extra high level of support, there is little or no chance of success. The requirement to provide more transport would also adversely affect viability.

The Conservative Family Campaign warmly welcome the government's proposals to extend parental choice by allowing maintained schools to opt out of LEA control. We hope that all schools, even those with less than 300 registered pupils, will be able to exercise this option as soon as possible. In rural areas, there may be even more support for a local school opting out of the LEA.

The one major area where we would disagree with the current proposal is that the school is not going to be allowed to change its character. This seems to us to be an unnecessary restriction, and given the clear wishes of a majority of parents in the United Kingdom (as expressed in an opinion poll in September 1987) that the majority of parents wish to have grammar or selective education for their children from the State system, then a change from for example comprehensive to selective should be allowed and indeed could be one of the major reasons why parents would wish to see a school opt out of the LEA. In any case, the definition of 'character' needs very careful writing because it could be again that parents have been unhappy about the approach of an LEA's teaching towards for example peace studies, sex education, race relations or Christianity, and this is the main motivation for them wishing to take a school into a more independent relationship. Are we to say that these matters, which concern many parents and which are the cause of much discontent, would not be allowed to be changed if the school were to become grant-maintained?

All the desired objectives in the consultation paper could be achieved, and more besides, and for all parents, if the Government were to commit itself to a system of education vouchers. In many ways this would be even more administratively simple to operate than the structure now being put forward for opting out.

We disagree with the concept that grant-maintained schools should not be able to charge fees. Autonomy means independence, and we do not for one moment believe that a vast majority of the schools which become grant-maintained would wish to become fully fledged private independent schools with extremely high fees. They may however wish to offer certain extras which may require greater funding than the Government feels willing to provide. They should therefore have the possiblity of charging fees.

Bow Group – Although not stated in the document it seems that the proposals were formed with left-wing LEAs in mind. They would enable schools to escape the clutches of the 'loony' Left to return to the more conservative views of the parents and school governors. However, this could easily prove a very blinkered view and the whole situation could be reversed if, for example, a school were to be in a right-wing LEA with a left-wing governing body. Becoming grant maintained would enable the school to continue along a left-wing path regardless of more moderating influences from the LEA. This is surely not what the present Secretary of State intended. In addition, is a socialist government going to allow a school with a right-wing governing body to become grant maintained in order to escape a socialist LEA? The proposals put too much emphasis on the power and ability of governing bodies.

The Council on Tribunals has responsibility for supervising appeal committees dealing with admission to schools, special educational needs and, latterly, permanent expulsion and reinstatement. The document is silent on how admission policies would be formulated and whether parents who wished their children to attend grant-maintained schools would have a right of appeal against a refusal. It is unclear whether there would be any right of appeal against expulsion or how these proposals would affect children with special educational needs. At first sight this appears to be a weakening of parental rights of appeal, and the council would therefore like to hear more detailed proposals.

The Association of Voluntary-Aided Secondary Schools is extremely concerned at the possible effect on schools acquiring grant-maintained status of their ceasing to enjoy the benefits of the advisory services provided by local education authorities. Particularly in connection with in-service training, appraisal of teacher and the handling of organizational and disciplinary problems involving teaching staff, these benefits are very substantial. The association urges that renewed attention should be given to the future viability of local authority advisory services in the new situation. If any appreciable number of LEAs find themselves unable to continue offering a comprehensive advisory service to grant-maintained schools, consideration will need to be given to setting up a separate centrally financed advisory service, possibly organized regionally and linked to HM Inspectorate.

Special Education Needs, National Advisory Council – We consider that it is unacceptable that parents who are temporary users of a school should be given the power to change the character of the school for ever. We consider that the LEAs task of providing efficiently for children across the full range of needs will be made more difficult by the combination of the Government proposals. The net effect of some children could be a worsening of educational opportunity.

If schools may opt out of LEA control, we would wish to be assured that parental and governing body responsibilities under the

Education Act 1981 still apply. We would like to know the nature of the arrangemetns whereby the informal and statutory involvement of advisory support services would continue to be available to children with special educational needs and how any additional teaching or ancillary support, regular support to the child or to the school staff by specialist advisory teachers as recommended in the statements under the Education Act 1981, and in-service education of teacher would be secured.

The National Deaf Children's Society is alarmed that the document contains no reference to schools which make provision for children with special educational needs, whether these needs are the subject of a statement or not. Absence of such mention indicates that the Secretary of State has not considered this substantial group of children in his deliberations. We cannot accept that the proposals are conducive to the principle of parental choice in special educational provision, nor do they show an understanding of the machinery of such provision or the needs which make such provision necessary.

The Children's Legal Aid Centre believes that, if this scheme does go ahead, school students as well as parents should participate in the vote as to whether or not the school should opt out of local authority control. Since it is their education which is being determined, they are as entitled as their parents to have a say.

We would also like to express our general disappointment at the way the consultative papers fail to take account of children with special educational needs, and thus discriminate against them. The national curriculum document virtually ignores them, and the opting-out proposals pose serious threats to them, as others have pointed out. We trust the legislation will properly safeguard the needs of these children.

Campaign for the Advancement of State Education – We totally oppose this scheme. The best guarantee of an effective and responsive system is the vigilance of those who lie nearest. Locally elected members are accountable to their citizens. We support the measures in the 1986 Act to give school governors and parents more say within the local system. This in itself is a check on the abuse of power. We think it morally wrong that one generation of governors and parents should be able to remove from community control schools which past generations have worked and paid for, and future generations look to. Education is not a transaction but a shared responsibility. Schools are ours in trust.

The proposals for the future management of these schools seem incoherent and offer frightening uncertainty for children. Like the authors of the 1986 Act we believe that a school succeeds through the living interest of its parents, staff and community, not vague 'local worthies'. No such living interest will be guaranteed by cutting schools adrift. We are shocked that schools which opt out should be able to appoint unqualified staff. We object to asking LEAs to finance schools over which they have no control. Above all we believe that this plan, with open enrolment, will lead to racial tension and ultimately apartheid.

5

Local Financial Management

THE PROPOSALS

All secondary schools, and all primary schools with more than 200 pupils, are to be given responsibility for managing their own budgets. Each education authority, after consulting school governing bodies during 1989, is to publish proposals for allocating its resources among its schools. Governing bodies will become responsible for expenditure on staffing, books and equipment, heat and light, cleaning and rates. LEAs will remain responsible for home-to-school transport; for providing advisory, inspection and other services; for the administration of pay, tax and superannuation. Governors may provide meals if they can offer as good a service at the same or lower cost.

Governors will be responsible for selecting heads and other teachers, for promotions and decisions on redundancy; but (except in voluntary-aided schools) LEAs will remain the teachers' employers, and will have to serve any notices of dismissal. Governors could also take on extra teachers if they could meet the cost. Governors will be offered training for their new responsibilities.

(Responses to the consultation document led to certain changes. When the Bill was published it placed an obligation on governors to consider the advice of the Chief Education Officer when appointing staff. It excluded the proposed requirement that every LEA should submit a scheme of delegation by September 1989, although Mr Baker has said that he thinks that date is 'a realistic target'.)

THE DEBATE

What limits to self-sufficiency?

Philip Merridale
Chairman, Hampshire Education Authority

The principle that delegated management produces effective decision-making should need no advocate. Many schools already have
control over substantial parts of their budgets and can decide
priorities within them. This trend is growing and would inevitably
continue to do so without the Bill. Few sensible people would wish
to defend the notion that the head of a multi-million-pound enterprise should have to seek consent before having a broken window
repaired.

However, in seeking *total* financial delegation, imposed by the
force of law, the beguiling simplicity of the original proposition
collides sharply with vexing problems. How is the money to be
fairly distributed between schools? Can a formula be devised which
is sensitive enough to reflect the many differences between schools,
but yet not so complicated as to defy understanding? The daunting
example of the rate support grant mechanism springs to mind –
constantly adjusted, this way and that, and yet always producing
seemingly perverse results; understood by nobody and reviled by
all. Councils that have experimented for some years with financial
delegation have yet to be fully satisfied with the outcome.

Where some of the total money available is held back, then the
distribution formula is perhaps not so critical. The aggrieved or
crisis-striken can do an 'Oliver Twist'. The present wording of the
Bill, however, clearly intends that the LEA bowl shall be well
scraped at the first delivery. Is the school to be responsible for
maintenance and repairs? Will parent governors then be tempted to
postpone long-term needs in favour of short-term advantages like
extra books or staff? Should this happen, what would be the legal
position of the LEA which owns the school?

Other powers to be delegated include the hiring, firing, promotion and deployment of staff and most of the other actions normally
regarded as those of an employer. The Bill says that the LEA will be
the employer and thus, normally, would be answerable as such
under the Employment Acts. Since, manifestly, the LEA cannot
usurp the delegated powers of the governors, it cannot be held
responsible under the Employment Acts. To reconcile this paradox,
clause 139 has been grafted into the Bill. It seeks to give the
Secretary of State powers to 'make modifications' to the Employment Acts as they relate to this Bill. Seldom can it have been felt

necessary for an Act of Parliament to be proposed which gives a
minister power to make up the law as he goes along. Patently it is an
honest attempt by civil servants to draft an answer to the unanswer-
able. Either teachers are employees of the LEA or they are not.
They cannot be marooned in a kind of legislative limbo. A possible
suggestion would be to give teachers access to the LEA appeals
procedure, which they have at present, and then the LEA would be
answerable for its decisions.

If the local education authority employs the teachers in its
schools, it should, of course, be required to offer not only the
'bread-and-butter' administrative services like payroll and
pensions, but also an active training and staff career-development
policy. If, on the other hand, schools are to become islands of self-
sufficiency, then an alternative source of support must be found.
Support has always been forthcoming over the vital task of appointing a new head teacher. The Secretary of State has responded in the
Bill to the many fears, expressed during consultations, about
leaving schools to face this entirely alone. The advice of the Chief
Education Officer must now be asked. Will this prove enough to
ensure fully considered appointments?

Delegated self-sufficiency may well make a strong appeal to some
staunch and supportive governors, to the great benefit of schools.
Others may perhaps blench at the full magnitude of the tasks
confronting them. Training, advice and support will clearly be
needed, together with the diplomacy to offer it without offence. It
will not be achieved without costs being incurred, which should be
recognized.

It is clearly apparent, throughout the text of the Bill, that most of
the confusions in the wording arise from the built-in conflict
between the philosophy of retaining the ultimate accountability of
the local authority for the provision of education, and the opposing
view that education should be provided by free-standing institutions in competition with each other. It is not possible for either
argument to be wholly victorious; hence the need to reconcile
contradictions.

One contradiction from outside the Bill could perhaps helpfully
be removed. The Local Government Bill, at present before Parliament, requires local authorities to take steps to organize competitive
tenders for services – including such things as school meals. The
Education Bill will, of course, give this responsibility to governors
and not the local authority. It would be a useful first step to decide
which of the two Bills the Government wants to apply.

THE ADVICE

The Association of County Councils wholly endorses the principle that decisions on priorities and spending should be taken by those closest to the point of delivery, provided that the decisions are consistent with needs, overall policies (from central and local government) and proper management of public expenditure. Those concerned need to be trained and suported and they must be accountable. Resources must be adequate.

The Government's proposals stress the importance of LEA initiatives and experience in developing schemes for local financial management (LFM) in schools. The document admits these are experimental and mentions the development of 'appropriate management systems to underpin them'. LEAs who have moved down this road have encountered a number of problems and none has claimed, yet, to have overcome all the difficulties. The consultative paper moves directly from a development which is still at the pilot stage to propose legislation to enforce it on all LEAs. Sound administrative practice would suggest that compulsion where there are still problems to overcome would be inappropriate.

LEAs will have been required to reconstitute governing bodies on the lines laid down in the 1986 Act by the time they undertake consultation on schemes for delegation. These newly formed bodies may, understandably, have some concern about governors' individual or corporate legal and financial responsibilities, including questions which the paper does not address. It is suggested that governing bodies, at least for a defined period, should be allowed to indicate that they do not wish to accept the responsibility for local financial managment and that the local authority should be enabled to prepare schemes for a limited number of schools.

The Secretary of State intends to take powers to approve, amend, or reject LEA schemes of delegation. There is a welcome and realistic recognition that authorities might wish to vary schemes in the light of experience. The consultative paper goes on to propose that such varitions would need to be submitted to the Secretary of State for approval. This seems to illustrate neatly the paradox which arises from a proposal to impose a detailed local freedom through central legislation. The procedures will be cumbersome and unnecessary, and involve civil servants in making narrow judgements on matters which could vary considerably according to local circumstances. The legislation, although directed towards devolution, removes many critical decisions from those most closely involved.

The document sets out in some detail the points which LEAs would be required to take into account in preparing their proposals.

They would be expected to calculate central expenses first and deduct these in aggregate from the total amount to be spent on all schools. The remainder would then be allocated to schools on a formula (agreed with the Secretary of State) which would have to take some account of differences between types and sizes of schools. The list of items of central expenditure contains serious omissions. A number of vital central functions would need to be added. The strict overall formula funding approach is a reflection of a 'top-down' approach to management and, as such, an inefficient way of assessing the needs of individual schools. This goes to the heart of the proposals. They are intended to give as much freedom of decision as possible to governors so that they can take full account of the particular needs of their own schools. There is however a potential contradiction. The wider the area of activity covered by the formula (and therefore the less money available outside it) the higher the possibility that some schools will be adversely affected. For example, a school with a less than averagely efficient heating system would suffer badly from a severe winter. A school with a large proportion of staff at the higher points of their incremental salary scales would find that it could afford to buy fewer books than its neighbour. A school which experienced a sharp drop in numbers would need support above the level of the formula. If that was not available the school would probably be unable to meet commitments such as the proposed national curriculum. Unless the LEA was able to hold money back in order to give these schools some special assistance, inequity would be built into the system.

The adoption of local financial management would mean that LEAs would no longer be able to make an assumption about aggregate underspending and would therefore have to budget for the full amount. As that would then be disaggregated by schools, which would have an incentive to spend, overall spending would be higher (or 'savings' lower).

The need to be able to respond flexibly to the different circumstances of schools provides one reason for retaining additional moneys in the central fund and therefore limiting the scope of the formula alloctions. There are others. For example, the Government has wished to encourage the development of computer education programmes in schools. LEAs need to be able to hold a central reserve to foster such developments. In a different way central government's emphasis on 'value for money' can sometimes only be satisfied if there is a capacity to enter into contracts covering a number of institutions or even the whole of an LEA area. Block purchasing arrangements for fuel, food and even books and arrangements for such work as grounds maintenance to a number of establishments all provide examples of the potential economies of scale – and value for money. They can, equally, be seen as inhibiting freedom of decision at operational level. There is always a balance to be struck, and LEAs are familiar with the problems. LEAs are better placed to judge the balance of advantage than civil servants, who are inevitably remote. If the Government still believes it necessary to legislate, it should simply require LEAs to prepare schemes for financial delegation to governing bodies which must include a substantial part of school's recurrent expenditure excluding staff salaries and which may include an element for salaries.

The paper proposes that governors' responsibilities might be limited to internal repairs, maintenance and decoration. This would not mean that governors could avoid all difficulties if the money for these elements had to be included in the formula. The repair of a central hearting system could absorb a disproportionate amount of a school's formula budget in one year, and schools which had not been redecorated in the relatively recent past would similarly be at a disadvantage. It would be more reasonable to give governors responsibility for work up to a fixed cost.

If schools were allowed to transfer expenditure from youth, adult and community education budgets under local delgated schemes it could disrupt LEA planned provision over an area and bring conflict with other groups, such as district councils in the operation of joint-user schemes.

The ability to carry forward underspending is not a feature of central government's own funding practice. It must be an important feature of any scheme intended to give more freedom for local decisions on priorities if, for example, a school is to accumulate sufficient money for the purchase of a major item of equipment. However, it is obviously important that there should be safeguards to ensure that schools do not become involved in situations where they would have difficulty in meeting their liabilities and it would be essential for central government to ensure that its own arrangements for grant to local government would not lead to penalties to the authority as a result of variations in the aggregate of schools' end of year spending.

The consultative paper suggests that schools might need additional guidance in the light of health and safety responsibilities delegated to them. It is not clear whether LEAs would in fact be able to delegate their own responsibility, and it is clear that schools would need not only guidance but expert opinion.

The paper identified some of the factors which could affect predetermined school budgets. These include variations in the number of pupils on roll and pay increases. These and other contingencies (such as unexpected increases in inflation rate or mid-year government reductions in public spending) would constitute a case for adding to the central fund. It is at this point that the

consultative paper seems to come closest to recognizing the problems that would undoubtedly arise from a strict application of the
formula funding approach.

The document proposes that, having determined the amount to
be spent on central services, LEAs should then calculate and
publish the notional share of that expenditure 'which *might* be
attributed to each school'. It is not at all clear what value this paper
exercise would have for the schools concerned. The notional calculations will seldom have any direct relationship to the actual
spending on individual schools. The calculation will provide a basis
for determining the amounts which would be paid to grant-maintained schools but appears to have no other relevance or purpose. At
the end of each year LEAs would be required to publish information
on the actual expenditure at each school and governors would be
required to demonstrate how the school has responded to the
national curriculum. The paper sugggests that parents would then
be able to 'evaluate whether best use had been made of the resources
available'.

This proposal is obviously intended to provide some sort of
accountability links between governors and parents, but the picture
that will emerge could all too easily become confused. A reduction
on spending on, say, science equipment might be necessary as a
result, for example, of a combination of a cold winter with above-
average heating bills and an unusually large entry for GCSE. The
relationship may be obvious, but parents and others might take the
view that the problem was caused by an overall shortage of resources. Governors, who would have no responsibility for the primary
decision about the level of resources available, would be likely to
support this view. The proposals seem designed therefore to ensure
the establishment of more active and better informed pressure
groups for additonal spending on school-based education. That will
be a welcome outcome for many but it also demonstrates a major
flaw in the proposals for accountability. No evaluation of a school's
performance can be complete unless it is seen against the background of local and, increasingly, central government policy on
overall resources.

Although much of the detailed prescription for financial delegation appears unworkable to authorites which have had experience of
developing such schemes, most LEAs would accept the broad
principles. The proposals for control of staffing raise a number of
even more difficult points. They are impracticable, expensive and
inefficient. The LEA would continue to be the employer, with
responsibility for appraisal, probation and in-service training.
LEAs' powers however would be restricted to setting minimum and
maximum limits to the number of staff employed at a school, to
vetoing the appointment of teaching staff without appropriate

qualifications, to seeking to reach agreement with governors where early retirement or dismissal seemed appropriate and to trying to persuade governors to accept redeployed staff. LEAs would no longer be able to use their experience and expertise to support the appointment of the most able staff and, most important of all, would be unable to take part in the appointment of heads and deputies.

Most members of governing bodies will be involved in only one headship appointment during their term of office. Experience shows, too, that governors are likely to give undue weight in appointments to the merits of known internal candidates. LEA members and officers have wider experience of appointments. The previous Secreatry of State was particularly concerned about the quality of procedures for the appointment of heads, and HMI have regularly stressed the importance of ensuring that the leadership of schools is in the most capable hands. It is difficult to see how LEAs' continuing overall responsibilities as employers, can be properly discharge if they are unable to lay a part in the appointment of senior staff in schools. The appointment of heads and deputies should be the responsibility of joint committees of LEA members and non-LEA governors, and the advice of the CEO or his representative should be available at all times in the appointment of staff.

The proposals will seriously reduce LEAs' capacity to manage the largest group of professional staff in their employment. Central government's grant arrangements include assumptions about the efficient use of staff. An LEA which wished to transfer staff from a secondary school where pupil numbers had dropped would be unable to proceed if other schools were not ready to accept the redeployed teacher. LEAs would be seriously handicapped in trying to plan for the best use of resources, and the proposal would lead directly to unjustifiable expenditure. LEAs should retain the right to redeploy staff after consultation with the governing bodies concerned.

It is proposed that a governing body may 'instigate' a premature retirement or dismissal 'with which the LEA did not concur'. The proposal implies that governors, having decided *without the agreement of the LEA* to dispense with the services of a teacher, then ask the LEA – as employer – to dismiss the teacher. If a case is subsequently brought before an industrial tribunal the LEA – as employer – would be required to defend the dismissal to which it had not agreed. If damages were awarded they would presumably fall to be paid by the LEA, which could then decide to recover the amount from the school's allocation, although it would be concerned about the effect which such a deduction could have on what should be a finely judged budget. The LEA's position as employer might best be described as untenable. It is suggested that, while governing bodies should be able to propose the dismissal or early retirement of a member of staff, the final decision must rest with the LEA.

Delegated budgets would, rightly, be subject to internal LEA audit. The new procedure will generate a need for significant increases in staff at school and LEA level. The document suggests that LEAs should have the authority to withdraw delegations over both staffing and finance if it is satisfied that the governing body was unable to manage effectively. Governors would have a right to appeal to the Secretary of State against such withdrawal. This seems to be a case of too much and too late. The mismanagement may be limited to a relatively small part of a school's affairs and, in many cases, LEAs would be able to foresee problems that could arise in future year. It is suggeted that LEAs should retain power to vary a scheme of delegation, subject to a review, where they have good grounds for believing that a school might otherwise face difficulty in adequately managing its affairs.

The introduction of the schemes of delegation suggested in the paper will require substantial additional resources on training and on staffing at both LEA and school level. LEAs should be enabled to develop the most appropriate arrangements for their own schools in the light of experience over a period of years.

The Association of Metropolitan Authorities does not object to the principle of delegation; our main concern is that such delegation should be properly carried out, with all parties fully understanding the nature and limits of their responsibilities. We are not sure that the DES understands the complexities of devising satisfactory schemes. We would not dissent from the comment of the Audit Commission that 'establishing a scheme of delegation can be a long-term process taking perhaps 5–7 years'. This is demonstrated by the most developed of the existing schemes.

We also note, and agree with, the commission's requirements for increasing delegation successfully: that the 'strategy for change should be gradual and confined to selected schools in the first instance; that time must be allowed to make the necessary organizational changes in the local educational service; that provision for 'accurate and timely' financial information has to be made to maintain a proper overall level of financial control, which will 'probably involve extensive use of new information technology with remote terminals linked to the central financial information system'; that staff support and management training should be made available to headteachers in those schools given additional delegated powers. Clearly, additional governor training will also be necessary.

These are fundamental requirements: they indicate a significant level of investment, for which Government support will be necessary. The more far-reaching the scheme of delegation, the more likely it is that school non-teaching staff levels will have to be increased, and salary gradings of some existing staff adjusted to take account of their new responsibilities. Most secondary schools will need to appoint a bursar to deal with the large sums of public money for which they will be accountable.

We understand that Government thinks the extra staff costs at school level will be offset by lower central administrative costs. If that view is held, it is quite wrong. For example, in a medium-sized LEA with 119 nursery and primary schools, 19 secondary schools and one sixth-form college, nine staff handle a repairs and maintencance budget of over £3,000,000, as well as taking responsibility for over 700 caretakers and cleaners. Even if most of these functions could be delegated in their entirety to schools, which is very unlikely, there would still be a need to retain staff centrally to deal with duties which remain the responsibility of LEA. Economies of scale centrally would be lost. It is also likely that there will be increased auditing requirements, if individual school accounts have to be closed individually. Delegation is not a cheap way of running schools, and if proper control of public finance is to be maintained, schools cannot be allowed to sever the majority of their links with their maintaining authority.

The list of centrally determined items omits the careers service and fails to refer to the local authority's need to operate central services based on the needs of pupils – for example, home or hospital tuition and various types of peripatetic teaching. Schools deciding to provide their own meals could materially affect the costs of provision both of the local authority and of private contractors. We also wonder whether governors will be subject to the tendering requirements. If governors did decide to provide their own meal service the LEA could presumably require that local nutritional standards, or policy on menu content, would be followed.

Agreeing a workable funding formula appears to have eluded the authorities with the most experience in managing financial delegation. It is essential that this issue be resolved locally: the Government should resist the temptation to become involved in disputes over the basis of allocation to individual schools. There must be some danger that in seeking evident fairness tthe formula becomes excessively complicated. It is very doubtful that any division between responsibility for repairs to the structure of the building and internal repairs and maintenance could be made to work effectively. The only sensible division would be one based on cost, with all major items of repair and maintenance being carried out by the local authority, leaving the governors to deal with minor repairs up to a certain cost limit. The ability of a school to operate tendering procedures, draw up work specifications and supervise large contracts without outside assistance is uncertain.

In many cases, community facilities are provided by joint action betwen the education committee and other committees of the local authority and specifically designed for wider community use. Governors should not, for example, be permitted to close down such facilities in order to save money or to divert funds elsewhere, and the local authority must be free to exercise its responsibilities to other members of its community by fixing concessionary charges or giving priority to particular activities or particular groups.

We see no alternative to the LEA retaining contingency sums for pay awards, it being understood that if an authority cannot anticipate a pay award, it cannot provide for it either in its own or in school budgets. To that extent, schools cannot be protected from financial uncertainty as they assume their wider responsiblities.

The proposals on staffing are among the most unsatisfactory. We specifically disagree with the statement that 'the benefits of financial delegation would only be fully realized if governing bodies were given discretion in respect of how many, and which, staff they should employ'. Of particular concern, at a time of falling rolls, and in the context of the Government's proposals on open enrolments, is the apparent loss of ability to conduct a redeployment policy. It will become increasingly difficult for the LEA to maintain its curriculum policies or to make accurate assessments of recruitment needs, either in total or according to subject areas.

We find the proposals for selecting headteachers and their staff extraordinary. It is a feature of this consultation paper, and of those dealing with grant-maintained schools and admissions, to regard schools as independent entities and not part of the overall provision in a locality.

Cambridgeshire County Council – We welcome, in the main part, the proposals for delegating new powers to school governors and heads. As you know, Cambridgeshire and other LEAs have been operating schemes similar to the one suggested for some time. The consultation paper benefits from having taken account of our experience; it is to be regretted that some of the other proposals for education have not similarly been tried and tested.

The need for local diversity and the need to build confidence in the schools both imply a need for a slow build-up to implementation. Each LEA should operate 'pilot' projects in a few schools. The necessary management information systems will also take time to design and install. There will be a need for very extensive management training for heads and governors, and that will again take time. It is important to get these things right first, before committing the majority of schools to the new system.

Delegation to schools, as practised in Cambridgeshire and as outlined in the consultation paper, goes beyond financial matters. It is about local management of the whole school. Nevertheless there are some aspects of school education which demand an overview of educational needs and good practice which no one school can be expected to have. These are the proper concern of the local education authority, and the proposals suffer from a failure to take account of some of them. The proposal that governors should be empowered to hire and fire heads and other staff makes nonsense of the LEA's status as employer. There will be a need, therefore, to make teacher a special case in law, uniquely exampted from normal employment protection; this will hardly encourage people to join the profession. This authority has for some years been committed to the principle that schools should be free, within certain limits, to transfer between staffing and other budgets; the LEA as employer will wherever possible take account of schools' wishes in this direction. That is quite different from being forced into an untenable position by circumstances beyond its control.

The partnership between schools, LEAs and central government has worked well in the past. Delegation of new responsibilities to schools implies a shift of emphasis in that partnership which is to be welcomed. But it must not be a shift which leaves LEAs with all the responsibilities and none of the powers or prevents LEAs from providing those elements of the education service which only they can offer.

Solihull Metropolitan Borough Council – We would question the viability of the proposal to delegate financial responsibility to the governors of primary schools with 200 or more pupils of statutory school age. In Solihull, this would mean that, of our 71 primary schools, 39 would be eligible for a scheme of local financial management. A choice of 200 pupils is somewhat puzzling, given the fact that a one-form-entry infant school would have a normal limit of 105 pupils and a two-form-entry school 210 pupils. Similarly, a one-form-entry junior and infant school could have a role of 245 pupils, but commonly this will fall below 200. It would be far more sensible to prescribe for the admission to a financial delegation scheme of separate two-form-entry junior and infant schools or combined one-form-entry junior and infant schools.

The reference to parents being able to 'evaluate whether best use had been made of the resources available to governors' seems questionable, particularly in view of the stronger representation of parents on governing bodies for which provision is made in the 1986 Education Act. At best, it seems that evaluation by parents would be superficial and depend more on physical resources – the state of the premises, etc. – than on the quality of education.

The principle of the school determining the precise level of staffing in relation to books, equipment and support staff has been considered central to the Solihull scheme, but at the same time it has raised largely unresolved questions. The policy in Solihull has always been that headteachers are appointed by a joint panel (in equal numbers) of LEA representatives and governors, with chairmanship resting with the LEA. This procedure has been codified in the 1986 Education Act and the council has also agreed a policy of applying the same procedures to the appointment of deputy headteachers. A joint panel approach has many advantages, chiefly the development of expertise in interviewing at this level the benefits of comparative knowledge across all schools, an avoidance of parochialism in appointments and preserving the overriding duty of the LEA to staff schools satisfactorily.

South Tyneside Metropolitan Borough Council – There is a longstanding interest in the granting of a greater measure of delegation to governors and headteachers, and had it not been for the financial stringency of recent years there would undoubtedly have been more widespread experimentation. The assumption in the consultation paper that more information and freedom lead to greater efficiency in the use of resources is by no means proven. These proposals, especially in respect of staffing, will restrict the ability of the local authority to reallocate the resources of the whole service.

A scheme of financial delegation works most effectively during a time of change and growth. The problem at the present time is the coincidence of many and rapid changes, affecting all aspects of the life and work of a school, with the imposition of extremely rigid financial controls. The fomer trend cries out for delegation to cope with the initiatives and priorities faced by each school. The falling rolls in many schools could release the necessary finance for these growing curriculum and community needs, but the demand for substantial savings year after year necessitates firm central decisions by the authority and the ability to implement such decisions without delay.

The Secondary Heads' Association welcome any opportunity for its members to take a greater share in the management of schools. There is considerable enthusiasm within SHA membership for the principle of financial delegation, and many members with appropriate experience strongly advocate it. Despite this, we advise the Government to proceed with the utmost caution. Financial and resource control is vital if we are to create and maintain good schools. In order to achieve this objective, however, we would put forward these necessary conditions:

(1) There must be provision for the widest consultations between the LEA, its schools and governors.

(2) Heads and deputies should be appropriately and effectively trained.

(3) Staff and parents, as well as governors, should be properly informed and involved in the preparations for the decision to delegate.

(4) Sufficient support staff of the right quality must be available in every school.

(5) The salaries of heads and deputies must reflect the extra responsibility they will incur.

(6) All schools must be funded equitably to ensure that no school community suffers from the change in policy.

(7) LEAs must have sufficient liaison staff to co-ordinate the scheme adequately.

SHA supports the proposal that parents and the community should receive full information about LEA and Government funding of the education service. It is equally important that schools should be recipients of this information, so that staff are properly appraised of the financial implications. SHA also agrees with the objective of giving schools 'freedom to take expenditure decisions' but hopes it will be a real freedom, through the provision of sufficient funds to make choices possible.

SHA welcomes the Government's intention to build on successful pilot schemes. Evidence suggests that, where these have been developed in consultation with schools, rapid and satisfactory progress has been made. These LEAs will clearly be at an advantage following legislation. Pilot schemes have been successful because schools have volunteered and have participated enthusiastically; they have also benefited for the concentrated attention of LEA officers who, for the most part, have been committed to the scheme. The immediate future will be fraught with difficulties, however, in those LEAs where discussions have not yet begun. It is to be hoped the Government's assertion that it will 'draw on the views of LEAs before issuing general guidance on more detailed aspects' will lead to thorough research and realistic guidelines.

The development of an appropriate funding formula is probably the single biggest problem in the entire proposal. A simple formula will not meet the needs of all schools. In order to protect the educational and social requirements of each school an LEA will need time and patience to devise something that is sophisticated and yet comprehensible. The document is almost nonchalant in its failure to grasp the complexity of devising such a formula.

SHA supports the involvement of governors; evidence from the pilot schemes is that there is no better way to persuade them of their accountability. The role of the new governing bodies after 1988 will, of course, be crucial, so it will be incumbent on LEAs during the coming year to ensure that all nominees for governorship, particularly those parents standing for election, are fully appraised of their future responsibilities under financial delegation.

SHA is very concerned about the legal implications for its members, as well as for governors, in the face of requirements of health and safety legislation, and will seek the most stringent safeguards.

The Secretary of State's warning that he will take statutory powers to override an LEA's failure to delegate is presumably a necessity. But the consequences of such an imposition could be disastrous for the schools, as a scheme is unlikely to be effective without the agreement and understanding of all those charged with its implementation.

SHA does not agree that the selection of heads and deputies should be delegated solely to the governors. However knowledgeable individual governors might be, collectively they lack the professional experience to make the wise judgement that is essential when appointing the leaders of a school. The current system in most LEAs with the checks and balances of shared responsibility between officers, advisers and governors, a reasonable blend of professional, lay and community opinion, seems to offer the best procedure.

The proposals that staff reductions should be the responsibility of governors are contentious; their practical application will be extremely difficult, creating tensions between LEAs, schools and teacher unions. Redeployment and redundancy will be central to the effective management of the teaching force, and a failure to devise acceptable local agreements will have serious implications. Because of their responsibility to meet costs of compensation, LEAs could set staffing complements at their lowest level in order to minimize possible redundancy payments. SHA stresses the need to close the many loopholes apparent here.

Training facilities must be extended to deputy heads. In large secondary schools in particular, the detailed management of the school's budget is delegated to a deputy; whether that is so or not, following legislation most deputy heads will share some of the responsibility with head, and many will serve as acting head for a short or long period, carrying the direct delegated responsibility. The paper fails to acknowledge the crucial role of deputy heads in the administrtion of effective financial management in any school.

SHA sees the major advantages of financial delegation to be:

(1) the freedom to make effective decisions at the point of action,

i.e. within the school community;
(2) the opening of the Pandora's box of LEA expenditure;
(3) the raising of governor and staff perceptions of the processes of financing and resourcing schools.

The major problems could be:

(1) the difficulty of identifying an equitable formula which will mean that some schools, for all sorts of historical reasons, could be unfairly treated;
(2) unscrupulous LEAs will 'pass the buck', leaving unpleasant decisions and public accountability to the schools;
(3) hurried implementation at a national or local level, leading to inadequate preparation, thereby endangering the stability of local educational provision at a time when there are many policy changes and conflicting demands. With the best will in the world, in such circumstances, some schools, through no fault of their own, will not be up to the task.

National Association of Head Teachers – A common objective of pilot schemes has been to allow for as much devolution of the school budget as possible, with the exception of those items which would cause overriding difficulties. A typical list of included items could be: teacher staffing; supply cover for teachers (including maternity and long-term sickness cover); administrative and clerical staff; caretaker, cleaners, maintenance staff and ancillary helpers; rent and rates; fuel, oil, gas, electricity and water; furniture and fittings; text books, library books, stationery and materials; examination fees; administrative, educational and domestic equipment (including purchase, hire and repair); printing, office stationery, postage and telephones; educational visits (including field study courses, staff advertising, staff travelling and subsistence expenses); income, including sales and lettings; repair and maintenance of buildings; maintenance of grounds; refuse collection; INSET (including GRIST); laundry and protective clothing; toilet and first-aid requisites; transport of pupils, other than home to school; school catering; school funds.

This places considerable additional responsibility on heads. There is an increase in the importance of consultation and negotiation at school level. There is no need to: direct resources into priority areas; obtain maximum value for money; conserve resources by effecting economies where possible and avoiding unnecessary expenditure; maximize the use of school assets to generate additional income; create greater financial awareness; improve management information; produce greater job satisfaction.

Delegation of budgetary control constitutes a major change in the role of the maintained-school head and must be accompanied by increased remuneration.

The extension of local financial management to smaller primary schools, in which the head has a class teaching commitment, will require a special consideration and perhaps a different scheme from that for larger schools.

Scant reference is made to the need for training. We believe that every secondary head and primary head with 200 or more pupils must undergo a centrally funded and approved course of training before delegation takes place. All such schools will have to have additional administrative staff who will also require training.

The crucial role of the head and his or her legal responsibilities are consistently ignored throughout this paper, even in such vital areas such as the appointment of staff. LEAs should be required to consult with heads, as well as governing bodies, on how school budgets might best be delegated. In our experience governing bodies do not have expertise in business and financial management, nor the ability to commit themselves to the time needed. In practice the major responsibility will fall to the head, and the Government's proposals must recognize this fact.

In many schools with community facilities the governance and management of the youth and adult activities do not fall under the control of the school's governing body (to whom financial control is to be delegated) under existing articles of government. Such activities are managed by a separate body on which the governors may have a co-opted place. It is not uncommon for such activities to be outside the control of the head of the school, which is clearly undesirable. Community activities can place an unfair and unrecognized drain on the resources intended for the school's pupils. The additional wear and tear by community use on buildings and on expensive equipment, for instance in the home economics, science and computer departments, is often not recompensed by the LEA. Provision must be made for this.

Clarification is needed as to the position of the head – who is after all to be responsible for discharging the decisions of the governing body – in the event of the governors failing to manage the budget effectively.

National Union of Teachers – The greater the extent of financial delegation the greater the diversion of the head's professional skills, and the greater the temptation to seek to appoint heads for their business acumen rather than their qualities of leadership within a team engaged in providing effective, as well as efficient, education. This would change the role of the head very significantly and alter irrevocably the relationship between head and staff. All would have less time for their professional responsibilities. The undoubted effect would be to change the whole nature of leadership in schools.

While the first objective of ensuring that the resources available to each school are known is in itself laudable, the union does not believe the measures proposed will achieve it. There will be a greater availability of information and therefore opportunity, but to assume that parents and the community will therefore know, let alone understand, the complex nature of each school's financing is another matter. The Government is avoiding the question of the proper resourcing of the education service and is seeking to obscure the fact by these proposals. It will be more difficult for the public to make judgements as to whether the total funds made available are adequate, so that the blame for any shortcomings in the service will be laid at the door of the school rather than where it belongs.

A number of central activities, such as the imposition of a national curriculum, will significantly diminish the 'freedom' to take expenditure decisions which governors will be in a position to exercise, though again the objective is acceptable.

Schools differ widely in their physical condition; many schools are in a poor state of repair and decoration. An agreed baseline and common formula for the fair allocation of funds will not be easily achieved.

There must be opportunity for schools to carry forward an underspend where they wish to finance an item of larger expenditure such as furniture, large or expensive equipment or provision for significant curriculum development or innovation. It is sufficient to recall the question of asbestos in school buildings to make clear that account will need to be taken of the financial implications of health and safety requirements, as well as providing the guidance suggested in the consultation paper.

Provision for children with special educational needs, as described in the Education Act 1981, is totally inadequate. Some differential provision amonst mainstream schools is bound to be required on this account.

The provision of additional information on expenditure per pupil at each school on services not included in the allocation formula will be of little public value in view of the wide variation in the way services not included in the formula are used. It may well lead to misunderstanding, according to whether a school does or does not make extensive use of transport, education welfare officer, educational psychologists and so on. The union doubts if parents or the community in general will have the financial expertise to interpret the results. The publication of the budgetary information as set out, together with the results of 'benchmark' testing, will give a completely misleading basis for comparing the performance of schools. The union deplores such an attempt to develop 'performance indicators'.

The matter of the financial responsibilities incurred by governors in relation to premature retirement will need considerable amplification. The document appears to raise the severest difficulties in the path of negotiated redeployment agreements. The union deplores the proposal that governors should be able to dismiss teachers regardless of the attitude of the LEA, and is firmly opposed to declarations of teacher redundancy.

National Association of Schoolmasters/Union of Women Teachers – Before the introduction of any schemes, staffing base lines, both national and local, should be agreed.

The NAS/UWT is not opposed in principle to school-based financial management. It does object strongly to the giving of financial responsibility to governing bodies without any of the checks and balances needed to ensure that schools are so managed as to add to the quality of education provision. By no stretch of the imagination can local financial management (LFM) be seen as an issue of high priority. It is under-researched, and the limited pilot schemes that have been tried have revealed problems to which, so far, no answers have been found. In Cambridgeshire, where it is claimed LFM is 'flourishing', a funding formula which will adequately meet the needs of all schools within the scheme has not yet been found – and this is an authority where LFM has been piloted for five years.

Since resources are scarce, unpleasant choices will have to be made, and there are serious problems in meeting basic educational requirements. The problems arising in the formative stages have little chance of being resolved satisfactorily in the atmosphere of resentment and non-co-operation which the imposition of LFM upon reluctant and unprepared governors and headteachers may well engender. A more sensible strategy would be the use of positive incentives for an increasing number of local authorities and schools to explore cautiously and fully monitor the expansion of delegated financial management.

Health and safety must be given priority. Contractors for repair and maintenance work must be restricted to a local authority approved list. There is need for a local authority contingency fund to meet repair costs which are beyond the reasonable limit of a school's annual budget.

The NAS/UWT is totally opposed to governing bodies being given the sole responsibility for matters such as premature retirement, disciplinary procedures or dismissal. These procedures are determined by negotiation between the local authority and teachers' representatives, and the association will resist any attempt to change existing arrangements. Consultation between governing bodies and local authorities, with the local authority having the final responsibility, is the best working model and this should be retained.

The Professional Association of Teachers supports the introduction of financial delegation to schools but is anxious to ensure that the many problems are resolved before a new system is implemented. We note that the Secretary of State intends to have overall control of the LEA schemes. These powers appear to be setting a precedent for central control, which the association regrets.

Health, safety and welfare in schools are a matter currently exercising the association. The annual conference in July 1987 expressed concern that educational establishments are not covered by certain provisions of: the Fire Precautions Act 1971; the Offices, Shops and Railway Premises Act 1963; the Health and Safety Act 1974; the Education (School Premises) Regulations 1981; the Health and Safety (First Aid) Provisions 1981; and the requests that the Secretary of State for Education and Science rectified the situation by using the powers instead in his office. It follows that schools should be required to provide much more by way of first aid, nursing facilities, training for staff, etc. than is presently the case. Financial delegation to schools will need to take account of these and other very important matters affecting the safety of all who work or who are taught within the confines of the school.

Security for teaching staff in schools must not be lessened as a result of devolved financial control. Account must be taken of the fact that the less scrupulous governing body might seize upon an opportunity to dispense with staff in order to balance the books. We understand that existing LEA redeployment agreements would cease to apply. It could be detrimental to teachers where a reduction in staffing of a school was insisted upon by the governors, the result being redundancy, as no redeployment agreement would be operative.

Governing bodies and headteachers of special schools may wish to be involved in local financial management. They should not be prevented from being so involved in the first place, despite the Secretary of State's intention to consider the position at a later date.

We consider it essential that adequate training is provided for headteachers and governors *before* they become involved in financial control of schools. However, in some cases, schools might ultimately be governed by influential financial 'experts', intent of self-aggrandizement, to the detriment of the good of the school as a whole. The balance must be struck.

National and Local Government Officers' Association – As the major union representing administrative, professional, technical and clerical staff employed in schools and in LEA central education departments, NALGO is extremely concerned at some of the implications for jobs and service conditions.

The consultative paper seems to assume that the new arrangements will not lead to any changes in the levels of funding. NALGO believes that, on the contrary, financial delegation will mean that the unit cost of the central service the LEA must continue to provide will increase, and that it must be more expensive for individual schools to operate a new layer of administrative responsibilities. The paper makes no reference to the work of administrative and clerical staff, despite the importance of their role in providing the essential support for headteachers and governing bodies to carry out these and other proposals. Under the proposed system, spending on these staff would have to compete for priority with spending on teachers, books, teaching aids, building maintenane and so on. The paper seems to presume that most of the extra duties would be undertaken by headteachers. NALGO does not believe that this would or should, be the case. Experience in those LEAs conducting pilot schemes has been that much of the work is, in turn, delegated to senior teaching staff *and* school office staff. If such arrangements are to operate successfully, it is essential that sufficient office staff are employed to cope with the workload and to free teaching staff and headteachers to concentrate on their teaching and educational roles. In many schools this will mean additional office staff. It is also essential that gradings fully reflect the additional complex duties they would be taking on.

The whole concept of delegated financial management on the scale proposed cuts across the lines of accountability which the Government seems so keen to reinforce through separate proposals on local government finance. Schools can effectively go their own way, using public funds disbursed by LEAs. What then becomes of the accountability of the LEA to the ratepayers who fund the system?

Institute of Economic Affairs – The proposals in many respects are too timid, retaining too much central control at LEA level. The following paragraphs are intended to strengthen the Government's proposals for full financial delegation to schools, leading eventually tó full management delegation. In inviting schools and LEAs to learn from the experimental projects already embarked upon in this country, Solihull and Cambridgeshire in particular, we would suggest that the experience of publicly funded schools elsewhere in the world is also worthy of study – in particular, Australia, parts of

Canada and parts of the USA.

The proposals exclude certain items of expenditure from the schemes of financial delegation, retaining these at LEA level. Whilst the LEAs may continue to supply such services centrally, the cost of such services on a per-school or per-pupil basis should be contained in budget statements and included in the allocation of funds on a school-by-school basis, rather than be available on a 'for information-only' basis. Schools themselves should be able to 'purchase' service from their LEA, using sums allocated in their budgets. This would identify clearly the cost of such services. It should be open to the schools to purchase such services from elsewhere if the cost and quality can be bettered. For example, it should be open to the school to arrange cheaper and/or better transport for the pupils than the LEA can provide; better and/or cheaper legal and medical advice, financial advice and other advisory services.

In that same context, it should be open to the governors to choose to purchase school meals from the LEA or from an outside caterer or to make their own provision, and it would be up to the governors, no doubt guided by the parents, whether the alternative provision was 'comparable' (to use the term in the consultation paper). It should be for the schools to opt into the LEA's school meal service rather than, as presently proposed, opt out.

It should be made clear that the funding of each school is to be on a per-pupil basis. There should in addition be the minimum number of 'differentials' modifying such a basis, otherwise the basis of financial delegation would quickly be discredited as a bureaucratic 'fix'. We recommend that the provisions be extended to all maintained schools from the commencement of the scheme, including those with fewer than 200 pupils. The 'norm' should be financial delegation to all schools, with discretion to LEAs and governors, by mutual agreement, to exclude some smaller schools from the initial scheme. The maximum financial delegation to schools is highly desirable, with the minimum of costs retained for central direction by the LEA. Schools should be free to obtain guidance on financial management from whatever source, including the management consultants appointed by the Secretary of State to devise models of financial management. We trust that the Secretary of State will welcome competitive provision, by independent groups, of financial consultancy.

There is a strong case for devolving management to county and voluntary controlled schools at least as much as to the voluntary-adied schools. Since voluntary-aided schools are employers of staff, so too should county and voluntary controlled schools be. The consultative document says that the Secretary of State notes the degree of autonomy in staffing matters enjoyed by aided schools; it should also be enjoyed by the other maintained schools.

There is no reason why in-service training should be the sole responsiblility of the LEA. That too could be devolved to governers, and the school's budget include an item to cover in-service training. The governors would then be free to purchase training from the best sources available, which may or may not be their own or another LEA.

We suggest that the legislation should be extended now to all special schools but, as with smaller schools, allow for those not yet ready for it to opt to delay.

The training requirement for governors, headteachers, deputy heads and others implicit in these proposals is most important. It should not, however, be just in financial management but in management *per se*, and should not be exclusively provided by the LEAs. There are severe reservations over the quality of the statutory training to governors now being given by LEAs as required under the 1986 Act. It would be better to allow an item in the school's budget for such training, and to allow the school to purchase it from its present LEA if it wishes, but also to purchase it from elsewhere – most notably from consultants and organizations expert in management in the full sense of that word. We seriously doubt the ability of many LEAs to offer competent training in management. This scheme should not fail because of inadequate preparation given to headteachers and others.

Society of Local Authority Chief Executives – The general impression given is that a number of authorities have *successfully* introduced schemes for the devolution of financial resources to schools. This is not the case. Those few authorities that have introduced schemes similar to that which the Government is proposing have done so only in pilot schools.

The difficulty of producing appropriate distribution formulas goes without saying, and it is interesting to note that this particular problem has been delegated to local authorities to solve. The document makes a basic but incorrect assumption that existing resources will be carved up and, on that basis, that the existing resources must be correct. In other words, the allocation will be resource-based instead of needs-based. Just about every survey since 1974 has shown a wide disparity between what local authorities spend on education. Most of all, this disparity relates to the number of teachers employed and the amount of money available for books, equipment, materials, etc. It would appear that, in each case, whatever the authority spends at the present time will be regarded as being 'right' and that no additional resources will be made available.

It is easy to state that governors will be responsible for the allocated budget, but what does this mean in practice? Will it be delegated to the headteacher for him or her to act, without the need for any supervision other than periodic reports to the governing body? Before governors can take any decisions they and the head-teacher will need sound financial and possible legal advice. Who is going to provide this?

Present expenditure patterns form the basis of the proposals. This is a major flaw which needs to be reconsidered. Take the case of a small county council. It spends £10m a year more on education than is the average for its 'audit commission family'. It has a number of aspirations: to maintain some policies which contribute to that 'excess spending' (admissions for 4-year-olds, nursery education, generous transport provisions and extensive use of school facilities for community leisure and education are examples); to continue to transfer funds from education to social services; to keep the rate precept at a reasonable level. Both of the latter aims depend upon the council's ability to translate savings in the education service to other purposes. It is of great importance, therefore, that present patterns of expenditure do not become institutionalized by the financial devolution proposals, with savings made unavailable to the county council by the Government's guarantee to governors that 'their own school will benefit from efficiency savings'. The Audit Commission comparative expenditure figures probably provide a starting point. Average spending, or even lower quartile spending, might form the basis. This would leave the county council in control of that part of its expenditure which might be considered excessive in Audit Commission figures, and in a position to benefit from 'managing down' its school places as rolls fall.

Increased central cost can be expected in budget preparation and matters arising from the allocation of budgets, financial monitoring and related information technology requirements, increased calls on audit, and closure of accounts on a school-by-school basis, with great attention details in arriving at over/underspendings. Although savings might be expected at school level from closer financial monitoring, these savings will be available for the school to spend, and not available to reduce costs of the LEA. Overall, increased LEA expenditure is inevitable.

Maintenance expenditure is typical of large areas of a school budget, which will be a source of conflict between the LEA and the school. If a school has a light year on maintenance it will divert the resources, but when a heavy year comes along they will scream for help, particularly if the circumstances are unusual or unexpected. If every school in that borough overspent by 5 per cent it is likely, under present regulations, that an area which is totally outside the control of the council could lead to that council becoming rate-capped and, subsequently, penalized.

It is all very well to allow under- and overspendings to be carried forward between the years, but this carries with it a loss of flexibility for the committee as a whole to divert underspendings in primary and secondary education to meet any pressing problems that they might have in another area of their budget. There is also a very real issue of financial control, because experience tells us that if there are not adequate 'teeth' in the system then there may be a tendency to overspend in the knowledge that no severe action will follow. The LEA will be spending more money than it has raised from the ratepayers, etc. The need to maintain an even more sophisticated monitoring system raises itself, and this of course carries costs with it. It will require adequate computer systems. The present systems would not be able to cope. Nationwide implementation of recommendations may be impossible because of a surge in the need for financial/administration/computer hardware and computer staffing.

Society of Education Officers – If overall costs are not to rise, the likely movement of expenditure will be towards the administration of the financial delegation scheme, and away from the classroom.

Responsibility for the delivery of the service remains with the LEA. It is difficult to see how the LEA will be able effectively to carry out its duty when there could be a conflict of standards between the LEA and the governors. The responsibilities of the CEO need clarification and definition in statute.

It will not, apparently, be possible for the LEA to retain central funds to support developments in schools which the LEA considers desirable, although the DES will not be similarly constrained. Where elected members now become convinced by the electorate that resources should be allocated to, for example, school furniture, the development of pupil records or the use of micro-electronics across the age range and curriculum, they are able either to raise additional rate income or to reallocate existing rate-borne expenditure to that end. This will no longer be possible. Chairmen of education committees will no longer be able to guarantee to ratepayers that money allocated and raised for a particular purpose will be spent in the planned way.

In amplification of this point, the recent letter to CEOs (21 July 1987) 'New Technology for Better Schools' seeks a statement of the authority's development policy over the coming five years for the use of new technology in schools. The removal of an authority's power to 'top slice' its budget before allocation to schools will reduce this statement from being what is sought, 'a coherent schools IT policy for the authority's area', to the level of a hollow exhortation to governors.

The question of supply cover is vexed. It would be more desirable for the authority to provide supply cover costs centrally for all sickness and maternity absences. Where a school does not use supply staff for sickness, in cases where it would have an entitlement to do so, it should be possible to devise a system for the school to claim an additional financial reimbursement. This might provide an appropriate incentive for a school to cover absences within its own staffing resources.

Governing bodies are often reluctant to see their school premises used for a wider public and accept more intensive use only under the persuasion of an overriding authority policy. The insertion of a financial dimension will cause unwelcome difficulties in many instances. It will not lead to a wider use of school premises by the public.

The document envisages publication, at the outset of the year, of information on each school's proposed allocation of resources. At the end of the year the actual expenditure would also be published on a school-by-school basis. Bearing in mind that these sets of figures will be affected by changes in pupil numbers, the amount of long-term sickness experienced by staff, the number of maternity leave absences, together with pay and price increases in the year in question, the view that this information will 'provide the basis on which parents could evaluate whether best use has been made of the resources available to the governors' is unlikely to prove well founded.

It is assumed that the LEA is not to have the power to recover funds from governing bodies where they have spent outside their powers and the district auditor has no power to surcharge governors. Unless governors who fail to take proper decisions are to be free simply to resign and leave the problems to their successors, consideration might be given to allowing the withdrawal of delegation when, in the view of the authority, mismanagement is proposed or appears imminent.

On staffing, the scheme proposed, though practically feasible, will make it very much more difficult for LEAs to manage the teaching force. SEO hopes that the Secretary of State will be convinced of the wisdom of allowing LEAs to have coherent authority-wide policies in such spheres as redeployment, and a continuing major influence and involvement in the appointment of headteachers.

It is not clear whether the governing bodies of LEA-maintained schools will be free, within the limits of their finance, to determine the number of incentive allowances to be paid over and above the main salary scale and to pay heads and deputies salaries appropriate for schools in higher groups. The spirit of LFM as spelt out in the paper seems to demand that freedom, and yet in the consultation paper on grant-maintained schools there is a reference to governing bodies having the same discretion as LEAs to decide the number of incentive allowances to be paid and the salary grades appropriate to headteachers of higher groups.

Parallel legislation is proposed to extend competition into the areas of cleaning of schools and ground maintenance. This legislation will be taking effect while LFM is being introduced. Schools will be able, under the proposals, to opt out of contracts let by the authority. The extent of the possible opting out will not be known to contractors. Complications will result both for contractors bidding for a market of unknown size and for authorities drawing up contracts which will not bind schools to their use.

Church of England Board of Education – We accept in principle the two main objectives. One important condition is that the implementation of the proposals is not rushed to the detriment of a sound scheme being formed.

We have some concerns arising from the proposal for there to be a range within which a governing body may decide the number of staff. Some schools with financially supportive parents and/or independent trust funds will be able to employ staff at the top of the range and enjoy a better pupil–teacher ratio than those less favourably placed. Is this example of 'to them that hath shall be given' accepted and encouraged? The opportunity for some governing bodies to 'vary the mix' will be very limited compared with others.

We very much hope that implementation of these proposals will not be imposed until there is general confidence that a sound scheme is available. The last thing that is needed in schools, when so many are crying out for a period of stability and consolidation, with headteacher having suffered increasing strains in recent years and governors undertaking many extra responsibilities, is for them to be floundering in a financial morass.

The Association of Voluntary-Aided Secondary Schools is surprised to find in the consultation paper no reference to the need for any school with extensive financial delegation to have the services of a (not necessarily full-time) bursar. The role of bursar will be vital, as it is in independent schools and will be in grant-maintained schools. The full-time value of the bursar's post ought to be equated with that of the deputy head's post, and its establishment should be a statutory requirement.

Governing bodies of schools accorded financial delegation should be statutorily provided with the opportunity each year of drawing up estimates of their own spending requirements for the following year and passing them to their local education authorities, which would be obliged to take them into account when formulating their own estimates for their school service.

National Confederation of Parent–Teacher Associations – The two main objectives as stated in the paper are: to ensure that parents and the community know on what basis the available resources are distributed in their area and how much is being spent on each school; to give the governors of all county and voluntary secondary schools, and of larger primary schools, 'freedom' to take expenditure decisions which match their own priorities and the guarantee that their own school will benefit if they achieve efficiency savings.

The proposals contain no provision which would result in parents and the community (or schools themselves for that matter) knowing on what basis the available resources are distributed. Nowhere does the requirement appear for LEAs to publish the basis of the expenditure breakdowns. The term 'freedom' as applied to expenditure decisions is illusory. All aspects of educational finance are so tightly constrained that little flexibility exists in decision-making – particularly when one component, staff costs, forms 70 per cent of the budget. The national curriculum, if implemented as proposed, will determine such a large proportion of the curriculum, and thence staffing levels and resources, that a governing body would have little room for manoeuvre.

There is no 'guarantee' that a school will benefit from any efficiency savings achieved. If a school benefits from a saving in the financial year the saving is made, there is no guarantee that such saving will be included in the allocation the following year. It is a matter for 'local resolution'.

NCPTA concludes that the proposals will satisfy only one of the four constituent parts of the two objectives and they therefore need extensive revision. More autonomy will be both meaningless and unacceptably onerous unless the following conditions are satisfied:

(a) The budget allocation must be seen to be adequate.
(b) There must be an absolute guarantee that any savings made can be used to benefit the school and will be left untouched in future allocations on a recurring basis.
(c) The allocation must be protected against the effects of inflation and any other extraordinary increases in cost. This is no doubt an ideal, but schools should be first and last places of learning for children, not implementors of centrally determined fiscal policy.
(d) The governing body and headteacher must have access to such expertise as they may require to fulfil their responsibilities, the cost of such expertise to be included in the allocation.
(e) The situation must not arise where any governors, particularly

parent governors, are prevented from serving, on the grounds
that they do not possess some particular expertise.

(f)   Governors must be clear about their legal position in the event
of an overspend occurring. They must be assured that they
cannot be held personally responsible.

Subject to the conditions being met, NCPTA would like to see the
devolvement of financial responsiblity at the earliest opportunity,
phased in to suit the pace at which schools are prepared to accept the
change without undue disruption.

Advisory Centre for Education – With the cake diminishing, it will
be convenient for both Government and the LEAs to lay the
responsibility for making unpopular decisions on spending upon
the shoulders of governors. With such a burden of responsibility,
governors will feel pressurized into becoming fund-raisers for their
schools, the divide between those in affluent and those in poor areas
will grow and the fear of the creation of a large number of 'sink'
schools will become a reality. Local financial management must not
become a smokescreen for the real problems of many schools as
identified by HMI – inadequate resourcing.

Governors' new duties under the 1986 Education Act, coupled
with those envisaged in the new Education Bill, will make the role of
school governor even more onerous and daunting. Parents passing
through a school may feel less willing to take on such unpaid work.
The demands upon a governor's time already make it difficult for
parents with young families or full-time jobs to take on such
responsibilities. Unless there is adequate training, guaranteed paid
time off work and the full back-up and support of the LEA, which
must be allowed to respond to local needs in the most appropriate
way, these plans will leave schools floundering.

The Association of British Chambers of Commerce very much
welcomes the objective of giving more authority for expenditure and
other decisions to governors and headteachers. We regard extensive
training of headteachers in management as critically important, and
the same applies to all governors to a very considerable extent. This
should not be solely in financial topics, but also in such as staff
selection and appointments, disciplinary processes and the like.

No governor should be permitted to take up an appointment
without the prescribed training. Governors could be well advised to
ensure that one of their number, by co-option if necessary, is
experienced in financial management: a local accountant or bank
manager, for example. Clear specifications of the duties and responsibilities of governors will be required and, in addition, the matter

of any personal financial liability on the part of a governor needs to be explicit. Our experiences show that, to get a high standard of person to devote time to such duties, he or she has to be given real responsibilities.

It is essential that schools should carry forward an underspend or overspend from one year to the next. They should have the incentive of being able to utilize subsequently any savings they achieve, should have to cope with any mistakes they make and generally be able to plan beyond an arbitrarily restrictive date. Further financial delegation is also appropriate, namely: the authority to transfer between accounts at their own discretion, to operate their own bank account and to earn interest on deposited balances of moneys not yet utilized. All this should encourage a proper business approach to financial management,

National Association of Governors and Managers – There is an important distinction between decision-making and administration in the governor's role. It is right and much more efficient for governors, who know the school well, to take decisions about the selection of staff and the allocation of resources. But much of the administrative work can usually be done more efficiently by the LEA. Otherwise it would impose many additional burdens on the lay governors, and the school staff, which they are not specifically qualified to perform and which they may be unwilling to shoulder. The new proposals expect a very great deal from governors, who in the past have been given little preparation and support for their role. It is unreasonable to expect them to give up the time that will be needed to do the job properly without compensation for financial loss, including loss of earnings, and without adequate training. NAGM believes that well-informed governors can help schools to make a better use of the resources available to them. But there is a short-term cost which has to be met.

The Library Association – The Secretary of State will be aware that there is widespread concern over the lack of books in schools, and aware of the dismal state of school libraries highlighted in recent reports. Unless steps are taken to improve school library provision, some of the current financial proposals could negate the modest progress made since the publication of these reports. We would urge the Secretary of State either to give consideration to legislating for minimum standards of provision in schools, including the provision of school libraries, or to make the provision of a properly resourced school library a statutory responsibility as part of his strategy for enabling a national curriculum to be effectively delivered in all schools.

Education Resources – With enough additional financial support, the proposed financial devolution might contribute to a more cost-effective management of schools. However, we are convinced that the proposal will cost both the schools and the LEAs considerably more than the present arrangements. It is crucial that financial training be given both to headteacher and to governors, who will have to become, respectively, managing director and boards of directors if they are properly to carry out the proposed duties. A bursar and the bursar's clerical assistance must be added to the existing staff of each school. The bursar's work must not be foisted on to the over-burdened shoulders of the head, the deputy heads or the senior teacher, and certainly not on to the secretarial or administrative staff. It will be necessary to appoint auditors for each school as well.

School governors, who work only in their free time, may find the extra financial responsibility too great a burden; it will become more and more difficult to find willing parents, community volunteers and even LEA appointees who will take on this responsibility. Perhaps you should consider providing attendance allowances and, when necessary, remuneration for loss of earnings.

Your consultative document is not clear about the proposed sharing of responsibility between the LEAs and the schools. Please make it clear who has ultimate responsibility for what.

We are especially concerned that not enough time has been given to the various pilot schemes around the country, and that those that have reported have not been very successful. Mr Peter Edwards, the Chief Education Officer of Berkshire, has been quoted: 'People tell us that local financial management is going to be effective and it is going to be cheap. The first proposition is quite possible, but there is no possibility whatever in our county that it is going to be cheaper.' Is it not possible for you to extend the current pilot schemes before introducing wholesale delegation? Why not find out how much it really will cost?

6

Open Enrolment

THE PROPOSALS

The Government considers that no child should be refused admission to a school unless it is genuinely full. Many parents get their first choice because the Education Act 1980 gives them the right to name their preferred school, but too often they are disappointed because artificial ceilings are put on the numbers of places available at popular schools. That barrier needs to be removed.

New arrangements will apply to both primary and secondary schools, but to secondary schools first – from the school year 1989–90. Schools will have to admit pupils at least up to their 'standard number', as defined in the 1980 Act, which is usually the number admitted in 1979. Where admissions are higher in 1988, that higher figure will become the standard number. In primary schools, the standard number will be raised to take account of all pupils admitted to a reception class, including those below the age of 4½ and any who have come up to the main school from a nursery unit or class. The LEA or governors can ask the Secretary of State to agree to a lower number if they can prove that the school no longer has the space to take the standard number; but the number will not be reduced simply to divert pupils to less popular schools. Dissatisfied parents will have a right of appeal.

Governors of voluntary schools will keep responsibility for admission arrangements, in consultation with the LEA; and arrangements which reserve some places for pupils of particular religious affiliations will continue, even if it means that places are not taken up. Transport arrangements will not change.

THE DEBATE

Who'll pay to prop the school gates open?

David Hart
General Secretary, National Association of Head Teachers

Open enrolment – or parental choice – should, in theory, be the least controversial of all the Government's proposals. Most people would subscribe to the right of parents to choose the school for their child or children; yet the Government's commitment to securing wider parental choice has been the subject of fairly widespread criticism. This is quite simply because there are doubts about whether the Education Reform Bill will achieve Kenneth Baker's objective. There are several reasons for this.

First, the whole object of the Bill is to change from a system where control is exercised by local education authorities to one where market forces will reign supreme. This tends to ignore the fact that local education authorities are being urged by the Government in its White Paper on Public Expenditure (1988–9) to take some half a million surplus school places out of use. Those same market forces will make it very difficult for local education authorities to manage the contracting pupil numbers in secondary schools either economically or efficiently. Parental expectations will have been raised but in a number of cases those expectations will not be met.

Secondly, the operation of market forces will inevitably mean that oversubscribed schools will quickly fill up to the limit of their physical capacity, and disappointed parents will be offered undersubscribed schools. At the same time, severely undersubscribed schools will have to close because surplus places will have to be taken out of use. This will lead to fewer schools and a further reduction in parental choice.

Thirdly, the whole thrust of the Bill is to put future funding via financial delegation very largely on a per capita basis. Nothing much has been said about the plight of undersubscribed schools, but this means that such schools will begin to be stripped of funds unless the local authority can in some way boost these funds by recognizing the special factors that exist. My guess is that the economics of the situation will force LEAs to close them rather than to keep them open with additional financial support.

Fourthly, some undersubscribed schools will have to stay open, either because they will have to take the pupils who have been turned away by the oversubscribed schools or because of geographical or social reasons for their retention. The narrower curriculum that these smaller schools will inevitably provide will have to be expanded by the provision of additional money if they are to meet the demands of the new national curriculum. Accordingly the resource implications will have to be recognized.

Finally, the understandable attraction of parental choice is undermined by the Government's refusal to extend the current legislation governing the provision of free school transport. It will not be much use telling some parents that they can choose a school anywhere in the authority, or indeed within the area of another authority, if they cannot get free transport for their children to the school of their choice.

The corner-stone of the proposals on parental choice is the creation of a new 'standard number' – the measurement of pupil admissions which is to be based on the 1979–80 admission numbers. Schools will be allowed to take pupils up to that number and will not be circumscribed by any artificial limitation which an authority may wish to place by way of a reduction of that number. This fails to recognize that the physical capacity of many schools has been reduced since 1979–80. Surplus places have been removed; unused capacity has been converted for use as laboratories, resource areas or staff rooms.

It is therefore strange that the Bill states that, whereas the local education authority and the governing body can agree to admit pupils in numbers *greater than* the 1979–80 number without the consent of the Secretary of State, they are not allowed to state a *lower number* unless they first agree among themselves and then obtain the specific approval of the Secretary of State. If there is one modification that the Secretary of State should make to the Bill, it is to allow LEAs and governors to fix such a lower level without having to go through the bureaucratic procedure of obtaining Government consent. There comes a time when we really must trust LEAs and governors to act by joint agreement in a responsible and proper manner.

Parental choice, like some other aspects of the Bill, such as a national core curriculum and financial delegation, is a sensible concept. But the detailed application of the idea has not been thought through clearly. In this it is similar to other parts of the Bill which contain provisions which are anomalous. For instance, the requirement for the Secretary of State to approve a reduction in the standard number of pupil admissions is an excessive power which can be set alongside the fact that there are 181 other powers granted to the Secretary of State by the Bill. Similarly, the insistence upon the Secretary of State having such a power contrasts oddly with the principle that as much responsibility as possible should be devolved to school-based level, as set out in the proposals for financial delegation. It is my belief that the Bill heralds not just a shift of

power downwards from local authorities to schools, but a shift of
power from local authorities upwards towards central government.

THE ADVICE

Nottinghamshire Education Committee – Last year in Nottinghamshire, 99.88 per cent of parents were satisfied that children
were admitted to schools of their first choice; only 171 appeals were
lodged with this authority. How much is wider choice possible?
Where is the evidence to suggest that the proposals will improve the
quality of education and raise the standards for *all* pupils? The
committee believes the proposals will lead to stronger preferences
for full schools and fewer for the undersubscribed ones. This will
seriously erode the concept of access to equal opportunities. There
is evidence, including significantly from HM Inspectorate, that
undersubscribed schools suffer a loss of curriculum opportunities.
Yet if some schools are allowed to fill to their 1979 capacity, there
much be undersubscribed schools elsewhere. What choices exist for
these parents?

The committee is satisfied that, within its present arrangements,
there is already wide scope for parental preference; there is parental
confidence resulting from proven worth; the choices of parents are
protected in a wide range of communities in this geographically and
demographically disparate county.

The proposals in the consultative document appear to be founded
on the concept that market forces must be allowed to prevail. If
these proposals were to be enacted, Nottinghamshire would be
faced with a situation in which a planned and coherent approach to
the distribution of a comprehensive system of education would be
impossible; management of its staffing and limited resources would
become reactive to the market forces and thereby prevent strategic
and development planning; there would be a wholesale waste of
resources and a loss of proper accountability.

The committee believes it is right that parents should be helped to
secure the admission of their children to the school of their choice. It
also believes that all parents are entitled to have access to the same
choices. The proposals will mean that some parents will be able to
choose from all the options and others from some of the options,
while many will have no choice at all.

Definition of the capacity of a school by reference to a standard
number is a wholly arbitrary and impractical device. Since 1979
there have been significant changes in the size of groups taught,

curricular developments, specialist and practical room requirements, adaptations to the premises or the removal of surplus places,
annexes and temporary accommodation. The best advice available
persuades LEAs to enrich the processes of learning by providing an
appropriate physical environment. Does the Secretary of State
expect the committee to put back in place the temporary and
HORSA huts that were in use in 1979? Would he be satisfied with
arrangements which involved the dismantling of libraries, staff
rooms, common rooms, technology suites and science laboratories,
for these are all developments that we have been able to effect
during the last eight years?

There is a further flaw in the proposals. On the one hand, the
Government intends to legislate to enable schools to raise admission
limits to this arbitrary standard number which has been set at a date
before the Government's policy on falling rolls took shape. On the
other hand, since 1981 the Government has sought to remove up to 2
million surplus places by 1992. The consequence of implementing
that policy since 1981 and taking out surplus places is that the LEA
is now, in 1987, incapable of responding to the new proposals in
ways which will produce educational improvement. It will have to
reopen old buildings, put back into use temporary accommodation,
transfer practical equipment, refurbish rooms and redesignate
teaching spaces. In the case of some schools, new or more appropriate accommodation may be left unused as parents see as more
fashionable another school which may have less appropriate facilities. The committee, even if it were able to effect such changes,
dares not ponder the consequences if a previously preferred school
then becomes unpopular. The committee is most concerned that
schools which since 1979 have utilized surplus accommodation for
community use may now be required to forfeit this in favour of
accommodating more pupils.

In the even that a school, according to the proposed definition, is
designated to be full or oversubscribed, by what means or criteria
will it determine which pupils it accepts and which it rejects? In a
system based on market forces, what choices are available to those
who are neither socially mobile nor academically able? The
committee considers that one consequence will be an emigration to
the more favoured suburbs from the inner-city areas for those who
are both mobile and academically able, leaving those who are
already disadvantaged in other ways with no choice but to attend a
school which may not even be in their area. This will incur
additional costs in transport. The overall effect is divisive, expensive and educationally unsound.

HMI have emphasized, in their '5–16 Curriculum Matters', the
need for curriculum continuity. If parents of pupils at the age of
transfer can freely choose their secondary school, curriculum or

pastoral links between any one primary and its previously designated secondary school would disappear. Curriculum and pastoral
continuity will no longer be possible.

The system of appeals and appeals committees would also be
unable to function. The only reason for the refusal of a place [will
be] that the school is full. How then can any appeal be allowed
without alteration to these limits and without creating an impossible
situation for the school and all the children, with a consequent
requirement for extra resources and capital expenditure?

York Diocesan Council of Education – The proposals seems to rest
on the assumption that making parental choice paramount will raise
standards everywhere. There is general acceptance that in several
notable ways the legislation of the last decade has opened the way
towards more effective participation by parents in the running of
schools. And the right given them by the 1980 Education Act to
send their children to schools outside their immediate locality,
subject to availability of places, has served to strike a balance
between recognition of the administrative problems in running an
efficient education service, on the one hand, and respect for the
wishes of parents who previously had an extremely limited choice of
schools, on the other.

'Balance' is a key word in the discussion, and it provides the clue
to the approach which genuine concern for *all* the nation's children
should prompt. That priority requres efforts to preserve high
standards at schools which are already good (and therefore popular)
and to raise standards at those which are not sought after. At the
same time, LEAs must be able to make progress through rationalization of educational provision in their unpopular task of taking
surplus places out of commission – either closing small schools
where reasonable alternative arrangements are available, or taking
out of use parts of schools (or converting classrooms into needed
specialist facilities).

The effect of making consumerism sovereign may well be to
reduce the quality of education in the schools that are judged
successful, because the pressure of extra pupils will counter the
imaginative use of teachers, facilities and space which under
existing legislation helped to create their reputations. However, the
more articulate parents will always find a way through the system
for their children.

The real anxieties are for the children of the less articulate parents
and the less motivated. The Welfare State embodied the principle
that all children should receive an education suited to the fulfilment
of their potential. Although home circumstances have always been a
powerful influence on the futures of all children, there was built into

that concept the deliberate aim that those from less favoured backgrounds should through their schooling be brought within reach of higher goals than their parents attained or dreamed of attempting. With a network of schools set in a static situation, advance towards fixed targets would bring assured improvements for all. But that is not how things are. Thus, while the better schools may be expected to continue to do relatively well, the less fortunate schools will be struggling against (a) lower resources on account of reduced capitation, (b) poorer buildings, (c) plummeting staff morale and (d) the concentration in them of pupils heavily weighted towards the lower end of the academic scale – the children of parents who are less successful or less informed and forceful.

The resources made available are ever more limited. To talk of choice is therefore misleading, for it is used in the consultation paper to describe a system which is geared towards the children who reach the security of a good school and which stacks the odds against the rest. The proposals will deliver a body-blow to hopes of improving standards across the maintained sector – and nothing less than that is a worthy target.

The National Confederation of Parent–Teacher Associations accepts that some parents have been concerned at the school allocation arrangements in some authorities, and would like all parents to be happy with the allocation of the school their child should attend. When parents have a feeling of unease or frustration it undermines confidence in our educational system. An attempt to resolve this problem is welcomed.

The number of parents not achieving the school of their choice is, however, proportionally small, and NCPTA questions whether 'open enrolment' is the answer. If it were to become an actuality it might appear to satisfy parents by allowing choice, but we fear, it is almost impossible to apply. 'Popular' does not necessarily mean 'good', and good schools might be destroyed by an ill-founded comment. Further, the reputation and popularity of a particular school can change with an alteration in staffing, and simply the unfounded rumour of change or closure can cause an exodus. To ensure that all schools are good, well resourced and enjoy the understanding and support of the community they serve appears the better solution.

NCPTA supports the view that the governors should have the final decision on setting and any alteration in the [standard number of pupils] – after due discussion with LEA, headteacher and staff (teaching and non-teaching) and existing parents – while supporting the power of independent appeals committees [to decide individual cases] within the number.

It is essential that there be a final admission date: at present, schools need to have reasonably reliable figures by 31 March to lose/recruit staff. Will parents be able to change their mind after that date? If a pupil moves, what addition or subtraction might be made to financial allocation after planning is under way? We feel strongly there should be no negative change in budget allocations until the following year. There are arguments for stipulating that transfer between schools in the same age range and area should normally occur only at the beginning of a school year.

What provision will there be for entry to a year group as it moves through the school? NCPTA feels it essential that there should be provision to allow for the mobility of labour in the economy. If this provision is implemented, parents will expect funding to be available. LEAs should not be expected to meet costs from existing funds.

What will be the definition of 'prejudice [to] the provision of efficient education or the efficient use of resources'? What guidance will be given to appeals committees? Who will be empowered to make the final decision? There is considerable support for local pupils to have priority.

NCPTA is also concerned about the wider staffing implications of fluctuating enrolment. Teaching and non-teaching staff need to feel a sense of commitment to the school and a constant sense of insecurity will not help this. Well-qualified and dedicated staff are not always easy to find at short notice.

Will 'less popular' schools be supported for full curricular provision? NCPTA is anxious that an emphasis should be placed on finding out what makes them less popular and on improving them – or their image, if that is where the problem lies. There will be a need to ensure that they have good specialist staffing and offer the full provision appropriate to their pupils' ages and abilities.

NCPTA would remind the Government that the cost of transport effectively removes choice from some parents. In many areas geography also limits choice, and there is often a sensible wish for pupils to have the opportunity to attend a good school near home. Liaison between secondary schools and their feeder primaries is of great importance, and this will be difficult to achieve if pupils are able to go to one or more secondary schools from a wide range of primaries.

Secondary Heads' Association – DES *Circular 3/87*, dated 6 May 1987, was explicit about the need for forward planning to deal with the problem of falling rolls and to make the education service cost-effective. We therefore find ourselves astonished that, by 9 July of the same year, the DES, under the same Secretary of State, has brought out proposals, obviously forged in the heat of an election campaign, which will undermine completely the principles of its circular. While we clearly support the principle of a degree of parental choice, the changes needed in our educational provision must be planned and not whimsical. The Government's present plans will make any rational planning of school places impossible.

The year selected to determine the 'standard number', 1979–80, was the peak year for admissions to secondary schools, and the numbers admitted in that year were frequently housed in temporary accommodation. We would hope that a school operating at 100 overall places below its standard number would not find itself with an extra 100 first-year pupils. The circular is silent on this and all other management problems. The Secretary of State must realize that variation in intake of as much as 10 per cent can cause organizational difficulties of a major kind, with huge staffing and resource implications. Schools need at least six months to plan and put into effect all the necessary adjustments. We know this length of notice will not be available under the proposals.

'Popular schools': there is an unbelievable naïvety about this phrase. Frequently, a school's popularity in a town has far less to do with its effectiveness than its past history, especially when, out of three or four comprehensive schools, only one was based on a grammar school and inherited its name, its academic reputation and freqently its endowments. In other cases popularity is so fleeting that parental opinion will change with the fashions, the incidents and the accidents of the day, and schools will not have the period of stability to build up the long-lasting reputation that they all would wish to have.

There are serious consequences, too, in allowing popularity to determine admission limits in areas where there are large numbers of children of overseas origin. Does the Secretary of State really want to see Muslim schools, Afro-Caribbean schools and white schools in our inner cities, or would he want, as we do, to follow the recommendations of the Swann Committee and strive for integration of all our children in local schools with some attempt at racial mix? The same argument applies to working-class and middle-class children, and we are particularly concerned for those children for whom no one will be able, or interested enough, to make a choice.

Professional Association of Teachers – The paper makes the fundamental assumption that parents make judgements about schools as a result of careful thought and informed observation. It has not been the experience of this association that this is inevitably the case. Parents, like other people, sometimes make judgements on the basis of incomplete, biased or out-of-date information. A school's reputation can be a volatile thing, and an admissions policy which takes so much more note of parental choice may well result in greater fluctuations between one year and another than is currently the case.

While it is true that, at present, sometimes parents are refused admission to a school which could accommodate more children, the problem is not so simple as this bald statement implies. Leaving aside the question of human resources, we note that there is throughout this paper great emphasis on the physical capacity of a school. It is not, however, made clear what this is to mean. A school may be assessed in terms of its simple capacity to seat children at desks, or in terms of the facilities it can offer. A library which is adequate to the needs of 600 pupils will not be adequate to the needs of 900, for example, even though the school could offer enough unadorned classroom space for the extra pupils. The counting method using work-stations is woefully inadequate. Given the great emphasis on science and technology in the national curriculum proposals, a critical aspect of school capacity in the future will be laboratory capacity.

The association agrees that there has been widespread use of the flexibility available under the 1980 Act to spread intakes among schools. We accept that, in some cases, this has delayed a programme of necessary rationalization. We do not accept, however, that this has acted as a barrier to effective parental choice. On the contrary, it has sometimes been the very strong feelings of the local community, as expressed by parents, which have prevented that rationalization of schools provision which the DES would have liked to see. It is our fear that the heightened parental expectations which have already resulted from the publicity given to these proposals will exacerbate this problem.

An assumption underlying the paper is that a school is simply an administrative unit, the effectiveness of which is assessed by the parents as consumers but determined by such matters as its physical capacity. It is not. A school is also a community of people working together, long-term, at a task which is both demanding and complex. Any admissions policy which omits to remember this will not only be ineffectual: it will be dangerous.

Association of County Councils – The proposals would actually make matters more difficult for schools and LEAs to manage sensibly and for parent in general to be confident about the provision that will be made for their children. A preferable system would be for LEAs to be obliged to agree admissions limits with governors of schools and that the matter should be referred for adjudication to the Secretary of State only where there is irreconcilable disagreement. If parents are to have real opportunities to make choices it is essential that they should be able to do so within a system which operates fairly, efficiently and openly, and which can safeguard the features which led to the choice in the first place. The present proposals do not guarantee those outcomes for the majority of parents and are therefore seriously flawed.

We wholly endorse the importance of paying the closest possible attention to the wishes of parents. The practical problems arise when a marginal increase in meeting the preferences of some has to be set against a general reduction in the preferences of others.

Admission limits may be set lower than the 1979 intake (or a subsequent higher intake, or a school's theoretical physical capacity) in order to protect the quality of provision at a school in terms of sensible organization, reasonable class size and access to specialist provision. It is not at all clear how the proposed machinery, with its emphasis on highest possible admissions, could preserve this use of reasonable limits. Primary schools, for example, could be pushed back up to class sizes of 40 if successful appeals have created a high standard number and further appeals are successful in the following years, taking numbers beyond an already inflated intake. The standard number may also be unrealistically high where turnover has allowed extra admissions during the year.

The sensible use of limits to protect the quality of provision for all pupils over a period can be illustrated by the example of a town served by four secondary schools which, in the bulge years, were overcrowded and using extensive temporary accommodation. As numbers fell it became possible to remove the temporary accommodation, reducing the potential as well as the actual intake at all the schools. It might since have become possible to manage with only three schools, but numbers in the pre-school and early primary years already make it clear that a fourth school will be needed again. The LEA cannot assume that capital will be available for a future new school if one is closed now, and cannot anyhow sustain a closure proposal where there is clear evidence of future need for the provision.

The expressions of preference will inevitably not produce equal numbers for all four schools in the meantime, and it is likely that one or more will be fully subscribed and one or more undersubscribed. This does not necessarily mean a great difference in the esteem felt for schools or the quality of schools. The system requires an expression of preference, but that preference may be only a marginal decision taken on balance. If numbers at one or two schools are allowed to run down too greatly while the others remain full to capacity, the quality of education in the undersubscribed schools will suffer and they will be more costly to maintain than if all had a reasonable share of the numbers. In such circumstances it is reasonable to use reduced admission limits to spread numbers more evenly. Failure to manage admissions will increase the problems in many areas.

Association of Metropolitan Authorities – The present arrangements are in part a means of keeping a range of choices open, so that parents can have a reasonable scope for exercising preference. They allow LEAs sensibly to manage falling rolls and achieve the kind of rationalization which they and successive Governments have regarded as essential to deal with the effects of demography and to respond to unavoidable expenditure constraint. In common with proposals on financial delegation to schools and for grant-maintained schools, the new admissions proposals will run the risk of jeopardizing policies on joint and community use of school premises. Inflexible application of the proposals as presently outlined could mean that communities will be deprived of facilities which have been imaginatively opened up for their use as LEAs have taken advantage of declining pupil numbers overall.

The other risk in the proposals is that they will make schools experience fluctuating numbers, which will make for management problems. Financial management within school, the provision of school meals and the Government's intention that there shall be open tendering for specified services would all be made the more problematic if numbers in school varied sharply and at short notice from year to year.

Apart from recourse to the arbitrary limit prescribed by 1980 Act, LEAs ought to be able to refer to national standards in assessing the accommodation of their schools. The school premises regulations, which become mandatory on all schools from 1991, are an obvious reference point. If they were applied now, however, many existing schools would be found to have proper accommodation for numbers well below those admitted in 1979 and more recent years. Furthermore, LEAs should be able to have regard to the state of temporary and dilapidated buildings, which ought soon to be taken out of use. There is an unhealthy emphasis in the consultation document on premises alone.

Parent–Teachers Association of Wales – The broad objective of providing more choice is welcomed. The current arrangement whereby a parent has been able to express a preference, as distinct from a choice, has been misunderstood all too often and has led to resentment. A clarification of the procedures would be beneficial, and a readjustment to place more emphasis on parents' genuine and reasoned wishes is welcomed.

PTAW is concerned that the consultative paper does not appear to recognize the importance of a school within its community. Statements such as that the preferred school may be 'anywhere in the LEA, or within the area of another LEA' should be moderated to indicate that pupils would normally attend schools within a reasonable distance of their home. If the effective recruitment area is large and diffuse, the community relationship will become difficult to maintain. Parents and families will be less likely to participate fully in the school activities, both educational and social. PTAW maintains the promotion of improved home–school links as one of its foremost objectives and would not favour any proposal that might diminish this relationship.

The London Board of Jewish Religious Education point out that many parents are unable to select the school of their choice if it is in the area of an LEA other than that in which they reside, since in many instances the home LEA refuses to meet transport costs. Many parents residing outside the areas concerned are inhibited from expressing a preference when travelling costs are not met. This, to a very large extent, negates the principle of parental choice, and we urge that the new Education Act remedies this.

Commission for Racial Equality – It is essential that parental choice of schools be based on sound educational grounds and not on prejudice or racial considerations. It would be extremely damaging to race relations if, for example, a school was considered unpopular by the parents of prospective white pupils simply because their children would be educated next to black children. The possibility that this might lead to a degree of *de facto* racial segregation in education must be seriously considered. The commission recommends therefore that consideration should be given, in the drafting of the legislation and/or subsequent DES circulars, to what can be done to ensure that the image and performance of schools can be judged on a rational and informed basis by parents when selecting a school for their children.

The document refers to 'removing artificial barriers to recruitment'. The term 'artificial barriers' should be extended to include admissions arrangements and criteria that indirectly discriminate against particular racial groups. Since the purpose of the proposals is to secure wider parental choice, the forthcoming legislation should encompass any admissions criteria, such as school uniform requirements, catchment areas or language tests, that may exclude a significantly higher proportion of pupils from particular racial groups and so artificially limit parental choice. If such arrangements cannot be shown to be justifiable on educational grounds they will be unlawful under the Race Relations Act; the proposed legislation therefore presents an opportunity to ensure that this does not occur.

National and Local Government Officers' Association – The proposals assume an infinite flexibility in the movement of staff (both teaching and non-teaching), materials and other resources between schools in response to the fluctuations in the market for places in schools.

An outcome of these proposals is that schools will need to compete with each other for admissions. Resources which hitherto have been put into the education of children will need to be devoted to attracting parental choice in the market-place. When allied to the planned freedom of schools to spend their allocated budgets in line with their own priorities, there will inevitably be a concentration on those criteria which are deemed – rightly or wrongly – to be the measures of popularity at the expense of the other just as worthy pursuits.

These proposals, in undermining the role of LEAs in planning provision of schooling for all children within their own area, introduce market forces and competition into schools. They are concerned to meet parents' needs for the children solely by allowing 'popular' schools to increase in size, and show a complete disregard for the future of other schools and, more importantly, the children in them. We fail to see how this offers any improvement in real parental choice. The only way of ensuring quality education for all – which is what parents really want – is to raise the standards of *all* schools. And the only way of ensuring the Government's aim that 'pupils should be entitled to the same opportunities wherever they go to school' (as stated in the national curriculum proposals) is to promote equality of education provision for all pupils.

Children's Legal Aid Centre – The Government's plans, proclaimed under the banner of making state schools increasingly subject to market forces, seem concerned with parents rather than children. Giving parents greater choice of school will not help those children whose parents are unable or unwilling to exercise that choice in the full interests of their children. In other areas of 'consumer choice', purchasers who make the wrong decision suffer the consequences themselves, but in the field of schooling it is their children who suffer. So the simple 'justice' of the market-place is clearly inappropriate.

Unless minimum standards of provision are increased in all schools, the proposals in the consultative document will leave some children in inadequate, unpopular schools which they themselves have not chosen to attend.

We would also urge you to amend the law so that, as in Scotland, rights to choose a school transfer from parents to children when they reach 16. If young people of this age can decide whether or not to leave school, they are quite capable of deciding which school they should go to if they stay on; and English and Welsh school students are clearly as capable of exercising this responsibility as their Scottish counterparts.

National Association of Inspectors and Educational Advisers – Late recruitment of well-qualified staff, especially in the reception infant year, and the problem of resourcing new classes formed late in the year, could mean children being given poor conditions at a new school or being placed in grossly overcrowded situations. This in itself could lead from year to year to violent pendulum swings of pupil numbers as rumours spread of their difficulties. It leads to the term 'popular school' becoming a misnomer. Already popularity and unpopularity can rest on rumour, a single incident or personalities. We don't see this new legislation as helping an already difficult situation in most LEAs.

National Union of Teachers – The most important factor in parental choice is that parents should have access to a good local school for their children, with adequate buildings, accommodation, equipment and staffing. The Government's proposal to abolish planned admission limits will threaten that right. The plan to let schools admit up to capacity would cut across other considerations such as those expressed by the Government in its recent circular *Providing for Quality*:

The assessment of the viability of an individual school is not solely a matter of the number of pupils on roll. Much will depend on the age range and character of the school, but a true assessment must also take account of its ethos, the quality and balance of expertise of its teachers and its non-teacher support, links with neighbouring schools and colleges, the fitness for purpose of its premises and the extent to which all these factors can be sustained. In rural areas, account must also be taken of the distances to be travelled to alternative schools in the event of closure, and of the age of children making these journeys.

Admission procedures which gave parents the right to choose a school anywhere in the LEA or in another LEA might prove totally impracticable with regard to the provision of transport and, indeed, might increase such costs drastically. Parents should be aware that it is they who might have to bear the cost if they choose a school outside their LEA area; thus there is a hidden price to pay for the privilege of choice held out as a prospect by the Government.

National Association of the Teachers of Wales (UCAC) – The wheel has turned. Forty years ago, in 1947, the first Welsh-medium school was established. But what a struggle it has been over the past decades for Welsh parents who wished to send their children to Welsh-medium schools! Throughout the 1960s parents sent their children on a daily mile journey to a school of their choice, and made sacrifices to achieve the elementary right to choose a school for their children. Now we see the Government legislating for all parents to be able to choose their children's schools. UCAC hopes that we will not see the parents of Wales presented with further problems in obtaining a Welsh-language education for their children. But there are problems. Although schools have the right to admit as many pupils as the building can accommodate, almost all Welsh-medium schools are already full, and in some counties Welsh units are established instead of schools. Will the same conditions apply to the 'units', particularly where the demand for places in the Welsh unit is increasing and there are empty rooms in the remainder of the school?

London Boroughs' Association – Where there are single-sex selective schools, currently of equal size by use of admission limits, the effects of abolishing the limits could be to admit a greater number of pupils to one school than the other, and this could lay the authority open to action under equal opportunities legislation. It is important therefore that the provision in the consultative paper [governing selective schools] should be interpreted so as to allow for a defined number of pupils to be admitted to any selective school, the number being fixed in relation to the level of ability, and to enable an equal number of boys and girls to be selected.

Assistant Masters' and Mistresses' Association – The proposals raise the disturbing threat of damage to community relations. If parents are given uncontrolled freedom of choice they may well elect against schools in which a mix of cultures exists. The recent dispute at Overthorpe School in Dewsbury offers a distressing example of this. The result could be the polarizing of pupils into 'single-culture' schools. The association is seriously troubled that the valuable policy of educational integration might be abandoned and that there could be damage to multicultural education.

College of Preceptors – Whilst the paper does not explicitly say so, it would appear that all schools are considered to have low standards. It seems that the underlying intention of the Government is rather more to rationalize provision by the elimination of a number of pupil places than to give parents better choice. Rather, parental choice is being exploited in order to shift the pupil population to fewer, 'popular' schools at the expense of others, which could then be declared redundant.

Popularity is not necessarily synonymous with quality. This proposal, therefore, does not accord with the Government's wishes in regard to the quality of education. If the proposals for a national curriculum are implemented as intended, should and will there be much, if any, difference between one school and another?

Campaign for the Advancement of State Education – The 1980 Act goes far enough. The 1980 Act, with its provision for appeals and further recourse to the DES and the courts, gives a good balance between the rights of the individual and the needs of all the children in an area. We believe that most LEAs of all political persuasions operate the Act sensibly, giving parent the maximum choice they can consistently with running a fair and efficient service. If a few 'over-manage' admissions, there are checks in the system already: these might be improved.

The Conservative Education Association warmly supports the Government's firm commitment to improve parental choice. However, the vast majority of LEAs manage to meet the first choice of nearly all parents, with a sucess rate of over 90 per cent the norm. In many LEAs the figure is well over 90 per cent. (The exceptions are those LEAs that operate selective systems, when most parents will not get their first choice, which is usually a grammar school.) Admissions policy has to take into account three different and sometimes contradictory factors. There is the need to meet parental wishes wherever reasonably possible. Secondly, there is the need to ensure a certain school size on educational grounds. Thirdly, there is the need, often stressed by this Government, to ensure the most efficient use of scarce resources. The first and third of these factors in particular can conflict.

Among the most successful initiatives introduced under this Government have been GCSE, CPVE and TVEI. They all require changes in teaching method and resourcing, including the need to use more space. For example, the teaching of science is more laboratory-based than it used to be, and LEAs have built more laboratories in schools despite falling rolls. All these initiatives have been introduced since 1979, and account must be taken of these changed needs in any new legislation. It is a matter of some concern that, in a number of places in the series of Government discussion documents, there seems to be insufficient recognition of the changes that these initiatives have brought about. It would be a tragedy if the new Education Bill were to undermine initiatives which the Government has only just brought in.

It should be remembered that the popularity of individual schools usually goes in phases, often linked to a particular and popular head. The idea that unpopular schools can simply be left to decline and ultimately close through lack of business is not one that the CEA can support. We do not believe that market forces alone should determine educational provision.

Society of Local Authority Chief Executives – The document notes that there has been widespread use of the flexibility available under the 1980 Act to spread intakes among schools, but it does not also acknowledge that these powers have considerably helped in the rationalization of education provision. These advantages will be undermined by the proposals, and the consultation paper, surprisingly, does not address this issue at all. It is remarkable, given the nature of the debate which has taken place about the use of school resources, not least the views expressed by the Audit Commission, that such a fundamental proposal can be put forward without any reference at all to this severe drawback.

The proposals also sow the seeds of conflict yet again between governing body and authority. If the physical capacity of a school exceeds the 1979 standard number it will be open to the governing body to seek to admit up to the physical capacity; and if the LEA object, the matter will be referred to the Secretary of State. It seems more than likely that the Secretary of State will opt for an admission limit equivalent to the physical capacity. In a few cases this could mean the difference between the larger primary school being able to seek grant-maintained status and not being in that position.

Society of Education Officers – The need for a standard number that reflects the capacity of a school is accepted and in conjunction with the 1980 Act has been useful. There are, however, a number of points that arise, and the definition of the physical capacity of a school is needed. The concept of a figure to which a school can fill does not include the identification of various kinds of accommodation necessary to meet efficient education provision. This must include the ability at secondary level to meet GCSE, CPVE and other requirements and throughout to meet the core curriculum as it is to be prescribed. The 1979 figures often conceal the fact that many schools were not properly resourced for the curriculum on offer. Since then, groups have had to reduce [capacity] to tackle certain curriculum changes, i.e. high technology, and other practical subjects.

Some schools are limited in the number of meals they can supply. Unless this informs the establishment of a standard number, it would be possible for more children to demand meals than can be provided.

Particularly at primary level, where schools are oversubscribed, authorities will have to establish initial guidelines to which to work in allocating places, e.g. the closest residents have first claim. There is a need to recognize that this will be so, otherwise parents will have false expectations aroused. In addition, there is no guarantee where a 'feeder' school system has been successfully established that this will be able to continue.

The reference to the date of enactment as being September 1990 is unrealistic unless Royal Assent to the Bill is achieved by Easter of 1988. Many of the essential processes begin before the autumn term for the following autumn term, twelve months. The summer term is needed to prepare for this.

London Diocesan Board for Schools – Included in the proposals should be an assurance that teacher–pupil ratios will not be lowered as a result of admitting pupils up to the physical limits of the school.

Several schools in 1979 were able to take higher numbers because pupils occupied temporary buildings; these buildings in some cases have been removed and in others patched up; in either case it would be unrealistic to enforce the present proposals. It is commonly estimated that the nature of the work for GCSE requires approximately 10 per cent more space, so many secondary schools are already experiencing acute problems through shortage of teaching and storage space. This again is inconsistent with using a 1979 standard number.

Church of England Board of Education – In so far as Church schools tend to be popular, the proposals could be seen to be advantageous to Church schools. With the present position, governors, diocesan education committees and LEAs by and large negotiate to try to share the impact of falling rolls. We wonder whether the long-term effect of the proposals might not be to build up considerable bitterness between those representing county and Church schools respectively. In certain areas the ration of children attending voluntary schools to those in county schools could be significantly affected. One practical point needs to be borne in mind when the relevant legislation is being framed. Governing bodies must be given the power to recruit temporarily to less than the physical capacity of the building, (a) when a new school is building up numbers year by year and (b) whenever a primary school has three intakes of pupils per year.

The Salford Diocese Schools Commission is in favour of parental choice but is concerned to ensure that today's choice does not become tomorrow's compulsion. Whilst seeking to provide the widest choice for parents, the Government and the Roman Catholic providing bodies must pay due attention to making the best use of the available provision and ensure that adequate and reasonably accessible provision is retained to enable future parents to have a choice for their child.

The admission proposals as they would relate to Roman Catholic schools require specific amendment. They would in some cases remove the Catholic parents' valued opportunity of choice for a Catholic school. The Schools Commissions ask that a clause be added to the effect that, in the case of an aided or special-agreement school, admission [limits should] be compatible with arrangements published by the governors to preserve the religious character of the school.

Methodist Church Division of Education and Youth – Many schools from time to time and for various reasons experience periods when local opinion, rightly or wrongly, is critical of them. Under normal circumstances with LEA support and advice they can be helped to overcome their difficulties or to present themselves in a more favourable light. There will be little chance for them to recover from the sort of setbacks which can sometimes affect schools if their rolls are allowed to fall substantially – as they well may, under these proposals.

Empty desks and empty classrooms are not conducive to good staff morale. There is little doubt that staff will be affected by the proposals. Their chances of redundancy will be greatly increased. At best they will be redeployed within the area. At worst they will be unemployed, since it appears that under the proposals for financial delegation to schools LEAs will be able to do no more than recommend their appointment to another school in their area.

Association of Career Teachers – Some ACT members consider that the present proposals are using a sledgehammer to crack a nut and make the point that, if LEAs could be prevented in some way from tinkering with admission limits, then these proposals would be unnecessary. The appeals machinery which exists at present was set up by the then Secretary of State to deal with this precise problem, and it has proved to be less than satisfactory in many LEAs, particularly those where the concept of parental choice is not supported.

Some members were worried that a local child could be squeezed out of a place at a popular school by a child from outside the area whose parent had 'booked' his or her place in advance, and it was felt that preference should be given to local children, otherwise they could be penalized because of the system. Parents whose children were unsuccessful in gaining a place at the local school of their choice should not be expected to bear the costs of transport if they subsequently chose a school outside the area. It was also feared that parents from outside the area could persuade the governors of a local school to change their status and become grant-maintained against the wishes of local parents.

The North Yorkshire Education Committee challenges you to produce evidence: (1) to suggest that this is a widespread problem; (2) in what particular respects the service provided in North Yorkshire is so lacking as to justify the sort of measures proposed; (3) in what respects [these proposals] are likely to improve the situation in North Yorkshire.

The committee is opposed to the detail of many of the proposals which it considers variously dictatorial, ill considered, overhasty, simplistic, unsupported by research evidence, not apparently meeting with the favour of those they are intended to help and unlikely in many cases to lead to the desired outcomes or to justify the increased expense and disruption involved (not least since the ability of the Secretary of State to deliver must be seriously questioned).

Birmingham Education Authority – The absence of reference to the Education (No. 2) Act 1986 is surprising, since section 33 requires authorities to strengthen the position of parents very firmly, by the requirement that governors of schools be consulted annually about admission arrangements, including the number of pupils to be admitted. Birmingham LEA is consulting governors, and admissions for September 1988 will not be set until their responses have been considered. Given the Government's intention to delegate more power and responsibility to governors, it is surprising and inconsistent that they are not trusted to be the best judges of a school's capacity. The Secretary of State's aim, which Birmingham shares, can be achieved – and is being achieved in our case – without new legislation. We would rather work with the Secretary of State to clarify existing arrangements, if this is necessary to fulfil his purpose nationally.

Buckinghamshire County Council in its admissions policy in recent years, has given strong support to the general principle of enabling schools to admit the pupils who want to go there. There have, however, been a number of situations where the authority has felt it important to balance its support for this general principle with action under the provisions of the 1980 Act to plan admissions and to fulfil its responsibility to provide appropriate and efficient education for all pupils.

In the secondary sector, the provisions of the 1980 Act have been a corner-stone of Buckinghamshire's work. It has helped the authority to plan so that all schools kept open after a review will achieve an adequate level of admissions to ensure continuing viability. The authority has aimed at a ten-year period of broad stability from the proposed date of implementation of its proposals. This has been very much welcomed and has given people reassurance which has been important in helping them to accept the period of upheaval which inevitably goes with reorganization. Buckinghamshire has been able to plan admissions which will sustain all schools required in the longer term through the trough years, in the interests of the pupils and the curriculum they can be offered.

Our experience is that it is not possible or prudent to remove all surplus places from an area, and we deliberately retain places as a 'cushion' to allow for some flexibility over the ten-year planning period. This kind of prudent planning by LEAs could well be negated by the loss of control over admission arrangements.

Surrey Education Authority – The need for flexibility is paramount. In the case of primary schools, any rigid application of a 'standard number' formula could lead to insuperable problems in so far as the admission of rising-5s is concerned. The authority is committed to a policy of increasing opportunities for the under-5s. This will require the provision of additional accommodation; and, at the present time of 220 first schools in Surrey, 104 would be overcrowded if summer rising-5s were included as part of the standard number.

Governors of Hove Park School, East Sussex – Market force education provision is unacceptable. There are better ways of ensuring that schools operate effectively than throwing them into competition with each other. There will be winners and losers: the losers will suffer exponentially as they further lose the resources whereby they can get better.

Planning education provision becomes impossible – this is not simply closing one supermarket because it is unprofitable and opening another somewhere else. Headteachers will have to 'market' their school, and some will be better at it than others – hardly a rational basis for parents to exercise choice.

Headmaster of Hove Park School, East Sussex – The removal of admission limits for schools will result in an undesirable situation in which schools will be encouraged to sell themselves in the market-place, losing sight of their true purpose and directing the energies of their staff into areas which have little to do with the education of children. The proposal will result in a hierarchy of schools, with those at the bottom of the league table becoming increasingly undersubscribed and therefore undesirable. It will create a crisis of confidence in many schools, causing them to shift their ground according to misconceived external criteria. The proposal will encourage complacency among schools at the head of the league. In these schools it is likely that classes will be large and the wider elements of education ignored. The competitive ethos will permeate a school's organization at the cost of educational philosophy.

Chairman of Governors, Prudhoe County High School, Northumberland – We gave full marks to the paper. It seemed to us entirely reasonable that a ratepayer should be able to obtain for his children what he considers to be value for money. At Prudhoe we would certainly not want to enrol children whose parents felt they could obtain more appropriate education elsewhere. Likewise, we would welcome youngsters from beyond our catchment area who preferred our scenario. Several governors from rural areas have expressed concern that this freedom of choice might prejudice the viability of their small-roll schools. My response has been that, if village schools claim to offer particular qualities of excellence, parents will opt for them. If parents secede, then the remedy lies in the hands of the schools themselves.

(The question of opting out of the State system has led to an awful lot of huffing and puffing by Northumberland Education Committee – quite needlessly in our view. The idea is a daft one, and it merely needs governors and teachers to tell parents this forcefully. What councillors (and perhaps Mr Baker) seem to forget is that schools have a vast built-in resistance to change. Education never leads a social revolution. Politicians can legislate as fervently as they like, but the pace of progress is essentially geared to the tempo of Form 2c.)

7

Charging for School Activities

THE PROPOSALS

*In a consultation document (published in October 1987) Mr Baker
sought advice from education authorities on how to clarify the law
governing charges for certain school activities. The document said the
Government remained firmly committed to the principles of free school
education established by the Education Act 1944; but that since that Act
became law there had been a widely accepted understanding that this
principle was not intended to prevent LEAs or schools from charging
parents for what were generally described as 'extras'. The range of extras
had widened, and almost all LEAs and schools now passed on some or all
of the cost of certain activities.*

*However, the judgement in the 1981 Hereford and Worcester case
concerned with charges for instrumental music tuition – the only occasion
when the relevant section of the 1944 Act had been tested in the courts –
had called into question the legality of much current practice. So had
recent reports by the local government ombudsman dealing with charges
for board and lodging. These developments had caused concern to LEAs
and schools that long-standing arrangements were under threat, and they
had asked that the legal position be clarified. There was no question of
requiring any LEA or school to charge for any service, but Mr Baker
wanted views about the need for legislation expressly allowing them to go
on charging for certain limited activities. He suggested a list of categories,
to be included in primary legislation, for which it would be unlawful to
charge.*

*He might also take power to make regulations (which would be subject
to Parliament's approval) specifying items for which charges could
lawfully be made, subject to full remission for those receiving income
support or family credit and subject to governors giving help in other cases*

of hardship. These chargeable costs might include such things as individual music tuition; theatre tickets; transport to a swimming pool or field study centre; board and lodging at a residential centre; and extra insurance for activities away from school. Regulations might require that certain charges could be levied only with the agreement of parents.

Advice was also sought on whether the law should be changed to prevent parents being obliged to pay charges in kind by providing essential equipment or materials.

THE DEBATE

Who knows when an 'extra' is essential?

Christopher Everest
Headmaster, Drayton Manor High School, London Borough of Ealing

Charging for certain school activities is a difficult and emotive subject. In the comments on the consultation paper there are two main themes, one simple and essentially political, the other complex, many sided and practical. The first concerns the principle of charging, which is seen by some as almost wholly unacceptable; the second is about the detailed proposals set out by Mr Baker. Subject to suitable arrangements for remission in cases of hardship, some charges are acceptable to many of the respondents. They are not felt to be incompatible with the universally approved principle of free education. At this point difficulties are seen over the definition of free and chargeable areas, over 'essentials' and 'extras' and over the cost of remission and the division of control of charging between LEAs and governors.

Beyond these issues is a third dimension, part history, part long-term policy. Society has changed greatly since 1944; the average standard of living has more than doubled and may well double again in the next 30 years. Custom and practice in other countries, mentioned only once in the responses, cannot be wholly irrelevant. In some countries parents pay more, sometimes substantially more, for stationery and books than is ever expected in the United Kingdom. The problem of financing a good education service will not go away. The shortage of teachers of mathematics, physics and CDT and the very unequal provision of books and maintenance in different areas are just two aspects of a problem which has existed, with different degrees of intensity, since 1944. Against this background it is possible to see the proposals in the consultation paper as reasonable in many respects for the present, but full of uncertainties over interpretation in the future and rather restrictive in their impact on the education system's development.

The argument for a totally free education service is always attractive. Full funding at an adequate level from central and local revenues, with charges limited to activities outside the school day and unrelated to the curriculum, may indeed be the only way of ensuring that no pupil is ever prevented by limited means from taking part in educationally desirable activities. Such a policy would relieve the pressure on low-income families and fulfil the apparent intentions of the 1944 Act. This view, however, ignores both the changes in parental expectations of education and the fact that there has to be a limit to what local authorities can be expected to provide. In some areas certain activities would simply stop if all charges were illegal. A totally free, fully-funded service is not on the agenda.

Fundamental to any consideration of the Government's proposals is the attempt to define those parts of the education service which must be free and those parts for which charges are allowed. In the responses doubts were expressed about the wisdom of attempting a definition of the free areas. More widespread was concern over the interpretation of an 'adequate provision of books, equipment and materials'. Frequent interpretation in the courts is an obvious danger; inflexibility in changing circumstances in another. Although the idea of entrenching the free areas in primary legislation has strong support, it may be wiser not to invite judicial interpretation of the adequacy of LEAs' or governors' arrangements. If a full list of the free areas is undesirable, it will be best not to form an incomplete list.

Apart from references to 'adequacy' the principal comments about the free list were that voluntary contributions should be allowed for improving school premises, and that examination fees should be chargeable for resits, unacceptable absences and unsuitable entries. On charging for individual or small-group music tuition, opinion and current practice vary widely, with the argument cutting across the usual divisions. The argument for free provision, as put forward by the musicians is very persuasive, especially in the light of GCSE requirements and the fact that ongoing charges for tuition are for many parents much more onerous than other charges such as those for day visits. An immediate ban on charging might mean the end of instrumental tuition in some areas. An acceptable compromise could involve two provisions: no LEA or school to charge for individual or small-group if a charge was not in force in January 1988; all such tuition either in school time or examination-related to be free from September 1990.

The list of chargeable areas was largely acceptable to those not wholly opposed to charges. But, in addition to the question of instrumental tuition, some difficulties were anticipated over transport costs, home economics and CDT materials, charges in kind (calculators, writing materials, etc.) and the proposed remission arrangements.

LEAs clearly want to control charging policy and remission. They are opposed to the different practice within areas which governors' discretion might produce. In some responses the difficulty and the cost of implementing remission arrangements were recognized. A statutory requirement for remission schemes was welcomed, but there will be a net cost to public funds in respect of increased claims for exemption from charges and the administrative costs of such schemes at LEA or school level.

Whether considered as a matter of policy or of law, charging is a difficult area, a minefield of problems and inconsistencies. In practice, in many schools – perhaps most – it is not a big issue. The best solution, therefore, may be to deal only with the situation created by the Hereford case and the ombudsman rulings. If instrumental tuition became free from 1990 and if charges were specifically authorized, though not required, for residence and for visits, whether or not exam-related, the principal areas of uncertainty would be removed. There need be no reference to other charges. Schools would continue to deal appropriately with cases of hardship. Without a statutory requirement, the problem of remission arrangements under local financial management would not exist. The 'free' and the 'chargeable' parts of education would neither be set in tablets of stone, nor be opened to more frequent legal action. Parents would continue to pay for some extras, and the question of hardship would be dealt with by the school, or, if preferred, by the DHSS.

Such a policy would be compatible with the Government's determination to make substantial changes in the education system. It would avoid the most obvious problems over charges and allow time for a thorough look at continental experience and for full consideration of how these issues may appear in future years.

THE ADVICE

Association of Metropolitan Authorities – We are pleased to see the explicit commitment to the principle of free education, and we recognize and applaud the evident care which has been taken by the paper's authors to suggest acceptable ways of resolving what are often intractable problems . . . although we have very serious reservations about the implications of a number of the proposals.

We were pleased to note that there is no question of *requiring*

LEAs or schools to charge for any service. We support that, but we would go further and say that we expect that, if any discretion to charge is given, Government will not assume in setting expenditure levels that charges *will* be made. A number of our member authorities have noted that where a power (not a duty) to charge exists, district auditors have pressed for charges to be levied. If there is a discretion, it should be a genuine one. When the clarifying legislation is in place, the individual authority should state its policy on charging which would have the form of a direction to governing bodies (which governors might in any case welcome). Governors could depart from that policy only to better it: they should have no power to derogate from it.

We see the best approach to the general problem as being, first, to specify in legislation those aspects of provision for which charges would be unlawful, and then to go on to specify in regulations those limited areas in which charges might be made. Aspects of provision not specified in one category or another would be deemed not normally chargeable. We find the list [covering categories for which it would be unlawful to charge] broadly acceptable.

The formulation should protect the right of the LEA to require payment of fees if pupils were entered for examinations against the advice of the school, to recover fees if exams were missed for no good reason or to cover the cost of late entries and perhaps resits.

We should deal separately with the issue [of books], equipment and materials. There will always be parents who will wish to supplement the provision made by the school. However generous the local authority, it may not in most cases be able to provide, for example, commentaries on set texts, or dictionaries for personal use.

As to chargeable items, the procedure suggested is acceptable, but the regulations should permit LEAs, not governors, to make charges. Of the possible areas of permitted charges listed, it is not clear why [the first category] refers only to individual music tuition; it is possible that sports coaching, or speech and drama work might be treated similarly. Where visits and journeys are made by groups of pupils as an integral part of their curriculum (by which we do not mean simply the core subjects in the national curriculum, but the full range of studies undertaken), then it seems unreasonable to charge them either for transport or insurance; but many LEAs would probably be content to have discretion to recoup admissions charges and board and lodgings costs. If the visits are for recreational or social purposes, or for purposes deemed as enhancements to the curriculum, then the other costs could be recouped. The list of aspects of provision for which charges might be made largely reflects current practice.

Editorial Board of *Forum*, while welcoming the government's affirmation of commitment to the principle of free primary and secondary education, believes it is now necessary to ensure that the principle applies universally, without discrimination in respect of school location or access to any area of the school curriculum, as an essential prerequisite for equality of opportunity.

We are concerned at the increasing erosion of that principle, especially over recent years, and the growing disparity in its application which has resulted in educational disadvantage for children attending certain schools – often those in economically and socially disadvantaged catchment areas – where the provision of books and other essential learning materials is so inadequate that there is now reliance on parental contribution or individual purchase as well as shared use by pupils. We have noted that HMI have expressed similar concern in their annual reports on the effects of LEA expenditure policies, and have identified the inadequacies as a significant factor accounting for poor work and inhibiting independent work. The financial circumstances of parents or guardians must not be allowed to debar from participation in mainstream educational activities available to their peers; to do so is further to disadvantage precisely those most likely to be already experiencing disadvantage through straitened home circumstances and restricted educative experiences outside school.

The location of the school means that certain facilities essential for children's physical development, health and a properly balanced curriculum may be available on the premises or within cost-free walking distance or require transport. Free access to such facilities must fall within the principled guarantee [of the 1944 Act] and must therefore apply to such curricular activities as games and swimming, regardless of the location of playing fields and swimming-pools. Whether or not a child learns to swim may be a life-or-death matter.

Forum is strongly opposed to the suggestion of giving the Secretary of State a new power to make regulations listing those items for which charges might be passed on to parents. We consider that such a new power would be dangerously open-ended and could be used seriously to undermine the principle enshrined in the 1944 Act.

Forum recognizes and welcomes the many initiatives now taken by teachers, schools and LEAs to offer a great variety of opportunities for children to participate in a wide range of activities never envisaged at the time of the 1944 Education Act. We would wish to encourage such developments. We would also hope that the community, industry, voluntary organizations, parent–teacher associations, etc. will support them financially so as to widen access for children who cannot participate for financial reasons in the rich array of extra-curricular 'extras' offered by many schools and for which charges have regrettably to be made.

Forum considers that LEAs should be required to publicize their remission arrangements for hardship cases; and that, while ensuring that families in receipt of income support or family credit pay no charges, schemes should be flexible enough to cover others identified by the school as needing such help. *Forum* is concerned that charging for any school-based activity within the normal school day can lead to some children to absent themselves, with or without their parents' knowledge, and then to associate with delinquent truants. We urge the Government to heed this warning when formulating its policies on charging for school activities.

Secondary Examinations Council (Sir Wilfred Cockcroft) – Once again, what we hoped was a reasonably simple matter is turning out to be complicated. In geography the problem of deciding between 'required' and 'recommended' is so often left to teachers, who are then put in the dilemma of trying to act in the best interests of their pupils. The examining groups seem to almost take a delight in leaving matters to teachers' judgement. I have asked about geography in general, but we cannot stop there: each group, for example, has a geology syllabus and fieldwork (usually equivalent to about three days of work) features in them all. The word 'trips' is not used as such, but I am willing to wager that teachers will not think much geology can be done in the school back-yard.

Syllabuses in agricultural science, environmental science and rural science also all make reference to work outside the classroom. One (WJEC rural science) recommends 'visits' as such. Without appropriate investigational work in such subjects, we would of course probably have taken the groups to task on a 'fitness for purpose' tack, within the national criteria. The same applied to biology.

Similarly, the understanding of subject content in GCSE history and performance in the assessment objectives of empathy and 'handling' of evidence can be developed very effectively through visits to museums and historical buildings. In social science, survey work will be necessary but this can be instigated on a local, probably no-cost basis. There are also GCSE catering syllabuses (approved under the general criteria) which require visits to hotels and restaurants – it is sometimes possible to avoid this if the school meals kitchen is cooperative.

The above relates only to field-trip costs and does not of course cover other 'costs' in following syllabuses. For example the GCSE music criteria state that candidates who receive no instrumental tuition outside the course should be able to gain high grades. This indicates that instrumental teaching must be seen as an integral part of the course – and therefore free? The question lies in the extent of that tuition and over what range of instruments. Also to be remembered in non-free education are the costs of material in such subjects as home economics and CDT. Oh dear!

Camden Community Law Centre – It is pleasing to note that the Government is firmly committed to the principle of free school education. It should also be equally committed to acknowledging that charging for 'extras' is not necessarily acceptable simply because the 'practice is long-standing and of almost universal application'. To suggest that the 'legal basis for such charges has become unclear' is an understatement. There is no legal basis in section 61 of the Education Act 1944 for much current practice.

The consultation document clearly identifies itself as a response to the concerns expressed by LEAs and schools which fear that they will no longer be able to continue the practice of charging as a result of recent court and local ombudsman decisions. In light of this, it is understandable that the document does not fundamentally question the whole practice of charging for so-called 'extras'. Instead it merely seeks to legitimize and regulate this practice. The concern is for a means of alleviating the burden for LEAs and schools rather than for parents.

However, it is vital that parents are not forced into the position of taking on greater financial responsibility for the education of their children by new legislation in the form proposed in the consultation document. Although it is not intended to require charges for any education service provided by LEAs or maintained schools, it is likely that there will be few, if any, schools/LEAs which will not take advantage of the opportunity to offload some of their costs on to parents with legal backing. Yet such costs would be better met by increased central/local government expenditure on maintained schools.

National Confederation of Parent–Teacher Associations – Home economics and possibly craft are areas where the family can benefit from the pupil's activity, and it is traditional in many schools for payment to be made for the products of these areas. As long as schools are realistic in their demands for these subjects, and do have a discreet fall-back system for families that are really unable to budget for these, the system is not unreasonable. An exception would obviously have to be made for examination course demands that were likely to be beyond the realistic expectations of the everyday family for everyday food or home ornaments.

Trips are an essential aspect of the wider part of a school's curriculum. They will introduce some pupils to theatrical, historical, geographical and residential experiences that they might not otherwise experience. NCPTA welcomes this aspect of school life but recognizes that where they are not an essential part of the examination curriculum they could cause a considerable burden to the school's budget. The saddening point is that for some pupils it will only by the school that might suggest these experiences, and those may well be the very pupils who could not afford to pay.

Means-testing and other ways of directing money to those who need it can be divisive and open to misuse by those who could afford to pay but see a way not to. NCPTA would like to be assured that ways of actively helping children to greater opportunities and experiences are being sought and would not like to see legislation foor charges making it difficult for this to occur. Allowing governing bodies to set difference charges would in essence make schools selective on the grounds of ability to pay. This would put the parent rather than the child at the centre of the state education service and so not be in accord with what the NCPTA sees as the principle behind the provision of free education.

When we look at out 'competitor countries', we acknowledge that there is sometimes a stark difference in the expectation placed on parents to provide. It is, however, unfair and foolish to look at the difference in parental contribution alone. In many of these countries education enjoys a significantly higher position in national esteem. Parents may pay more, but so often does the State. The buildings and standard equipment are often superior to those in England and Wales; so also are the esteem and financial reward afforded to the teaching profession.

Surrey Education Authority welcomes the general trend of this paper, particularly the recognition of the fact that a clarification of policy is needed. The authority welcomes a specific list of items for which no charges can be made, and also the regulations which would allow charges for certain items to be passed on to parents. However, many reservations have been expressed in connection with the freedom of governing bodies to vary the permitted list. This freedom will lead to the fragmentation of the LEA's policy and will produce a variation in practice which would present an incoherent picture to parents.

The list of categories for which it would be unlawful to charge has received general agreement, particularly individual music tuition. It is particularly important that only those examinations approved for payment by the LEA should be free to pupils. If this were not the case schools operating local financial delegation would be subject to the financial exigencies arising from parental whims. Schools and

LEAs should also be allowed to charge for resits and for examinations in which pupils disqualify themselves. At present the schools in this authority charge for link course travel pre-16. Schools also charge a nominal fee for transport to games matches.

Within the 'central core' [of items protected from charging] it is important to include provision related to learning difficulties, in order that 'remedial' or 'dyslexic' support is protected from charging.

In principle the list [of items for which charges could lawfully be made] is welcomed, but concern has been expressed at the use of transport to the local swimming-pool as an example of a permitted charge. This arises from the presence of swimming-pools on the sites of some schools and the fact that many people view swimming as part of the school curriculum. The list of items for which charges might be made needs to be more comprehensive.

It is possible to summarize Surrey's *de facto* charging policies under the following headings:

(1) Material and ingredients: (a) charges for items if taken away or consumed; (b) indirect charging through students bringing ingredients and materials.
(2) Optional activities to extend PE programme: transport and cost of using facility, e.g. sports centre, bowling alley, skating rink.
(3) Curriculum enhancement through additional activities: transport, entry costs and residential costs, e.g. theatre groups in school, theatre and concert visits, fieldwork throughout the school, general educational visits.
(4) (a) optional additional equipment to support the curriculum – general indirect charging through pupils providing items, e.g. calculators, optional reference books (dictionary, atlas, bible), mathematical equipment; other optional books as opposed to basic texts; (b) basic equipment pupils are required to provide, e.g. writing implements, PE kit, protective clothing (aprons, laboratory coats), computer disks for BIS.
(5) Examination fees, i.e. private entries; resits; pupils who disqualify themselves without good reason.
(6) Individual music tuition outside curriculum time.
(7) Match fees: refreshments and transport.
(8) Deliberate vandalism.
(9) Optional extra-curricular activities, e.g. ski trips, foreign travel.

The above list of present charges in Surrey would give an indication as to what an LEA should and should not provide.

Sheffield Education Committee – In framing regulations, some key principles should be followed:

(a)   The basic principle of free education must be maintained. The proposals must not be seen or used as the thin edge of the wedge to introduce fees progressively into any maintained schools.
(b)   The power of any body to levy charges should always be discretionary and not obligatory.
(c)   There should be a continuing equity between schools so that the range and level of charges for activities at any particular school do not become a barrier to choice of school for some parents.
(d)   As charges should be limited to desirable but not essential activities, parents should not be placed in a position where, in practice, their children have little option but to take part in those activities.

The document suggests that the governors of any school should, after having considered the LEA's policy, be allowed to adopt their own policy within the national framework. It would seem inequitable and inconsistent with the principles outlined above for the governors to be given such powers. A better approach would be for the LEA to be required, from the national list of items for which charges might be levied, to state its policy on any particular item which should be free in its area and to show how its allocation of finance to the school covers such a policy. It would thus be open to the governors to be more generous, i.e. not to charge for other items, but not to be less generous.

Manchester Education Authority – The criteria for remission of charges are to include (at the least) that the pupil's family receive income support or family credit.

Who will be responsible for inquiring into parents' financial circumstances and for checking up on the various benefits which families might be in receipt of? Who will take on this major administrative task? Does the Secretary of State recognize the stigma associated with receipt of public benefits, and the consequential under-claiming this causes, particularly for means-tested entitlements?

Manchester LEA welcomes the proposal that parents should be fully informed about the 'extras' for which they are charged for their children's education. Will the Secretary of State go further and require governing bodies to publish annual accounts of charges and remission, and give to individual parents an itemized 'invoice' of the costs which parents will have to meet each term? Does the Secretary of State accept that, for parents in financial hardship (whether or not they are eligible for remission), a school's policy on charging will have a bearing on parental choice of schools? Is this the Government's underlying intention?

Lancashire Education Authority – Taken in isolation, it is doubtful whether there should be a statutory requirement for LEAs to establish and publish their underlying policy on charges and remission arrangements. However, given the whole package of legislation now proposed, and particularly the introduction of mandatory financial delegation to governors, it would appear highly desirable that the LEA policy should be published in order to inform governing bodies of the basis on which schools were funded. The legislation should go further and require governors not to charge parents for activities specified by the education authority. For example, an authority may have developed a clear policy on swimming, and it should be open to it not to charge for swimming activities for, say, a basic two-year programme that applied to all pupils.

Hertfordshire Education Department would wish to make three main points. The first is that it would be quite wrong to oblige parents to pay *any* fees. It follows from this not only that parents should have the right to opt out of any paid-for activities but also that, if necessary, schools have to be prepared to offer alternative programmes. It is recognized that this could have an inhibiting effect on the arrangement of activities and also that the alternative programmes may be somewhat limited if this inhibition is not to prove too discouraging.

Secondly, it is on balance considered preferable not to seek to itemize through regulations those areas where charges may be made. The problems of definition are real, and there is a danger in seeking to codify existing charging practices that the regulations could become impossibly complex. Moreover, there are two safeguards. The first is the good sense of authorities in the operation of such arrangements. The second – but this is dependent on the acceptance of the authority's previous comment – is that any such payments should be completely and genuinely voluntary. If this fundamental point were not to be reflected in the legislation, the authority would prefer to see the items for which charges might be made defined and thereby limited.

The other principal point is in part linked to what is said above. The view is strongly held that the question of what, if any, activities are charged for should be entirely a matter for the local education authority; and that it is not appropriate that such decisions should be capable of being varied on an individual school basis. It is considered incumbent on a local authority to seek to ensure that its services are available to ratepayers on as even-handed a basis as is reasonably practicable.

The authority doubts whether the distinction between voluntary contributions from parents, and items or services to which a specific charge may be attached, is always as clear as the document suggests; and questions whether the proposed legislation ought not to re-inforce the test stated here, namely that such contributions are known to be voluntary and that pupils do not receive any different treatment whether or not their parents have paid.

Birmingham Education Committee – The issue of individual music tuition is complicated. It is surely invidious to single out music as an area for charging, while individual sports coaching, which is a developing area, is not mentioned. In some authorities instrumental music tuition is provided in groups – is this intended to be defined as individual tuition for the purposes of charging? The paper makes no mention of the provision of instruments. Although charges may be made for tuition, will the authority be obliged to provide an instrument as one of the 'adequate materials' for the curriculum or will it be made clear that instruments are provided at the discretion of the authority?

European String Teachers' Association – Virtually all LEAs since 1944 have considered instrumental music as an integral part of the curriculum, and there has been little suggestion that it should be considered an extra. Administrative memorandum 15 and the 1981 Hereford and Worcester judgement merely underlined and clarified this point. The proposal to allow charges is therefore not intended to clarify the law but to change it with the express purpose of trans-forming instrumental music into an extra-curricular acticity. It is outrageous and unjustified to single out one category of teachers who will be under contract to a LEA but whose services will not be free to children. It is as arbitrary as if the teaching of remedial reading, a second foreign language or further maths were to be charged for. It is also ironic that the greater emphasis on practical music in the new GCSE syllabuses will go for very little if adequate teaching is not made available – as for other GCSE subjects.

The Incorporated Society of Musicians asks that the DES explicitly declare it unlawful to charge for instrumental music tuition which is given as an integral part of the music curriculum during school hours, considering that music is one of the foundation subjects in the proposed national curriculum, that performance is a requirement in the GCSE and other external music examinations and that instrumental tuition is the mean by which collective musical activities in schools become possible.

Modern Language Association – In the vast majority of cases, all visits abroad have always been funded entirely by the pupils. It has been a source of irritation to language teachers that some school visits, such as geography trips, have received financial assistance because they are linked to an examination syllabus. We maintain that our visits are inextricably linked to syllabuses, too. With the introduction of graded objective tests, GCSE and certain modifications to A-level examinations, all of which emphasize authenticity of language, it becomes even more important for pupils to vist the country or countries of their target language. It is therefore disappointing to see that the document appear to rule out any hopes we might have had of assistance towards visits abroad.

The Association for Science Education Science Advisers Groups wishes to underline the fundamental importance of fieldwork activity of all kinds, both residential and non-residential, in a programme of broad, balanced and relevant science education for all pupils, regardless of the individual requirements of examination syllabuses. Under the list of items for which *no* charge should be made should be included any charges relating to provision of tuition, transport or materials for the fieldwork activity. Under the list of items for which charges could be made should be included a nominal figure allowing for the cost of board and lodging, related to the cost of providing the same at home.

North-Eastern Counties Amateur Swimming Association – Members have considered the consultative document on charges for school activities and expressed great concern at the proposal to levy charges for children having to travel to local swimming pools. This will have an effect on the numbers learning to swim and consequently on the numbers joining our affiliated clubs, which will also reflect a loss to competitive swimming. Many children will be deprived of taking part in the many water-sports where it is essential to be able to swim. Many children live close to open water and they are constantly at great risk from these hazards. We hope that this proposal can be given further consideration and that trips to the swimming-pool can be made without charge, as is the case with other subjects in the school curriculum where travel is involved.

The Association of Higher Education Institutions Concerned

with Home Economics expressed grave concern regarding the perpetuation of present practice where in many areas practical workshops are resourced by parental provision. This arrangement is considered wholly unacceptable, and the provision of food in this context should be on precisely the same basis as chemicals for science workshops. Food-preparation activity in home economics is not solely concerned with finished products. The analytical, investigative aspect of the exercise forms the focus of the study, and the end product may frequently be unsuitable for consumption.

National Union of Teachers – The evidence that school fund-raising has become not merely a matter of paying for desirable 'extras', but an essential means of paying for centrally important provision, is incontrovertible. HMI have estimated that two-fifths of primary schools parental contributions are topping up the capitation by over 30 per cent. It is no longer simply a matter of traditional fund-raising through school fêtes and jumble sales.

Vast disparities of provision between schools within the maintained sector, and between the maintained and the private sector, are appearing. Hertfordshire County Council, an authority in which a relative evenness of provision might have been expected, discovered in a recent survey that the richest primary schools had 14 times as much additional money as the poorest, while the best-off secondary schools had an astonishing 37 times the additional funding of the least well off. Few of the heads questioned in the survey denied that these additional funds were used for essential items such as science equipment. In the light of this extensive evidence, the Government's statement of firm commitment to the principle of free school education 'irrespective of parents' financial circumstances' is simply not credible.

Music, swimming, domestic science, craft, technology and field trips, which form part of the curriculum in history, geography or science, for example, should therefore under no circumstances be considered 'chargeable'. The consultation paper is doubtful or even contradictory on some of these areas. It suggests for example that 'a trip to the local swimming-pool' might be chargeable. The union would argue that if swimming is considered a necessary part of educational provision – and few parents would argue that it should not be – then it ought to be provided free of charge. After all, whether or not a trip to the local swimming-pool is required is a function not of educational argument but of whether or not a school has its own pool. Why should parents be asked to pay for swimming because their children attend a school without a swimming-pool?

On musical provision the document is similarly dubious. It states that charges should not be made for a 'school activity such as an orchestra' yet suggests that individual music tuition should be chargeable. How does the DES expect the school to provide an orchestra without also providing individual music tuition, or is it suggesting that school orchestra should only be made up of those who can afford to pay for such tuition? If so, the Government is denying the possibility of thousands of pupils participating in an activity at the heart of Western culture on the basis, not of 'abilities and aptitudes', but of parental income.

The union is not opposed to schools also providing optional extras which might be considered chargeable. This would include items which are voluntary leisure activities such as participation in school journeys not related to the curriculum.

Society of Local Authority Chief Executives – If primary legislation is necessary at all to clarify the position over which extras may be the subject of charging, we would expect to see only very simple and straightforward legislation which prescribes the activities for which charges should *not* be made. We would not expect this to be supplemented by prescriptive and detailed rules about what may be charged for and the nature of that charging. Whilst there may be problems in using such words as 'adequate' in the legislation, it is preferable to leave the LEAs to determine what [educational provision] is adequate rather than attempt to define this in legislation or regulations.

National Association of Governors and Managers welcomes the proposal that no LEA will be *required* to charge for any service it provides, as we believe that enabling legislation is preferable to prescription. LEAs should be able to decide for themselves what charges should be made, within a framework of provision that protects the poorest families everywhere. We cannot, however, see the logic of allowing individual governing bodies to impose charges that the LEA does not recommend. The financial pressure on governing bodies to impose charges in order to improve provision elsewhere would be great. This can only be divisive, potentially unfair to individual parents, and could act as a financial barrier to parental choice.

The draft lists of chargeable and non-chargeable items give some cause for concern. The expansion of music education is one of the big successes of comprehensive education. Collective musical activity such as the school orchestra has to be underpinned by individual tuition, and many children would never have the chance to learn an instrument without LEA subsidy. Some LEAs encourage class-based tuition, and we believe that this is a positive way to bring music to all pupils. Some LEAs then go on to provide free tuition to those pupils who have reached a certain standard through this class-based tuition. This could be an acceptable compromise that would protect musical education.

The Southern Examining Group notes the responsibilities placed upon the Secondary Examinations Council with respect to the approval of examination syllabuses and the scrutiny of examinations. It believes that the groups should have regard for costs when they develop and revise syllabuses, and that the council should monitor very carefully this aspect of submissions and subsequent examinations. The introduction of the national curriculum should assist in the specification of the curriculum.

R. G. Smallshaw **Headmaster, Hugh Sexey Middle School**, Blackford, Somerset – Previous to the Hereford and Worcester case, when Somerset did not operate a free instrumental tuition programme, we organized our own, using private tutors. We were able to offer tuition in any instrument to all children who wished to take part. Following the above court decision and the county's introduction of a free scheme using county-employed tutors, we were forced to abandon our scheme. Because of the limited resources available to the county scheme we now have 108 pupils receiving tuition (school roll 449), with 71 waiting. This means that pupils in our first year can no longer be offered tuition, nor can all second-year pupils. Thus the 'free' scheme has resulted in a reduction in the amount of musical tuition in the school. I therefore feel that some degree of fee-paying must be introduced, to allow freedom for growth in the system and to protect the excellence of the school corporate musical activity.

W. L. Carlyon, **Headmaster, Launceston County Primary School** – In rural areas the cost of transporting children on a regular weekly basis to the local swimming-pool is a crippling burden. This LEA, although funding the hire of swimming-pools for 2 ½ terms, in the year has never provided funding for transport in order to get there. Far from considering a reduction in funding for so-called 'extras in children's education', we should be considering the plight of these rural schools for which an important part of their education is in danger of being omitted. Our rural areas have frequently higher rates of unemployment and lower incomes [than the inner cities] so that the burden on parents assumes a greater importance.

J. M. Goodier, **Headmaster, Bewsey County High School**, Warrington – The points contained in the document seem perfectly reasonable and are in fact statements of what is common and accepted practice in the vast majority of schools. The only area where I can foresee difficulty is that of visits in connection with external examination courses. In a number of GCSE subjects field-work is a necessary part of the course. This factor is not new; it has always been present to some extent but it will no doubt increase in the coming years. As an example I can quote the successful CSE mode 3 course in outdoor education which has been running at this school for several years and requires visits to Wales for canoeing, climbing, etc. There has never been any parental objection to payment despite the fact that we are an inner-town school in an area of some parental hardship.

Acle High School, Norfolk – Parents who are also teachers are most concerned over proposed charges to the education system. The concept of education for all will become education for some if parents pay for creative, artistic and athletic extras. This will introduce the concept of a two-caste education system. Since many of the suggested payment areas are on the arts/PE side it will widen again the gap between the arts and the sciences. Families with more than two children would be severely strained meeting the required payments, unless they restricted their offspring to a basic educa-tional diet. Stress could also be caused at school due to peer-group pressure because an individual was either receiving an extra or refusing, for whatever reason, to partake.

M. R. Jefficott, head of geography, **St Cyres Comprehensive School**, Penarth – Dear Mr Baker, I am writing to you to support your proposals for charging parents for essential A-level and GCSE field visits. For 11 years, St Cyres School has taken school parties on residential field visits to Malham in North Yorkshire. This is 'essential' since the school has developed its own WJEC examina-tion module entitled 'Landform Development in the Malham Area', and it is worth 12 ½ per cent of the final A-level geography mark. During this time we have taken over 200 students to Yorkshire (37 this year alone) and have never received a complaint from a parent concerning the £50 cost.

We now find ourselves in the position that South Glamorgan will ban this and similar visits in future in case they get a claim from a parent. It would be educationally detrimental if these visits were forced to cease. I hope that you will allow common sense to prevail and allow these activities to continue.

8

Inner London

THE PROPOSALS

The Government believes that in Inner London extra steps must be taken to make the education service more responsive to the needs of parents and employers. It says there has been severe criticism of the quality of the education service provided by the Inner London Education Authority (ILEA) despite expenditure levels far higher than those of any other LEA.

On 4 February, 10 weeks after the Bill was published, the Cabinet decided to wind up ILEA and transfer its functions to the 12 boroughs and the Corporation of the City of London for which it has provided education since 1963. Each authority will be required to publish plans for running its own education service, possibly through joint committees with other authorities.

The Cabinet's decision overturned the compromise for which the Bill first provided and which was described in a consultation paper published in September 1987. This would have allowed any borough wishing to run its own education to withdraw from ILEA from 1 April 1990. ILEA would have continued to run education in the remaining boroughs until eight or more had opted out.

Much of what was first proposed remains relevant. The Secretary of State will need to be satisfied that each borough is able to provide appropriate education for all, including those with special needs, and to provide support services and a youth and careers service. He will expect a borough to maintain provision in any institution London-wide or regional significance which it inherits. Students and children will still be able to seek places in schools and colleges outside the area where they live. As a rule, each borough will take over ILEA property within its boundaries if it applies to do so. Where an institution is mainly based outside a borough but shares facilities (e.g. playing fields) elsewhere, the Secretary of State will decide any dispute about ownership and may require the owner to afford user rights to others.

From April 1990 the new system of local government finance will come into operation with the product of a uniform business rate, levied by every rating authority in England, distributed according to the adult population of each authority. Exchequer grant will compensate for different levels of need. Under these arrangement boroughs remaining in the ILEA should not be adversely affected by others opting out.

The article which follows by Dr. William Stubbs was written before Mr Baker announced that ILEA was to be abolished. The representations to the Government which occupy the rest of this chapter were also made on the basis of the original proposals. Many critics, including Dr Stubbs, objected that the orderly administration of what remained of ILEA would have been impossible, and Mr Baker indicated in his Commons statement that he was meeting that criticism. Most of the objections and arguments which follow, however, have yet to be answered and are still being pressed with equal anxiety.

THE DEBATE

What hope for London's education service?

William Stubbs*
Education Officer, Inner London Education Authority

The consultation paper *The Organization of Education in Inner London* published on 11 September 1987 was notable more for the matters on which it remained silent than for the information it contained. The outline of the proposal – that inner-London boroughs should be able to apply to become local education authorities – had been included in the Conservative Party manifesto at the general election. The consultation document contained a detailed description of the proposed mechanism to enable boroughs, individually or jointly, to apply to the Secretary of State, and for the Secretary of State to consider such applications. It contained however only the briefest of references to the Government's reasons for making the proposals and no reference at all to the effect on the remainder of the ILEA of one or more boroughs opting out.

The period for consultation extended only to five weeks. Nevertheless it is understood that well in excess of 2,000 responses – over a third of them from individual parents – were made to the Secretary of State. The responses were overwhelmingly opposed to the proposals. The main areas of concern appear to have been:

- the unsatisfactory nature of the consultation process;
- that boroughs would be unable to sustain the current quality of education;
- that the level of resources available for the education service might be inadequate;
- that boroughs would be able to opt out without a ballot of parents or local people;
- the disruption to the education service during transition;
- that boroughs would need to duplicate functions, at unnecessary expense.

Given the narrow focus of this consultation document, in that it dealt only with the procedures for 'opt out' and failed to address the wider London issues, the replies related mainly to the details of the proposal itself and not to the wider implications. Readers may be interested in knowing more about these.

The first important point to make is that the proposals for the ILEA are not new. They have been previously considered four

times in the last ten years. Three of these reviews were in the life of
the present Government, which, after each one, concluded firmly
against proposals to break up the authority. While only the first of
these reviews, the 1977–8 Marshall inquiry into London local
government, was an open process in which evidence was invited and
submitted, all the reviews were prolonged and gave detailed consideration to the various alternatives to the ILEA. The current
proposals have not been subject to such consideration.

The second point is that the proposals give no regard to the effect
on the remainder of the ILEA of one or more boroughs opting out.
The sole determinants of the future shape and size of the ILEA will
be the decision of a borough to apply to opt out and the decision of
the Secretary of State on its application. The financial implications
for other boroughs served by the authority and for the effect on the
service in the remaining area are not specified as being relevant
considerations.

It is perhaps worth recalling here that the education service in
inner London has been administered as an integrated city-wide
service since 1870. The location of school and college provision has
no regard to the old London borough boundaries, let alone those
laid down as recently as the 1965 reorganization of London government. Eighteen per cent of school pupils and 72 per cent of college
students currently attend secondary schools and colleges outside the
borough in which they live. To assume without a detailed appraisal
that a borough-based education system can be fashioned from the
existing provision simply by relocating administrative responsibility
is conjecture. There are alternatives to the present arrangement.
The Government, however, is proposing what is, in effect, an
unplanned combination of individual boroughs' LEAs with a resi-
dual ILEA responsible for an area determined by the random
decisions of an unknown number of borough councils. The Bill
itself now greatly increases that uncertainty by allowing borough to
opt out not only in 1990 but on 1 April in any subsequent year. If,
despite the conclusions of earlier reviews, change is perceived to be
necessary in the education service in London, then a proper study of
the possible options leading to a viable plan is surely necessary.

The third area of concern is the time scale proposed for implementation of these proposals. The education service nationally is
being asked by the Government to cope with major changes in both
schools and colleges. The 1986 Education Act, the teachers' pay
settlement, the present Bill and the Local Government Bill on
competitive tendering will all require attention. In London this is in
addition to the consequences of a severe rate limitation, requiring a
major contraction and restructuring of the service, as well as various
delayed consequences of the abolition of the GLC, including
replacement of all computer services and a requirement on the

ILEA to leave its headquarters at County Hall. The timetable proposed by Government would mean that the first boroughs would apply in late 1988 to take over the service in their area on 1 April 1990. The earliest approval that could be given to such an application by the Secretary of State would be on 1 April 1989 but it is likely in practice to be much later. Only then could a borough establish an education committee and seek to appoint the necessary officers. The demands on the ILEA in this period to respond to the needs of boroughs wishing to leave it are certain to be considerable, and this will add significantly to the other burdens to which I have referred. So serious do I judge the combination of these factors to be for the ILEA that I have been obliged to advise the education committee that the orderly administration of the education service cannot be sustained under these circumstances throughout this period.

Whatever the answer is to the question of which is the best way forward for the London education service, no informed observer is on record as supporting the present proposals. There is time for further consideration, and this is clearly necessary if the best interests of those for whom the education service exists, the pupils and students in our schools and colleges, are to be fully safeguarded.

*Dr Stubb's appointment to be Chief Executive of the Polytechnics and Colleges Funding Council, to be set up under Clause 93 of the Bill, was announced on 27 January 1988.

THE ADVICE

Sir Ashley Bramall – I am writing on behalf of the Governors of Pimlico School, London SW1 of which I am the Chairman, to express their unanimous opposition to the proposal that education in this area should be taken over by Westminster City Council and the service of the ILEA for the whole of the inner-London area broken up. We are also expressing the view of a large number of parents of pupils at the school. The strength of feeling of parents is intensified by the fact that well over half the pupils come from outside Westminster.

Once this decision is taken, the parents who live outside the city will have no opportunity of influencing as electors the authority which educates their children. This is particularly important when a new authority is taking over and especially now that authorities are going to be able to charge for many features such as music lessons and field study trips.

The presence of a large number of non-Westminster pupils in this and other schools is also significant when it comes to administrative costs. Westminster say that they will save money that the ILEA spends on administration, but one wonders whether they have taken any account of the enormous increase in claims for recoupment from a large proportion of the pupils, and in paying recoupment in respect of pupils in other areas.

A particular concern relates to music. Pimlico is, I believe, unique among secondary schools in running a course for talented musicians within an ordinary comprehensive school. There is certainly no comparable provision within the ILEA and, therefore, it follows that the majority of the up to 15 pupils a year on the course, with others joining in the sixth form, come from other boroughs. We wonder what chance there is that the council will want to continue this very necessary provision, mainly for pupils from other boroughs, except possibly on a charging basis.

The Pimlico building is also used for the authority's Centre for Young Musicians, which provides Saturday tuition for some 300 young musicians from the whole of the authority's area. It is extremely heavily used for adult education and, as with much of ILEA adult education, a good deal is of a specialist nature, provided in only one or two institutes and therefore attracting a clientèle from the whole of London. In this way Pimlico is a centre for many different communities. We are afraid that, unless this is allowed to be a building which the ILEA retains under [the terms] of the consultation paper, a great deal of this work will be discontinued or made impossibly expensive.

We are disturbed by the small size in terms of population of Westminster as an education authority. Westminster cannot be compared to other education authorities with a similar population, because of the large proportion of its population who send their children to independent schools. If 'opting out' by schools becomes prevalent, Westminster's involvement in local authority school education could become even smaller, and its willingness to maintain services (such as the inspectorate) be decreased.

There is growing concern over children with special needs and a great deal of opinion in favour of locating them wherever possible in ordinary schools. It is essential, if this is to be done successfully, that existing special schools shall be available to provide the resources and know-how to assist in ordinary schools. The only special schools in Westminster are one for moderate learning difficulties and one for severe learning difficulties.

The same problems arise with access to services for pupils, such as the ILEA summer courses, field study centres or sports facilities. It is not surprising that residential, field study, sports and water-sports centres are all located outside Westminster and, indeed, outside London in many cases. Will our pupils continue to have access to such facilities and, if Westminster are in charge, what are they going to have to pay for it?

Westminster City Council welcomes the proposals set out in the consultation paper on the grounds that local control of the education service by a multi-purpose authority will enable improvements in educational standards and enhanced cost-effectiveness, enable education services to be integrated with existing local authority services and increase the accountability of the service by bringing administration close to its customers. It will be preparing an application to the Secretary of State.

The council notes that the consultation paper requires an authority wishing to opt out to satisfy the Secretary of State that it can secure the provision of the complete range of educational services, including specialist and support services. The council also notes that the provision of specialist and supprt services is an area of particular concern to headteachers and principals of educational institutes. The council attaches the greatest importance to these areas and is determined that they will be adequately provided for.

The council notes that the ILEA's unit costs are significantly higher than the rest of the country and also significantly higher than comparable city authorities. The council will seek to concentrate resources on schools and other educational institutions by establishing a slim, cohesive system of administration. The council considers that the proposals for financial and managerial decentralization to schools will facilitate the concentration of resources in schools.

The council notes that the proposed date of transfer of education is coincident with the introduction of the community charge and uniform business rate. This will lead to Westminster's commercial rate being equalized across the country, and those boroughs which choose to remain within the ILEA will not, therefore, be adversely affected.

F Barrett, Chairman of Governors, Hallfield School – I and many others look forward to the time when we in Westminster can run our own schools, as we consider that 'Small is Beautiful'. It is then possible to be able to get in touch easily with the people running all departments.

Hackney Council – The ILEA at present serves as a mechanism for equalizing education resources between richer and poorer boroughs across inner London. We are acutely aware, therefore, of the severe financial difficulties likely to face the authority if the few wealthier net-contributor boroughs, such as Westminster, were to opt out as anticipated, leaving only the poorer boroughs such as Hackney which have been net gainers from ILEA.

The education service in Hackney has undergone and continues to experience radical change. Continuity of education has been seriously affected by the teachers' action; and many of the Government's current proposals, if adopted, will mean further change and disruption, affect the ILEA's staffing and morale and take up time and effort at the expense of education in Hackney and elsewhere. The case for stability in London's educational adminstration – which does not preclude improvement – seems very strong at the present time.

While there is a general presumption that all ILEA properties in a borough would transfer, there is no indication of the criteria to be adopted, although it appears that the borough may have to indicate they are needed for effective operation as an education authority. It may therefore be that the borough would have to make a clear and detailed case for transfer of each and every property. From experience of abolition of the GLC, detailed property information may not be held by the ILEA valuers in a readily available form. Asset transfer could be complex and time-consuming. It does not appear that there would necessarily be any ability for a borough to inherit 'surplus' properties and then dispose of them, utilizing the proceeds towards its overall educational budget, whether to purchse/repair/ improve property for any needs it may have or for other reasons.

It requires further work to estimate the effect on Hackney if particular boroughs opt out of the ILEA. However, since the new system of local government finance will include a grant from the Exchequer 'so as to compensate for the different levels of need', and since there is an initial assumption that the ILEA currently spends far too much in relation to its level of need, and since the new system will include powers to limit precepts and community charges, it is logical to conclude that large spending cuts in education will be enforced whether the ILEA is dismembered or not. The paper suggests that boroughs which opt out may initially be less severely affected by the community charge limitation 'where they were actively seeking to reduce expenditure'. But if the Exchequer grant were grossly inadequate to needs, it is likely that the complementary sums required from the community charge to sustain provision would be excessive in relation to the incomes of most residents in a poor borough like Hackney.

Furthermore it is clear that any transfer would impose major adminstrative and financial problems, both in the transfer itself and in the subsequent management of a local education service. Government funding of such a service would be through the normal GREA process which automatically disadvantages areas such as Hackney where levels of need are consistently higher than the national averages used by the Government to estimate expenditure.

Mrs Carlis Richards, co-opted nursery school governor – I am totally convinced that Hackney's children will suffer from this scheme if it is allowed to go ahead. If wealthy boroughs choose to opt out of the ILEA, no doubt their funds would also opt out. This would lead to less money in the kitty for the boroughs which are still in the ILEA. This would in turn force even more cut-backs in education. I assume under-5 schooling would be the first to go. The first five years of a child's life are crucial in mapping out how he or she will progress through life. Children in Hackney do not have the best start in life and they need all the stimulation and education they can receive. Are we to have the sentence of no education for the under-5s hanging over the children's head if this Act is to become law?

Kensington and Chelsea Council warmly welcomes this consultation document. The ILEA is both the most expensive and the least efficient education authority in the country, and inner London's educational service should therefore be devolved to the boroughs. The current ILEA precept on the Royal Borough of Kensington and Chelsea represents about two-thirds of the total rate bill of commercial ratepayers and about three-quarters of the bill of domestic ratepayers. We confidently expect to provide a first-class education service and at the same time reduce the burden on ratepayers. The council looks forward to preparing its educational scheme in consultation with borough residents, especially those concerned with education: parents, governing bodies, teachers and local employers.

The council warmly welcomes the combined effect of existing legislation and the new Bill to allow the widest possible choice of educational establishments by parents and young people without regard to LEA boundaries.

Hammersmith and Fulham Council – The prime consideration in any reorganization should be the interests of those being educated; in contrast, issues such as the structure of the authorities administering the service are secondary. We are unhappy that it is proposed to dismantle the ILEA for financial (as well as any other) reasons. We are also unhappy that the proposed date for the transfer of education (1 April 1990) comes in the middle of the academic year and only weeks before GCSE and A-level examinations are due to begin, and thus that dislocation to the education service and to students will be magnified. The paper focuses on educational administration rather than on the problems of inner London, which we had been led to believe were one of the new Government's priorities.

The ILEA has a fine record of innovative educational provision, and it is unfair to say that it has shown little sign that is ready to tackle the root causes of its educational and financial problems; the entire public sector which is endeavouring to serve and govern London is facing comparable problems.

In view of the Government's determination to cut ILEA spending in the next two years, the council needs to know more about the assurance given that boroughs remaining in the ILEA will not be adversely affected as a result of others opting out, providing that the ILEA makes commensurate savings in its overhead costs. It seems to us that a smaller ILEA will experience a proportionate increase in its overheads.

Wandsworth Council intends to proceed – in consultation with all interested parties – with drawing up a scheme for opting out of the ILEA on the earliest date (1 April 1990), so that benefits such as the following can be reaped at the earliest possible stage:

(1)   improved standards achieved by applying the council's sound management practices and building upon the joint efforts of teachers, governors and parents.

(2)   a fully resourced service with a capital programme benefiting from the finanacial rewards of the council's robust capital receipts policy;

(3)   improved accountability – instead of the present remote ILEA bureaucracy with its several tiers and diffused accountability, there would be an education authority that is local, is concentrating only on Wandsworth's problems and is, therefore, much more responsive to local needs and preferences;

(4)   better management, illustrated by the council's track record and commitment to providing a good quality service by the most cost-effective means;

(5)   better planning and co-ordination with many existing council services – under-5s, play, latchkey, youth training and employment, welfare and children with special needs; and

(6)   dual use of facilities – allowing schools to benefit from daytime use of the council's existing wide range of facilities and permitting the community to benefit from the use of school swimming-pools, halls, playing-fields, etc. when not required for school use.

Tower Hamlets Council Policy and Resources Committee – The proposals do not fully spell out the implications which will arise either from opting out or, indeed, from remaining within the rump of the ILEA. They are to be deplored because they give those most involved – parents, teachers, pupils and others – insufficient opportunities to express their views, and they therefore fail in their stated aim to make education provision in London more accountable. They appear undemocratic in that they follow on from one set of local elections and are to be implemented before the next set, denying people their voice through the ballot box. The consultation paper should be reconsidered, and more detailed proposals should come forward with a fairer time scale.

These comments should not be construed as a statement that the council is nervous about its ability to provide an accountable, dynamic and efficient education service. When the Government provides detailed proposals, and the position of other authorities is clear, the Council will have to decide upon a method of proceeding in the best interests of the residents of this borough.

National Union of Teachers – No one would pretend that the ILEA is perfect. Like many large bureaucracies there are examples of inefficiency. However, the union would argue that the ILEA is no worse that a great many education authorities in the shires and provincial cities and that is a great deal better than some (including a few in outer London, which the consultation paper mentions in passing as models for the future of inner London).

As regards the transfer of assets, the consultation paper lays down the basic rule 'that all the ILEA property within the boundary of the opting-out borough should transfer when that borough becomes an LEA'. This clearly discriminates in favour of those boroughs which, through accidents of history or geography, have the heaviest concentrations of ILEA establishments. The ILEA has established a network of support services, at present available to all teachers in inner London, which under these proposals could become the sole property of one borough. The paper disregards the fact that whether a teachers' centre is in Westminster or Lambeth it is the property of the ratepayers of all twelve inner-London boroughs.

National and Local Government Officers' Association – Opting out by particular boroughs could have a very severe effect on the financing of education in what remains of the ILEA. Redistribution of resources through the pooling of borough contributions has always been a characteristic of the ILEA and it enables the provision of schooling and further and higher education across the whole of inner London at an equivalent cost to ratepayers. The possible departure of Westminster, Kensington and Chelsea, and the City – which together account for over 60 per cent of the ILEA's income –

would effectively cripple education in the remaining boroughs. Maintaining the same level of services would put an unacceptable burden on the revenue to be raised from the poorer boroughs such as Hackney and Tower Hamlets. The ILEA would be left with the task of meeting the needs of the most socially deprived areas without access to the resources of the better-off areas.

The stipulation that the decision by a borough to apply to opt out needs only a simple majority in the full council is astounding. Such councils have not been elected with reference to the running of an education service, and the political complexion of certain authorities considering this course of action does not suggest any clear mandate for the views of the majority party (in Wandsworth, there is a majority of only one).

National Association of Teachers in Further and Higher Education – Further and higher education has an important function in relating to the needs of the labour market in London. This labour market is not borough-based. It is all-London-based and draws upon the whole community. Without the co-ordination that a unitary authority can supply, the needs of the labour market cannot be adequately provided for. Without the educational opportunities at present available across London – particularly the opportunities of access and progression to AFE – offered by a coherent system, the population of inner London will be less able to compete in the job market.

Camden Adult Education Institute – In London, adult education is within the reach of the whole of the adult population. The ILEA's policy has been that no adult should be denied access because of high fees. Pensioners, the unemployed, the disabled and those in basic education classes pay a concessionary fee. It is argued by some that a 'market price' fees policy should be used. In other parts of the country where this approach is current, adult education is a middle-class activity. In London the service is used by adults from all walks of life. 260,072 adults used the service last year, and it cost 3.6 per cent of the ILEA budget.

Adult education in London has a combination of some full-time staff and a large part-time highly professional workforce, on sessional pay. Many part-time tutors work effectively full-time across several institutes, while others teach only once or twice a week. This combination offers a wide-ranging and cost-effective curriculum across the ILEA as a whole. The ability to enrol students from across the whole of London allows some highly specialist provision. In some areas of the curriculum, links with industry and business are already strong, as part-time tutors also work in industry, commerce, the media and the arts, and new technology. If boroughs opt out of the central organization, it is doubtful if either the opting-out or the remaining boroughs would be able to mount such a varied programme.

National Institute of Adult Continuing Education – A particular concern has been expressed about the future of inner London's three grant-aided voluntary adult education institutions: the Mary Ward Centre, the Working Men's College and Morley College. All three have a London-wide remit, and none is attached to any one borough. The position of these institutions, combining a reputation for specialist work unrivalled in the country with integration into a city-wide service, perhaps epitomizes the fear and uncertainty which now hang over the whole education service for adults in our capital city. They find no clear provision in the consultative document for their continued support after perhaps a century of service to the changing needs of Londoners. Their worries must be shared by a large number of voluntary organizations whose support from the ILEA and partnership with it in providing comprehensive services are now called into question.

The Advisory Committee to the ILEA Education Resource Unit for Older People seeks assurance of its future in a devolved or fragmented London organization. This central support structure includes liaison with voluntary organizations, many of whom operate across London and have neither the time nor the personnel to liaise with many smaller authorities. We are concerned that a declining resource base for adult education would reduce opportunities for all kinds of specialist development.

What is your understanding of an 'efficient education service'? What measures of effectiveness would include the benefit received from adult education by older people, many of them otherwise isolated and with dwindling opportunities for self-development? What will be the criteria for assessing whether boroughs are proposing an 'adequate organization' for adult education? What are the criteria for deciding whether the combination of proposed reorganizations will damage central services to the point of serious loss? We wish it were possible to respond with a discussion of you approach to, and aims for, education in inner London, but we find no such statements there to engage with.

London Voluntary Service Council – The paper makes no reference to the acute social needs of inner-London residents. It is not enough to simply assert that the ILEA is relatively expensive as an authority. The authority must be evaluated, with recognition of the needs that have to be met. Inner-London boroughs show up among the most deprived areas of Britain on Department of Environment indicators (Urban Deprivation Information Note no. 31983). Further studies have shown that poverty is widespread. In 1985–6 just under half of ILEA primary pupils were eligible for free meals; one in five schoolchildren have unemployed parents, and more than one-quarter (twice the national average) were from single-parent families. A further strain on the ILEA is caused by the homelessness crisis; in 1984, 12.7 households per 1,000 were accepted as homeless (the national average is under 4 per 1,000). Such deprivation is rapidly worsening. Thus in only two years, between 1983 and 1985, the percentage of primary schoolchildren with both parents unemployed rose by 33 per cent in ILEA Division 5 (Tower Hamlets and the City of London), and the percentage eligible for free meals by 21 per cent (*Children in Need*, 1985). Voluntary groups working with families in bed-and-breakfast accommodation are conscious that ILEA-supported youth and community centres become essential sources of housing advice and that schools have severe problems with high proportions of transient children.

Voluntary Youth Service – Voluntary organizations provide around three-quarters of the youth service in inner London, and the high level of voluntary contribution in resources of all kinds ensures that the voluntary sector is extremely cost-effective. Support from the ILEA is crucial to the survival of many units. The likely effects of withdrawal of support by a number of boroughs upon the resources available to those which remain is likely to be very serious.

Society of Education Officers – It is asserted without evidence that 'special considerations' make it necessary to ensure 'responsiveness to local needs', that very large LEAs find it difficult to be 'responsive', that the ILEA is a high spender and poor performer and shows little sign of tackling its problems. These assertions apparently comprise the sum total of the reasons for introducing an opting-out process which would fragment the education service in the capital. SEO believes that the future of the education service in London deserves much fairer and more thorough scrutiny than these paragraphs accord it.

Very little time is allowed for planning, for making and considering objections and for implementation. The contrast with the procedure under which LEAs have to follow when they propose changes to schools under section 12 of the 1980 Education Act is marked and raises doubt about whether the Government intends to weigh proposals and objections fairly and objectively. The transfer date (1 April 1990) is in the middle of the academic year and is only about 7 months after the 'shadow' authorities are established. Little regard is paid to the need for continuity and orderly planning, nor to the effect such haste could have on children's education. SEO has grave doubts whether adequate machinery can be established to deal with the complex issues involved in transferring staff and property and preserving continuity and stability in schools and colleges under the pressure of this timetable. In making this comment, SEO members speak with real experience of local government reorganization in 1974 and reorganization in outer-London boroughs in 1965.

The Government proposes that 'opting out' and the introduction of the community charge and the uniform business rate should coincide in April 1990. Because of that it is argued that 'Boroughs which choose to remain in the ILEA should not therefore be adversely affected as a result of the decisions of other boroughs to opt out, providing the ILEA makes commensurate savings in its overhead costs'.

It is naïve to suppose that an LEA which contracts in size can make savings in support costs and centrally incurred expenditure which match the scale of its contraction. The boroughs which opt out are likely to have a lower need for educational spending than the boroughs which remain with the ILEA. They will have fewer social and economic problems, a higher proportion of children in private schools and a lower proportion of school-age children in relation to their population. If these more favoured boroughs opt out, the education component of their community charge will fall. In the boroughs which remain in the ILEA, community charge payers will face an increased burden. This result will not arise from reasons of efficiency – but simply because of the different levels of educational need in the relevant school populations. In the first few years of the new arrangements part of the costs will still be paid for by domestic ratepayers. There are substantial differences in the total domestic rateable values in each borough. Richer boroughs will have an extra advantage during the transitional period. The remainder of the ILEA will have a corresponding disadvantage.

SEO believes that the consultative document should have exposed these difficulties to public discussion. If the arguments presented to the public in the consultative document are superficial and one-sided, discussion will be equally superficial and ill informed.

Methodist Church Division of Education and Youth – Because of the resources which the ILEA is able to command, and because of the large area which it covers, the reports of its commissions of inquiry are of national importance. In recent years there have been three widely acclaimed major reports on schools: the Hargreaves Report *Improving Secondary Schools* (1984), the Thomas Report *Improving Primary Schools* (1985) and the Mortimore Report, *The Junior Schools Project* (1986). The authority has also recently published reviews of advanced further education and work-related non-advanced further education. Its treatment of its five polytechnics has pointed the way to 'corporate status', now part of the Government's plans for higher education. No other single authority is able to match the ILEA's record in this respect, and any impairment of it ability as an education provider will impoverish the national system.

London Diocesan Board for Schools – The rationale for the proposal is inadequate. The ILEA has its virtues as well as its vices; there is no attempt to acknowledge those, nor to balance the one against the other. The allegations of inadequacies in the ILEA are not backed up by any reference to research data, to HMI reports or to any other authoritative independent source. Although we acknowledge the need for a measure of administrative reform it also remains true that the ILEA, because of its scale, is able to retain professional teams and facilities that are second to none (for instance, some of the teams within the inspectorate, architects' branch and research and statistics branch, to take a widely varied sample; also various specialist teachers' centres). The loss of these teams and facilities will be felt well beyond the boundaries of the ILEA itself, fulfilling as they do a quasi-national role, albeit with a local emphasis. The recent series of fundamental reports on secondary schools, primary schools, special needs education and nursery provision bears abundant additional witness to that.

London Churches' Group – Piecemeal opting-out is hardly a planned response to the educational needs of London. The inability of boroughs such as Tower Hamlets and Hackney to cope with their housing problems after the abolition of the GLC underlines the dangers of the proposed break-up of a unitary authority.

Save the Children Fund – The ILEA suports voluntary provision for pre-school children by giving grant aid and by acting as a strategic planning agency developing co-ordinated policies across the inner-London area. The loss of such a strategic body would mean the loss of planning and appropriate support for the field of under-5s services. Any changes to the organization of education in inner London should ensure that alternative planning and co-ordination structures are created. The Save the Children Fund also collaborates with the ILEA in the provision of educational play facilities for travellers' children. In the London area this is an issue which is extremely difficult to manage within borough boundaries, and a London-wide approach is needed.

One of our current concerns is the plight of children in homeless families accommodation. Few children are able to attend their normal school, and many are temporarily lodged out of the borough where their family is registered as homeless. The ILEA accepts responsibility at the moment for their education while in the hostel, because they are drawn from the inner-London area. Considerable resources have been directed by the ILEA to meeting their needs. Problems would arise in future if children from boroughs which opt out of the ILEA were to be temporarily lodged in boroughs remaining in the authority. The numbers of children involved are not insignificant. Any borough proposing to opt out should provide evidence that it expects to make effective provision for the appropriate support of voluntary organizations in the pre-school field as well as in the youth service.

Greater London Action for Racial Equality – The ILEA has taken positive steps towards eliminating the possibility of black and ethnic minority children being removed, unfairly and in disproportionate numbers and placed in special schools. The justifiable concern of parents, and especially Afro-Caribbean parents, about this practice was highlighted by the Swann (then Rampton) Committee in 1981. The ILEA has set up procedures for ensuring that the assessment and 'statementing' of special educational needs (SEN) is properly carried out, and is pursuing a policy of integrating as many SEN children as possible into mainstream schools and of providing them with specialist teacher support. Present policies and practices should not be lost as a result of any forthcoming reorganization of education in inner London.

The consultation paper nowhere gives even passing recognition to the fact that London is a multiracial city, in which one in five residents is of ethnic minority origin (with an even higher proportion of black residents in the inner-London boroughs). It does not refer to the work done by ILEA in making such provision and in pursuit of that objective, and consequently is silent on the question of how that work would be continued after reorganization.

The SMILE Mathematics Project – SMILE is an ILEA mathematics project which produces learning materials for children of all abilities in the secondary age range. The materials are sold throughout the country with schools across 50 LEAs basing their mathematics curriculum on SMILE. Its international reputation as a centre of excellence means that SMILE materials are now used in India,

New Zealand, Spain, West Africa and many other countries.

The proposals make unsubstantiated assertions about the cost and quality of education in inner London and imply that a transfer of responsibility to borough level would lead to a more 'efficient' service. The ILEA serves a population of 2.3 million people, yet Strathclyde LEA serves 2.4 million, Essex, Hampshire and Kent LEAs each serve 1.5 million people over a far wider area than the ILEA. It is the compact size of the ILEA that has allowed a project such as SMILE to develop. Far from finding it 'difficult to keep in touch with . . . the requirements . . . of different areas', the nature of the ILEA has meant that communication between all those involved in the project has been much more straightforward. The nature of the ILEA has enabled the project to match the requirements of its users in a unique way, confounding the assertion in the proposals.

The SMILE project has meant a significant improvement in the mathematics education of a large number of secondary school pupils. Entries for the SMILE O-level have almost doubled each year since 1981. Given the shortage of mathematics specialists nationally, the existence of SMILE and the INSET possibilities available within the ILEA are important factors attracting well-qualified teachers.

City Lit Centre for Deaf People and Speech Therapy – The ILEA has created a team at this centre that is without equal in this country. The team includes teachers of the deaf, speech therapists, teachers of sign language, hearing therapists, a student counsellor and a college social worker. About a quarter of the staff have significant hearing losses themselves. This breadth and depth of expertise enables us to offer educational opportunities that no single London borough could contemplate sponsoring from its own resources, due to the comparatively small number of students involved. The inter-disciplinary service we offer is of value in raising the quality of life for its users. The investment of time and effort in our students is cost-effective in that much of our work is directed to training people who are entering the job market for the first time; to teaching further skills to achieve promotion or change of job; or to helping people re-enter the job market after a period of unemployment.

Any Act of Parliament that leads to the diminution of this centre by leaving it as the responsibility of an impoverished or contracted ILEA, or by devolving it piecemeal to the boroughs of London, will remove a centre for education and training, that is valued highly throughout the United Kingdom.

National Union of Students – Over the years the ILEA has been able to develop a coherent strategy for student grants across London. We are concerned that, with no mention of this area within the consultative document, there will be a messy transition period whereby students, especially those receiving or hoping to receive discretionary awards, could well be disadvantaged depending which side of the boundary they fall following 'opting out'.

Chelsea Open Air Nursery School governing body – We appreciate the high standard of nursery education provided by the ILEA, bearing in mind that it is not a statutory requirement. We wish to express our concern about the lack of opportunity for consultation with parents, governors and teachers; that there is no democratic mandate for the decision of the Royal Borough of Kensington and Chelsea to opt out; that the borough council has not the expertise or the experience of running a local education authority.

Governors of Parkwood Hall School, Swanley, Kent, a residential coeducational school for pupils with learning difficulties from inner-London boroughs – The document states that London boroughs should have the *opportunity* to demonstrate that they could provide an efficient educational service, but what does this mean? Does 'efficient' mean that educational standards will be higher? Does it mean that it will be more cost-effective? How will such judgements be made, and what will happen if the standard is not reached?

The document states that boroughs cannot opt back into the ILEA, but will the Secretary of State intervene where standards are not maintained and will he consider returning such LEAs to the ILEA after a minimum period?

The proposals have far-reaching effects for all staff, whether teaching, child care or ancillary, at a residential special school. There are no indications on how teaching staff would transfer *en bloc* to a new LEA, or the implications this may have for family resettlement, etc. No teacher or member of the child-care staff would be protected from redundancy. In fact the whole issue of transfer of staff seems to be a minefield of complexity. It is difficult to imagine, in a period of uncertainty, staff being able to carry out their duties with enthusiasm and commitment. This would inevitably result in the education and care of the pupils suffering. Not to be forgotten are the equally highly motivated ancillary staff of cooks, cleaners, gardeners, etc., usually engaged locally, who have no indication of how they would be affected by these proposals.

Brent Knoll School, London SE23 – As the governing body of a special school, we are deeply concerned about the ability of individual boroughs to meet the wide range of needs of those with special educational requirements. Coherent wide-scale planning is necessary to provide the range of specialist provision and services for those with disabilities and learning difficulties. How can an individual borough with, say 35 primary schools and 5 secondary schools possibly meet the range of provision necessary?

Mrs Jean Calcott, governor of an ILEA special school – Although the Government states that the proposed legislation is to improve education in inner London, as it is very critical of the service supplied by the ILEA at present and considers it excessively expensive, there does not seem to be any saving in having many small boroughs each having to run their own education service with all facilities being supplied. This will severely penalize those areas in inner London which already suffer from overcrowding, poor housing and many social problems. I feel that this will lead to many teachers leaving the service because of the uncertainty of their future career prospects, and will lead to a far inferior service in inner London, which already is under severe pressure from all the problems in inner-city schools.

Mrs Catherine Porteous – I write as a governor of Holland Park School, Kensington. I am not a member of any political party, but was a Conservative appointee to the governing body of Ladbroke School ten years ago. I oppose the proposal that the Royal Borough of Kensington and Chelsea should set up its own education authority under the Government's new legislation. My principal reason is that we have been furnished with no figures showing what the likely financial outcome will be, and I feel that it would be improper, indeed extremely irresponsible, to take any decision of this radical nature without proper information.

Dr Lynn Bindman, London N6 – The suggestion that local borough councils should organize educational provision is grossly irresponsible. They are amateurs in this field, in contrast to the ILEA, which is staffed by experienced professionals.

The document does not justify the *costing* of its proposals on financial grounds. Since about 40 per cent of pupils cross borough lines, the administrative work in clawing back fees would be heavy and absurd. What is the *evidence* of educational benefit, and detailed evidence of financial benefit on which the Government is basing its present proposals? It appears extraordinarily doctrinaire to fly in the face of recent reviews and put forward far-reaching proposals with no evidence that they are justified.

Richard Black, inner-London school governor – What appears to be a trick, to rush the entire process through before the next local election, is all the more serious since the change-over period comes just a short time before the most important part of the academic year in which pupils will be taking public examinations. Simply on grounds of fairness to the children, I would strongly urge that the process of change-over from one authority to the next is postponed until after this period, i.e. the summer of 1990.

Honeywell Schools (London SW11) Parent–Teacher Friends' Association – We note that the timetable envisaged provides for opting-out boroughs to assume responsibility for education in April 1990, one month before the next borough elections. This creates the possibility that, should a council majority change, the incoming council would inherit arrangements to which it was not committed but would have no power to change. We do not think that this would be in the best interests of education. A change of power is a clear possibility in boroughs such as Wandsworth where the parties are very evenly balanced.

Eve Oldham, primary school governor – Transfer of assets – this section of the report utterly appals me. What you suggest would open the possibility of public-sector resources very quickly ending up in the private sector, at a cost to the private sector no doubt of a minimal amount.

Barbara Nathan, teacher-governor, Merlin Primary School, Bromley – You mention providing a better service for parents and employers, but what about the children? A blood tie should not automatically assume that a parent knows what is educationally best for his or her child.

Hugh Tessier, Chairperson, National Union of Public Employees, Greater London Technical and Scientific Officer's Branch – The malevolent arrogance in this 14-page hymn of hate exposes the cant and hypocrisy so characteristic of this Secretary of State for Education's iron-headed regime. Disraeli's famous maxim, 'Conservatism discards Prescription, shrinks from Principle, disavows Progress; having rejected all respect for antiquity, it offers no redress for the present, and makes no preparation for the future', neatly parodies this paper's delinquent marauding into London's education. You can be assured that our membership will enjoy the spectre of your disgrace and relegation to the dustbin of ignominy, if you should be so foolish as to pursue this disastrous, reckless adventure.

9

Higher and Further Education

THE PROPOSALS

Forty-eight polytechnics and other large colleges in England – those with 350 or more full-time-equivalent students, of whom more than 55 per cent were in advanced further education on 1 November 1985 – are to be separated from local authority control and given corporate status, in recognition of the fact that they now have strong national as well as local roles and provide for more than half the higher education students in England. With voluntary and other grant-aided colleges which offer predominantly higher education they will form a new polytechnics and colleges sector. Seven colleges which had fewer than 350 students on the qualifying date will also be incorporated with the agreement of their LEAs. A new body, the Polytechnics and Colleges Funding Council (PCFC), will be established to plan the sector and allocate public funds. The National Advisory Body for Public Sector Higher Education will cease to exist. The Bill allows these provisions to be extended to Wales, by order.

A Universities Funding Council (UFC) will replace the non-statutory University Grants Committee (UGC) to administer the public funds provided for education, research and other activities at 46 of the 47 universities in the United Kingdom (the exception being the University of Buckingham). It will not be empowered, as is the UGC, to offer the Secretary of State advice on the needs of universities. The Secretary of State will appoint the members of each Funding Council who will include people from industry, commerce and the professions as well as academics. The UFC chairman will be non-academic, the PCFC chairman an industrialist.

The Funding Councils are to contract with universities and colleges to supply public funds for education and research. The Secretary of State will be empowered to attach conditions to funds paid to the councils, and they will have power to attach conditions to payments which they make. Contracts are described in a consultative document as key features distinguishing the new regime from the old. The advantages are described as: greater precision in the specification of what is expected in return for public funding; closer links between funding and institutions' perform-ance; and periodic renegotiation of contracts. The objectives to be secured are described as being to encourage institutions to be enterprising in attracting contracts, particularly from the private sector; to lessen depen-dence on public funding: and to sharpen accountability for the use of public funds. It is recognized that some work, 'such as the advancement of learning', cannot readily be embraced by contractual commitments.

Academic tenure is to be abolished. Commissioners will be appointed with power to amend charters and statutes so that academic employment contracts made since 20 November 1987 cannot preclude dismissal on grounds of redundancy or financial exigency or inefficiency.

New arrangements are proposed for internal and external audit of the Funding Councils and of bodies receiving funds from them. A new Higher Education Internal Audit Unit is to have access to institutions' books, and value-for-money audits of universities and colleges may be required.

Local authorities, whose duty *to provide further education and* power *to provide higher education will be redefined, will be required to delegate financial and other powers to all colleges with 200 or more full-time-equivalent students, and to reform the size and composition of their governing bodies. Not more than a fifth of the governors will represent the LEA; at least half must represent employment interests or be co-opted.*

THE DEBATE

Who'll use these new levers of State control?

Michael Brock
Warden, Nuffield College, Oxford

The Education Reform Bill embodies the Government's plans for altering the funding of higher education and the terms on which the teaching and research staffs are employed. In dealing with the consultative papers and discussions which preceded the Bill the Secretary of State for Education and Science was reassuring about the intended use of the powers sought[1]. 'The Government', *The Times* has responded, 'should not take powers it has no intention of using or, much less, that it would not like any other government to use.'[2]

The greatest change in the governance and funding of higher education is that nearly all of the non-university sector is to be removed from the control of the local education authorities, and put under a Polytechnics and Colleges Funding Council. Here the Government has a strong case. This sector now constitutes more than half of the system. The orientation of its leading institutions is national rather than local; and its degree students resemble their university counterparts in receiving maintenance grants which enable them to study away from home. Controversy centres on the fact that there are to be new funding arrangements for the whole of higher education. The universities are funded at present by the University Grants Committee, which was established by Treasury minute in 1919. The majority of its members, including the chairman, are from universities: two are drawn from industry.

The replacement of the UGC by a Universities Funding Council, composed of broadly equal numbers from the universities and the non-university world, diverges from the recommendations of the Croham Committee (February 1987) in several ways. The committee recommended that their new body should be charged specifically:

To make recommendations on the levels of public funding for the universities over a span of years, in the light of the practical options available; and to assess the implications for the universities of the Government's public expenditure policies.[3]

This represented a sharper version of the UGC's duty 'to inquire into the financial needs of university education in the United Kingdom'. The Universities Funding Council is given no such duty in the Bill, its principal remit being to 'administer funds made available . . . by the Secretary of State'.

In reply to criticisms about these limited terms of reference, Mr Baker told the Vice-Chancellors: 'I recognise the crucial importance of having an intermediary body that can make disinterested and fearless assessments of the financial position of universities.' He added, however, that the UFC and PCFC 'should not come to be seen primarily as lobbies for more money'. The assumption here seems to be that advice to the Government from such councils always becomes publicly known. The Croham Committee, reviewing the UGC's record, had reached the opposite conclusion. Defenders of the terms of reference in the Bill have also suggested that the Funding Councils 'will give general advice whatever their terms'. The effect of restricting the terms must be to reduce the authority of any general advice on funding levels which the councils may give.

Secondly, the Croham Committee recommended a University *Grants* Council, whereas the theory underlying *Funding* Councils is that higher education should be based not on grants but on 'contracts'. This part of the Government's planning is opposed no less strongly from the political Right than from the Left. Professor Elie Kedourie has been critical in a pamphlet published by the Centre for Policy Studies of which Lord Joseph is chairman. After reviewing the 'contract' proposals he concluded: 'that detailed controls are in contemplation cannot be doubted'.[4] The official voice has become cautious here. 'The Government', wrote the Parliamentary Under-Secretary of State, Mr Robert Jackson (23 January), 'has not yet reached conclusions on the exact nature of the proposed contracting regime; and it welcomes further discussion.'[5]

'Some of you', the Secretary of State told the Vice-Chancellors, 'see these policies, taken together, as tending to intrude on the proper freedom of universities to manage their affairs. That is not the direction in which I want to move: quite the reverse.'

In support of Mr Baker's contention it is argued, first, that following the Croham Committee's advice in substituting a statutory for an advisory body in the intermediate layer can hardly represent an increase in *ministerial* power; and secondly, that if the Secretary of State's statutory powers to direct the Research Councils have never been used, the two new Funding Councils must be safe from direction. The force of these arguments may be doubted. It would seem paradoxical to deny that replacing a well-tried system of usage and convention with a tightly controlled statutory apparatus can represent anything but a move towards *dirigisme*[6].

The part of the Bill regulating the tenure of university staff (clauses 130–136) has been criticized for the omission of any statement about academic freedom. The redundancy which gives ground for dismissal is precisely defined in clause 131(3). The fact that there can be no dismissal for voicing views objectionable to the authorities is left unstated. Drafting difficulties have been adduced to explain this omission. The Secretary of State assured the Vice-Chancellors that he would instruct the University Commissioners, who would be regulating each university's statutes on tenure, to see that the 'responsible exercise' of academic freedom was properly safeguarded.

The universities, polytechnics and colleges may in the end be affected less by the clauses dealing directly with their affairs than by some which concern secondary education. Under clause 13, for instance, the Secretary of State may make an order extending the national curriculum scheme so that it covers those aged 16 to 19. The sixth forms may not dance much longer to the universities' tunes.

Notes

1 Speech to the Vice-Chancellors' Committee, 30 October 1987, sections 3, 18, 39. The Bill was published on 20 November.
2 27 January 1988.
3 *Review of the University Grants Committee* (Cm 81), p. 33.
4 *Diamonds into Glass* (January 1988), p. 25. The pamphlet does not represent the 'corporate view' of the Centre. The author's agreement with Professor John Griffith is significant. See also Lord Beloff, *Parl. Deb.*, Lords, vol. 488, col. 164, 30 June 1987.
5 *The Times*, 23 January, 1988.
6 For ministerial denials that the Government could interfere in allocations by the UGC see *Parl. Deb.*, Commons, 27 October 1981, col. 707 (Waldegrave); 7 July 1987, col 186 (Jackson); Lords, 10 February 1987, col. 513 (Earl of Dundee). For indirect pressure on Research Councils see *Oxford University Gazette*, 28 January 1988, p. 493 (view of Sir John Kingman, chairman, SERC, 1981–5).

The Government's plans for extensive changes in the structure of higher and further education were prepared in less apparent haste than those for English and Welsh schools and the consultation period was slightly longer. The main outlines were published in a White Paper, Higher Education: Meeting the Challenge, *in April 1987. (Lord Croham's committee, which reviewed the University Grants Committee, had reported the previous February. The Government announced that it accepted the 'broad thrust' of Croham's recommendations, but it soon became apparent that its proposed Funding Council was to be a much feebler creature than the reconstituted and wholly independent University Grants Council which Croham had recommended.)*

More details of Government thinking emerged in consultative documents on the polytechnics and colleges sector (in April); on the UFC and on contracts (in May); on the abolition of tenure (in July); on the reordering of the maintained sector (in August); and on accounting and audit in higher education (in October). (The intention to legislate on tenure was first announced in July 1984.)

As more details emerged, the tone of the responses changed. For this reason, the date is given of each response printed below. Publication of the Bill on 20 November, with the revelation of the extensive powers to be taken by the Secretary of State, provoked indignation from the universities. As this book went to press, and the Government showed no willingness to amend the Bill, the anger of the Vice-Chancellors was mounting, emerging in an unyielding statement by the Hebdomadal Council of Oxford University on 28 January, of which an extract follows.

THE ADVICE

Oxford University Hebdomadal Council (January 1988) views with deep concern those provisions in the Bill which affect the universities. As drafted the clauses represent a major threat to the independence of the universities. That independence is crucial to academic freedom and so to freedom of thought in the country as a whole.

Under the Bill, Government is to be given statutory powers exercisable through the Universities Funding Council by which control could be exercised over every activity carried on within a university. The Bill heralds a wholly undesirable change in the relations between Government and the universities. It may well be that the UGC as at present functioning is in need of reform. The Croham Committee, which reported in February 1987, certainly thought so. But it insisted that the new council which it recommended should be 'visibly its own creature, enjoying the confidence of the Government, the universities and the community at large' and that its independence 'ought to be given formal recognition with appropriate safeguards included in a founding instrument'. Not only are there no such safeguards, but the Bill expressly provides that the UFC shall comply with '*any* directions' given to it by the Secretary of State.

The UFC will be in a position to dictate to universities what activities they must carry out (and, indeed, must *not* carry out). This is achieved by statutory language empowering the UFC to pay money to universities 'subject to such terms and conditions' as it thinks fit. The obedience of universities is secured by a remarkable clause which accords to the UFC the right to require repayment of the entire grant in the event of any breach, in any respect, of the conditions of the grant. If repayment is delayed, for whatever reason, interest becomes payable. Of course, the universities accept that they must be able to demonstrate good stewardship of public funds entrusted to them, but such accountability is not incompatible with autonomy.

One line of defence adopted by Government is to say that the powers will not be used in disregard of the views of the UFC and of the universities, and that the minister's power to give directions will be used only as a 'last resort'. No such limitations appear on the face of the Bill. One reason for this could be that the limitations are incapable of being precisely drafted. Another reason could be that an unfettered power is preferred to a restricted one. Neither reason affords any comfort to the universities.

More recently a fresh defence has been advanced. The Secretary of State has stated that the new UFC will have 'greater independence from the department' than the UGC. The minister believes that not enough people 'realize that the UGC only *advises* the department on grants to universities. At present the holder of my office could reject this advice and make grants on some different basis. The Bill therefore *reduces* the department's currently unlimited powers.' Such statements are wholly inconsistent with established practice. Ministers have repeatedly assured Parliament that the UGC is quite independent of Government. As a minister told the House of Commons in July 1981: 'By convention the allocation of recurrent grant to individual universities by the UGC is not subject to ministerial intervention.' By long-established convention the independence of the UGC from Government has been carefully preserved.

The change is that the convention of UGC independence is to be replaced by statutory powers of intervention by central government in the affairs of the UFC and through the UFC in the affairs of individual universities. The Bill makes no attempt to codify the convention which now protects the UGC's independence. The universities and the public are asked to accept Mr Baker's statement that the UFC has 'statutory independence' and Mr Robert Jackson's assurance that the convention 'will continue to operate in the new era'. Statutory existence does not by itself guarantee statutory independence, and Mr Jackson's assurance is negatived by the two unrestricted powers of interference expressly written into the Bill, the power to attach conditions when paying money to the UFC and the power to give *any* directions to the UFC. The independence of the statutory UFC should be made manifest and not be allowed to rest upon non-statutory comments by ministers. Nor should the

UFC itself be allowed to have an unqualified power to impose on universities any conditions it wishes.

The clauses of the Bill relating to the universities are unacceptable as they stand. They should never have been put forward in their present form. The amendments required are that the powers of the Secretary of State should be limited and the independence of the UFC safeguarded, though with its powers to impose conditions properly circumscribed.

Council most earnestly hopes that the Government, mindful of our universities' long tradition of independence, and of the Government's own professed desire to delegate control and responsibility, to encourage individual initiative and to diminish the need for centralized bureaucracy, will give most careful consideration to the criticisms of the Bill which have been made and the amendments which this and other universities have proposed.

Professor J R Quayle, Vice-Chancellor, Bath University, to Mr Kenneth Baker (January 1988) – I am writing to express my deep concern over certain aspects of the Education Reform Bill now in passage through Parliament and the House of Lords. I would not cavil at a properly designed system of contracting with the UFC. Bath University, like many of the newer universities without substantial endowments, has always had to depend on its wit and outside contracts to supplement its block grant. Nevertheless, the fact that the UFC, having made a contract with the university, may have the right to terminate it and call back the money with interest does indeed sharpen the managerial tools in the new Council's tool-box.

The really key issue is, however, the new powers to be given to the Secretary of State in clause 94. These powers, if used, would open the way to direct control by the Government of the country's universities – whom and how many they may teach, what subjects they may teach, what they may do research in, what they may publish, what libraries they may keep and who may read in them and so on. Such direct powers are inappropriate in a non-totalitarian civilized country. You have frequently assured vice-chancellors that these powers would be used only as a last resort, but your idea of a last resort may be very different from future Secretaries of State and their civil servants.

It may be argued that more riches and greater prosperity will flow back into the country by harnessing more of the universities' research talents and resources into research as defined by tightly drawn contract from the UFC. Of course a balance must be struck between basic, strategic and applied research, and striking the right balance is, indeed, one of the most difficult aspects of management of research resources. What makes it so difficult is that it is rarely possible to predict at the time what, if any, scientific and technological breakthroughs will emerge in 20 to 30 years from every new and recondite finding or new line of work. What is certain, however, is that if we are not able to fund and retain our best scientists and engineers and enable them to devote an appropriate part of their time to curiosity-driven research (and that means, I am afraid, mostly public rather than private money), the seed-bed of new discoveries will grow but little. It is therefore most important that, in drawing up UFC contracts, overheads could contain a 'profit margin' for the chosen universities themselves to plough back into their own curiosity-driven research.

Sir John Kingman, Vice-Chancellor, University of Bristol, to Mrs Angela Rumbold, Minister of State, DES (December 1987) – I read with great interest your speech in the Second Reading of the Education Bill. Like many in the educational world, I support most of the intentions of the Bill, but I greatly regret the way these are being implemented in the clauses relating to the universities.

My eye was caught by your statement that 'the power of . . . the Secretary of State to give direction . . . follows a well-established precedent of the Research Councils, and no one has ever seen it as a threat to academic freedom'. I spent four years as chairman of the SERC, and I have to say that the precedent does not support your case. Although the power was never formally used, its threat was ever-present and was used by civil servants as a pretext for continual interference in both major and minor matters.

The fear in the universities is not that ministers will give formal and public directives but that their civil servants will use the legal power as a deterrent to independent action by the UFC. And the universities will not have the power to intervene because of the two-stage mechanism of the Bill. The DES can direct the UFC to impose a condition of funding. The universities can protest to the UFC, but cannot force the UFC to appeal to ministers. In the jargon of the spy novels, the UFC is the 'cut-out'.

At the end of your speech, you made the strong point that your policies on education had been endorsed by the electorate. For the universities that is not so. Your declared policy was that of the White Paper, which proposed that universities would operate as contractors, being judged by the success with which they fulfilled the contracts and not by the details of their internal affairs. There was no hint that central control from Whitehall was to be strengthened by the absolute powers of clause 94.

I do not believe that this was the intention of ministers. But the policy clearly stated before the election has been distorted by your civil servants, who have long been contemptuous of the government of universities by their councils and senates. Their ancient ambition to grasp the reins of power themselves is now within sight of achievement. I am deeply ashamed that it is a Conservative Government which is letting it happen.

University of London (May 1987) – The 5 per cent growth in student numbers proposed up to 1990 is not supported by any commitment to additional resources, but rather is dependent upon achieving 'better value for money from the public funds made available to higher education'. This is a matter for particular concern, as Government expenditure plans for further and higher education published earlier this year show a fall in real total spending of £126m between 1986–87 and 1989–90. It is simply not possible to continue to produce graduates and research of an international standard under a regime of continuously falling unit costs. The White Paper notes that 'the Government accepts the broad thrust' of the Croham recommendations for the future of the UGC, but states that the successor body will be the Universities Funding Council and that the payment of grants to universities will be 'replaced by a system of contracting'. In practice, the reservation of powers to the Secretary of State for Education, and the apparent elimination of the right and duty of the UGC to advise on the resources needed to sustain the university system, constitute a fundamental change in the university/Government relationship. The university would greatly regret a decision to make the UFC simply an instrument of Government, abolishing the UGC's historic and widely-admired quasi-independent role. The proposal is not consonant with the need for higher education to remain as independent as possible from the apparatus of the State, even when largely funded by it.

Likewise, the implications of the contracting concept imply deep-seated changes in the roles of individual university institutions. It is hard to see how any system of contracts could apply to the bulk of a university's teaching work, without the basis of a national manpower plan so detailed as to be wholly unrealistic. The implied move towards a planned economy seems surprising in view of the Government's general economic stance.

The key recommendation in both the Croham and Jarratt reports for a firm and longer funding horizon is rejected by the White Paper in favour of the UFC providing 'planning parameters for the medium and long term'. It is disappointing that the Government, while pressing the need for change on all other groups concerned with higher education, refuses to act on a matter within its own competence to which successive independent reviewers have drawn attention. Universities are not, as the White Paper suggests, seeking to insulate themselves from the need for change (few organizations can themselves have initiated and sustained rationalization programmes on the scale which the University of London has) but rather to be enabled to improve their efficiency further by obtaining a commitment for stable incomes for periods for which they have to make their own commitments to students.

The University of Edinburgh (May 1987) has already communicated its serious concern that the proposed Universities Funding Council should have as its remit that it should 'make money available on contract' as the sole form of allocation. It believes such a limitation to be unwise and unduly restrictive, that it would militate against the flexibility and responsiveness of the system and could cause legal problems for the proposed UFC and the universities alike. There is clear evidence that the authors of both the White Paper *Higher Education: Meeting the Challenge* and the consultative paper *Contracts between the Funding Bodies and Higher Education Institutions* had serious doubts as to whether contracts could cover all the essential items to enable universities to operate effectively.

It needs to be recalled that the universities are now in the throes of adapting to a new and untested funding system introduced by the UGC in 1986–7. Even though it differs in only a limited number of ways from the previous system, this has resulted in significant discontinuities in funding. It would be disastrous for the universities and the educational system if inadequately framed contracts were issued, since these would lead to inefficiency and to unpredictable and uncontrolled changes in the provision of services and other activities. Further disruption of educational services and diseconomies, such as those experienced in the period since 1981, must be avoided.

Sir Edward Parkes, Vice-Chancellor, University of Leeds (June 1987) – We are especially concerned that the terms of reference proposed for the UFC would provide for it to advise Government on the needs of the universities *only when the government actually asks for such advice*. The terms of reference of the existing UGC enjoin upon it a responsibility 'to inquire into the financial needs of university education in Great Britain' and 'to advise the Government as to the application of any grants made by Parliament towards meeting them'. The Croham Committee, similarly, proposed that the UFC should have a responsibility 'to make recommendations on the levels of public funding . . . and . . . assess the implications for the universities of the Government's public expenditure policies'. We can see no logic in a system which allows the funding body more or less complete freedom over the allocation of funds but does not allow it the right, for example, to advise Government that the objectives set for the system require a certain level of resources.

There must be a suspicion that the Government is simply trying to avoid the possibility that it might, at some point in the future, be embarrassed by criticism from an independent body. It would be difficult, we believe, to attract lay members of the appropriate calibre unless the UFC had the independence to offer advice to the Government.

Our second principal point concerns the nature of the contractual relationship envisaged between the UFC and the universities. We are firmly of the view that, whatever relationship is developed, it should preserve a number of essential advantages inherent in the present block grant system. The block grant system underpins speculative research into untried areas, research which is fundamental to the country's long-term economic well-being. Such research would be jeopardized by any contractual system (such as the one posited in the consultative document) which entailed a university having to secure a specific contract for every research programme it wished to carry out.

Let me quote an example. Work at Leeds on a slowly dissolving glass pellet to release essential trace elements in ruminants' stomachs was supported for many years only on block grant; an application for funding from a research council was turned down on the grounds that the idea lacked promise. It seems to be reasonable to assume that any application for a 'contract' from the UFC would have met a similar fate. But the idea did bear fruit: the glass pellet is now known as Cosecure and is being manufactured by Pilkington Brothers. In an extensive national advertising campaign about 18 months ago, Pilkingtons indicated that Cosecure could become the biggest product in the animal health market, worth over £2 billion world-wide. Three possible forms of contractual system are mooted in the consultative paper. Only the first, the 'single comprehensive contract', is guaranteed to preserve the advantages of the block grant system.

Whilst there are aspects of the Government's proposals for the UFC which we would endorse, we should like to conclude by expressing our disappointment at the general philosophy which seems to underlie the proposals. It does not seem sensible to base the whole of educational provision upon exercises in manpower planning. The nation's need is for a well-educated population firmly rooted in an improved base of literacy, numeracy, the humanities and scientific knowledge. We are not convinced that the model proposed by the Government is sufficiently flexible or broadly based.

Professor Michael Thompson, Vice-Chancellor, University of Birmingham (June 1987) – The document on contracts provides me with a serious problem. In a sense the universities are already in a (consenting) contractual relationship with their clients – the students and their sponsors, the research funding bodies and the Government. However, the present arrangements admit a great degree of autonomy on the universities' part, though not nearly so much as they had in the days of quinquennial planning. The concept of detailed contracting is in itself inimical to the principle of university autonomy and could result in greater hindrances and expense than we have now in terms of bureaucratic and financial controls. We are particularly concerned at the long-term damage a system of contracting will inflict upon scholarship in this country. Not only would apparently purely academic projects not be possible to anything like the same extent, but the side-effects of these abstract projects might not reach the stage of practical fruition. At a more basic level the present drive to maintain and improve academic standards would be put at risk by the universities' reluctance to quarrel with their monopolistic paymaster.

The Standing Conference of Arts and Social Sciences in Universities (October 1987) is opposed to the substitution of contracts for the present system of university funding. To fulfil their purposes, teaching and research in higher education must be critical and exploratory. A contractual system can only undermine this, since its intention is to press institutions of higher education to conform to objectives based on considerations of short-term utility and formulated by politicians, industrialists and others not directly motivated by academic ideals.

[Of the three stated goals in the consultative document] the third appears to embody the real purpose of the new system: 'to strengthen the commitment of institutions to the delivery of the educational services which it is agreed with the new planning and funding body they should provide'. What plainly concerns the DES is commitment to goals set from outside by political or economic considerations. Since financial power will lie on one side only, and that side will also be the sole judge of fulfilment of the contract, the use of the term 'agree' in this context is sophistical. In plainer English, this goal can be stated as being to force institutions to do what those with political power want them to do, by denying them money if they do not. This is precisely why SCASSU opposes the entire notion of contracting.

Association of University Teachers (June 1987) – We see no clear argument in the text of the White Paper for the system of contracting. It is predicated upon the unsupported assumption that institutions have in some way failed to meet the requirements of the nation; we do not believe this to be a basis for introducing damaging changes in higher education as a whole, or a cause for the disruption of the entire funding basis of the university system. One of the stated aims of contracting is 'to encourage institutions to be enterprising in attracting contracts from other sources, particularly the private sector'. Universities already have a good record for attracting funds from this source. However, the private sector will normally only fund specific activities or pay for specific services. Only in very rare cases will the private sector support general funding or basic research.

The process of interactive planning of the university system which used to be employed by the UGC provided an adequate balance between the needs of the institutions and the requirements of the nation. The great national contribution of the universities has been that of an independent response to the mixed demands for education from the Government (channelled normally through the UGC), from employers and professional organizations, from the wider community and from the students seeking places. We reject the implication of the consultative document that contracted educational services can better reflect and balance these needs. Nor do we in any way accept that the work-force planning implicit in this process is likely to be effective or desirable. The vast majority of recent experiences has indicated that 'manpower planning' at first-degree level is at best imprecise as the basis of forward planning and at worst grossly misleading.

The supply of degree places should not be seen simply as a 'training' function, but as having a wider educational purpose. The aims and purposes of higher education were defined clearly by the Robbins Committee, and repeated in the Green Paper, as 'instruction in skills, the promotion of the general powers of the mind, the advancement of learning and the transmission of a common culture and common standards of citizenship'. It is difficult to envisage how these objectives could be achieved under a system of contracting for degree places. Contract funding would only be able to comprehend the functions of the universities narrowly defined, and would tend to damage the wider academic and scholarly functions of the system which are not susceptible of narrow definition and costing.

Any extensive price competition between universities would be extremely damaging to the quality of teaching, scholarship and research and could potentially threaten the existence of institutions. Even pressures to admit large numbers of additional students 'at marginal cost' would damage the research and scholarship of the universities while threatening the quality of their teaching.

Planning and teaching degree courses, scholarship and research all take place on long time scales. It takes many years to build an excellent department or team, but only months to destroy it. Contracting, especially on relatively short time scales, with attendant uncertainty about renewal, could destroy much of what is excellent in our universities.

Professor John Ashworth, Vice-Chancellor, University of Salford (January 1988) – In the 1987 White Paper *Higher Education: Meeting the Challenge* the aims of higher education are said to be to serve the economy more effectively; to pursue basic scientific research and scholarship in the arts and humanities; and to have closer links with industry and commerce and promote enterprise. The universities would claim that they have adapted to serve these aims and purposes loyally. This Government is clearly impatient, however, because the mechanisms which have facilitated this adaptation are about to be changed in a radical and dramatic way.

The University Grants Committee is to be replaced by the Universities Funding Council, which will reflect a greater weight of non-academic opinion, and the UFC will distribute funds amongst the UK under novel, contractual arrangements. The question is whether the new arrangements will be more or less effective than the old in achieving the aims set out in the White Paper. It is useful for us to have had the opportunity in this instance to define a clear performance indicator (another phrase beloved by this administration) for the new UFC. It will have to aim to achieve a productivity increase from the university system in both teaching and research of at least 5 per cent compounded for at least four years to do better than the old UGC. Faced with these statistics, it might strike you as odd that the Government should not have heeded the old American adage 'if it ain't broke, don't fix it'.

What the universities could do if they were to be let off the Government leash is probably best shown by the way they have responded to the opportunities presented by the market overseas. There is no quota for overseas students, and since the imposition of so-called full-cost fees in the late 1970s univerisities have fiercely competed to attract foreign students. They have set up special 'access courses', provided tailor-made courses in English and study skills and adapted their course provision to the special needs of specific groups of foreigners. The University of Salford now earns over £2.5m per annum from foreign students and we, like most other UK universities, are now entirely dependent financially on such a revenue stream continuing.

I can only wish and hope that the Government takes note of this astonishing way in which the universities have responded to this challenge (there are now more foreign students in UK universities than ever before) and asks itself what might happen if the universities were allowed to make contracts not of some wishy-washy, rhetorical kind with a bureaucratic quango like the UFC but real, legally enforceable contracts with their true customers – their students and the potential employers of their students.

If, instead of the Government giving money to the universities and thus keeping them in a state of continuing dependency, universities were allowed to charge full-cost fees to UK students, then we would see the enterprising, flexible and socially responsive higher education institutions that are extolled in ministerial rhetoric. This is a much more hopeful and exciting avenue to explore than the one outlined in the consultative documents – redolent of the centrally planned, UGC-supervised, Government-funded, dependent past in which the country's commerce and industries have suffered (and continue to suffer) from a chronic shortage of suitable educated and trained graduates.

Professor Graeme Davies, Vice-Chancellor, University of Liverpool (July 1987) – The general reaction in this university to the consultative papers is one of unease. They reflect changes to the present system which, generally, would be to the advantage of the Secretary of State and to the disadvantage of universities. Concern has been expressed about the proposed reserve powers of the Secretary of State. The possibility that the Secretary of State might exercise these could act as a considerable disincentive to the chief executive and to the members of the Universities Funding Council.

It is also considered that the terms of reference of the UFC are one-sided, being loaded substantially in favour of the Secretary of State. Its responsibilities are negative and restrictive, concentrating on methods of administration and monitoring, rather than on the search for an imaginative enhancement of higher education provision. A general concern has been expressed about who would be responsible for its operation and about the procedure for advising Government on the total level of resources required by the university system.

On the subject of the proposed contracting arrangements, concern has been expressed that the 'dual-support' system is threatened. Charities give valuable short-term support to universities, with long-term support for research provided by the UGC. The fear has been expressed that stable long-term support would disappear. Long-term planning in universities requires long-term contracts, not contracts for three years only. It is proposed that, as a minimum, five year contracts are introduced, with no bureaucratic interference within the contract period. Long-term research is planned to some extent, but its direction and emphasis will change over the years. There is some concern as to whether or not the contract system would be able to cope with this need for changes over time in the nature of a particular research project. It is likely that the proposed arrangements would lead to increased selectivity in the funding of research, with opportunities restricted for research into new areas of study. Pump-priming funds are often needed for the early stages of preliminary research, and it is doubtful whether contracts would cover this type of funding. Much research is also fundamental and not targeted towards commercial exploitation. Concern has been expressed that fundamental research would not prosper under the proposed new arrangements.

A general concern has been expressed about the danger that research undertaken under the proposed new system would reflect what the Government wants to be done and not what may be needed or worthwhile. It is considered essential to attempt to ensure that the academic initiative remains with universities as of right.

University of Bristol (November 1987) – The consultative document *Accounting and Auditing in Higher Education* is unacceptable even as a basis of discussion with universities, because it is totally inconsistent with Government policy for universities as recently explained by your Secretary of State and by the White Paper and its dependent consultation papers.

The whole thrust of ministerial statements is to regard universities, not as non-departmental public bodies or as nationalized industries, but as independent contractors to the nation (with the DES/UFC as proxy customer) for the supply of degree-level education and basic research. They are to develop other sources of income, and in particular to build much closer links with industry.

The accounting arrangements should therefore be those appropriate to independent contractors, and to contractors moreover on a 'fixed price' or 'payment by results' basis rather than on a 'cost-plus' basis. The public interest requires that universities should fulfil the contracts into which they enter, and that the UFC should use its monopoly position to help universities to do so. It does not require that the DES should exert central control over the way in which universities manage their internal affairs.

The particular arrangements at Bristol apply with only minor changes to almost all British universities. The exceptions are the federal universities of Cambridge, London, Oxford and Wales.

At Bristol financial responsibility is vested in the Council, a body with a substantial lay majority appointed largely by the local authorities and by the Court. Council must present annual accounts to the Court, audited by a professional firm appointed by the Court.

These accounts are effectively public. Court also elects the Treasurer, a distinguished layman with financial experience who then sits *ex officio* on Council. Council appoints a Finance Committee, chaired by the Treasurer and with a lay majority, which decides financial policy and acts as the audit committee. Day-to-day management is in the hands of a qualified Finance Officer, answerable to the Vice-Chancellor, to the Treasurer and to the Finance Committee. The university's internal auditor has direct access to the Finance Officer, to the Vice-Chancellor, to the Treasurer and to the Chairman of Council. He submits an annual report to the Finance Committee, and has an annual meeting with the Vice-Chancellor and Treasurer.

The external auditor (one of the major international accountants) reports to Finance Committee, Council and Court and meets routinely the Finance Officer, Vice-Chancellor and Treasurer. The Finance Officer makes returns regularly and in agreed form to the UGC. And all the university's books are open to the National Audit Office.

This provides a system of checks and balances much more complex than you would find in industry, in government departments or in non-departmental public bodies. It is probably too complex, but what is quite certain is that we do not need any more. The proposed Higher Education Internal Audit will add nothing to the economy, efficiency and effectiveness of the universities, but will confuse the pattern of financial responsibility in a way which will lessen, not increase, confidence in the financial integrity of the universities.

The point can be illustrated by the repeated references in the document to value-for-money studies (which incidentally are not synonymous with examinations under section 6(3)(c) of the National Audit Act 1983). According to the document, these can be instigated by universities' external auditors (para. 21), audit committees (para. 25c), Comptroller and Auditor General (para. 27), the UFC (para. 28), the Permanent Secretary, DES (para. 31) and the Director-General, UFC (para. 31) – all of these independently of the responsible Council, Treasurer and Vice-Chancellor. Who is to decide whether these studies are themselves worthwhile? How are these arrangements consistent with the Jarratt concept of the Vice-Chancellor as chief executive?

Lest I be thought alarmist in seeing in the document a malign strengthening of the DES central control, let me take one more example, the proposals about audit committees. It is to be (para. 24) a condition of funding that we should have an audit committee, that it should consist of between three and six lay people, and that it should exclude those (like the members of the Finance Committee and in particular the Treasurer and the Chairman of Council) directly concerned with financial management. The chairman of this committee will be another lay member of Council, with a duty (para. 25e) to report in certain circumstances directly to the Director-General of the UFC. This is the first time the DES has laid down the committee structure for universities, and the precedent may prove uncomfortable for the department as well as damaging for universities. In Bristol we have concluded that the Finance Committee is a more effective watchdog than a separate audit committee would be, and we do not intend to dilute its responsibility or that of the Vice-Chancellor or the Treasurer.

These are just a few of the objectionable points in a document misconceived in principle and likely to make it more difficult for your ministers to achieve the restructuring of higher education which is their aim. I hope there is time for second thoughts.

Chartered Institute of Public Finance and Accountancy (November 1987) – There are a number of points relating to external audit which could with advantage be clarified. The justification for the C&AG to have access to the records of bodies funded by Government is that he should be able to carry out whatever inquiries are necessary to assure Parliament that the funds which they vote are property used. However, universities and colleges are under pressure to attract funding from outside sources. It is not clear whether the C&AG will have access to all records or only those relating to the expenditure of Government funds. In practice it would be unrealistic to restrict the C&AG's access to records, but his prime responsibility is to monitor the use of Government funding.

Coopers & Lybrand, accountants (December 1987) – Overall, we believe that the consultative document provides an appropriate framework for ensuring adequate accountability of polytechnics and colleges, in the light of the changes in their status proposed by the Government, and of universities. The proposals in the consultative document are likely to lead to a greater degree of scrutiny of the activities of institutions by auditors. The proposed involvement of external auditors, the Comptroller and Auditor General and the new higher education internal audit unit in value-for-money issues may give rise to concern by the management of institutions. We believe, however, that provided this work is properly co-ordinated, it should be of major assistance to those responsible for the management of institutions in achieving improved services from the resources available to them.

The University of London Court (November 1987) fully recognized the importance of the need for effective and proper accounting and auditing arrangements in universities. Universities collectively receive and spend over £1.3 billion of public money and are charitable corporations. On both grounds it is imperative that high standards of accountability for public funds are maintained. Many of the procedures referred to in the consultative document are already applied or have been accepted for adoption as best practice by universities.

Against the background of developing mechanisms within the university, it is a matter of great concern that the consultative document proposes several new tiers of outside scrutiny. The UFC is to have its own internal audit arrangements which will monitor institutions' systems, while the DES accounting officer will deploy the department's internal audit to monitor the UFC. A new Higher Education Internal Audit Unit is also to be established, with access to institutions' books. Furthermore, issues raised by universities' external auditors must be reported regularly to the UFC, and their reports made available. Finally the UFC itself may commission 'value-for-money' studies from external agencies on universities. These new elements are to be added to the existing access of the National Audit Commission to universities' books. These proposals will produce a confusing network of overlapping responsibilities rather than a developed and rational system of accountability.

A veritable army of accountants and management consultants will be required apparently to check and double-check one another's results. This must all be funded from the diminishing resources available for a higher education system expanding to meet national needs. The Government should be in no doubt as the (unproductive) extra costs which much of this writing will generate – perhaps well in excess of £1m per annum for the University of London alone.

The university believes that a clear choice must be made. Either the Government must rely on the independent professional work of universities' external auditors and accept the certificates that they give that universities' accounts give a 'true and fair view' of their financial position, and that grants and other receipts have been properly applied for the purposes for which they were given; or the external auditing of universities should be placed squarely in the hands of the Audit Commission. The university believes the former approach accords best with a developed system of higher education.

Professor John Ashworth, Vice-Chancellor, University of Salford (September 1987) – Our first concern relates to the very wide scope of the Secretary of State's power. There are worrying signs that these powers will be used vigorously to control every aspect of a university's activities, whether these are primarily dependent on Government funding or not. In the recent consultative document entitled *Accounting and Auditing in Higher Education*, for example, a new auditing body, the Higher Education Internal Audit Unit, is proposed to oversee the four other layers of audit that already burden this and other universities. This new audit unit, together with the other innovations proposed in the document, will add significantly to our administrative costs but, worse, will inevitably lead the senior management of the universities to become more risk-averse. We have been concerned, since our grant from the University Grants Committee was virtually halved in 1981, to diversify our sources of income. We have been quite successful at this and the financial viability of the university is now wholly dependent on the continuing success of such activities. They have to be managed in a commercial manner, and I am accountable for their performance to the Finance Committee of my Council. At the moment this committee has on it a number of very experienced and hard-working industrialists and bankers who understand the nature of the risks (and rewards) that are involved in these kinds of activities. To have this committee being 'second guessed' by a group of civil servants in the Higher Education Internal Audit Unit will mean importing into the university those features of the management of the nationalized industries which has made the commercial performance of those industries so lamentable. At the very least amendments should be made so that the powers of the new University Funding Council and its minions apply only to monies provided by the Government.

Committee of Vice-Chancellors and Principals (interim response, 7 August 1987) – Tenure is a valuable right. Academics are prepared to accept lower salaries than their counterparts elsewhere because they enjoy a security of employment which does not exist in business and industry. It would seem to follow that academic staff who in the future do not enjoy tenure should receive enhanced remuneration. The Government's proposals in this regard are awaited with interest. There is a further consideration. Academics are frequently expected by their universities to possess and extend their expertise in specialisms for which there may be little or no demand outside the university system. It may well prove increasingly difficult to recruit first-class staff to pursue such non-marketable specialisms if neither security of tenure nor a salary which would take account of the lack of such security can be offered.

The note indicates that tenure will be lost if an academic currently enjoying tenure transfers to another institution whether at the same level or on promotion. This a short-sighted proposal. The inevitable effect will be to create a disincentive against making a move to another university. Yet mobility is always a highly desirable factor in the university world and now more so than ever when so many ideas are under consideration which involve the movement of staff from one university to another in furtherance of 'rationalization' or 'restructuring'.

The note makes no reference whatever to academic freedom. At an earlier stage, when Sir Keith Joseph was intimating the possibility of a change in the law in relation to tenure, he clearly recognized that his proposal might be regarded as a threat to academic freedom and he thought that safeguards ought to be provided. The fear (to put it crudely) is that academics expressing unpopular opinions or pursuing studies stigmatized as 'irrelevant' by those in authority will simply be forced out of their jobs by the withholding of the money required to pay their salaries. That this can happen where there is no tenure to protect academics can be amply demonstrated by events elsewhere in the course of the present century. It was therefore welcome that Sir Keith Joseph was at pains to stress that the abolition of tenure in its present form was not intended to be a covert means of undermining academic freedom. He made it plain that he was anxious to ensure that adequate safeguards to protect academic freedom should be enshrined in legislation.

CVCP further response, (23 October 1987) – We have little to add, apart from emphasizing two main points. The first is fundamental. We consider it essential that the Commissioners, when considering the statutes or other instruments of government of the various institutions and the changes which may be needed to secure Parliament's main objective, should be required to ensure that those instruments include explicit safeguards for the protection of academic freedom. Concern on this point was very strongly expressed at our meeting in Manchester last month. By protection of academic freedom we do not, of course, mean unqualified job protection. We mean the freedom within the law for academic staff to question and to test received wisdom, and to put forward new ideas and controversial or unpopular opinions, without placing the individuals in jeopardy of losing their jobs. The present proposals are wholly silent on this point. The silence might be taken to indicate that the Government has lost sight of the basic justification for any form of tenure in universities, and is ignorant of what has been done to universities elsewhere in the course of the present century. Public reassurance on this would be welcome. There should be in the statutes of each university something to which an aggrieved academic could point if he or she believed that termination of employment was due, not to misconduct, financial exigency, redundancy or incompetence, but to the nature of the opinion or beliefs or the work which he or she was undertaking.

The Association of University Teachers (September 1987) is opposed to the legislative proposals designed to limit tenure. We find it particularly disturbing that the proposals contain no reference at all to the need to safeguard academic freedom, despite the universally accepted view that such safeguards are essential to a free society and the clear evidence that tenure provides a strong and effective means to protect that freedom. It appears that the Government is unable to answer the arguments advanced, and therefore chooses to ignore them. This Government has consistently misunderstood the importance which academic staff attach to tenure and greatly underestimates the damage and dislocation that its current legislative proposals would cause. We believe that the proposed changes would add significantly to the 'brain drain' and would do much to frustrate the Government's own declared intentions of maintaining and concentrating excellence in UK universities. The proposals seem designed to reduce mobility and flexibility rather than increase it.

Attention might be given to one curious anachronism which might at some stage be raised in the courts by someone of a sufficiently perverse degree of ill will. We refer to the possibility that accepting a pension for early retirement as compensation for giving up an office or fellowship may well be a technical offence under section 2 of the Simony Act of 1588. The DES might care to refer this point to the Law Commission, since it seems a peculiarly inappropriate and obsolete provision in the light of the Government's approval for the early retirement schemes which have operated in the university system for the last ten years or so.

University of Salford (December 1987) – The Bill refers to academic tenure. Council is a little puzzled about the fuss that sometimes seems to be made about this. We take the view that academic tenure is one means that has proved useful in the past to preserve academic freedom. Tenure has now outlived its usefulness in this respect. It is the end (academic freedom) that is important, not the means (academic tenure) whereby it is achieved.

The Committee of Directors of Polytechnics (May 1987) particularly welcomes the Government's intention to put all major institutions of higher education in a similar relationship with their respective funding bodies. Inevitably, separate organizations will develop their own identities and procedures. Great care will have to be taken to ensure that, at least as far as the nature of their contracts is concerned, the Polytechnics and Colleges Funding Council and the Universities Funding Council adopt the same approach, criteria, procedures and performance measures. One great benefit from the PCFC and the UFC operating on a similar basis will be that, for the first time, it should be possible to obtain comparable data and to use comparable measures when assessing the cost efficiency of institutions.

We welcome the Government's intention that the system of contracting should encourage institutions to be enterprising in attracting external sources of funding. Nevertheless, resources attracted from external sources should not be regarded as a substitute for any support from the public purse. In the Government's 1985 Green Paper, *The Development of Higher Education into the 1990s*, it was clearly stated that it was not intended to regard externally attracted resources as replacing public funding. It was stated that 'donors can be assured that their gifts will result in a genuine increase in the (institutions's) resources'. We regret, therefore, that the consultative paper is equivocal on this point, referring only to avoiding 'damage to aspects of the work of institutions'. An institution must be assured that all aspects of its core activities will be protected by public funding (provided that it satisfies the conditions laid down by the funding body) and that it will not have to rely upon an injection of external funding to safeguard those activities.

Proper recognition will need to be given to the support of research when developing the contractual system. To enable institutions to develop a base on which to build their research work and attract external funding from different agencies (including the Research Councils and industry), part of their core funding should contain a significant element for research. The size of that element might well reflect an institution's proven success in attracting external funding for research.

There will need to be close co-operation between institutions and the funding bodies on the identification, development, application and interpretation of appropriate performance indicators. There should be a small number of key indicators that can be readily applied and be capable of producing measures of cost-effectiveness and well-understood criteria. Performance indicators should be applicable to all major institutions of higher education. Nevertheless, we realize that the distinctive character of many institutions might make it easier to apply some indicators more easily to some institutions than to others. Each institution, and each contractual area, should be assessed on its merits and in the context of its particular circumstances. No two courses are identical, no two research projects the same, each institution has unique characteristics and requirements. The criteria established by the funding bodies, such as SSRs, unit costs, weighting by mode of study, level of course and academic discipline will need to be applied sensitively and intelligently to give institutions a degree of flexibility.

Due account will have to be taken of the acute lack of investment in polytechnics, the severity of which varies. Aequate provision will have to be made to enable the PCFC to redress the situation in the immediate future.

Institutions should be given a clear statement of what is expected of them. Such a 'mission statement' might be regarded as part of the overall contractual relationship between an institution and the PCFC or UFC. The statement would constitute a recognition of an institution's ethos and of the distinctive contribution which it would be expected to make to higher education.

Association of Colleges for Further and Higher Education (May 1987) – The White Paper claims to have three main policies we need for economic success; to secure centralized control of free-standing polytechnics and colleges; and the replacement of the University Grants Committee by a Funding Council with a strong presence of economic relevance and a remit to shape policy more closely. These policies are not followed through consistently. Neither the White Paper nor the consultative papers outline a plan to encourage access. The consultative document on contracts reveals no thinking at all as to how the contracting system will be used to pursue this.

The only reason given for the increase in student numbers is the call from industry and commerce for more highly skilled, better-educated people. The four Robbins aims (instruction in skills, promotion of the general powers of the mind, the advancement of learning and the transmission of a common culture and common standards of citizenship) are quoted and endorsed. There are reassuring statements about the Government's commitment to the arts, humanities and social sciences, but there is to be an additional emphasis on science and technology. The White Paper endorses the aims defined in Robbins but changes their balance fundamentally.

Because of the need to encourage more people to become highly skilled, the Government intends to widen access, by increasing the participation rate at 18 and of mature people, and by encouraging more women into higher education. These intentions are all to be welcomed. A further 30,000 full-time and 20,000 part-time places are planned. We doubt whether this increase is enough. The report of the council for Industry and Higher Education, *Towards a Partnership: Higher Education Government Industry*, expressed doubts as to whether a 4 per cent increase in undergraduate numbers by the end of the century would be sufficient.

Secondly, there is no indication that funding to establish the proposed further 50,000 places will be forthcoming. As the consultative papers show no awareness of the 'unit of resource' principle, the lack of clear statement on this matter opens the way to reduce resourcing below the level which is required. Government should make it clear that higher education will be properly resourced.

Thirdly, there is a serious mismatch between the intention to create more part-time places and the intention to rationalize scattered provision and 'to concentrate effort on strong insitutions and departments'. If the intention is to widen access, then geographical availability of opportunity becomes important. Concentration is the enemy of improved access.

Brighton Polytechnic (May 1987) welcomes the broad approach to higher education outlined in the White Paper but urges that the development of the business commercial model for overseeing and assessing the effectiveness of provision should not be at the expense of safeguarding quality, standards and the ability to be innovative and flexible in the development of new educational opportunities.

The polytechnic welcomes the recognition that student numbers will grow and the associated commitment to increasing access to higher education. However, growth in numbers must be accompanied by (1) a student support system which will encourage entry to higher education and (2) an institutional funding system to provide the resources needed for the new types of courses required.

The polytechnic looks forward to being granted a form of corporate status designed to enable it to pursue agreed academic objectives. It looks to the Government for parity of treatment for universities and polytechnics. It acknowledges the good working relations that have been established with East Sussex County Council and its officers and would expect to be able to maintain them; and it will further develop its links with schools, local colleges and the University of Sussex.

The polytechnic is concerned at the nature of the contracts to be entered into with the PCFC and urges that these should take into account such factors as quality, regional requirements, institutional academic plans and the need to preserve a broad academic basis. It would be very concerned if cost was the overriding factor in determining contracts.

The polytechnic is seriously concerned at some of the proposals on the composition of governing bodies, particularly the suggestion that the group of representatives from commerce, industry and the professions should be essentially self-selecting. It believes that the members serving in this category should be chosen by the governing body as a whole. It also believes that there should be increased representation from staff and students.

The Polytechnic Academic Registrars Group (May 1987) represents key professional staff in the polytechnics who will have a major role in the implementation of much of the change envisaged by the White Paper. PARG welcomes the Government's long-overdue recognition that the polytechnics merit greater autonomy in the conduct and management of their own affairs.

The additional workload and responsibilities can be borne neither by existing staffing levels nor at current levels of remuneration. The new arrangements may provide some opportunities for making more effective use of existing resources. Opportunities need to be taken to relieve institutions of unnecessary bureaucracy. In this context the abandonment of the course approvals procedure is welcomed, and it is hoped that it will not simply reappear in the arrangements for contracting. Servicing the current student fees system consumes resources. The new arrangements, for both management and maintenance of standards, will work only if they are adequately underpinned by professional administrative support. The projected additional student numbers will impact on overstretched support services, as will the development of performance indicators.

Standing Conference of Principals and Directors of Colleges and Institutes in Higher Education (July 1987) – I have been asked to write to you to seek block contracts with a degree of flexibility yet carrying forward the good work of the NAB programme area funding allocations over a long period of time, e.g three or five year rolling programme planning cycles; to stress the need for bridging finance for the transitional arrangements providing restructuring money similar to that received by the universities and risk capital or seed money vital to any new business endeavours. It would also be helpful to receive any annual grant in full at the beginning of the financial year. The Standing Conference asked me to underline their positive commitment to a vigorous new higher educational system.

Committee on Polytechnics Local Links (June 1987) The local dimension to the proposals for reform of the higher education system will need clear definition at the outset because of two factors: the fear that the proposals and the process of change will threaten local links that are vital to the life of the institution and to the development of its strategy; and the opportunities offered by the widespread and often insufficiently recognized networking of local links which underlie much of what polytechnics and major colleges have become.

The support of a community reflects the degree of local pride and involvement that a town or city has in its college or polytechnic. The support may have accrued for various reasons, but it has given expression to a form of higher education which has national recognition united with local responsiveness. The institutions are proving to be attractive and accessible to sectors of the population previously under-represented in the traditional system. They have functional links with the local economy and industry and with the social and cultural concerns of the community. The principle of local responsiveness is crucial to the future development of higher education.

Recommendations

Any polytechnic or college incorporated under the Companies Acts should include in the memorandum that it shall have special regard to the educational needs of the community; promote courses and seminars for persons who may or may not be students of the instituions; provide advisory services and centres for information and documentation for the use of students or staff or the public.

Effective collaboration [should be] established between the institution in the new sector and all other educational establishments in its locality such as schools, colleges, universities and the local education authority itself. An effective partnership is essential to assess, and an obligation rests firmly on LEAs and on the institutions to achieve this, and to publicize by education shops and other means the opportunities that exist.

As a leading employer in its community, the new institution should seek to establish a closer relationship with other employers, joint their organization and become involved in employment affairs and other industrial concerns in the town and region. A similar obligation lies upon the local authority.

Industry, commerce and the professions should recognize that sending signals about likely future requirements, or attempting to influence the choice of subject, are necessary but not in themselves enough. Partnership in action calls for working contact and direct experiment on the shop-floor, in the office, in the boardroom or in the local community.

A committee should be set up in each institution to search in the community for people to serve as governors, in order to achieve a balanced governing body and to prepare people with an appropriate sense of commitment to succeed them.

The practice [should] be established at local level of systematically widening access to higher education without lowering standards. To achieve the Government's target figures for students, positive steps must be taken. A consultative document is needed on matters which affect students: their needs, enlistment, support, prospective employment and, not least, their own perceptions.

Scottish Joint Committee of Principals of Colleges of Education and Principals and Directors of Central Institutions (June 1987) – It appears that the Polytechnics and Colleges Funding Council will itself be a non-departmental public body (NDPB), and it seems possible that this may lead to the polytechnics and colleges in England being in a position analogous to the universities rather than the position which applies in Scotland, where the central institutions and colleges of education are themselves NDPBs. As this impinges on freedom of action and the ability to carry funds from one year to the next, we note that this might place the polytechnics and colleges in England in a more advantageous position than those in Scotland. Thus, whilst we welcome the move to implement a similar system in England to that which has applied in Scotland for a very considerable period, we would not now wish to fall behind the situation of the colleges in the South. We would regard it as essential that any developments in the management of colleges in England, which bring them closer to the university system than the present Scottish CI system, are also applied in Scotland.

It is essential that any system of contracts applies equally to the universities and the non-university sectors of higher education so that the latter shall not be placed in a disadvantageous position.

Voluntary Sector Consultative Council (June 1987) – Given that the White Paper places emphasis on quality, how will contracts encourage quality? Any system in which contracts are awarded to the bidder offering the lowest price might not give sufficient weight to the quality of service on offer. It would seem more appropriate for the Funding Councils to indicate a norm, a rate for the job or unit of resource, based upon some independent judgement of what is needed to achieve quality provision.

What indicators of performance will be used? Several indicators of administrative efficiency can now (thanks to the spread of computerized management information systems) be generated simply. Serious reservations have been expressed about most indicators of academic effectiveness currently under debate. There are fundamental theoretical difficulties, for example, in seeking to establish causal links between specific teaching inputs and learning outputs. No one's interests will be served by too crude an approach to this matter.

The length of contracts and how far ahead they will be announced are crucial issues to resolve. If contracts are awarded with too short a time between the award of contract being announced and a college implementing it, this would negate the process of sensible academic planning and probably stifle innovation and initiative. The PCFC could greatly assist college managers by moving towards a system in which the funding year coincided with the academic year.

The Confederation of British Industry (July 1987) welcomes the publication of the White Paper and in particular the plans for: increasing the access to higher education, while maintaining standards; raising the proportion of 18–19 year-olds participating in higher education from 14.2 per cent in 1986 to 18.5 per cent by the end of the century, though we fear this expansion may not be sufficient to meet industry's needs; achieving a further shift in the proportion of students involved in mathematics, science, engineering and vocational courses, though again we are concerned that the change sought may not be sufficient to meet future requirements.

Concern remains both about whether the provision for public funding of higher education will permit these plans to be implemented to full effect and whether the proposals as a whole overestimate the ability of industry to contribute to the funding of higher education. Industry should not be expected to make a direct contribution to the funding of conventional courses except at the margin, e.g. sandwich courses, although an innovative approach directed to high-quality updating and retraining could open up a substantial market for which companies would be prepared to pay.

The Government should issue a consultative document setting out the main options for the funding arrangements for student support. There should be an informed public debate of these options before decisions are taken. It is important that the system adopted should not, compared with the present system, deter suitable students of all ages from entering higher education. Industry shares the Government's view that continuing education has an important role to play in increasing and updating the supply of skilled members of the workforce. Making fees tax deductible for individuals could encourage more people to enter higher education in later life.

The following responses were to the separate consultative document, published on 7 August 1987, which outlined proposals for changes in the remaining (local authority) maintained sector of further education. It proposed changes in the composition of governing bodies 'to make them more responsive to the needs of industry and commerce'; and a duty upon local authorities to delegate financial powers to colleges (as to schools).

Association of Municipal Authorities – We find most of the proposals for the reform of governing bodies unsatisfactory. We question whether the contents of the paper address recognizable problems or deficiencies in existing methods of college government.

We know of little or no evidence to suggest that governing bodies are not at present 'independent', or that they do not already have 'a worthwhile and clearly defined part to play in determining the conduct of colleges', or that governing bodies composed approximately as at present would not be capable of assuming the extended financial responsibilities envisaged for them.

We find the suggestion that a local authority representative should not be permitted to chair the governing body offensive and vindictive. Many local authority representatives have long-standing relationships with institutions and often have enormous experience and expertise in FE. To fetter the discretion of a governing body to choose its own chairman in this way is wholly unreasonable.

The need for FE to make continuing adjustments and to remain receptive to the rapidly changing demands of employers and of the MSC is acknowledged. For many institutions, it will be a major exercise. The long-term health of the FE sector, with the implications that has for national training provision, will depend on the effective management of change. We do not think that the present proposals will help the process of change, though we acknowledge that much of their impact will be determined by the way in which articles of government are drafted. As they stand, they seem likely to introduce delay, uncertainty and inexperience where colleges need clear, agreed policy and proper guidance.

Engineering Employers' Federation – The Government's proposals should make a significant contribution to the ability of colleges of further education to respond effectively to changing employers' needs. The proposed changes in the composition and powers of college governing bodies are a vital part of the proposals. We welcome the intention that half of the governors of each college should 'represent business, industrial, professional and other employment interests'. But, as the Croham Committee pointed out, there appear to be three problems in recruiting and retaining suitable members from industry and commerce: the commitment of time; lack of familiarity with the conventions; the style of working, which is closer to that of an academic committee than a company boardroom.

There is an additional disincentive: college governing bodies have become political battlefields. Suitable employer candidates will not waste their time on governing bodies preoccupied with administrative trivia and political posturing.

The Government will not achieve more effective college management with governing bodies of 20 to 25 members. This is far too large. Smaller governing bodies would require fewer volunteers and increase the chances of obtaining good ones.

Inner London Education Authority – The greatest difficulty throughout the proposals is the apparent divorce of power from responsibility: the power of governors to appoint and dismiss staff – the responsibility of the LEA as employer; the power of governors to run or not to run courses – the responsibility of the LEA to fulfil its MSC contract; the power of the governors to undertake financial commitments – the responsibility of the LEA for the financial consequences thereof. The consultative document fails to deal with this essential aspect of delegated responsibility.

There is a major contradiction between this paper, which emphasizes the strategic role of the LEAs in the making of provision, and the proposals in the recent consultative document *The Organization of Education in Inner London* whereby the specialist FHE provision could be fragmented and the capacity of the ILEA to plan provision in inner London could be lost.

National Association of Teachers in Further and Higher Education – It is disturbing that the consultation paper admits that the legislation based on it will only be a 'framework of duties and powers'. This may expedite parliamentary business, but it is no way to allow for proper discussion of complex, controversial and, in many eyes, highly unnecessary, undesirable and even unworkable proposals. If these matters are to be the subject of legislation, then their full implications should be the subject of debate. The Education Bill is likely to be a massive compendium, and it will be difficult to give the attention to the further and higher education issues in it that they deserve. The vital issues of principle and practice that have been raised merit proper discussion in Parliament, and should not be largely relegated to secondary legislation or to the discretion of the Secretary of State.

NACRO, the principal national charity working for the resettlement of offenders, wishes to express concern over the effects on prisoners of some of the proposals. The prison education service is currently offered through local education authorities and financed by the Home Office. Prison education departments often have strong links with further education establishments. Should governing bodies be appointed with more locally focused interests and increased powers, linked prison education departments could suffer. Prisoners often come from and will be released to widely dispersed geographical regions, and it is important that prison education departments should have access to educational expertise on a regional rather than a local basis.

Society of Local Authority Chief Executives – There is some muddled thinking about the consequences for the college and the LEA on appointments and dismissals of staff. The existing provisions for appointment and dismissal of teachers involving governors and local authorities have given rise to some complex issues of employment law. There are really only two possible models. Either the LEA becomes the employer and has the last word on appointments and dismissals of all staff, or the college becomes a corporate body with all the responsibilities of an employer. In either case the employer should be free to enter into contracts of employment which meet local needs including where appropriate departing from national agreements.

National Union of Students – A primary concern is the proposed reduction of student representation to a single place on governing bodies. The Audit Commission has criticized colleges in the past for the lack of student participation in decision-making. With so many changes taking place in the FE sector at present, it is vital that the primary clients of further education – students and trainees – are able to provide regular feedback [to help] the smooth running of colleges. At present most colleges have two student governors, some three.

The NUS totally rejects the inclusion of 'parent governors' on governing bodies. Such a move is unnecessary, irrelevant to FE and patronizing to young people. Students and trainees are quite capable of representing themselves.

The National Bureau for Handicapped Students must express very deep concern at a move towards unit costing. Without adequate safeguards there will be no incentive and every disincentive for a college to cater for students with special needs when, in many instances, the support required for them to function within college is relatively expensive. In practice, this suggests the need to 'weight' students who have special needs in whatever formula is applied to determine the college budget.

10
The Constitutional Dimension

THE PROPOSALS

The Government did not put out consultation papers to gather advice on the constitutional aspects of its proposals. All the same, among the replies to other papers lodged in the library of the House of Commons, especially those dealing with the universities and the national curriculum, are many protestations that the proposals will give too much power of decision to central government. The arguments do not vary much, and for that reason only a small selection is given here. What is notable is the frequency with which respondents turn aside from their testimony to express their disquiet at the powers that Mr Baker is asking Parliament to give him.

One of the more eloquent voices raised before the Bill was published was that of Sir Peter Newsam of the Association of County Councils, who spoke in Birmingham on 26 October at the first Standing Conference on Education, organized by the Council of Local Education Authorities. He said: 'We appear to be moving closer to direct ministerial control of the education service and of the many institutions within it . . . What if one day this country were to find itself with a Secretary of State possessed of a narrow vision of what education in a democracy should aspire to be, coupled with a degree of self-regard and intolerance of the opinions of others that caused him or her to seek to impose that vision on others? Are we, however unintentionally, creating the machinery through which such an imposition could occur?'

It was no doubt in response to misgivings of that kind that Mr Baker turned to the constitutional question in his speech to the North of England education conference in Nottingham on 6 January, when he asked his audience not to misrepresent the Bill's nature and purpose. He said: 'It is about the devolution of authority and responsibility. It is not about enhancing central control.' The purpose of the national curriculum was educational; it was not concerned with the distribution of power, and the role given to the Secretary of State in respect of it was 'clearly consistent with both constitutional doctrine and the 1944 Act'. Financial delegation was 'a devolutionary and not a centralizing measure', shifting responsibility from local authorities not to the centre but to the colleges and schools. He had been accused, he said, of wishing to impose his will on the two Funding Councils: 'Yet my record belies that charge.' In this he was on a false point: neither his past nor his likely future behaviour were under attack. Critics like Sir Peter Newsam were troubled, and remain troubled, about the use to which one of Mr Baker's successors may one day put the armoury which he is assembling.

THE DEBATE

The Constitution: does the Bill offend it?

Patrick McAuslan
Professor of Public Law, London School of Economics and Political Science

To talk of the constitutional dimension to this or any other Bill is to run into an immediate difficulty. We do not have in this country a constitution in the sense of a fundamental body of rules of pre-eminent importance against which all other laws, and all actions and decisions of public and private bodies, may be measured and struck down if they offend the provisions and principles of 'The Constitution'. To talk of constitutional or unconstitutional laws and conduct is to run the risk of being accused of dressing up political arguments in a pseudo-legal garb to make them appear more important than they really are.

Such an accusation can be overdone. We may not have a constitution but we do have constitutional principles against which the laws, actions and decision of Governments may be and frequently are measured. These principles are generally accepted and acknowledged to be relevant guides to assessing Governments and may be used therefore in assessing this Bill. Two relevant principles are the sovereignty of Parliament and the separation of powers. The first refers to the principle both that anything Parliament enacts as law is the law and must be obeyed as such thereafter, and that only Parliament can alter or amend what it has passed as an Act of Parliament. The separation of powers in its modern formulation directs attention to the importance of a dispersal of governmental powers among different governmental institutions and bodies so that they can act as a check on each other and help avoid undue concentrations of uncheckable power in the central government, experience having shown that such concentrations tend to be abused.

Measured against these principles, how does the Bill fare? On the first principle, there are many provisions where the Secretary of State is taking to himself powers to amend the Act once it is enacted. A few examples may be given. Thus, he may amend the provisions of clause 3, which specify the foundation subjects and the 'key stages' of pupils, an absolutely fundamental part of the reforms. He may by order repeal the provision which limits to primary schools with more than 300 pupils the eligibility of any county or voluntary primary school to transfer to grant-maintained status. Perhaps more alarmingly, he may by clause 94 confer such additional functions as

To talk of the constitutional dimension to this or any other Bill is to run into an immediate difficulty. We do not have in this country a constitution in the sense of a fundamental body of rules of pre-eminent importance against which all other laws, and all actions and decisions of public and private bodies, may be measured and struck down if they offend the provisions and principles of 'The Constitution'. To talk of constitutional or unconstitutional laws and conduct is to run the risk of being accused of dressing up political arguments in a pseudo-legal garb to make them appear more important than they really are.

Such an accusation can be overdone. We may not have a constitution but we do have constitutional principles against which the laws, actions and decision of Governments may be and frequently are measured. These principles are generally accepted and acknowledged to be relevant guides to assessing Governments and may be used therefore in assessing this Bill. Two relevant principles are the sovereignty of Parliament and the separation of powers. The first refers to the principle both that anything Parliament enacts as law is the law and must be obeyed as such thereafter, and that only Parliament can alter or amend what it has passed as an Act of Parliament. The separation of powers in its modern formulation directs attention to the importance of a dispersal of governmental powers among different governmental institutions and bodies so that they can act as a check on each other and help avoid undue concentrations of uncheckable power in the central government, experience having shown that such concentrations tend to be abused.

Measured against these principles, how does the Bill fare? On the first principle, there are many provisions where the Secretary of State is taking to himself powers to amend the Act once it is enacted. A few examples may be given. Thus, he may amend the provisions of clause 3, which specify the foundation subjects and the 'key stages' of pupils, an absolutely fundamental part of the reforms. He may by order repeal the provision which limits to primary schools with more than 300 pupils the eligibility of any county or voluntary primary school to transfer to grant-maintained status. Perhaps more alarmingly, he may by clause 94 confer such additional functions as he thinks fit on the Universities Funding Council and the Polytechnics and Colleges Funding Council to be established by the Act. Finally, tucked away inconspicuously at clause 139 of the Bill, is the largest power of all: a power to make such modifications in any enactment relating to employment – and in particular any enactment conferring rights on employees – as he considers necessary or expedient in consequence of the delegation to governors of schools and higher education corporations of powers to appoint and dismiss staff.

he thinks fit on the Universities Funding Council and the Polytechnics and Colleges Funding Council to be established by the Act. Finally, tucked away inconspicuously at clause 139 of the Bill, is the largest power of all: a power to make such modifications in any enactment relating to employment – and in particular any enactment conferring rights on employees – as he considers necessary or expedient in consequence of the delegation to governors of schools and higher education corporations of powers to appoint and dismiss staff.

There are no restrictions on these powers which the Secretary of State may exercise, and no explanation of the need for them appears either in the factual summary of the Bill released as a news item in November 1987 or in the Financial and Explanatory Memorandum which accompanied the Bill when it was introduced into the House of Commons. A dangerous precedent is being set if matters as important as these, which go to the root of the reforms being introduced by the Bill, can be removed from the full parliamentary scrutiny which accompanies amending Acts of Parliament and is relegated instead to orders which receive to all intents and purposes no parliamentary scrutiny when placed before Parliament.

Much more significant, however, are the inroads being made on the principle of the separation of powers, a matter to which a good deal of attention has been directed by contributors to the consultation process and commentators on the Bill. A very significant transfer of powers is being made from local elected authorities to the Secretary of State. There are few effective safeguards on these powers. Such advisory and other committees and bodies which are to be established are wholly the creatures of the Secretary of State, being appointed exclusively by him. Where consultation is required before he exercises any of his powers, the time allowed for consultation is usually short. To argue, as it might be argued, that ministerial responsibility will provide all the safeguards necessary to expose the unreasonable use of the new powers by the present or any future Secretary of State is to fly in the face of reality. Modern governments are adept at using ministerial responsibility to conceal rather than to expose.

But it is not just local authorities which are losing powers to central government. An important feature of any liberal democracy of which the separation of powers is an aspect is the autonomy and freedom of universities and other institutions of higher education and research. It is no accident that illiberal regimes around the world reject and curb the autonomy of universities, often on the grounds that they are not serving the national interest or are inefficient. It is on these grounds that autonomy is to be taken away from universities and other institutions of higher education and research by the Bill, and they are to be reduced to dancing, by contract, to the Government's tune.

The Government will argue in reply to these points that it has a mandate to reform education and that, while some powers are being relocated upwards from local authorities to the Secretary of State, many powers are being relocated downwards to parents and other responsible people and away from inefficient and unrepresentative local authorities. The balance of power between central and local has been maintained; only the institutions have been changed. But the change is more than that. For all their deficiencies, local authorities are elected, and the electoral principle is at the root of our democratic traditions. For 150 years, since the Great Reform Bill of 1832, the extension and use of the franchise have been a major driving-force behind the development of an informed citizenry and a representative and responsible government at both local and central levels. The extension of the franchise and the universal provision of education went hand in hand. This Bill marks a step back from the electoral principle; in place of the universal provision of education by elected local authorities, it sets in train the differential provision of education by appointed bodies in which the elected element is in the minority and a specific group in the community is accorded a privileged place in appointments.

A final constitutional point is this. We live in a pluralist multi-ethnic society in which respect for and advancement of human rights are essential if we are to live in harmony and progress in peace. Slowly, inch by inch, local education authorities were coming round to the need to adapt their policies, programmes and practices to the kind of society in which children are going to grow up. In the 169 pages of the Education Reform Bill, which is going to allow devolution of school governance to parents and business people, there is not one word on this vital matter – the need to continue to make progress to a system of education which inculcates into those participating in it a respect for and acceptance of one's fellow citizens, whatever their race, colour, creed, religion or sex. Is this not, then, to be part of our new 'better education, relevant to the late twentieth century and beyond, for all our children' – words used by Mr Baker when he introduced the Bill in the House of Commons in November 1987?

THE ADVICE

Association of County Councils – Under the provisions of the Bill, the Secretary of State will have extensive powers in relation to the national curriculum and the day-to-day management of the education service and of individual institutions, of varying types, to be maintained out of public funds. It is at this stage less clear how the other parties to the education service (parents, governing bodies, those with responsibility for voluntary schools and the local education authorities themselves) will, between them, resolve a number of matters on which the Bill leaves uncertainties.

The Bill leaves unchanged the general division of responsibilities laid down in the 1944 Education Act. Section 1, which deals with the duties of the Secretary of State, as amended, reads:

It shall be the duty of the Secretary of State for Education and Science to promote the education of the people of England and Wales and the progressive development of institutions devoted to that purpose, and to secure the effective execution by local authorities, under his control and direction, of the national policy for providing a varied and comprehensive educational service in every area.

Within the allocation of responsibilities laid down in the 1944 Education Act (as amended), the manner in which the Secretary of State is to carry out his duties is to be varied or given a statutory basis [by the present Bill] in the following principal ways:

(a)   In relation to the school curriculum, the Secretary of State is to take powers to control both its content and the means by which it is imparted. The principal powers, or duty to exercise such powers, include the power: (i) to establish a national curriculum, consisting of a core and a number of foundation subjects; (ii) subsequently to vary either that core or those foundation subjects; (iii) to establish and thereafter vary the key stages to which a variety of attainment targets, programmes of study and assessment arrangements relate; (iv) to establish bodies appointed or designated by him to oversee syllabuses and approve external qualifications for which pupils may be prepared; (v) to establish curriculum councils to keep the national curriculum under review; (vi) to approve or disapprove of variations to the national curriculum proposed on behalf of particular schools.

(Special arrangements for the exercise of the Secretary of State's powers are to be taken in relation to Wales, and there are to be reserve powers to extend the approval of qualifications and syllabuses to the 16–19-year-olds in full-time education.)

(b)   In relation to determining the physical capacity of schools, ultimately the Secretary of State may vary the standard number of pupils arrived at by any one of a number of methods set out in the Bill.

(c) In relation to the local financial management of schools, ultimately the Secretary of State can determine the form any scheme submitted by a local authority is to take, and, by regulations, can extend the delegation requirement to primary schools with fewer than 200 pupils.

(d) So far as further education is concerned, the Secretary of State will also take similar powers to control the form of schemes of delegation to colleges of further education and, if he is not satisfied with the LEA's proposals, will have power to impose his own. He will also take powers to alter articles of government for FE institutions.

(e) In relation to grant-maintained schools (i.e. schools maintained and controlled by the Secretary of State), the Secretary of State is to have more extensive powers than a local education authority has in relation to schools it maintains. The Secretary of State is to have power to: (i) approve, vary or revoke the articles and instruments of government of the schools; (ii) modify the trust deeds or other instruments relating to a grant-maintained school; (iii) cease to maintain the school under specified circumstances or with appropriate notice.

(f) In relation to city technological colleges, the Secretary of State is in a position to participate in creating new independent schools, and, subject to due notice of withdrawal from the arrangement being given, continue to make payments of both capital and revenue, described in the explanatory memorandum as 'in line with' costs in an LEA-maintained school, to any person responsible for carrying on such a school.

To assist the Secretary of State in carrying out his functions, the Bill affords a statutory basis to a number of bodies to be appointed to advise the Secretary of State on, or perform other functions in relation to, schools or colleges at present maintained by local education authorities. Some of these bodies replace existing bodies with similar functions; others are new. A distinguishing feature of each is that, as they are to be appointed by the Secretary of State, the representative or elective element in their composition is excluded. The bodies to be appointed by the Secretary of State are:

(a) The National Curriculum Council – to advise the Secretary of State on attainment targets, programme of study and assessment targets at defined stages of the period of compulsory education.

(b) The Curriculum Council for Wales – to perform similar functions in relation to Wales.

(c)   The School Examinations and Assessment Council – to keep all aspects of examinations on assessment under revision and to advise the Secretary of State on a number of matters, including research programmes and courses of study and external qualifications for pupils of compulsory school age.

(d)   The Education Assets Board – the principal function of the board will be to arrange for the transfer of assets arising from the changed legal position of a range of educational institutions.

(e)   The Polytechnics and Colleges Funding Council – the principal function of the council will be to distribute funds made available by the Secretary of State to polytechnics and designated colleges of further education.

In the university sector, a Universities Funding Council will be appointed to replace the present University Grants Committee, and University Commissioners will be appointed with powers to oversee and modify university statutes.

National Association of Governors and Managers – We reaffirm our support for the principle that education should be a national service locally administered, and that powers should be distributed carefully within that framework, so that the functions of decision-making and carrying out decisions are allocated to the people and organizations that can perform them most effectively. The distribution of functions between the Government, accountable to Parliament, the LEA, accountable to the local electorate, and the individual school, accountable to the governors, provides a system of checks and balances that protects the independence of the education system within a secure framework. Remove or weaken one element of this structure and it becomes unstable. We are therefore concerned about the centralization of power implicit in these proposals.

Much of the proposed legislation could have the effect of weakening the power of the LEA to provide an appropriate pattern of education in its area, one that meets the needs of the whole community. And while we welcome much of the restatement of the governor's role, which we see as returning to the concept of school government envisaged in the 1944 Act, we know that governors would find it very difficult to carry out that role effectively without the support provided by the LEA.

National Union of Teachers – There will be created a massive new bureaucracy accountable to no one other than the Secretaries of State. Subject working groups and a Task Group on Assessment and

Testing are to be appointed, as are the National Curriculum Council (NCC) and the School Examinations and Assessment Council (SEAC). These are to be the machinery for the use of the Secretaries of State, themselves armed with enormously enhanced powers over the curriculum, examinations and ultimately the qualifications available to young people. Though provision is made for consultative procedures, the recommendations of even the NCC and SEAC need not be accepted. Despite the disavowals in the consultative document, the intention is a transfer of power to small groups representing special interests and so-called expertise. Even the limited exercise in shared responsiblity between LEAs and the DES, introduced after the demise of the Schools Council, is to be abandoned; the School Curriculum Development Committee (SCDC) is to be ended, and the NCC is to be totally controlled by the Secretary of State. The document portends a radical shift towards central control with no room for local consultation and, far from spreading responsibility, will severely limit the democratization of education. Parents' rights are restricted to complaining if the national curriculum is being ignored.

National Association of Head Teachers – The extent of the powers [over the curriculum which] the Secretary of State seeks to place in his own hands is alarming. By the end of this whole exercise he will have statutory power to:

(a) specify what qualifications may be offered to pupils up to 16;
(b) regulate what qualifications and courses are offered to full-time 16–19-year-olds;
(c) lay down foundation subjects;
(d) prescribe attainment targets and programmes of study; and
(e) set out arrangements for assessment (including testing and examinations).

We are seriously concerned that the Secretary of State is setting a dangerous precedent which will allow future, and possibly extremist, governments to introduce doctrinaire curricula into our schools.

Association of Municipal Authorities – It must be a matter for concern that all the appointments to the National Curriculum Council are to be made by the Secretary of State. The 1944 Act achieved a delicate balance which sought to ensure that the State did not prescribe what was taught in schools; the forthcoming Bill should contain some system of checks and balances to ensure that no one body can exercise sole power. Without such safeguards the way is open for the establishment of an education dictatorship of a type which this country has consistently resisted.

Socialist Educational Association – The democratically elected local authority is to lose powers, and new bodies such as the Statutory Assets Board will be set up to decide the allocation of buildings and equipment. The curriculum will be decided at the centre, and even the independent examination boards will lose power to the Secretary of State. Even the teachers will not be trusted to mark the tests. Moderators appointed by the Government will amend the results and then make judgements on the school and the staff.

The whole process is to centralize decision-making with the Secretary of State at the expense of decisions being made at local level. No evidence is put forward to suggest local authorities, teachers or educational officers and advisers are failing the education system. The desire is to reduce their initiative, power and influence and replace it with appointed boards, centralized power and a business approach to educational institutions run by an equivalent board of directors.

The Social Democratic Party feels that some schools have considerable justification for wanting to opt out of the control of extremist local education authorities. However, we believe that centralization of power in the DES does not offer the best solution to the problem, as such concentration of power is open to abuse itself. Extremism in local government, and therefore the extremism of elected members of the local education authority, would be severely curtailed if elections to such authorities were by proportional representation. This would ensure that the LEA was directed by a group or groups of people who were genuinely representative of the local community. The domination of LEAs by an unrepresentative extremist group elected without majority support would cease immediately. Such a reform would make it unnecessary for schools to opt out of LEA control.

Index of Contributors
and Respondents